THE RHESUS CHART

THE
RHESUS CHART

CHARLES STROSS

ACE BOOKS, NEW YORK

THE BERKLEY PUBLISHING GROUP
Published by the Penguin Group
Penguin Group (USA) LLC
375 Hudson Street, New York, New York 10014

USA • Canada • UK • Ireland • Australia • New Zealand • India • South Africa • China

penguin.com

A Penguin Random House Company

This book is an original publication of The Berkley Publishing Group.

Ace Books are published by The Berkley Publishing Group.
ACE and the "A" design are trademarks of Penguin Group (USA) LLC.

Library of Congress Cataloging-in-Publication Data

Stross, Charles.
The rhesus chart / Charles Stross.
pages cm
ISBN 978-0-425-25686-2 (hardback)
I. Title.
PR6119.T79R53   2014
823'.92—dc23
2013048131

FIRST EDITION: July 2014

PRINTED IN THE UNITED STATES OF AMERICA

10 9 8 7 6 5 4 3 2

Cover art by Mark Fredrickson.
Interior text design by Kristin del Rosario.

FOR HUGH AND BECCA

THE RHESUS CHART

1.

PROLOGUE: ONE MONTH AGO

"DON'T BE SILLY, BOB," SAID MO. "EVERYBODY KNOWS VAMPIRES don't exist."

I froze with my chopsticks halfway to my mouth, the tiny corpse of a tempura-battered baby squid clutched precariously between them, while I flailed for a reply to her non sequitur. We were dining out at an uncomfortably pricey conveyor-belt sushi restaurant just off Leicester Square—it was my treat, although I had an ulterior motive. Unfortunately I was in the doghouse for some reason. I didn't know why, and it might not even have been related to the deed I'd brought her here to apologize for, but dinner showed every sign of turning into one of those rare but depressingly unfocussed marital arguments we had every few months. And the most prominent warning sign was this: the replacement of reasoned discussion with peremptory denial.

"We can't be sure of that. I mean, doesn't that take us right into proving-a-negative territory? The ubiquity of the legends, the consistent elements, all suggest to me that maybe we've been looking in the wrong place—"

We were here because I thought it might help soften her up before I apologized for what I'd done to her friend Pete the month before.

But instead of unwinding or letting me tell her about my latest office project, she'd switched into hypercritical mode as soon as we got to our booth. Apology shelved. Perhaps she'd just had a bad day at the office, but begging forgiveness for sins of necessity committed in the line of duty was clearly off the menu for the time being. Ten years together, seven of them married, have taught me to recognize the signs: right now if I reminded her that the sun rose in the east she'd start by stonewalling then escalate to a land war in Asia.

"Bob." When she said my name like that, it gave me flashbacks to Miss Pearson in Primary Two (*not* my favorite teacher): "Vampires *can't* exist. There'd be detailed records in the archives; they couldn't possibly evade detection by the state for any significant period. Besides which"—she aimed an alarmingly sharp wooden chopstick at my nose—"there'd be corpses everywhere. Human blood is a poor nutrient source; it's about 60 percent plasma by volume and only provides about 900 calories per liter, so your hypothetical blood-sucking fiend is going to have to drink about two and a half liters per a day. Those calories don't come in the form of useful stuff like glucose and fat: it's mostly protein from circulating red blood cells. Dracula would have to exsanguinate a victim every day just to stay alive, and would suffer from chronic ketoacidosis. The total number of intentional homicides for the whole country is around 700 a year; a single vampire would cause a 50 percent spike in the murder rate. Or they'd have to take transfusion-sized donations about two thousand times a year." She capped the boss-level takedown with a tight-lipped, triumphant smile, the better to conceal her incisors: "If you think you, or I, or anyone in the office could mind-control hundreds of people well enough to prevent at least *one* of them going to their GP to complain about the lethargy and anemia . . ."

I gave in to the inevitable. "You've researched this already, haven't you?"

"It came up in a brainstorming exercise about six years ago. We were investigating using ecosystem analysis to evaluate the probability of emergent new threat modalities. We also brainstormed golems, werewolves, and sasquatch." She took a spoonful of miso soup. "If they existed we'd know about them, Bob."

"But"—I paused to swallow my squid and pluck another one from the color-coded plate in front of me—"your model assumes they're obligate hemophages, doesn't it? And that they're endothermic, or at least have an energy budget not entirely unlike every other vertebrate known to science. What if that's not the whole story? What if they eat—"

"*Bob.*" She stopped short of rolling her eyes, but I could see she was bored, and growing more annoyed by the minute: "Eat your baby tentacle monsters before they go cold."

Mo has an aversion to pseudopods. When we first met, some very unpleasant people were trying to sacrifice her in order to summon an alien horror from beyond spacetime. I'd distracted them long enough for the seventh cavalry to arrive, and sometime after that Mo and I had started dating—but she still couldn't (and can't) stomach calamari. I cleaned my plate and watched as she finished her soup.

"I'm done here," she announced, picking up her violin case without asking whether I was still hungry. "I'm going home."

Which is why I didn't get a chance to apologize for dragging Pete into the business in Colorado Springs. Or to explain my hypothesis about what vampirism *really* was, and what I was doing about it. Or to save our marriage.

THE NAME'S HOWARD, BOB HOWARD. I'M A COMPUTER SCIENCE graduate and IT person, and I work for the British government in London, as does my wife Mo, Dominique O'Brien, who is a few years older than I am but still (in my opinion) a gorgeous redhead.

That's the mundane version, cleared for public consumption. It is also deeply misleading, but it's the version I'm allowed to give to friends and family without being required to kill them, so we'll call that a net win. It's also not *entirely* false.

The secret organization I work for is commonly called the Laundry because when it was established in its current form in 1940 it was based above a Chinese laundry in Soho. As Q Department, SOE, it was tasked with waging an occult war against the Ahnenerbe-SS. Today, the name may have changed several times but it's the same organization—the one you have just been admitted to, if you're reading this classified journal and your hair isn't on fire due to the security wards on the cover.

I'm actually a specialist in a field called Applied Computational Demonology: the summoning and binding to service of unspeakable horrors from other dimensions, by means of mathematical tools. Magic is a branch of applied mathematics: we live in a multiverse, there is a platonic realm of pure numbers, and when we solve certain theorems, listeners in alien universes hear the echoes. By performing certain derivations and manipulating theorems, we can make extradimensional entities sit up and listen, and sometimes get them to do what we want them to. True names have power: you should assume that any names or locations I give you may have been changed in the interest of security.

Although ritual magic has been around since the dawn of time (and indeed the Laundry's antecedents go back at least as far as Sir John Dee, in service to Queen Elizabeth the First under Sir Francis Walsingham), it was first systematized and placed on a concrete theoretical footing by Alan Turing in the 1940s. There are dark rumors that his "suicide" might have been a deeply misguided attempt to shut down a perceived security risk; if so, it was the organization's biggest mistake ever. Later on they took to recruiting anyone who rediscovered the truth by accident—which led, via the mushrooming popularity of computing during the 1980s and 1990s, to an increasingly unwieldy and overstaffed org chart full of disgruntled CS postgrad researchers and mathematicians.

I ended up in this line of work because once upon a time, my perfectly innocent master's thesis nearly summoned up an undead alien god in Wolverhampton. (We will step swiftly past the suggestion that this could only have resulted in urban regeneration.) Luckily the Laundry caught me in time and made me a job offer I wasn't allowed to refuse: take a nice civil service job in an obscure department where we can keep an eye on you, or be found crunchy and good with ketchup by a nightmarish monster from beyond spacetime.

That was about eleven years ago. Unfortunately, after a while I got bored with my tedious make-work job and made the cardinal mistake of volunteering for active operational duty. As a result of that error of judgment, I've had more encounters with nightmarish monsters from beyond spacetime than I care to think about, not to mention their deranged cultist worshippers. This doubtless sounds very exciting to you, but the committee meetings and form-filling that go with the job are a bit of a downer. And that's saying nothing about the hoops you have to jump through to satisfy the internal auditors that you did everything by the book. Adventures are something I try to avoid these days. Unfortunately I'm not very good at it.

Final wrap-up: on top of the ploddingly mathematical side of the job, I've stumbled into a specialized sideline as a trainee necromancer, which isn't a talent you'd wish on your worst enemy; and I work for an obscure boutique department called External Assets that provides—well, that would be telling.

Mo *also* works for the Laundry. She's not a computer geek. She's an academic philosopher and combat epistemologist, not to mention a talented violinist. The instrument she plays was provided by the organization and has exotic, indeed horrifying, capabilities: it's one of a kind. (If at this point you are thinking, "occult acoustic weapons," then pat yourself on the back.)

When I lay it out like that we sound like some kind of superhero team, don't we? But we're actually just a couple of married civil servants with day jobs that involve far too much paperwork, and the occasional terrifying incursion from another dimension. And we're probably doomed, but I'll get to that later.

AN EARLY AUTUMN EVENING IN CENTRAL LONDON CAN BE A FINE experience, or a lousy one. It depends on a variety of factors: on the weather, on whether you've just been sucked into a bad-tempered and pointless argument with your wife, on how worried you are about next month's credit card bill. Not to mention your uneasy anticipation of the meeting your new and somewhat unpredictable manager has scheduled for tomorrow afternoon.

That night I'd rolled ones on all of my dice: it was raining and gray, Mo was pissed off with me, the credit card bill was unpleasantly large, and Lockhart isn't the world's most forgiving boss. So I escorted Mo to the nearest tube station, then, rather than accompanying her home in prickly silence, I made a lame excuse and headed back to the office—not knowing that I was about to put myself in mortal danger.

I WORK IN A BUILDING CALLED THE NEW ANNEX. IT'S A LUMP OF mid-seventies concrete brutalism that squats above a closed discount store somewhere south of the Thames. The New Annex is one of the temporary offices we occupy while a public-private partnership rebuilds Dansey House, our headquarters building. Thanks to the current government's budget cuts, the months have turned into years and the Dansey House rebuild appears to have stalled. Turns out there's a nagging problem with long-forgotten and extremely powerful geases mucking up the foundations: we've run into the thaumaturgic equivalent of trying to rebuild a university campus and discovering that the walls are riddled with asbestos, the chemistry department used to pour mercury compounds and radioactive waste down the drains, and the admin block was built on top of a plague pit full of skeletons.

I'm resigned to working in the New Annex until I die. It wasn't furnished for comfort or convenience, even by civil service standards— nobody expected to be there more than six months—and these days it's just seedy, with peeling paint, cracked plaster, grubby uncleaned windows, and a persistent whiff of sewage in the basement levels.

THERE IS AN ENTRYPHONE BY THE SIDE DOOR TO A SHUTTERED discount shop in London. It looks abandoned, but works just fine:

it's our staff entrance. I stepped inside, pulling out my LED Lenser torch. "Hello?" I called.

Something hissed in the darkness nearby.

I raised my warrant card and pointed the torch in the direction of the sound. A withered face swung towards me: but then it recognized the warrant card and shuffled backwards, receding into the shadows again. (The lobby lights burned out six months ago and you can't get replacements for the type of bulb they use anymore: hence the torch and the shadows.) I headed directly towards the stairwell at the end of the corridor, itching to reach the relative safety—and working lights—of my office.

The night watch are confined to the ground floor except during emergencies, and they're only supposed to eat unauthorized intruders, and in any case I have special talents for dealing with their kind; but batteries have been known to fail, and anyway, who wants to be alone in the dark with a bunch of Residual Human Resources for company? Note: *never* use the Z-word to refer to them. Our Facilities Management people fastidiously describe them as Residual Human Resources, former employees who are still present in body if not in soul. When your mission involves binding and controlling mind-eating horrors, after a while it seems perfectly normal to use some of the leftover corpses to cut payroll costs on the late shift. Anyway, the Z-word is disrespectful, insulting, and considered politically incorrect around here. You might end up as one of them yourself: How would *you* feel about being called a zombie?

AS TO JUST *WHY* I WENT BACK TO THE OFFICE AFTER DINNER with Mo . . .

The Laundry marches to a different beat from the regular civil service, but we are not institutionally immune to outside influences. We do computery algorithmic stuff: this means we sometimes succumb to contagious management fads that are doing the rounds in the real world outside. In this case, the winds of change had blown in from Google (or, more likely, out of the arse of a senior management bod who had come down with a severe case of Chocolate Factory envy): management, bless their little cotton socks, decided that we needed to be Creative and Innovative and endowed with Silicon Valley start-up style va-va-voom. So they decreed that everyone above a certain grade was to spend four hours a week pursuing their own personal self-selected projects—which would have been great, if they hadn't missed the point.

At Google employees spend 20 percent of their hours on their own personal projects; in the Laundry we didn't get any extra time, or any extra budget. Also, we didn't get to pursue arbitrary time-wasting enquiries on our own initiative: there was a stack of vetted proposals for Creative and Innovative research ideas, and we had to pick one from the pile and sign our names to it. Our assigned jobs still came first, and in any case usually kept us busy for up to 110 percent of our working hours. In other words, the beatings were to continue until morale (and our va-va-voom) improved.

To be fair, we could also contribute to the suggestions box from which a committee selected the suitable candidates for working time. If you *really* worked hard to engineer it, you could probably run your own project—just as long as you could sneak it past the committee without one of the jobsworths shooting it down. Anyway, the Creative and Innovative self-directed work inflicted upon us from above now needed to be done—and with no hours allocated to it during the working day, it had perforce to be done at night.

I WASN'T THE ONLY NIGHT OWL WORKING IN THE DEPARTMENT tonight; the Laundry is eccentric by civil service standards, and although the fax machines and telephone switchboards were all switched off at night to stop employees abusing the facilities (per some ancient directive issued in 1972), the coffee machine and the network remain accessible. Quite a few employees choose to work outside core business hours to minimize the risk of being disturbed.

Tonight, the red NO ENTRY light above Andy's office was lit, suggesting that my years-ago former manager was burning the midnight oil; our current departmental admin asset—Trish: twenty-something, plump, amiably inquisitive in an utterly inappropriate way—was nose down in a book at her desk in the middle of the open-plan area.

"Bob? Oh, hi!" She deftly shuffled the book out of sight beneath a lever arch file full of forms, but not before I spotted the cover of *The Hunger Games*. "Can I sign you in?" I nodded, as she logged my badge and photographed me (duplicating a process that had certainly already happened before the front door closed behind me). "What brings you back to the office?"

"Couldn't sleep," I lied. "Also, got to finish writing up a report for the Auditors." The document in question was my report on GOD GAME RAINBOW—the apocalyptic clusterfuck in Colorado Springs a couple of months ago—but Trish didn't need to know that: mentioning the Auditors would put her off asking any more questions. (Our audits are not strictly confined to the realm of the financial, and the people who administer them are deeply scary.) "Is anyone else around?"

"Andy's up to something: he said he wasn't to be disturbed." Trish's expression of mildly affronted disapproval nailed it: she was bored. "But he requested night service because of some regulation or other about not working solo, and I'm top of the on-call rota, so it's overtime for me . . ." She mimed covering her mouth for a theatrical yawn.

I got it, although I disapproved: regs meet reality. Andy needed to perform some sort of procedure that the Book said needed two bodies present, but he couldn't be bothered waiting for a qualified pair of hands. Instead he ticked the checkbox by ordering up a receptionist, then did it solo. Once upon a time that kind of sloppiness had been my forté—I'd gotten over it, but Andy had always been a little too casual to leave in a hands-on role. (That, I theorized, was why he'd ended up dangling from the bottom rung of the management ladder—too high to do any damage, too low to make anyone else do any damage.) "I'll go see if he needs a hand," I promised her. "If you'd rather go home I'll sort it out." I walked over to Andy's office door—diagonally across the open plan/cubicle area from my own—and knocked twice.

There was an unhuman presence on the other side of the door: it made the skin on my wrists tingle and brought an electric taste to my tongue. I listened with my ears and an inner sense I'd been uneasily practicing for the past year. Tuning in on the uncanny channel brought me a faint sizzling, chittering echo of chaotic un-minds jostling for proximity to the warm, pulsing, squishy meatsacks. The lightning-blue taste of a warded summoning grid—not a large one, just an electrified pentacle unrolled on a desk—was like fingernails on a blackboard: Andy was conducting midnight invocations by the light of a backlit monitor. Okay, so he wasn't being *totally* stupid about this. But it still set my teeth on edge.

"Who's there?"

"It's Bob. Am I safe to enter?"

"I'm running a level one. Make sure you don't violate the containment and you should be fine."

"Not good enough, Andy. *Is it safe for me to enter?*"

Andy sighed heavily. "Yes, Mother, I'm deactivating it now."

"Good." A muffled click came from the other side of the door, and I felt the inchoate gibbering subside. I put my hand on the doorknob and pushed.

"Come on in, Bob."

I squeezed inside his office. Andy hovered over a home-brew lab, pale-faced and skinny, staring at me with bleary eyes. He was older than me, a member of a generation that had grown up wearing a shirt and tie to the office and who still tried to keep up appearances; he was the junior ops manager who approved my application and gave me my first ever field test. It was odd to see him in a polo shirt and chinos. "What's the project? Couldn't you wait for a health and safety check?"

He managed a self-deprecating shrug. "You know how it is; it's my weekly ten-percenter."

He'd built the summoning grid on a folding table that occupied about half his floorspace: by the look of it, it had started out as a NAAFI table tennis game sometime in the 1950s, before he repurposed it as an occult research workbench. I spotted peripherals: an Arduino controller, a laptop, a couple of wire-wrap circuit boards, a breakout box, and of course a summoning grid—which most people mistake for a pentacle.

"They roped you into the Google cargo-cult, too?" I asked.

"Yes." He shrugged again. "On the bright side, it gives me an excuse to brush up on my practical skills: I've spent so long shuffling reports that I'm in danger of forgetting what it's all about. If you're willing to watch my back I'd be very grateful, Bob, but you really don't need to; it's perfectly safe."

"Yes well, I can't help thinking that you've been here since at least the BLOODY BARON meeting this morning." He nodded instinctively. "Which means you've been in the office for at least twelve hours. If you were a pilot they wouldn't let you anywhere near the controls of an airliner when you're that tired: it's how mistakes happen—"

"Don't be silly, Bob! All it is is a 'hello, spirit world' demo. There's nothing *to* go wrong: all it does is execute a contained summoning of a class one voice-responsive agent"—a demon, to you—"make it do a handstand, then send it away again. With maybe a couple of optimizations to the grid controller, which I'm trying to prove with cheap off-the-shelf components. There's no agency outside the grid." He pointed at the Arduino board. "See? It's perfectly safe. Watch—"

My hair stood on end, I broke out in a cold sweat, and I was already in motion, halfway across the room towards him, when he began to utter the inevitable, fateful word—"*this*"—as his finger descended on the button wired to the breadboard beside the microcontroller, and power surged into the grid.

I SHOVED ANDY AWAY FROM THE TABLE, BUT I WAS TOO LATE: the circuit had been completed, and I could hear the chittering in the back of my head *much* more clearly, over a mumbling chewing sizzle like millions of mandibles on the move—

"Andy, get *out*!" I grabbed his arm and swung him towards the door. He resisted instinctively but ineffectually: I shoved him across the threshold. The alien gibbering was rising in pitch, and my skin crawled as we passed the side of the card table, where the grid was glowing with a rapidly brightening violet radiance. I felt a metallic taste on my tongue as we crossed below the lintel—

"Wait, what, I don't even—" *Finally* Andy began to move under his own steam.

Only a couple of seconds had passed since he began to say "watch *this*," but my Spidey sense and the frankly terrifying sense of wrongness in my guts told me that we might be too late: whatever the thing flooding into the powered-up summoning grid was, it certainly *wasn't* just a harmless class one emanation. I felt it tracking me as I stepped across the threshold, like a terrier that has spotted and locked onto a juicy mouthful of rodent on the run: cold and dank and terrifyingly alien, like something from the abyssal depths of another world's oceans. I turned and pulled the door shut, then leaned against it and reached instinctively for the ward I wear in a small leather bag on a thong around my neck. "Andy," I gasped.

"What? What?" He blinked, confused as I stared at him. Eyes: clear. No sense of possession—if I was a god-botherer I'd have given thanks right then.

The door behind me rattled. I shivered: it was becoming cold to the touch. I took a deep breath. "Andy, I need you to go get—no. First, I want you to send Trish home. *Then* I want you to go get Angleton." I took a step away from the door, and turned to face it.

"I don't understand! It's only meant to summon a class one—" I could barely hear his spoken words over the gibbering din in my head emanating from the other side of the warded portal.

"Andy." I spoke through gritted teeth. "Get Trish out of the building and to a designated place of safety. Then go and get Angleton *right now*. We will resume this conversation at a later date."

"But—"

I glanced at him and he shut up. I'd never seen his face turn that color before: he nodded stiffly, then broke into a stumbling trot in the direction of the corridor leading to Angleton's hole. *Finally.*

I drew another deep breath, heart pounding. The tense feeling between my shoulders was getting worse. Andy was old enough to know better.

A *class one manifestation*, in our charmingly indirect lexicon, is nothing you want to make physical contact with. Many years ago I'd been on a training course where a guy called Fred from Accounting—who'd been assigned to the course because of a typo on an HR form—ended up extremely dead indeed because he hadn't understood that a *voice responsive agent* is a nasty little cognitive loop that can run on (and burn out) a human nervous system just as easily as a computing device.

Whatever was on the other side of that door was most certainly *not* a class one manifestation.

I could feel it from the other side of the door, like the hum of a national grid high-voltage bearer. Our offices are shielded by wards—we frequently handle occult materials—but whatever he'd invoked was flexing its magical muscles and coming dangerously close to overloading not only the summoning grid on that flimsy card table but the more substantial wards on the door frame. Which was very bad news. I pulled out my phone and pointed the camera at the door itself, then called up OFCUT—our occult monitoring app in a smartphone-sized can—to take a look. Sure enough, histograms shading from blue to violet were chewing around the edges of the elder sign in the middle of the elaborate tracery. It confirmed what I could feel in my tingling fingertips and roiling stomach: I wasn't about to open my inner eye and have an eyeball-to-eyeball look at the void by way of a third opinion, but I was pretty sure that if I did I'd see something so *wrong* that it wouldn't even be visible at all, except as a sucking blind-spot distortion in my visual field, dragging everything around it together at the edges like a detached retina.

The doorknob appeared to be smoking. It was air condensing on the metal surface as vapor, then boiling off again. Elapsed time:

thirty seconds. And here I was, with just my regulation-issue class four ward, my OFCUT-equipped phone, and whatever native magical talent I happened to have, facing the *oh-shit* lurking on the other side of the threshold.

An equally chilly voice from behind me said, "*Speak*, boy. What are we facing?"

I glanced round. It was Angleton, with Andy trailing along wearing a hang-dog expression. If it wasn't for the deafening hum and gibber I'd have felt Angelton's presence as soon as he entered the corridor leading to this office space: as chilly and powerful as the thing beyond the door. Not to mention his speech patterns: he spoke to everybody as if they were naughty schoolchildren. Judging by Andy's expression he was expecting a caning.

"Andy's ten-percenter involves a non-standard grid designed to summon and contain a class one. He hooked something else. I reckon it's class five or higher, minimally sentient or stronger, still inside the grid but working to get free. Leakage through the door wards is over six hundred milli-Parsons per minute right now, and rising; the grid is still powered up so I figure the entity on the other side is still trying to squeeze through the portal—"

"Understood," Angleton said crisply. "Mr. Newstrom. How *exactly* does your grid differ from a standard design?"

I looked back at the door, but I could see Andy's expression in my imagination: a naughty boy who has had to get the headmaster out of bed because he's set fire to the chemistry lab. "It's not substantially different: I just used an Arduino microcontroller board and a bunch of control code I wrote for it to run a standard 'hello, spirit world' demo—"

"Did you use an off-the-shelf code library? Or write your own?" Angleton's interrogation was gentle, precise, and pointed. I could see him in my mind's eye, too: tall, cadaverously pale, thin as a mummy, with eyes like ice diamonds.

"I rolled my own code generator in FORTRAN77," Andy explained. "Atmel AVR machine code, not that high-level Arduino stuff. It seemed more efficient to get down to the bare metal . . ."

Angleton sighed. And *now* my blood ran cold. Because if there's one thing worse than an IT manager who's feeling the chill wind of obsolescence blowing down his neck and consequently trying to contribute code to the repository like an actual working developer, it's an IT manager who's getting *creative*. And Andy's project was nothing if not *creative*, for values of creativity that I don't want to go anywhere near without body armor and HAZMAT gear. "Mr. Newstrom. We will have words about this later." Angleton paused: I could feel his eyes on me. "Boy. Tell me what you hear?"

He always called me *boy*. From anyone else I'd take it badly; from Angleton it was probably a sign of affection.

"I hear termites," I said. "About a trillion sixteen-dimensional, elephant-sized termites chewing on the edges of reality."

"Did you wire in a remote kill switch?" Angleton asked Andy.

There was an eloquent moment of silence, punctuated only by the munching of metaphysical mandibles. Then the sound changed.

"Oh dear," I said, as Angleton simultaneously said, "Mr. Newstrom, evacuate the building. Mr. Howard and I will remain to deal with this." Then, on the other side of the door, the over-stressed summoning grid ruptured.

The immediate consequence of the summoning grid rupture wasn't that spectacular; the door grew colder and the runes engraved in it flared up, glowing the eerie deep blue of Cerenkov radiation. The office was warded to a high level, and would hold for at least half an hour longer than the grid on the card table. But the thing Andy had inadvertently summoned was now forcing its way into our universe directly, no longer confined by the meter-diameter circle on the table. And if it was powerful enough to overload one grid, it might well be able to overpower another, including the structural wards built into the walls, floor, and ceiling of the New Annex: in which case, we could have a real problem on our hands.

Angleton closed the gap and stepped past me, extending a hand towards the door. He looked at it quizzically, even hesitantly: an expression I'd never seen on his face before, and most unwelcome. Angleton is a DSS, a Detached Special Secretary: in our unofficial lexicon the acronym really stands for Deeply Scary Sorcerer. This is, if anything, an understatement: he's known to some as the Eater of Souls. That's because he's not actually human—he's an alien intelligence bound into a human body by a powerful necromantic ritual. Luckily for us, he's on our side. I'm his assistant, apprentice, whatever you call it. I don't know the real extent of his power, but I'm a moderately competent necromancer in my own right; anything that gives Angleton cause for concern is, by definition, frightening.

"Boy," he said conversationally, "this is going to be messy. Please verify that all the human staff are off the premises, then fetch the night watch."

"Fetch the—what, *all* of them?"

"Yes, Bob. We're going to need zombies. Lots of zombies."

"Wait, what—" I looked back at the door. Either I had a sudden eyestrain or the wards on it were bulging ominously. I glanced at my smartphone again. The thaum field was strengthening rapidly, and the flux had exceeded a thousand milli-Parsons per minute. "Er, yes. Right away." I fled in the direction of the front door, leaving Angleton to face the glowing door alone, like an eldritch remix of the little Dutch boy on the dyke.

There is a formal procedure for evacuating the New Annex: it involves filling out six forms in quadruplicate to obtain the key to a key cupboard containing the key to a cabinet containing a silver hammer (that bit would normally be done in advance, daily, by the Security Officer on Duty), then using the aforementioned hammer to break the glass cover on a brass box containing a bell inscribed with mystic runes—

I hit the fire alarm. Then I raised my metaphysical fingers to my astral lips and emitted the most deafening mental whistle I'm capable of. Then I began to chant doggerel in Old Enochian: *On Ilka Moor Bah't 'At*, or maybe, *Get your shambling undead asses up here on the double*. This saved a breakneck dash down a darkened staircase (not to mention all the SOD form-filling and the hammer stuff), buying me sufficient time to dash across to my own office and rummage around in the assorted crap on top of the filing cabinet for my pigeon's foot, cigarette lighter, silver paint spray can, packet of sharpies, and pocket camera—all the while carrying on the chant. Thus equipped I dashed back into the open-plan area just in time to see the first of the night watch shamble towards me, arms outstretched in classic Bela Lugosi style.

"Be so good as to make a new grid, boy," Angleton murmured, not looking away from the haunted office door. "Make it big; I need an airlock." I began to spray conductive paint in a big circle behind him, across the beige carpet tiles and continuing on up the walls and as high as I could reach.

I paused before sketching in the second arc, stopped chanting, and turned to face the night watchmen. *"Acknowledge my authority,"* I ordered them in my halting Old Enochian. Slowly, with creaking joints, the wizened corpses in their blue uniforms went to their knees. Eight mummified faces turned to blindly inspect me. I could feel their attention, eager for flesh and life but bound to obey. *"I am your lawful knight-commander,"* I added. *"Under oath by way of my liege."* They followed my gaze to Angleton, and cringed, suitably terrified. *"A hostile intruder lies past yonder portal. Attend."*

I went back to sketching in the new, larger grid around Angleton and the door. I could feel his concentration focussed on the wards around the office, intent and precise as that of any surgeon. "Nearly done," I murmured, sketching glyphs rapidly: Elder Sign, Horned Skull, NAND Gate. "What do you want me to do?"

"Move two zombies in here, boy." (Angleton predates political correctness.) "Then activate the grid as soon as I'm clear of it."

I waved the first two night watch shamblers forward, then ducked to connect the grid terminals to a clunky-looking wireless transponder controlled by my smartphone. "Ready when you are, boss."

Angleton stepped back sharply. "Now, boy," he said. I poked at the touchscreen and opened my inner eye. The new grid shimmered pale blue around a smaller violet doorway, fronting the roiling darkness around Andy's office—I could see the thing right through the walls and floor. *"Thou,"* Angleton said sharply, in Old Enochian, *"it is thine honor upon my word to open the door. And* thou *shalt step through the portal and be my ears and eyes and tongue for that which lies within—"*

I twitched slightly. Was Angleton really going to use a zombie as a webcam? I've gotten used to dealing with the metabolically challenged over the past year, but even so, that was a level of intimacy I wouldn't willingly approach.

"Sssss," said one of the night watchmen, reaching for the doorknob. I could feel the taste of its mind, half-afraid and half-eager to discover whatever waited behind the door, ready to *eat*—

It touched the doorknob. And pushed.

The door swung open to reveal a luminous chaos. Green-edged shadows flickered across the room, dazzling me, as the other zombie lurched forward, straight into the embrace of a tangled skein of many-jointed limbs and a hairball of writhing tentacles, some of them sprouting fern-like leaves that quested blindly around the edges of the door. One of them sprouted, extending swiftly into the room; it reached the edge of the inner grid and sizzled, recoiling violently. The mass of wildly waving intrusive appendages spasmed and twitched, pulling back—with the zombie dangling in its grasp, unmoving. "Close the door!" called Angleton, and the other zombie pulled, hard. The door scraped shut, the warding on it sucking it back into place in its frame.

"Well, that didn't go so well," he remarked conversationally, pulling a starched white cotton handkerchief from his breast pocket. He wiped his forehead: the cloth came away pink, smeared with perspiration and blood. Angleton glanced at the kerchief disapprovingly, then folded it neatly and tucked it away. Then he looked at me. "The natives are restless tonight." A mirthless smile. "A capital learning opportunity don't you think, boy? Quick. Tell me what you saw."

"I—" I swallowed. *You have got to be shitting me.* This was Angleton all over. What you or I would recognize as an alien invasion by tentacled horrors from beyond spacetime Angleton would see as a teachable moment. I could swear there was liquid helium running in his veins. "Morphologically diverse subsentient entity, didn't even notice it was in physical contact with a vessel for the feeders in the night; the usual death patterning didn't touch it." (One of the reasons the night watch are so dreadful—to most people—is that skin-to-skin contact with one of them is usually about as survivable as skin-to-metal contact with an electric chair. Angleton is made of sterner stuff, and I'm immune to them for a different reason. But even so.) "What next?"

The mirthless smile broadened. "You send in another body and watch what happens, while I see what I can find out about the world on the other side of that door."

I turned to the group of Residual Human Resources in the corner. They looked singularly unenthusiastic for the fate Angleton had in mind for them, even by zombie standards. "You can't just go using the night watch as meat probes!" A residual budget-focussed reflex prompted me to protest. "There'll be hell to pay in the morning! Security will have a cow!"

"Security will have a much bigger problem to deal with if we can't close down this portal by then, boy." Angleton glanced at Andy's office. The remaining zombie in the outer ward was still clutching the door handle. After a moment I realized it was frozen to it. "Do you have any suggestions?"

"We don't have any spare nukes on the premises, do we?" *Don't be silly, Bob,* I told myself. "Well, hmm. It depends if what is on the other side of the door is still Andy's office, with a portal inside it, or if the grid's ripped wide open and the door is actually opening into another domain."

"The latter, I believe." Angleton cocked his head on one side. "You are considering the question of damage containment?"

"Yeah." I scratched my head, then pulled my hand back when I felt my hair dripping with sweat. "Send a bomb through, kill or injure whatever is pushing through from the other side, use the opportunity to exorcise everything on the other side of the door—"

"I have a better solution than exorcism," Angleton stated. "Your camera, boy. Have you loaded the basilisk firmware?"

"Um, let me check." My pocket snapper is a hacked 3D digital camera, with firmware that turns it into a not-terribly-accurate basilisk gun. "Yes, but I wouldn't recommend using it at this range . . ."

Basilisk guns are a nasty little spin-off of research into medusae, and our happy fun way of dealing with other universes. It's an observer-mediated quantum effect that applies a rather odd probability field to whatever it focusses on. About one carbon-12 or carbon-13 nucleus in a hundred, in the target, is spontaneously swapped for a silicon-28 or silicon-29 nucleus. (Yes, this violates the law of conservation of mass/energy: we reckon it works via a tunneling process from another universe.) The effect is rather dramatic. Lots of bonds break, lots of energy comes spewing out. Protein molecules go *twang*, nucleotide chains snap, everything gets rather hot. To a naive bystander, the target turns to stone—or rather, to red-hot, carbon-riddled cinderblock.

On the one hand, it's a lethally powerful hand weapon. On the other hand, you really don't want to use one at close range—say, at something on the other side of a door. The smallest area of effect it has is a bit like a sawn-off shotgun; at worst, it's an air strike in a pocket-sized package. Right now I was standing close enough that if I pointed it at Andy's door the blast effect would probably kill me.

"I have an idea. Wait here, boy, I need to fetch something from my office. If the ward on the door fails, snap away by all means: you'll be dead either way." And with that reassuring message, Angleton turned and scampered helter-skelter back towards his den.

ANGLETON WAS ONLY GONE FOR A MINUTE, BUT IT FELT LIKE AN eternity as I stood watching the vapor-smoking door in the pentacle. The zombie with the handle was slowly slumping towards the floor, leaning against the side of the door frame; I could hear him in the back of my head, growing sluggish and faint as if the feeder that animated his body was slowly being drained.

I hefted my camera, checked the battery status, and pointed it at the portal, knowing that if the wards didn't hold it was probably futile; anything that could break in from another universe under its own motive power was out of my league. Possibly out of Angleton's, too. The night watch shuffled anxiously in the corner between the reception desk and the dying potted rubber plant; I could feel their unease gnawing at the back of my head. As a rule, Residual Human Resources don't *do* unease: they're placid as long as they've got some flesh to embody them and the occasional hunk of brains to munch on. (Any old slaughterhouse brains will do: they eat them for the fatty acids. At a pinch, you can substitute a McDonald's milk shake.) But these RHRs were definitely unhappy about something on the other side of the portal, and that was enough for me.

Man up, Bob, I told myself. I checked the camera again, double-checked that I had the basilisk firmware loaded rather than the charming novelty 3D snapshot firmware that had come with it, shifted from foot to foot. That's when the moment of blinding insight went off inside my head like a flashbulb. I peered at the display back and frantically scrolled through the settings menu. Pinky and Brains, our departmental Mad Scientist unit, had somehow gotten hold of the original source code and hacked the basilisk functionality into it, hadn't they? It had to operate as a stereo camera, or the medusa effect wouldn't work, but normally I just left it on auto-focus. But had they left the original features—the *other* features, like aperture, exposure, focus, special photographic effects—intact? Because if so . . .

Angleton cleared his throat right behind me and I nearly jumped out of my skin.

"Well, boy?" he asked as I spun round. He was holding a small black binder, open at a page of peel-off stickers. Three of the five circular symbols had been removed, leaving shiny grease paper backing. I tried to look at the remaining ones but they gave me a stabbing pain behind my right eye.

"The thing on the other side of the door is pretty dumb," I said. "I think I can take it out, if we open the door, but it'll be touch-and-go. And if it's actually inside the office, rather than on the other side of a portal with its end point in the office, it might make a mess of—"

"Leave that to me." Angleton hefted his book of stickers. "Harrumph. What do you propose to do?" I told him. "Harrumph," he said again, and considered the idea for a few seconds before nodding. "Yes, you do that, Bob. I'll sign off on the forms for the replacement kit tomorrow."

"Okay," I said. Turned towards the cowering crowd of Residual Human Resources. "Here's how we'll do it. Eenie, meenie, minie, mo, catch a zombie by the—"

I reached out with my mind and *grabbed*. He came, shuffling, re-luctantly: an older, more withered corpse, wearing the dress uniform of a funereal military policeman. The original owner of the body was long dead. What held it upright now was a feeder in the night, a weak demon with a tendency to embed itself in (and take over) the neural connectome of its victims. I think it knew that I had a fate in mind for it, and not a pleasant one, but it was bound into the body by a geas, a compact of power that required it to obey my lawful commands. *"Hear ye this,"* I said, in my halting Old Enochian: *"define new sub-routine basilisk_grenade() as callback from operator(); begin; depress red button on front of payload; aim payload at self->face(); walk forward for ten paces; halt and retain physical control of payload indefinitely . . ."*

I set the self-portrait timer on the camera to ten seconds, handed it to the zombie, and sent him into the grid and through the door to blow himself up. Then things got weird.

ABOUT THAT STICKER BOOK:

"I want you to turn off the outer ward, boy," he told me. "Then shove your zombie inside and turn it on again. And after another fifteen seconds I want you to turn it off. Can you do that?"

I nodded. I had the beginning of a throbbing headache: the crack-ling gibber and howl from beyond the portal, combined with the Residual Human Resource's whining sense of dread at its undeserved fate, was getting to me. Controlling the ward at the same time wasn't exactly demanding but required focus—especially in case anything went wrong. "Okay," I said.

"Good. Then do it now."

I switched off the outer ward, and the howl rose to a near-deafening roar, a silent arctic gale buffeting at my attention. *"Thou shalt advance!"* I commanded my blue-suited minion: *"Perform the operation as soon as the portal opens!"* Then, to the all-but-deanimated relic on the door handle: *"Open the door* fucking right now*!"*

I shoved the full force of my necromantic mojo into the doorman, who twitched slightly and moaned something inarticulate and inaudible. So I shoved again. I'm not sure I can describe exactly what it feels like to pump your will into an empty vessel, filling and inflating it and bringing purpose (if not life) back to lumpen dead limbs. The feeder was still there, so I wasn't entirely doing it from cold: but it was listless and tired, as close to exhausted as I've ever felt. I rubbed my forehead and concentrated. *"Go!"* I shouted.

The nearly twice-dead corpse lurched to its feet. Then it twisted the door handle and pushed, opening the path for my reluctant bomb carrier.

I'm not sure what I saw through the open portal. My memory is full of confused, jumbled-up images of tentacles and lobster-claws and crazy-ass stuff looking like industrial robots made out of raw sewage and compound eyes the size of my head. I can't really say what it was, though, because my inner ears were ringing. It was total sensory overload, backlit by shimmering curtains of light and electrical discharges and the screaming of damned telemarketers in hell. Okay, I made that last bit up. But it was *raw*.

"Close, dammit! *Close!"* I yelled in Enochian. The door-zombie moaned incoherently and stumbled, collapsing against the portal, just as a bouquet of tentacles reached across the threshold and wrapped themselves around my bomb-carrier zombie in something that was probably not intended as a loving embrace.

My bomb carrier groaned piteously, with an inner voice so loud that I could feel it in my head even over the unholy din from the tentacle monster. I shuddered. I've never actually seen something *kill* a feeder in the night before—disembodiment is all very well, but something told me my minion wouldn't be coming back for sloppy seconds. But he'd stepped up to the threshold, and he was carrying the basilisk gun, and he'd pushed the self-timer "start" button . . . "*Close the* fucking *door before I invent a whole new hell to banish you to!*" I screamed at the door-corpse. (I am taking a liberty here. I had, and have, no idea what the Enochian for "fuck" is. Probably because the beings who invented that language didn't have anything remotely approximating mammalian genitalia. Even before their final extinction rendered the whole point moot.)

I shoved, hard, with my mind. So hard, in fact, that everything began to turn gray and my ears—my physical ears—began to ring. *K syndrome here I come,* I thought with a resigned sense of futility. Angleton was in front of me, approaching the edge of the outer ward, but I could tell this wasn't going to work—

There was a soundless flash of light and a deep, resonant thud, as of a gigantic door slamming on the other side of a wall. I felt it in my gut as I stumbled. Another flicker: I couldn't see properly—

"Cut the ward, boy, cut it *now*!" Angleton snarled over his shoulder.

The ward? Oh, right. I fumbled with my phone and hit the "off" icon on the control app. The light show began to fade. "Hang on, have we closed the portal?" I asked.

The door to Andy's office was still half-ajar, a skeletonized hand dangling from the doorknob. Angleton stepped around the remains of the door zombie with the delicate gait of a man in expensive shoes avoiding a dog turd. He raised a hand: dust and bones and other disquieting shapes gathered themselves up from the pile on the threshold and rolled beneath the lintel, vanishing into the darkened space beyond.

Angleton waited a few seconds, then pulled the door shut with his fingertips. Next he raised the black folder and delicately removed a decal. "By the authority vested in me," he said, "I declare this office closed." Then he carefully applied the sticker to the center of the door, and stepped backwards.

"Have we closed the—" I began to repeat, then stopped. "Hang on. What's going on?" I stared at the mess of paint, charred patch of carpet, and graffiti'd patch of blank wall at the side of our office area. "Hang on," I repeated, backing up mentally. "Wow."

I took a step towards the wall. Angleton caught my arm. "You don't want to get too close until it's had time to anneal."

"Until what's had time?"

"The ward I placed on Mr. Newstrom's office. Class ten," he added, almost smugly.

"Class *ten*?" I'd heard of wards that strong: I didn't know we actually *had* any.

"Yes, boy. By tomorrow morning nobody except you, me, and Mr. Newstrom will even remember there was an office there—and Andy will only do so because he left his coat inside." He clapped his hands together. "I want you to prepare a report on this incident for me. But be a good chap and fetch Mr. Newstrom back inside first. I believe it has begun to rain, and as I mentioned, he doesn't have a jacket anymore."

I WENT OUTSIDE AND HAULED ANDY IN, AND THEREAFTER WE didn't get much work done, apart from the inevitable clean-up and sending the surviving Residual Human Resources back to their crypt. Then I made an executive decision that Andy and I needed to finish the night shift by performing a destructive bioassay on the contents of a bottle labelled "drain cleaner" I'd found in a drawer in my desk. After repeated oral analysis, we concluded it was mislabelled. It was a risky procedure—if the bottle hadn't been mislabelled we could have made ourselves *very* ill indeed—but certain traditions must be upheld. In particular, a young high-flying officer should not tell a former superior that they've been bloody idiots without the plausible deniability lent by a sufficiency of single malt whisky. Even if it's true.

"So what's *your* ten-percenter?" Andy asked after I finished explaining precisely why he needed the refresher course on health and safety procedures when conducting summonings. "Don't tell me you're working on an admin-side scheme?"

"Actually, I am," I said, hoisting a shot glass in his direction: "Prosit!"

"Up yours." He took a sensible sip. "No, seriously, they've got you on the hook, too, haven't they? That's why you came in to work late?"

Actually they didn't. The ten-percenter thing only really applied to staff with actual postgraduate degrees. I'd never finished my PhD, much less got to strut my stuff in a silly robe, but I'd jumped on the bandwagon with a carefully muted shriek of glee. I had my own entirely selfish reasons. Andy might have selected his project because he was suffering from that peculiar version of impostor syndrome to which researcher-turned-admin bodies are prone, but for my part I'd been bitten by a bug, and I needed a plausible excuse to spend 10 percent of my working hours on a scheme the suggestions box committee probably only authorized because they hadn't understood the full implications. (*I* had. And it was fascinating. I wish I knew who'd had the idea first, so I could shake their hand . . .)

Last year, a series of unfortunate events in Colorado Springs coincided with me being promoted onto the management fast track—and earlier this year a series of even more unfortunate events derailed me from said track, dumped me on a jet-propelled skateboard, and shoved me onto the career progression equivalent of a crazy golf course played with zombies for putting irons and live hand grenades for balls. Since then I've been subject to matrix management by bosses in different departments with diametrically opposed priorities who still think I work under them, while trying to establish just what is expected of me by much more senior people who think I work for *them*. It's extremely fatiguing, not least because the furrow I'm ploughing is so lonely that nobody's actually written a skills development manual for it: the Laundry is about procedures and teamwork and protocol, not super-spies and necromancers.

"I'm on the hook to the extent that I want to be," I confessed. "Lockhart insisted, actually. Told me I'd never get anywhere unless I 'set a course and stuck to it,' to use his words. And Angleton just laughed, then told me to fuck off and play with myself."

"Angleton said—" Andy's eyebrow twitched again.

"No, that's me; his actual phrasing was more . . ." *Schoolmasterly* was the word I was hunting for. A long time ago, Angleton spent a decade teaching in the English public school system (the posh, private school system, that is) and it had rubbed off on him—along with the extra special version of sarcasm generations of schoolmasters have distilled for keeping on top of their fractious charges. (Even his current nom de guerre, Angleton, was chosen with irony in mind: it irritated the hell out of our American opposite numbers, because of the one-time CIA legend of the same name. Really, he ought to be code-named SMILEY or something.) "But anyway, he gave me carte blanche, and my other boss expects me to—" I waved my hands, nearly knocked over my glass, and caught it just in time. "No, that's not right. He just expects me to keep myself busy between External Assets jobs."

"Paper clip audits." Andy took a sip of Laphroaig. I didn't bother to correct his misapprehension: External Assets, which Lockhart runs, is about paper clip audits the way the FBI is about arresting thieves, i.e. not at all but it's extremely convenient for them that most people outside the organization don't realize that. "Sounds to me like they want to see what you can do. Hmm." Rueful amusement tugged at the sides of his lips. "So what are you going to do?"

"I'm building a spreadsheet. One with a lot of very interesting pivot tables." Andy peered at me with an expression of mild disbelief. "Getting clearances for the data to feed it is a bitch, and it's anybody's guess whether it's going to deliver anything useful, but if you don't ask you don't get . . ."

"Ask for *what*?" He hunched down in his chair. He was still a little shaky from the events of a couple of hours ago, despite all the whisky. "You've *always* hated admin work."

"It's not admin; it's data mining." I smiled blandly. "Big data, forward threat analysis. It's a really neat idea from the suggestions box—my hat's off to whoever came up with it. What I'm doing is proof of concept; there's no way I could get a budget to do it properly. But if it works, then I can present it for discussion and maybe get something rolling."

"Threat analysis and data mining?" Andy isn't easily impressed: he has a habitual pose of arid detachment, an expression of distant amusement as if the slings and arrows of office politics (and the tentacles and curses of sudden-death engagement) are merely flying all around for his entertainment. But I'd got his undivided attention tonight: rescuing him from sudden death did that. "What kind of threats are you hunting, and where?"

"I'm looking for outbreaks. Not sure what, or where, so I'm trying to spread the widest net that comes to hand. Anything peculiar. A rash of spontaneous human combustion in Stevenage, or rabies in Ravensthorpe; could be anything. The point is to try and build a tripwire for anomalies."

"But the police already—" He stopped. I shook my head.

"Not the police. Sure they'll be on the line as soon as they confirm a fire-breathing lizard has come ashore in Liverpool, but what about the other stuff? We live in dangerous times. What got me thinking was, how many of the sort of problems we get called in to piss on start out small and get treated by the wrong emergency services? Body snatchers in Bath, zombies in Z—Zurich." My metaphor engine had just broken: I took another sip of whisky. "A lot of possession cases show up as anomalous behavior, and while the ambulance service often bring the police in, it's frequently mis-categorized as a mental health issue. So I'm trying to work out how to mine the National Health Service data warehouses for early signs of demonic possession. That's what the task was about. 'Everybody knows vampires don't exist,' it said: 'develop a data mining utility to provide three sigma confirmation of the null hypothesis based on evidence from the NHS Spine.' I don't know who put it on the stack but it's *inspired*! I mean I couldn't have come up with a better ten-percent project if I'd designed it myself."

Andy stared at me slack-jawed for a couple of seconds, then raised his left hand and theatrically closed his mouth. "Refill time." He shoved his glass across the desk, towards the bottle. "Then you're going to tell me why you're telling me this."

"You haven't guessed already?" It was my turn to raise an eyebrow.

"You need a minion to run interference for you with the nice Data Protection Commissioner with the taser, right?"

"Right." I topped up his tumbler.

He hesitated momentarily. "Deal. Because it's crazy but it *just might* work, and it sounds a fuck of a lot less dangerous than what I was working on turned out to be. What could possibly go wrong?"

WHICH IS WHY, IN THE END, ANDY DIDN'T GET TO DEMONSTRATE his coding chops by summoning up an Eater.

And why I eventually sneaked my way into the clearances I needed to log onto the SUS Core Data Warehouse.

And, ultimately, why all the deaths happened.

2.

MEET THE SCRUM

"Hey, Alex, did you hear the one about the dyslexic sailor?"

"No—"

"He spent the night in a warehouse!"

Alex threw a bean bag at the joker—John—who caught it out of the air. Their supervisor was unamused: "Pigs!" said Mhari.

"It's okay, hen, we're committed," said John.

Then she laughed. "You will be."

It was lunchtime in an open-plan office, eight floors above the lobby level of a tower in Canary Wharf. North of Barclays, west of Santander, deep in the beating heart of global commerce. The office was a small clot of strangeness congealed in the pulsing circulation of an investment bank. They were *in* the bank, but not quite *of* it, this scrum of half a dozen Pigs and Chickens. They wore the suits and sometimes talked the talk, but held themselves apart; and when they left at night, they passed through a glassed-in corridor lined with metal detectors before they retrieved their personal phones and wallets and watches from metal lockers beneath the eyes of security guards. Some of them had worked in proprietary trading before joining this group; others had come straight out of academia, trailing the long shadows of student loans behind them (taken on by the bank as part of their golden handshake). But now they were *in* the bank but not *of* it, for the Scrum were not permitted any customer-facing contact at all. Indeed, they were employed by a shell company, the better to enable the parent's corporate management to deny their very existence.

There were other signs of distinction about them. Their hours were not governed by the ring of the trading floor bell in Paternoster Square, or any other market for that matter. (Electrons never sleep.) Nor did they directly support any of the parent institution's trading teams. They had a designated Product Owner, it was true, to whom the Scrum Master (or in their case, Scrum Mistress) was answerable, both for handover of deliverables and negotiation of new goals, and the Owner actually worked with a committee of traders and analysts. But the office was carefully structured to keep the members of the Scrum as tightly insulated from their parent organization as possible.

That way, deniability could be maintained for as long as possible.

I WASN'T HERE, I DIDN'T SEE THIS, AND I CAN ONLY OFFER THIS fictionalized reconstruction, dredged from the turbid depths of my imagination and seasoned with facts.

I got to sit in on the autopsy later, as we uncovered the gruesome history of the Scrum. Not that it was particularly awful, up to this point. So, an investment bank has a bunch of in-house proprietary trading teams who specialize in taking positions on the basis of quantitative analysis of which way the markets are trending? There's nothing illegal, immoral, or fattening about *that*. Investment Bank has a group who work on minimizing the latency in their trades, to reduce the market spread? Ditto. Algorithmic trading teams shoveling out and revoking put offers every few milliseconds to see what falls out of the high-frequency trading tree? We're getting into dubious territory here, but everyone else has been doing it, ever since the Yanks deep-sixed the important bits of the Glass-Steagall Act and their commercial banks all sprouted high-stakes gambling arms—but that's ancient history. The point is, the Bank wasn't doing anything they shouldn't have been doing, at least within the context of the crisis of early twenty-first-century capitalism.

Until we get to the Scrum.

A scrum—generic—is, depending on which dictionary you look it up in, either an elaborate way of restarting play in a rugby match (rugby: sort of like American football only with less body armor and more biting and gouging—I was forced to play it at school: did wonders for my character), *or* one of the quirkier cognitive disorders to which software project management is prone. The rugby version involves getting head-down and having a shoving match with the other side, sometimes involving ear-chewing, scrotum-grabbing, and neck-breaking (although the latter is frowned upon); the software variant is not dissimilar. It has its origins in Agile methodology, although it's Agile hopped up on crystal meth and spoiling for a fight: exactly the sort of thing you'd expect a bunch of city high-flyers to find appealing (at least in principle, and as long as it didn't look likely to detonate a large landmine under their bonuses).

The Scrum, singular, was the brainchild of Oscar Menendez, the vast unsympathetic brain at the heart of *The* Bank's Data Analytics Support Division, and sometime Algorithmics star. Back in the prehistory of the early noughties they headhunted him from Google to show them how to apply map/reduce to the very large data sets they were processing in real time—

(You're not listening, are you? Damn it, I suffered through the briefing. I don't see why you shouldn't have to suffer, too!)

Moving swiftly forward: the Bank set up the Scrum to try and bring some of the culture of an agile, highly responsive software startup to bear on the job of developing new and improved tools for high-frequency trading. The Scrum was elite; the Scrum had esprit up to *here*; the Scrum's long-term planning threshold was about twenty-four hours, marching to the beat of the daily stand-up meeting. They had a monstrous array of high-power data mining tools, live feeds from every exchange on the planet, their own individual compute-server farms. They had a PhD to headcount ratio close to 1:1 among the pigs—the hard core of math quants and algorithm developers. And every day they went in search of new and better techniques for identifying patterns in the data, trends that might be good for an extra 0.1 percent margin on every transaction for the handful of seconds it took before their competitors cottoned on.

They were brilliant, widely read, incisive, and effortlessly effective analysts and programmers. Which is another reason why, ultimately, so many people died.

PICTURE ALEX, ALONE IN THE OFFICE ONE EVENING.

Picture a twenty-something with spectacles and the remnants of a late heavy bombardment of acne cratering the '80s designer stubble under his jaw. The spectacles are, of course, aggressively black-rimmed and thick-lensed. His suit is expensively tailored, his shirt of finest quality linen, and the collar is just slightly askew, because Alex has an image to defend: that he is a quant, that he is Oscar's intellectual successor, that his mind soars as high above such mundane preoccupations as the City institution's dress code as an SR-71 roaring on Mach 3 afterburner across the abstract vistas of category theory and algebraic topology.

It's actually a total bluff. Like many truly brilliant minds, Alex suffers from an inordinate case of impostor syndrome, with mild hypochondria on top. He routinely arrives in the office each morning as a sweaty, seething blob of fear, certain that at any moment one of his colleagues will expose him as a fraud, unable to prove something as basic as $A^n = B^n + C^n$ for any arbitrary integer n. He's convinced that the reason he doesn't have a girlfriend is that he has halitosis. (He doesn't; the real reason is that he works over fourteen hours a day, six days a week, and spends the leftover hours sleeping, eating, and trying not to fall apart.) And he used to think that his acne was a symptom of malignant melanoma; every winter cold is multidrug-resistant tuberculosis.

Right now he's a bundle of pure anxiety because of his salary. He's theoretically due for a bonus—determined by the overall financial performance of the entire Scrum at the end of the financial year—but his basic salary of a little over £60,000 seems as dwindlingly inadequate as a Jobseeker's Allowance when stacked up against the Croesian excesses on display in the basement car park. And he gets to see the basement car park every morning when he chains up his bicycle after cycling in from his room in a house in Poplar. He's only been in the City for ten months (although it sometimes feels like a life sentence superimposed on a millisecond), and the habits of impoverished frugality he learned as a student weigh him down even as he tries to put on a good face for the people he works with.

You wouldn't want to be Alex. Being Alex, aged twenty-four and alone in the City, is awful. But being Alex in three hours' time is going to be much, much worse—and he'll still be alive to feel it.

ONE OF THE GREAT BESETTING PROBLEMS OF THE MODERN AGE is what to do with too much information. This is especially true of high-frequency share trading, where every second a Sahara-sized sand dune of data must be gulped down and sifted for the fragrant cat-turds of relevant market movements. The ebb and flow of share prices is familiar from a thousand ticker-tape parades and ever-shifting number grids, but that barely scratches the surface of the problem. Your stake in a corporation that makes robot milking machines for the dairy industry can be affected by a press release from an upstream supplier announcing a better image recognition algorithm for udders. Or by a newspaper article in which a farmer explains that, because the release cycle for new cows (nine months and one week) is shorter than the release cycle for new udder-recognition software (eighteen months), they've been breeding cows for teats that are compatible with robot vision systems. Or by a supermarket capping the price of dairy produce, leading to a liquidity crisis in Ambridge.

The Bank had been addressing the problem of drinking from the data firehose for many years, of course. Indeed, one of the Scrum's major tasks was to develop the banking equivalent of a self-cleaning litter tray: tools to help traders visually explore dizzying multidimensional arrays of ever-changing data without oversimplifying it into uselessness or causing them to throw up last night's Premier Cru.

Alex was working late on a surge effort, trying to hook a new data set up to a funky fractal visualizer Dick and Evan had knocked up two months earlier: a Spanner-based widget that turned sixty-four dimensional data sets into rolling three-dimensional landscapes, the gradient and color and friction and transparency of each crusty outcropping encoding some aspect of the object of fascination. The goal: pour in the popularity of babies' names over the past decade, sales of movie tickets in matinee showings, the Top 40 tracks pirated on BitTorrent, and the phase of the moon: get out an ordered list of toy manufacturers to buy or sell on the basis of their spin-off movie merchandising prospects. The reality so far: get out a scary-looking ski slope with black flags on the off-piste runs, not entirely suitable for traversal by a trading desk strapped to a snowboard.

Not that Alex knew much about skiing—his early lessons at school had been terminated by an unpleasant fall that had convinced him he'd broken his fibula for three days—but after eight nearly uninterrupted hours of staring at the screen he'd begun to go scooshy-eyed, his bladder was filing for divorce, and the interlocking mass of Möbius gears squirming behind his eyelids still resolutely refused to come into sharp focus.

I should go home, he realized. *I'm not getting anywhere. Maybe if I sleep on it, it'll come to me in the night . . .* But what if it didn't? There'd be a reckoning at tomorrow morning's stand-up meeting. In the theater of his mind's eye he could see Mhari smiling at him pleasantly and voicing all the apologies he'd have loved to keep to himself. He could hear Evan exercising his sense of humor, warped and slightly patronizing, playing off the weaknesses of his pair-programming partner. Maybe Oscar gracelessly and grumpily demanding to know what his salary was good for, if not this? *I can't go home,* he thought dismally. *Not until I've eaten my dog food.*

He looked round. For a miracle he was on his own. Janice was out of the office, dragged down to one of the server farms to supervise installation of some new piece of kit—he vaguely remembered hearing mention of the bank's acquisition of a D-Wave quantum annealer. Dick and Evan had gone along to rubberneck. Mhari and Oscar were in a meeting, and John had left early to attend a summit conference in a pub. It was a rare and peculiar experience to be alone in the Scrum's offices during working hours. *Fuck it,* he thought tiredly, then pushed himself back in his chair, seeking the focal point at the exact center of the cluster of five monitors on swivel-arms that overhung his desktop. Trading had closed a couple of hours ago: he badly needed a break. *Do I have time for half an hour in EVE Online—*

He reached out to touch his mouse and stared into the off-piste depths of My Little Pony affiliate marketing futures, just at the moment that one of the stuck Möbius gears in his mind's eye clicked forward a notch.

HIATUS.

Consciousness crashed back into Alex's head like the shards of a broken stable door banging to the ground behind a fleeing horse. Personality congealed out of nothing, in the midst of a monstrous chittering buzzing like a swarm of bees assembling themselves into larger and more complex units, grabbing hold of each other, reintegrating his scattered thoughts in the aftermath of—what?

Alex opened his eyes and tried to make sense of the grainy black-and-white shapes around him. The side of his cheek was hurting; the small of his back ached. He breathed out. Inhaled again, and color flooded into his vision. He was slumped across his desk, and the sharp edges in his face were the keys of his keyboard. He was half out of his chair: *Glad I didn't fall—*

His arms felt like limp noodles. He tensed, then braced himself and pushed upright. For a moment the world spun around his head; then he realized that he was, in fact, moving: his chair was spinning frictionlessly around on the axis of its gas strut. Nausea racked his stomach as he dragged a foot along the anti-static carpet, slowing the gyration. *I must have blacked out,* he reasoned. In his head he watched as Möbius gear-trains shimmered and rotated through a five-dimensional planetary cycle, mysterious and ineffable. It made perfect sense, in a manner he couldn't quite bring himself to articulate. *That's it!* he realized triumphantly, and grabbed his keyboard to freeze his insight in code before the moment slipped away.

Fifteen minutes passed. Or it might have been an hour, or three. Alex saved a new snapshot of the project to the common code repository and leaned back, dizzy and still slightly nauseous. "What happened?" he asked aloud, then looked at the screen. Icy panic flooded through his guts.

I lost consciousness! a corner of his mind gibbered. *I had a mini-stroke! Just like aunt Alicia!* His great-aunt had undergone a series of transient ischemic attacks, then ended up in hospital just in time for the big one. In conjunction with too many gruesome public information ads, her experience had instilled in Alex a deep dread of cerebro-vascular accidents. He fully expected to die shuddering on the floor of a dirty toilet cubicle, paralyzed on one side, if he so much as drew breath in a room where one of his colleagues had been honking the Honduran high-grade. *Now* the electric-pink elephant of hypochondria sat on his chest, force-ventilating him until he felt as if he was about to black out: *I've got to get to hospital!*

He staggered woozily to his feet, clinging to the back of his chair. After a moment, he let it go. It spun lazily around and he wobbled, but kept his balance. *Hospital!* he whimpered. His employers would view it as a sign of weakness if they knew he needed medical help, but visions of grue danced through his mind's eye: struck down in his prime by a malignant brain tumor, stroked out at his desk in an epic case of City karōshi, slain by a—*Möbius gear-train sigil blurring in and out of three dimensions as it rotated through a fourth and fifth: flame-like fractals, Cantor's dust burning in infinity behind them like malignant fire-rimmed eyes—*

Through the airlock corridor he stumbled, grabbed his wallet and keys and bicycle helmet from the locker in the hallway outside the Faraday-caged security door. Keyswipe-elevator-basement-car-park strobed past his shocky vision, still fixed on an interior vista of numinous dread. He threaded his way betwixt Bentley and Range Rover to the bike rack in the corner, tucked next to the fire riser inlet by the garage door leading to the exit ramp. *Should I be riding if I'm feeling like this? No, but it's faster than waiting for—*

He fastened his helmet strap under his chin with shaking fingers, then clambered astride his steel steed and pedaled unsteadily towards the ramp. *Heave* and up, *heave* again and round the bend, a sharp-edged line of daylight advancing across the shadowed concrete towards him.

Pain scraped razor-edges across his knuckles. A moment later, it hit his face. Alex squeezed his eyes shut and gasped at the magnesium-flare brilliance flooding over him in place of daylight, forgot to keep his feet on the pedals and staggered, falling sideways. He landed heavily, rolling. *Car crash, explosion, terrorists* flooded through his mind, then a moment later he was back in shadow, halfway down the ramp, limp and enervated as a doll with its strings cut.

THIS TIME, WHAT AWAKENED HIM FROM THE BLACKOUT WAS THE mouth-watering aroma of roast pork flooding his nostrils. The pain was ghastly, sickening. He tried to open his eyes, then to move. Something sharp-edged and hard entangled his legs—the frame of his bike, a Cannondale hybrid that had cost him half his first month's wages. He pushed himself up on his hands and fought back nausea. The backs of his wrists and fingers felt as if they were on fire. His face . . . *Must be a bomb,* he thought, shocked completely out of rationality. His helmet rim had shielded his eyes from that terrible heat-flash: otherwise he'd be blind. *There'll be other survivors. They'll need help.* He grabbed the frame of the bike one-handed and pushed it away, then shoved himself to his feet.

He sniffed. The smell was coming from nearby. He tried to lick his lips and nearly bit his tongue with the effort of holding back a scream. Abandoning his bike, he stumbled towards the fire door leading back to the basement elevator lobby. For some reason it wouldn't open at first. *Key card,* he realized fuzzily. He'd put it in his jacket pocket. He tugged at the door handle in increasing frustration, afraid to push his burning hands up against fabric: push against the wall with one hand, pull with the other. Something gave way, and the door opened.

He zoned out in the elevator on the way up to the eighth floor. His next moment of lucidity came in the cool tiled sepulcher of the bathroom. Avoiding the stalls—for some reason they were always terrible, no matter how recently the cleaners had been round—he lurched towards the row of sinks and the wall-wide mirror. His face hurt, a constant pounding burn: whenever he flexed a muscle a shivery spike of agony lanced through the skin above it. His hands were less painful.

He opened up a cold tap, forced himself to wait until the stream ran cool, then shoved his hands under the water. The bitter stinging began to subside after a few seconds. He peered closely. The backs of both hands were crimson and sore, as if severely sunburned or scalded. Tiny blisters were forming under the skin. He glanced up, risking a look at his face in the mirror.

His face—

I can't see my face. But he couldn't see the row of toilet stall doors behind him, either: there was something in the way, something fuzzy that skittered around the edges of his perception like a bead of water on a hot stove top. *Drugs? Chemical weapons?*

The rest room door opened as somebody entered. Wide pin-stripes and an even wider wide-boy manner: it was one of the commodities team, known to Alex only by sight (swaggering) and by attitude (expansively annoying). "Wotcher, cock. Spent too long on the sun bed?"

Alex spun round, blood in his eye. "Fucking get *lost*," he snarled, pain momentarily goading him until he forgot to be afraid: "No, wait. Can you see me in the mirror?"

The smirking chimp was taken aback. "Hey, no need to get personal! You been hitting the whacky backy or something? Of course I can see—"

Möbius gears turned in his mind's eye, their teeth meshing at the center of a beautiful and terrible symbol engraved in his vision, the projection into threespace of an instrument of power that he somehow knew was axisymmetric in seven dimensions. Alex opened his mouth and the words came with a deep assurance he'd never known before, from somewhere inside him that he hadn't known existed:

"I told you to get lost. *Do it.*"

Chimp-Smirker's smile froze. Glassy-eyed, he turned on the heel of one quarter-brogue and marched stiff-legged out of the rest room.

Alex turned back to the mirror. "I can't believe I just did that," he told the whirling blind spot where his reflection should be. "Someone must have spiked my—" He looked at his hands again. The redness had faded and the pain was trickling away. And his face: he raised a finger and gingerly touched the tip of his nose. It merely ached. "Psychosomatic. That's it," he mumbled to himself. Focussing his inner eye on the swirling gear-mesh at the heart of the evil mandala: "Fuck. Someone spiked my coffee. Trying to screw me over, make me lose my shit at work, lose my job, too. Who? The fuck. Go home and call in sick tomorrow. Work out who's got it in for me later. Fuck."

Was it just his imagination working overtime, or was he feeling oddly thirsty—for something thicker and heavier than water?

A tiny freaked-out voice gibbering in the corner of his mind (the same corner of his mind that nudged him to hide behind the sofa while watching monster movies on TV as a child) prompted him to check his smartphone for that day's sunset time before he moved. And so, he waited out the remaining quarter-hour until full darkness, shivering in the least-filthy toilet stall, telling himself that even though it couldn't possibly be true—Where were his fangs? How did he sign up for the opera cape and the widow's peak?—it wouldn't do to risk another case of psychosomatic sunburn and mirror-blindness.

GETTING HOME SAFELY GAVE ALEX MORE TROUBLE THAN HE might have anticipated, even taking into account his newly acquired stepping-on-the-cracks-in-the-pavement aversion to daylight. When he tried to take the lift down to the parking level it stopped at the lobby and he was politely directed elsewhere by uniformed security. "I'm sorry, sir, there's been some sort of attempted forced entry. It's probably just those bloody hippies from Occupy, but we can't take any chances."

"But my bike's—"

"If you want they can call a car for you at Reception, sir. You can collect your bike in the morning. Right now we're in lockdown, just in case one of them made it into the building."

His head spinning, Alex made his way instead to the underground atrium level, and out through the door into the shopping center. Sunlight didn't filter down this far; you could live like a mole. He stumbled towards the DLR station, hoping he still had enough credit on his Oyster card.

The platforms on the DLR were airy glassed-over tubes, raised well above ground level. As he rode the escalator towards his homebound ride, for a few terrifying seconds he thought he'd made a mistake and that it was still daytime: everything looked preternaturally bright, the shadows diffuse and lacking in concealment. But it didn't burn, and as he calmed down he realized it was the ochre London overcast, lit from beneath by a million lights. *I must be photosensitive,* he realized. *A migraine?* That would explain the visual distortions in the mirror. Of course; and there was mild nausea, too. But he'd occasionally suffered from stress-related migraines before, and this felt different.

Alex's current home was a spare bedroom in an old and damp-smelling maisonette owned by a pleasant middle-aged couple (a nurse and a police support officer). They still thought he was a counter clerk, because he'd bottled out of telling them precisely what kind of bank he worked for, or in what capacity. It wasn't much of a home: it was more of an ellipsis between student squalor and the penthouse off Mayfair that he planned to take out a subsidized mortgage on the moment his first annual bonus came in. In the meantime, it allowed him to save up frantically in case his bonus *didn't* come in and he ended up having to look for another job while picking up his burden of student debt again (the golden handshake not being due to vest fully until he'd put in two whole years).

He was about to turn the corner onto his street when a knot of deeply intertwingled thoughts brought him up sharply. *Someone spiked my drinks* led to *I'm hallucinating*, which by induction allowed him to derive *I don't want Sam or Valerie to think I'm a user.* Knotted around it like a venomous snake was another strange loop of concepts: *But if I'm not hallucinating I really shouldn't be around them. Because: vampire. Right?* Alex quite liked his landlords, at least to the extent of not wanting them violently dead: the imminent prospect of sprouting fangs and ripping their throats out was profoundly, mortifyingly embarrassing. Nor could he risk them bursting into his room and opening the curtains to check whether he was sleeping through the afternoon or needed urgent medical help. *I need a hotel,* he realized.

There was a cheap Travelodge across the bridge from Poplar station. Alex headed for it, diverting on the way to pick up a carrier bag of essentials from a late-night supermarket. To his disappointment, the dazed-looking hotel receptionist didn't spare him a second glance. She barely looked at him as she took his credit card, billed him for two nights, and droned through the here-is-your-room-card spiel. (On his way over he'd obsessively concocted a cover story concerning a lost checked bag, a mugger, and a rainy night in Paris—entirely for nothing, as it transpired.) "Thanks," he mumbled, and made a dash for the lift, trying not to think about the way the arteries in her throat throbbed so seductively.

The hotel room was exactly what he'd expected: a minimal salary-man/family on a budget dormitory, with the basic fittings and no extras. First he hung the *Do Not Disturb* sign out, then for good measure he reinforced it with an improvised door wedge—a free newspaper he'd grabbed on the way in. The curtains gave him some cause for concern, but he'd thought to buy a roll of duct tape and a pair of scissors. Wobbling and unsteady, he knelt on the dresser to tape around the gaps. *They're going to think I'm mad,* he thought, and tittered to himself. Locked in a safe space with a bag of munchies and a bathroom, he ought to be okay—as long as he didn't wig out further before sunset tomorrow. *Have I lost it already?* he wondered.

It was barely ten o'clock. The question of what he was going to do for the next twenty-two hours was only just beginning to sink in. He lay on the bed fully clothed, and stared at the bone-white ceiling until dragons and Möbius gears began to uncoil in the corner of his vision. *If I'm not nuts already I'm going to be nuts by the time I . . .*

He snatched up his phone. The face recognition unlock worked and he could see himself in the phone camera's display: that ought to tell him something if he wasn't so overwrought. He dialed a work contact. As he'd expected, it rang through to voice mail. *Good.* "Uh, Mhari? It's Alex. Listen, I'm not well. Uh, actually, spouting at both ends. Really, it's a rotavirus or something. I'll try to make it in tomorrow morning, but if I don't, it's because I'm pebble-dashing the—uh oh!" He forced a nauseated gurgle (which came disturbingly easily) and killed the call. *Ass: covered.* Now to sleep, and see if he could see himself in the bathroom mirror in the morning or something.

Sleep, of course, didn't come easy, but there were movies on demand.

Lots of movies.

Movies about Lesbian Vampire Hunters and Blood-Sucking Fiends.

Movies with lots of gore and blood. Blood which, on screen, didn't make him feel faint and dizzy the way the sight of even a trivial graze did in real life.

Fascinating.

A SLEEPLESS BUT INTERESTING—NOT TO MENTION AMUSING AND educational—night later, Alex prepared to wait out the day in a state of numb boredom. Sleep hadn't come, and time had not restored his ability to see his own reflection: shaving had been unexpectedly hazardous. In a spirit of masochism, he stuck a pinkie through a gap in the duct tape around lunchtime; the resulting blisters took half an hour to subside. By noon he was reconciled to the horrible truth. *Face it: I don't need sleep. Daylight burns. I can't see myself in the mirror, I yanked the lock right out of the basement door and I distinctly remember bending my bike frame when I grabbed it.* He raised a finger to his mouth, ran it around the front of his upper jaw. *Is that my imagination, or . . . ?* No, it was imagination, at least for now. No fangs, thank God. *Fangs for small mercies, ha ha.*

There's no such thing as vampires.

There's no such thing as vampires.

There's no such thing as—

Research.

Alex spent much of the day with his smartphone, doing what research he could: mainly reading the Wikipedia and TVTropes articles on vampires, but also verifying that the camera could see him, but a left-for-right mirror flip turned his image into a blind-spot distortion. And that he could pluck falling objects out of the air ridiculously fast, on video. Some calculations in Wolfram Alpha confirmed that his reflexes had sped up to such an extent that they were not merely fast but biomechanically implausible, and while he couldn't see his own image, he could certainly see the hotel toiletries he was juggling. By the time his battery was down to 10 percent he knew even less than he had when he started: except that whatever had happened to him was real, or his pocket computer was in on the conspiracy to gaslight him. Also, despite eating all his munchies and drinking copiously from the bathroom sink, the enervating sensation of thirst wouldn't go away.

"What was I doing?" Alex asked the tiles in the bathroom. Introspection revealed a frustrating shortage of black-gowned Elvira wannabes slurping on his carotid artery; obviously there was something missing from the common lore that it takes a vampire to make a vampire. "I was trying to visualize the phase transition in—" He stopped dead, Möbius gears turning in his mind's eye. "Then I passed out and the weird visuals began. Hmm. I wonder if it's just me?"

A minute later, phone in hand, he waited for the call to connect. "Hi. Evan? Yes, it's me. Sorry I couldn't come in. I was still throwing up everywhere. No, really. You wouldn't thank me. No, I wasn't drinking. Rotavirus, I told Mhari—oh? She said what? The cow! Look, I'm a bit better now and I'm going to come in this evening, work the late shift to make up for lost hours. Thing is, I was hoping you could stay so I could talk you through my last commit. What, you didn't understand—look, I'm not surprised, I was already feeling ill so I didn't doc it very clearly. I'll talk you through it, okay? This evening."

Without ever saying so in so many words, Evan made it clear that he'd had other plans for the evening. No matter: Alex was at his most implausibly persuasive, and kept at it until he could feel Evan's resistance crumbling. *Bastard's probably got a hot date*, he thought resentfully. Evan had a way with the talent that Alex, despite diligent study, had never been able to emulate: something that enabled him to speak to pretty women without derping out like a refugee from the Island of Dr. Moreau. (Single-sex school followed by a de facto single-sex faculty and an obsessive-compulsive work ethic had left Alex with few opportunities to socialize with the opposite sex since the age of ten.) "See you there," Alex insisted. "You *are* going to stay, aren't you?" The same sense of assurance filled him: "You can go after we've gone over that visualization. Bye!"

SUNSET.

Alex left the hotel, not bothering to check out. A taxi to the office and a badge-swipe through the turnstile: he took the stairs to the office, intrigued to note that he didn't feel particularly breathless after sixteen flights. Passing through the airlock and into the Scrum's office, he had to narrow his eyes against the glare of the screens.

The office was empty but for Evan, who was waiting for him with a pained expression, as if desperate for the toilet. "Couldn't you have left this until tomorrow morning?" he demanded. "I had to bail on Candace and she's going to be—"

"*Trust* me." Alex leaned over his teammate: "If my hypothesis is correct, it's going to be totally life-changing . . ."

. . . AND THEN THERE WERE TWO.

3.

KGB.2.YA

MO AND I HAVE BEEN MARRIED FOR YEARS: ONE OF THE SE-
crets of our success is that we don't harbor grudges in silence. If Mo
figures I deserve it, she vents at me and we hammer out an apology
or an agreement or a peace treaty or whatever it takes immediately.
So it's a sign of how serious this quarrel is that she sat on it for nearly
a month. And when she finally decides it's time to draw it to my attention, it's very ripe and stinky.

"You shouldn't have dragged Pete into it," she tells me one mid-
week evening as I'm clearing the kitchen table of the remains of a
passable lasagne, and topping up our wine glasses. "It wasn't fair on
Sandy. Or the kid."

"I—"

She raises her hand, and that's when I work out she still needs to
vent. "I know what you're going to say. You're going to insist that it
was time-critical, that you didn't think we had anyone on tap who
could do whatever it was you needed Pete to do, and that the survival
of the human race depended on it. And you're ready to back up those
talking points with a well-reasoned, sensible explanation. But I'm still
angry."

The worst part of it is, she's right about everything *except* my having an arsenal of well-reasoned, sensible explanations to back this up.
The sad fact is, Gerry Lockhart emphasized the level of confidentiality
attached to that last job by ordering me not to talk about it to *anyone*.
And the geas that's part of my oath of office won't let me break that
order. It's extremely heavy-handed of him: Mo has been working as
an external asset since before I heard the term, and I've been part of
her support framework, and hitherto it's been mutual. However, I
can't tell her a word about GOD GAME BLACK without his permission unless I want my hair to catch fire and my brains to leak out of
my nose. The geas is intended to maintain internal security, but sometimes it has unpleasant consequences.

So I just sit there and take it, with a defensive grin on my face.

"It was grossly irresponsible of you to drag him into—whatever."
(So Pete hasn't told her exactly what I asked him to do for me, which
was to read a stolen scan of the appendices of a rather variant version
of the Bible, and give me an opinion on the sanity of the cult who
were using it. It turned out to be a road map for engineering the Second Coming—not of Jesus, but of an ancient undead nightmare from
the deep cosmological past. The cult was a mega-church in Colorado
Springs, yours truly was part of the team trying to stop them, and the
consequences are classified GOD GAME BLACK.)

"Sandy depends on him. The kid"—due in three months—
"depends on her. And he's a vicar. You just casually poked a hole in
his universe. Didn't you expect that to have any consequences? He's
got a family and several hundred parishioners to look after, and regardless of what you think of his belief system"—misguided at best,
because regular Christianity doesn't have much space for the Black
Pharaoh or the Sleeper in the Pyramid, or even the normal run-of-the-
mill tentacular horrors we deal with—"he fills an important niche in
delivering hope, comfort, and support to vulnerable people.

"And you tore down the curtain and exposed him to *our* world.
Which is inevitably going to screw him up, and, indirectly, screw up
hundreds of other people. Some of whom might go talk to the vicar
if they're feeling depressed or suicidal. Drop that stupid grin, Bob. By

destabilizing Pete you could have killed people. *Civilians.* The people we're supposed to be protecting."

The skin on my face feels taut. I cross my arms. *How much can I say?* "Remember Amsterdam?"

"What, the first time? Or—" she pauses. "You aren't allowed to talk about it?"

I manage to nod. My internal censor approves. "You can ask"—I check with my censor—"Gerry Lockhart, in External Assets. Please, Mo? I can't defend myself. I can't even apologize. *I am not allowed to talk about this.*"

"Well *shit!*" This is strong language for Mo. Her gaze flickers away from me, some of her electric anger seeking a new channel to earth. She knows about the geas, the binding compulsion to silence. We usually have a waiver that allows us to talk about work. A year or so ago she had to do a job in Amsterdam—wet work, because that's what Agent CANDID sometimes does—and came home in pieces, because some idiot up the line had explicitly forbidden her from talking to me. I'm her support system: I'm not in the same line of work exactly, but I'm close enough to understand what she goes through and help her deal with it. *That* time I hunted down the idiot in question and sorted it out, probably saving our employers a very expensive medical leave bill. *This* time the boot is on the other foot. If I could tell her what happened in Colorado Springs she'd . . .

(Well, no, she probably *wouldn't* forgive me. But she'd understand *why*, and take it into account, which amounts to much the same. Hate the sin, love the sinner: it's hard to stay pissed off at someone for doing something wrong if you know you'd have done exactly the same thing if you'd been standing in their shoes.)

I shove a topped-up wine glass across the table towards her. "You need Pete and Sandy for your own reasons."

She nods. Her neck muscles are still tense, but she takes the glass. "I can't afford to lose track of normal, Bob. Most of our friends *aren't* normal anymore—neither are we."

I take a sip (okay, a mouthful) of pinot noir and swallow. "Dead right." Pete (vicar) and Sandy (teacher) are some of our few remaining friends outside the organization. If I was a Harry Potter fan (and offensively stupid besides) I'd call them "muggles." But that's exactly the wrong way to look at the picture. Those of us who have too much to do with the supernatural aren't wizards, but monsters. Or in danger of becoming monsters.

Over time, most of our circle have either moved away or started families; we increasingly socialize with workmates because it's safe and easy. They understand why we can't talk about certain parts of our office days, and we don't risk endangering their world view by accidentally exposing them to the nihilistic truth. Our grip on everyday normality is, shall we say, eroding like the cliffs north of Aldeburgh. Lose that grip, and . . .

"We need more normal in our life," I say. "Especially now that I've been roped into, into . . ." I can't say it. Into the irregular twilight at the edge of the organization that she's been quietly slipping in and out of for so long, carrying that damned violin.

"Easier said than done." She takes in some wine, then slowly twirls the stem of the glass between her fingers, staring at the film of red washing up the sides of the bulb. I've seen this often enough to realize that right now she's in danger of tipping from anger into bitterness. "We haven't been normal since—"

"We could go out more often," I suggest. "Do normal things, meet normal people. Take up"—I search for a good idea, come up blank— "going to the theater? Opera?" (I detest opera and have no time for classical music in general, but Mo is rather a keen violinist.) "Bingo?"

Her cheek twitches. "We're a bit young for that, dear."

"We could get a cat." I'm not sure where *that* idea comes from, but it's an ordinary people kind of thing to do. Normal folks can also have children, but in our line of work that would be highly inadvisable. Even if we wanted kids, knowing the nature of the world we'd be bringing them into would give us second thoughts. But a cat . . . what could possibly go wrong with *that*?

"Are you volunteering for litter tray duties?"

I shrug. "It can't be worse than riding herd on software updates for six computers, two phones, and a tablet. Can it?"

"If you're *sure*—" Her eyes narrow. "Hmm. A cat." Pause. "Have you ever lived with a cat before?"

Vague memories of a purring warm lump sitting on my lap during family visits to my great-aunt percolate to the surface. (Ellis Billington's Fluffy I can safely discount. We are discussing standard-issue, non-supernatural felines, after all, not the alien-in-a-cat-suit kind.) "Not personally, but I've had visiting rights—"

"Oh, good. Well, I think it'd be really nice to know that when things go bump in the night it's just a cat knocking over the glassware to hear it shatter, so why not?" She knocks back half the contents of her wine glass in one. "Yes, let's do that."

It suddenly dawns on me that I know about as much about looking after a pet cat as I know about flying a jet fighter: it's all MEOW DAKKA-DAKKA ZOOM to me. "Um. I think we need to do some research first. Vets, food, that sort of thing?"

"No, Bob." She smiles at last. "*You* need to do some research. Litter tray duties, remember?"

"Oh bloody hell." It slowly dawns on me that while she can't justify berating me over Pete anymore, she can still extract a cold revenge: making me responsible for a small furry life-form's well-being, meanwhile adding an extra kilogram or two of ballast to help anchor her fraying connection to normality. "Well, I suppose so . . ." I finish my wine. "But if I'm looking after it, I get to choose what we adopt. Okay?"

AFTER WE DO THE WASHING-UP, I GET TO SPEND THE REST OF the evening reading FAQs on cat maintenance on the web. It takes about half an hour to come to the unwelcome realization that they're almost as complex as home-brew gaming PCs, and have even more failure modes. (When your gaming PC malfunctions it doesn't stealthily dump core in your shoes.) But I have made my bed and I must lie in it, so I pencil in a date at the nearest RSPCA shelter for next Saturday.

On the other hand, for the first time in nearly a month I don't get to sleep on the sofa-bed in the spare room. So perhaps the worst is over.

* * *

TWO DAYS LATER I'M IN THE OFFICE, WORKING ON A PILE OF virtual paperwork (you would not *believe* how many hoops you have to jump through to gain access to the NHS's core statistical data warehouse if you're not a sixteen-headed committee from a designated Strategic Health Authority), when there's a knock on my door. I hit "save" and look up, then mash my finger on the button that flips the red "secret" light to green. (What I'm working on isn't actually secret in the first place; just mildly embarrassing. But secrecy is a reflex.)

"Come in," I call as the door opens, then I do a double take. "Pete?"

His head is swiveling like a bird-scarer, taking in my twelve square meters of squalor. "Bob? They told me you worked here, but I didn't quite realize . . ."

"Come in, sit down."

I suddenly realize there's nowhere to sit—the visitor's chair is currently occupied by three broken computers. The uppermost one is a floppy-disk-only 286 lunchbox that somebody forgot to check back into inventory in 1994: I've already spent a couple of days trying to figure out a way to legally decommission it, because current regulations insist that all computers must have their hard disk or SSD shredded and disposed of securely, and any exceptions require sign-off by a security audit team which was unfortunately dissolved two years ago. I sweep the detritus onto the floor and turn the chair to face him. "You're, uh, well, you're here now . . ."

Pete sits on the edge of the chair, his expression somewhere between mildly puzzled and pained. "Yes," he says, and waits.

That's when the *oh shit* moment hits me.

"This is my fault," I say in a small voice.

"Is it really?" His expression brightens abruptly. "I thought you probably came into it somewhere along the line. Was it that fragment you sent me?"

I sigh. "How long since they swept you up?"

"About three weeks. I had a visit from a couple of polite gentlemen who asked me to sign the Official Secrets Act. In *blood*." Pete is clearly mildly perturbed by this, as so he should be: his faith doesn't have much room for sanguinary magic, unless you count holy communion. "Then they explained that you do secret work for the government and if I talk about it to outsiders without permission my eyeballs will boil. Is it true, Bob? I mean, how true *is* it?"

I oscillate for a moment between a frantic urge to run for the hills, a residual instinctive urge to flannel Pete with half-truths, and the doleful realization that it's probably best to tell him the unvarnished truth. That way there's no room for misunderstandings later.

"It's mostly true, I'm afraid. This organization, the Laundry"—I'm watching his eyes for any sign of surprise, and I don't see anything, which means he already knows too much for his own good—"is the part of the secret service that deals with occult and magical threats. I've worked here for some time. Since before I met Mo, actually." (About twelve years ago.) "I'm a, a specialist." I can't quite bring myself to say *necromancer* to a vicar.

"Well, I suppose that brings me to my next question. Mo—does she work here, too?"

"Part-time," I admit. "Yes, we've been holding out on you. We were required to, actually. We deal with stuff that's best not talked about in public."

I watch him, but he doesn't look surprised. He just sits there, marinating in the ambiance of my most secret office, nostrils flaring at the faint pong of *essence de spook*.

I crack first. "If we talked about it, it would scare people," I tell him.

"Stuff like that piece of apocrypha you emailed me last month?" he asks.

"Yes." I unwind infinitesimally. "It's our job to protect people from, from that sort of thing. And worse." I instinctively glance towards my bookcase. There, sitting in front of a pile of CS textbooks, is a Bible. It's the one the Golden Promise Ministries used, with added special sauce in the apocrypha. I make a judgment call and pass it to him. "I'm not sure how much I'm allowed to talk about what happened out there, but here's the original source material." Or rather, a copy we bargained with the Black Chamber—our American opposite numbers—for. Not that they had any reason to withhold it after we saved their ass.

Pete holds the Bible uncertainly, as if he's afraid its cover is coated in contact poison. "They told me their last expert on Aramaic studies and Biblical apocrypha died some years ago. And would I mind very much taking on that role on a part-time consultative basis, as and when."

"Yes." I didn't know about the *last expert* angle, but it sets my mind at rest somewhat. "How about we get a mug of coffee and I show you around?" *Whatever you're cleared for, once I've established your access controls,* I add silently, for my own benefit.

"Coffee would be great. But as for the tour . . . I'm not sure it's necessary." He looks slightly sheepish. "They told me they won't be needing me here routinely; I'm supposed to look at your archives and learn the procedures for accessing files and, um, that's all for now and they'll call me if anything comes up." He makes a dust-off gesture with his left hand.

"That's probably all for the best." I stand and lead the way towards the coffee station. "It's not as if you don't already have a job, is it?"

"A vocation, actually. But yes."

He ambles along behind me like an oversized penguin, glancing amiably from side to side, taking it all in: the heart of the secret state, all puke-green paint, chipped lino, and LOOSE LIPS SINK SHIPS posters left over from the last war but one. (Our decor is so cheesy it's almost regained a hipster-ish modicum of cool.)

"So is it true, then? That you single-handedly turned back an alien invasion of tentacle monsters who were being summoned by our dispensationalist brethren with the non-standard user manual?"

I wince. "Is that what they told you? Because if—"

"—Not in *quite* so many words—"

"—so they exaggerated my—"

"—but they were quite effusive about—"

"—success what?"

I grind to a halt, two doors past the gents, and take a deep breath.

"I'm not James Bond, Pete. Just a bad occasional stunt-double. For the extras," I add, before he gets the wrong end of the stick. "You know, the ones who get beaten up?" I cross my arms defensively, wrapping a hand around my upper right bicep, which has a curious rectangular dent in it. (Covered by a skin graft about ten centimeters long, a souvenir from some very unpleasant people I met a couple of years ago.) "It's nothing like as romantic as movies or TV make it out to be. Or books, dammit."

"But you're in the job of protecting us from . . ."

"Yes, exactly." I start walking again. Round the bend, then we come to the coffee station. "We tend to pool mugs here." I grab a couple of chipped promotional beakers left over from a long-defunct minicomputer vendor and slop the evil-smelling brew into them. *Milk, one sugar,* I remember on Pete's behalf. "Seriously, I didn't want to trouble you with that stuff. But I was out of options and you were the only person I knew who stood a hope of delivering an interpretation in time. Looks like Upstairs agreed with me, unfortunately, which is why it's entirely my fault you're drinking London's worst institutional coffee right now. I owe you a huge, groveling apology—"

"No you don't."

"What?"

Pete waves his mug around, eyes gleaming: "This is amazing! It's all real!"

"Um?" His response is so enthusiastic, and so unexpected, that he's reduced me to monosyllables. That's a *bad* sign.

"Bob. First of all, I like to think that the most important point of my vocation is *helping* people. Helping with grief, with love, with faith, with life's challenges. You've given me a *better* way to help *more* people. Do you really expect me to object to that? And secondly, you've given me some pause for reappraisal. The demon business, the whole nightmare monsters from beyond spacetime thing, the zombies: yes, I can see why you might expect that to shake my faith in God's love. But don't you think that's a little superficial? There's another way of looking at them, which is as evidence that the supernatural exists and is important. Where God fits into all of this I can't say, but I *can* say that these so-called elder gods don't invalidate His existence. They don't prove a negative. If anything they make God's message of love *more* important, in a human context."

I take a mouthful of lukewarm bunker-oil-flavored cow piss and try not to gag as my Weltanschauung strips its gears. His optimism is sunny, invincible, and just slightly pitiable. I'm about to open my mouth and say something inadvisable when I realize that, actually, I don't want to do that. I may be turning into a cynical old fart, but that's no reason to drag down everyone around me at the same time. So I open my mouth and say something else instead: "I think I can agree with the sentiment, if not the details." Then, moving swiftly on, "But they wouldn't have dragged you in here just for a mug of coffee, would they?"

"No. They said they want me to know where the archive stacks are, and how to access them. Then I've got what they called a 'training wheels' assignment, after which I go back in the box until they need me." He sniffs, mildly disapproving. "It's supposed to demonstrate competence with the library system, I gather. *After* I told them about my doctorate."

"Yeah, right." I roll my eyes. "They're big on that. Assuming the 'they' we are talking about is someone in Induction and Training . . . ?"

"Does Ellen McQueen ring a bell?"

"Yes, yes it does." I shrug. "Did she give you a time scale or a classification level for this assignment?" I begin walking slowly back towards my office.

"Yes: it's open-ended and the material is intended for public dissemination when the time comes—meanwhile, it's considered confidential. Is that . . . ?"

"Huh. The confidential bit is reasonable; no offense, but we don't hand secret materials to trainees, even if they've passed positive vetting. But open-ended?"

"Apparently it's expected to take some time. 'You are not expected to finish this job,' she said. Those were her exact words."

"What—?" I think for a moment. "That doesn't make any kind of sense to me. What did she say you were to do?"

"There was some sort of civil defense program from the 1970s called PROTECT AND SURVIVE, she said. That was back during the Cold War. It was a booklet and posters and a bunch of recorded radio and TV broadcasts about how to survive a nuclear attack, and in event of a war situation breaking out they were going to distribute the booklets and run the broadcasts. Sort of a public information thing, I gather, although the main effect was to drive graphic designers to suicide." He chuckles.

"Oh dear fricking . . ." What he's telling me finally sinks in. "You mean the Laundry has a public information campaign stored up and ready to roll in event of CASE—sorry, in event of us being invaded by tentacle monsters from another dimension?"

"Yes! That's exactly it. Only it was last updated in 1983. 'Take a look at it,' she said, 'and write a proposal for bringing it up to date.'"

"Did it have a name, this project?"

"Yes. The books and posters are called MAGIC CIRCLE OF SAFETY, but she said I'd find it in the stacks under a very strange reference—KGB.2.YA—what's so funny? Bob? Are you choking? Bob? Bob? Do you need help?"

Kiss Good-Bye 2 Your Ass: I *love* the Laundry sense of humor.

"I'm okay," I finally wheeze as I exhale the last of my half-lungful of coffee. "Let's go check it out."

KGB.2.YA. How bad can it be?

IN THE END WE GO BACK TO MY OFFICE, WHEREUPON A COUPLE of emails and a phone call confirm that Pete has actually been sent an orientation pack (not arrived yet) and assigned to my guest chair for the next week. Doubtless this is my punishment for increasing the departmental headcount and simultaneously downsizing our office floorspace with Angleton's help. (I gather Andy is still in full-on Office Flying Dutchman mode . . .) "Looks like we're hot-desking or something," I explain. "Let's do lunch and I'll take you to the archives afterwards."

The Dansey House refurbishment may be stalled, but the archive stacks, deep beneath the basement, are still in business. They're built inside segments of deep-running tube tunnels that were excavated before and after the Second World War, to double as air raid shelters and blitz-proof government offices. Nuclear weapons made them obsolete for their original purpose and the London Underground never asked to have their tube station back, so we hung on to it and filled it with microfiche cards and, latterly, storage servers. You thought the gigantic new London water mains were installed to supply the capital with drinking water? Well, yes they were—but only after we've used them as a heat sink for our equipment racks.

But we don't end up in the deep stacks. Before lunch I take Pete to visit old Basil in Archives to ask for the shelf locator of KGB.2.YA. This is necessary because Basil is one of our pensioners—the ones who don't retire so much as they subside into the furniture—and the most advanced technology he can operate reliably is his hearing aid (which whistles irritatingly, like a mosquito scraping its fingernails down a blackboard). He doesn't answer his email, instant messaging might as well be rocket science, and a voice call is inevitably frustrated by the intermittently faulty induction loop on his desk phone. Luckily Basil is okay if you visit him in person, so I procure a map and a signed authorization chitty before taking Pete to the canteen for lunch (British Institutional Keg Curry and naan for me, beans on toast for him).

Afterwards, back in my office: "You have got to be shitting . . . sorry." I peer at the hand-scrawled carbon-copy again, double-checking it. "You're sure that was the right reference?"

Pete rummages in the ring binder that Trish inflicted on him when he arrived. "Yes, that's the one."

"Well, it's in a warehouse in Watford, most of the way out to the M25. I didn't even know we *had* a warehouse in Watford. It'll take us three hours to get there and back by tube, so I suppose—"

"I brought the Vespa." Pete diffidently jangles a bunch of keys. "Can you ride pillion?"

Vicars on vintage scooters; what is the world coming to? (I'm just glad I don't have hemorrhoids.)

Pete has parked in an alley round the back of the New Annex, between two dumpsters full of non-office waste. It's raining, and I'm glad I decided to wear a parka to work, even though it makes me look like a dork. He passes me a spare helmet and I'm busy fiddling with the chin strap when I get a peculiar feeling that I'm being watched.

I open an inner eye and whip my head around. There's a startled hiss and a black bolt of lightning scoots under the nearer dumpster. It's not a feeder, nor is it a human intruder. I gulp with relief. Green eyes flash at me from the shadows, then retreat into darkness.

"What's up?" Pete asks, noticing my startle reflex.

"Just a stray cat." Maybe feral. *I need to stop jumping at shadows,* I think. "Let's go."

I have heard that the second fastest way to get around central London is on two wheels. Well, if your range needs to encompass the entire area within the M25 orbital motorway, you either need Lance Armstrong's prescription cabinet or a motor. Pete gives me a demonstration of the latter. We make it out to Watford in less than half an hour, faster than I could have managed even given a bicycle and access to the ley-line paths of power that thread the capital's disused railways and cuttings. Unfortunately I also discover that riding pillion in the rain without leathers is a great way to get soaked to the skin and chilled, and while I don't get car-sick or plane-sick I am quite capable of getting nauseous on the back of a scooter.

Nevertheless, Pete gets us there in miraculously short order. We dismount in a car park round the side of an anonymous-looking industrial unit with roll-ups, and I stumble dizzily towards the windowless door. There is a doorbell, and a small camera. I ring the bell and present my warrant card to the camera. After a moment, Pete remembers to pull out his shiny new ID. It doesn't come with the special sauce yet, but at least it'll get him in the door if he's accompanied by an irresponsible adult.

"'Ooozare?'"

"Bob Howard and Pete Wilson, Capital Laundry Services."

"C'min."

There's a buzz, and I push the door open. The office inside is tiny, occupied by the middle-aged security guard who was playing solitaire on his phone when I interrupted his brilliantly exciting afternoon. "Yus?" he asks resentfully.

"We called ahead." I try not to look disapprovingly at his game: rule #1 of working at remote offices is never to piss off site security. "We need access to the stores." I hold up the slightly rusty key ring I checked out from Archives Reception, and Pete produces a file from somewhere inside his bulky leather jacket and slides out an authorization form.

"G'wan in. You gointa be long?"

"Don't know yet." I glance at Pete, make eye contact, and nod infinitesimally. "We'll let you know. When do you go off-shift?"

"I gotta be out by five."

"Okay. If we're still going, knock on the door ten minutes before you're ready to leave and we'll wrap up."

"Lemme see that badge again?"

I show him my warrant card, and he scrawls something that might be cryptographically related to my name and departmental number on a dog-eared sheet clipped to a board hanging by the door. Then he goes back to his solitaire game.

I turn the key, reach round the door to flick on the light switch, and together Pete and I enter the KGB.2.YA archive.

IT HAS BEEN SAID THAT HER MAJESTY'S GOVERNMENT FINDS IT *extremely* difficult to throw anything away. Like your mad old aunt who lives in a flat with sixteen commemorative Royal Family tea sets, thirty cubic meters of yellowing newspapers, and an incontinent dachshund, the government hangs on to stuff until long after it becomes obvious that it lacks any conceivable use:

- As late as 1982, they kept a strategic reserve of 160 steam locomotives in a vast underground complex at Corsham, near Bath, in case they had to rebuild the British railway network after a nuclear war. (They also kept a Second World War jeep factory, five million battery-powered radios, and twenty-three million body bags at the same depot.)

- The official Government Random Number Generator used for seeding new encryption keys is a thing of legend, running as it does on a type of punched paper tape that hasn't been manufactured since the 1950s. (We had to invent some really neat hacks using digital cameras to read it into our oldest trailing-edge minicomputers in order to *use* those numbers . . .)
- And rumor has it that the Central Ammunition Depot hanging off Box Tunnel still contains two thousand barrels of iron-tipped English longbow arrows, in case it becomes urgently necessary to re-fight the Battle of Crécy.

But these pale into insignificance compared to the glorious, pointless obsolescence that fills the MAGIC CIRCLE OF SAFETY warehouse.

"Dear *God*," whispers Pete, "it's full of posters!"

He's not wrong. The warehouse is full of floor-to-ceiling, heavy-duty steel shelves, construction built to take timbers. The nearest aisle to us is not full of wood, though. Instead, every available niche is jammed with pallets laden with broadsheet-sized posters, stacked half a meter deep and strapped in place. I do some quick mental arithmetic and realize there has to be upwards of a hundred thousand public notices here. I really don't want to risk any of the shelves falling on me.

While the pallets are tagged for easy identification, someone has taken the trouble to hang a copy of each poster by the side of the shelves that hold the stock. The design values are classical, and not in a good way. Two-color printing on plain white paper: *Here* is the parliamentary portcullis-and-crown symbol, sitting atop a perspective-flattened summoning grid, menaced by cartoonish green tentacles to ram home the message—STAY IN THE CIRCLE. And *there* is a symbolic nuclear family (tall male toilet-door figure, shorter female toilet-door figure, two small mini-me's) gathered under an Elder Sign—CULTIST DANGER: WATCH YOUR NEIGHBOURS FOR THIS SIGN. I wince at this latter. (The next cultist I meet who can tell an Elder Sign from Transport for London's new logo will be the first. And don't get me started on the occult symbol they used for the Olympics . . .)

I look down the aisle. Yes, there it is: **PROTECT AND SURVIVE** with added magic circle goodness. Tentacles replace mushroom clouds in the variant semiological design language of pants-wetting despair at imminent brain-eating catastrophe.

"Is that," Pete says in an awe-muffled voice, pointing, "a box of LPs?"

I follow his aim. Yes, there is indeed some sort of ancient gramophone contraption sitting on one of the shelves, next to an open box containing black plastic disks about thirty centimeters in diameter. "You mean the things they used to use before compact discs?"

"Yes, Bob. Surely you must remember—"

Yes, I remember. (Just.) I walk towards the music player. There's something wrong with these disks, they're not quite the same as the ones my dad used to play. I get a bit closer before I can see properly. "They're too thick."

"That's bakelite, Bob, modern disks are made of vinyl. Ahem." Pete carefully extracts one of the disks from the velvet-lined box they're racked in. "Wow! Look, these are 16s."

"What's that?"

"You play them at 16 revolutions per minute, not 33 or 45. Lousy high-frequency response but great for speech, and they run for twice as long. I bet these were specially mastered in the late sixties. They didn't know how well magnetic tape would survive."

"But what would they do with them?"

"Broadcast them, probably. From the emergency command and control bunkers they had set up for running the country in event of a nuclear war: they had radio transmitters, didn't they? I saw a TV drama about it years ago, called *Threads*." He looks at me, curiously: "Would public broadcasting still work after an invasion of wibbly-wobbly nasties? What about the internet?"

I scuff my shoe on the bare concrete. "This stuff is useless. They haven't blown the dust off it in thirty years!" I look around. "I mean, it's useless except for kitsch value. Well, that's not quite right. You might get the service museum curator excited. But I don't see any of this junk going viral like **KEEP CALM AND CARRY ON.**"

"It lacks a certain *je ne sais quoi*," Pete agrees. "But what am I going to do?"

I shrug. "You're going to dig out the original brief for the folks who came up with this stuff. I figure it'll turn out to be 'come up with a public information campaign' or something along those lines. Then you're going to write a proposal for how to update the brief for a new generation, so that the New Media hipsters can all point and laugh at us. It'll get outsourced to a security-cleared agency, who in turn will pitch an iPhone app and a Facebook page, but by then you'll be signed off the job, so tearing off their heads and shitting down their necks as you explain in words of one syllable that we can't trust Apple or Facebook won't be your problem." I pause. "I can help you with that: it shouldn't take more than a couple of days. On the other hand, I've got a little project of my own I'm working on, and I could do with some help. And a library researcher is *exactly* what I need. Are you up for it?"

Thus I seal my fate.

4.

VAMPIRE START-UP

"DUDES, THIS IS *NOT* WHAT I SIGNED UP FOR! WHERE ARE MY fangs? Why can't I turn into a bat? This *sucks*!"

"Silence, minion!" Mhari turns her nose up with turbocharged hauteur and places one hand on her hip, theatrically poised, as she faces down Evan. "There will be no whining among the pigs!"

"Vampires."

"Goats, chickens, whatever." She waves it off. Alex stares at her, enthralled. They had to duct-tape Mhari to her Aeron and lecture her for six hours straight before she could wrap her head around just enough of the Core Theorem (as he and Evan had named it) to open her inner eyes to whatever they were all seeing in the visualizer, but eventually she got it. Vampirism becomes her. Her skin is paler and clearer than before, her hair more golden-blonde, as if some personal contrast slider has been turned up; and the city slicker uniform of sharp jacket, black dress, and heels goes well with the territory. The effect of turning post-human on the boy-pigs isn't quite as obvious— they already had the self-aware swagger of the masters of the universe, apart from Alex—but the change has bestowed an odd desmodontid magnetism on the Scrum Mistress, and Alex is an iron filing trapped in her field.

"We need to try the blood thing. I'm *dying* for a drink," says Dick. It's true: every last one of them has become aware of an unpleasantly intimate thirst since the change, a thirst unslaked by water or champagne. Denial isn't an option.

"Where are our fangs?" Evan deadpans compulsively.

"Who the fuck knows? Maybe they don't come out until we hunt." Dick hunches around his stomach as if he's in pain.

"Teeth don't grow overnight," Evan says, more thoughtfully; "maybe we ought to book a dental X-ray?"

"We could corner one of the cleaners," suggests Janice. The Scrum's sysadmin got with the program immediately, and now she's even scarier than ever: her hair spikier, her trouser-suits sharper. Alex half-expects her to whip out a red and black armband and announce that backsliders will be shot. "Use the hypnosis thing. Even if it doesn't work, how are they going to identify us? We all look the same to them—pasty-skinned Anglos in suits."

"Have they found Mr. White yet?" Alex had coughed to telling the smirking chimp in the bathroom to get lost during the daily stand-up meeting. (That was when the sprint on vampirism had been proposed and unanimously actioned as an emergency spike.) Oscar's discreet digging had subsequently revealed that one Barry White from the Rare Earth Futures desk had not returned to work since the evening of the confrontation; according to the police he was last seen booking a one-way flight to Mataveri airport on Easter Island.

"Not so far." Mhari wrinkles her nose. "That's a loose end we'll have to tie up. What *were* you thinking, Alex?"

"I was thinking I had sunburn and someone had slipped me some acid."

Mhari turns away dismissively, focusses on Janice instead, eyes gleaming. "The cleaners are a bad idea, Janice. We might—have you ever watched *Buffy*?—end up tearing them limb from limb. Or losing control and killing them. Cleaners have team leaders and contract management. Families, even. It could get messy, unless we know ex-

actly what we're doing. I think we need to deal with this in a business-like way. Oscar . . . ?"

Until now, Oscar has been sitting in his office at the far end of the boardroom, door flung wide so he can watch from afar. It's a pose he has: one ankle crossed over the other knee, brooding in his super-villain's swivel chair (a horribly expensive luxury item modeled after a Blofeldian excess from one of the earlier Bond movies). Now he stands.

Forty-ish, bald and skinny and intensely animated, Oscar is both the Scrum's leader and their interface to the institution they are embedded in. They all know it, and as soon as he steps forward they all look towards him. "Okay, people. Here's what I'm hearing: we have a huge opportunity, but it doesn't mesh with our deliverables list. And it certainly doesn't play to any of the user stories I'm seeing here." He looks at Mhari. "It comes with certain costs attached, the stomach ache and sunburn. But it also comes with some remarkable value-proposition increments"—Mhari had sold him on it the instant she regurgitated Alex's *get lost* anecdote—"and I think it constitutes a net benefit that we should add to our core skills matrix for all personnel." Everyone nods, glassy-eyed, unable to look away. Oscar in full flow was charismatic even before they sat him down in front of Alex's tracer bullet demo and turned him into one of them. Now he's positively mesmerizing, able to turn the driest of spreadsheet statements into a Shakespearean soliloquy.

"We need to explore the envelope of this new capability *immediately*, then determine how to apply it to our core production targets. We need to learn what it takes to deal with the stomach ache. We need to explore ways and means of minimizing daylight exposure. We need to identify the existential threats we face and develop procedures that maximize our chances of surviving them. You've all seen the movies: you know what happens to the unprepared, the unfit? *We are not going to be unfit.* We are going to confront this challenge and surmount it together.

"For my part, I'm going to feed a stall warning up the pipeline and tap-dance around it to give you a one-week window of opportunity.

I repeat: regular work is *cancelled for one week*, and I'll do whatever it takes to cover for you while you get to grips with our new toolkit. Unless anyone wants more than that one-week extension?" (Nobody nods.) "Good. So right now you're going to sit down and we're going to brainstorm the stories we're going to generate tasks from for the one-week sprint on vampirism. On this theme, *you* are the customers and your work is going to define our deliverables. The definition of done for this sprint is: we will know what hurts us, we will know what helps us, we will know what we can do that we couldn't do before, and we will know what extra things we can do when we go back to business."

He grins, toothily. Is it Alex's imagination, or are Oscar's canines longer than they were yesterday?

"Note that I didn't say 'back to business *as usual.*' Because I don't think we're going to be playing the same game again. We just got a power-up, people. And once we find out how big it is, we'll be in a better position to know how high we can raise our game . . ."

MIDNIGHT IN THE SPRINT PLANNING MEETING. ALL THE PIGS and most of the hens are present, standing around the table (to keep things moving). They've barricaded the door to the suite to keep the cleaners out, ordered in a pile of pizzas (for though the stomach ache is ubiquitous and insatiable, the old mammalian metabolism still demands food), and Mhari is keeping track on the whiteboard.

"Okay, what else?" she demands, brandishing a red marker.

"Sunlight, threat, or menace?"

"Thank you, Evan." She swings to the board, writes SUNLIGHT and circles it in yellow. After a moment she adds rays. "Well?"

"I got burned," says Alex, "but only my hands and face."

"Protective clothing," mumbles Dick. His suit probably qualifies as such, at least if it's his virginity he's trying to protect—it came from a charity shop, a coarse green tweed pig farmer's number that is more effective dissident garb in this environment than any amount of tie-dye and patchouli oil. "Hey, what about latex face paint, like in *Mission: Impossible*?"

Mhari adds two linked circles to the board: PROTECTIVE CLOTHING and LATEX MASKS.

"Hats," offers Janice. "Becca gave me a lovely new trilby . . ."

HATS goes on the board.

"Keep it moving, people," Mhari says briskly. Alex's attention wanders. He notices she's wearing opaque black leggings under her dress.

"Shouldn't we move the office down a few levels?" he asks. "And further away from the exterior?" The Scrum's office is already shielded in the heart of the bank's building, well away from any possible exposure to laser microphones or long-lens cameras.

"I'll action that with Oscar, but that's not strictly a user story," she reminds him. "Stories, people!"

"Blood: animal or human?" offers Evan.

"Good one. Does it have to be fresh from the artery, or can it be stored?" This from John.

"I saw this film once," Alex stumbles momentarily; "in it, the vampire had taken over a local hospital—it was set in the mid-west—and was using the blood bank . . ."

"Jolly good!" BLOOD BANK and FRESHLY SQUEEZED BULL went on the board. "Next?"

"Mind control." Janice took her turn. "We need to explore it. Can we all do it? *How* do we do it? What are the limits? What if the target is resisting?"

"Excellent points, one and all." Mhari turns to the board and scribbles: HYPNOSIS, RESISTANCE, LIMITS. After a moment she scrubs out HYPNOSIS and writes in BRAINWASHING instead. "Anything else?"

Alex rubs his jawline. It itches. "The mirror thing. How does it apply to cameras? Because if—"

"Nonsense, Alex!" Janice is nodding along with Mhari. "We already know that one."

"But—"

"Because I had to use FaceTime on my fucking iPad to do my makeup this morning. It can't fool cameras, or I'd be a real mess."

Janice holds up a cautionary finger: "Unless you swap the image right-for-left. Is that what you were wondering?"

"No, but—" Alex stares at Janice, then at Mhari. "It's a mental effect! Whatever stops us seeing our reflections, it's in *us*, not in the mirror or the camera."

"Huh." Mhari sounds skeptical, but turns back to the board anyway and adds: FACE BLINDNESS. "Anything else?"

"Garlic."

"Coffins!"

"Holy water."

"Anyone got a crucifix? Or going to holy communion?"

"Wait up, if you believe in the strict trans-substantiation, then if the host and wine turns into the body and blood of Christ, does that mean it could fix the stomach upset? Or would it set fire to us?"

"Dude, *consecrated ground*. Also: holy water!"

(Mhari doesn't interrupt the flow, but writes JESUS STUFF on the board.)

"But what if someone invites you in?"

"I can settle that one," says Janice. "The thing about needing an explicit invitation? Is nonsense." She sounds a little too smug, to Alex's ears.

(LET THE RIGHT ONE IN goes up on the board. RIGHT ONE is then struck out and replaced by WRONG 'UN.)

"Stakes," says John. He is greeted by stony, unwelcoming silence. "Did I say something wrong?"

"There is an obvious joke," Mhari says tightly. "You're all thinking it, so you can pat yourselves on the back and keep it to yourselves. But in current company if you say it *aloud* I will have to make a determination whether it constitutes workplace harassment and/or discrimination against persons-of-hemophagia. *Am I clear?*"

Alex bites his lip. The moment passes; nobody utters the words *stakeholder management* in any context, tasteless or otherwise. But he's managed to make his lip bleed, and the trickle oozing onto his tongue tastes like, no, it smells like, *no*, it reminds him of . . .

Mhari is saying something about teams and assigning a sprint backlog and prepping a new burndown chart and who takes on what roles. Alex shivers imperceptibly, and tries to shut the memory of his first orgasm back in whatever dusty memory box it crept out of: this is no time to be distracted. "John, Dick, you're on BRAINWASHING: go find a bar and practice your pickup lines. Janice and Evan, you're taking BLOOD BANK. Those are tonight's tasks. Tomorrow Janice can return the samples while Evan and Alex tackle the JESUS STUFF items. If you need support I'll pitch in. I'm going to take PROTECTIVE CLOTHING and LATEX MASKS but I've got some shopping for equipment to do first, so we can work on it tomorrow; I'll need one of you boys. And Dick and Alex can team on FRESHLY SQUEEZED BULL. Okay, on to phase two: let's start drawing up our work units . . ."

A PAIR OF VAMPIRES WITH CLIPBOARDS WALK INTO THE ACUTE Receiving Unit at a busy London teaching hospital, shortly after eight o'clock at night.

One is male and one is female. They're both smartly dressed, with badges on lanyards around their necks. Everything about them screams *outsourced private sector management*, except it's nine in the evening and there is no way that consultants from Accenture or PwC would be seen dead working this late amidst the vomit and screams of the unwashed sick plebs.

The male discreetly elbows his companion (pin-striped trouser suit, short spiky hair with racy violet highlights) and whispers, "We should have come as doctors. All it takes is a stethoscope, how hard can it be?"

"Don't be fucking stupid," she hisses at him. "What if somebody asked us to *fix* someone?"

"We could tell them they feel better? They'd believe it." (It was true: to everybody's astonishment, they'd sent John and Dick to test it. John, because he fancied himself as a pickup artist, and Dick because he was clearly a hopeless case, the twenty-something programmer most likely to still be a virgin. But Dick had scored with his first attempt. *Despite* his pig farmer's suit, questionable personal hygiene, bulging, watery hyperthyroidal eyes, and the miasma of squalid dissipation that trailed around behind him at all times, he'd slouched into a high-end club and squelched out again after half an hour; wearing the stunned, toad-like grin of a first-time winner in life's lottery, sandwiched between a pair of mistrustful anorexic blondes who clung to his arms possessively and glared daggers at one another across his prematurely thinning pate. John, aghast, had stuck around only long enough to obtain photographic evidence of the coup, then chickened out of his own chicken run and went home to commune with a bottle of limoncello instead, depressed by the ease with which Dick had devalued his expertise with the ladies.)

"Yes, but that wouldn't be—" Janice shuts up as a harried-looking bloke in blue scrubs marches briskly towards them.

"You can't wait here, you're blocking the—" he begins, then stops as Janice stares into his eyes.

"Health and Safety Inspectorate spot-check. We're here to verify that your unit is following approved hazardous waste disposal procedures during non-core business hours," she informs him.

"But you—"

"*Believe* it," she emphasizes.

The A&E nurse blinks a couple of times as he assimilates this new information. "You need to go and talk to janitorial services, then. Not here, this is the triage and control post. You're in the way, we have ambulances—"

"Which way?"

"There." Their unwitting informant points along the corridor, past curtained-off bays and an empty stretcher. "Turn left past the crash cart, through the double doors, third on your right."

"Thanks. Forget we were here." Janice hauls Evan along behind her, hurrying to clear the area lest a real emergency blow in, trailing too many medics and relatives and police officers to subdue by force of will alone.

"Now what?" mutters Evan.

"We ask more questions. Let's see, we're looking for the blood transfusion duty registrar. They'll be on-call and the internal phone book will take us to them. They'll know where the blood components are stored; probably a special refrigerator in a hematology lab, but there'll be supplies close to A&E."

"Where did you figure that out from? Did you work in a hospital before—"

"I used Google. Duh."

Badges, clipboards, and self-confidence will get you past the human gatekeepers in a hospital, but they won't help you with the combination locks on the doors. But if you have a vampire's talent for convincing people that they want to help you, you can move around relatively easily: just wait for someone to come along, then get them to invite you in. Over the next twenty minutes Evan and Janice inveigle themselves into the hematology lab, and corner the duty hematology technician: forty-ish, maternal-looking, and very surprised to see them standing in the doorway to the lab office.

"We're here to do a spot-check on the blood fridge," Janice announces forbiddingly. Evan, standing behind her, holds his clipboard before him like a weapon. "We are auditing supply levels and expiration compliance throughout the primary care trust, and we've been tasked with making spot-checks on hematology services to monitor wastage. Where's your supply manifest? We need to do a stocktake against it."

The tech looks surprised. "Can I see your ID, please?" she asks. "Nobody told me to expect—"

"Here's my ID," Janice says, holding the faked-up laminated badge. "You will recognize this as valid. There's no need to confirm it with management. *Everything is in order.*"

"Yeah, baby." Evan leers over her shoulder.

"Supplies." The technician shakes her head. "What do you mean?"

"Plasma. Platelets. Whole blood to hand for transfusion."

The technician frowns. "Whole blood? Someone's misinformed you. There's a single unit of screened O negative blood in the blood fridge by Theatre One, strictly for emergencies, and about six units of various types in the Resuscitation Ward on A&E, but we don't handle bulk supplies here; we handle immunohematology testing and order in supplies from the blood bank on a per-patient basis, as needed. And if they don't have enough, there's a blue light taxi service from the nearest NHSBT center. We don't just keep units of whole blood hanging around unused! The stuff's too valuable, and it has a short shelf life—"

"You're telling me you run a fractional reserve blood bank?"

"What?" The technician is perplexed by Janice's incredulity. "But you can't possibly imagine that—"

"Leave her," Evan suggests.

The hematologist shakes her head and blinks at them, leaning away. "Let me see your badges again. Who did you say you were from?"

The mind control thing clearly isn't working too well. Janice sighs, leans nose to nose with the woman, and slams the full force of her willpower into her: "Get a syringe and draw a sample from your left arm. I am a vampire and I *vant* to suck your *blood*."

"WAS THAT STRICTLY NECESSARY?"

"Shut up and drink."

"Prosit. Pro—oh." (Pause.) "Oh!"

"Jesus Christ."

"Oh."

"You're disgusting." (Pause.) "Please tell me you haven't wet yourself."

"N-no. Bitch." (Pause.) "Look, there's a drop left in the tube, I can't lick it out . . ."

"Rinse."

"Jesus Fuck, that was, that was amazing. Better than smack."

"Better than sex."

"Guess you've never had good sex, then."

"Animal."

"Dyke." (Pause.) "It felt amazing. But I need more. There's one tube left. Can I have—"

"No, it's for Oscar and Mhari."

"Come on, there's twenty mils, we can split it, tell them there wasn't—"

"You're not thinking this through, Evan."

"What?"

"We've got a problem. According to Google the NHS prices blood internally at £120 per unit, and a unit is only about a third of a liter. They never have more than about ten days' supply in the Blood and Transplant service's stores and she just told us they track it to the individual unit, on a per-patient basis. And I don't know about you, but I could get used to this stuff."

"Shit. You know what that means, then?"

"Yes. We're going to have to convince Oscar to buy us a hospital. Which is why you're not to drink the rest of the merchandise. Shit's *expensive*."

A PAIR OF VAMPIRES WITH CLIPBOARDS WALK INTO THE BACK of a church in time for evening mass.

They do not burst into flames. Nor does the sight of the crucifix on the altar cause them to cringe or convulse, but the incense gives Alex a sneezing fit, at which point an elderly parishioner turns and glares at him with muted outrage. That is the worst reaction that makes it into the task tracking grid on Evan's clipboard.

"Dude, not cool. Try to look like you're praying."

"How?"

"Copy the peeps in front of us. Them over there, they seem to know what they're doing."

The building is cold and dimly lit, the air dank with the chill of autumnal stonework. It seems almost deserted, but for a small cluster of officiants around the altar and pulpit at the front, and a scattering of worshipers, mostly old. The music sounds doleful and strange to Alex's ears. As with many other natives of the British Isles, he has grown up in a family that fills in the "religion" question on the census forms with "Church of England" but only bothers with the institution itself when they want something: an impressively traditional venue for a wedding, or a place in a highly rated C of E school for the off-spring. Consequently, he has only the vaguest grasp of the format and running order of a service, much less the audience participation bits. Evan, for his part, is no better off: he clutches the dog-eared Book of Common Prayer with both hands, trying to make sense of the card with its cryptic list of hymns and page numbers.

"This makes no sense," Alex complains, but help is at hand: Evan pulls out his phone—a ridiculously hypertrophied slab of black glass—and googles. After a moment he shoves it under Alex's nose: "Follow this," he whispers. They peer, shoulder to shoulder, through the narrow window onto churchofengland.org's website, gaping in perplexity at an alien universe of liturgy and prayer.

The service proceeds. There are prayers; there are hymns. There is a reading from the Holy Scripture. More prayers follow, and then the ritual preparation of the table. "Are you up for the free booze?" Evan asks as he prepares to join the queue of communion participants forming in the aisle.

"No, I'll just keep track in case you burst into flames or some-thing." Alex, to be honest, is somewhat bored: the religious symbols at the front of the church are no more cringeworthy than they would have been a week ago.

"Coward." Evan heads towards the queue. A few minutes later he's back. "Cheap wine, and not enough of it," he says.

"And the, um, Eucharist?"

"Tastes like chicken." Evan elbows Alex in the ribs. "Incoming collecting plate! Let's roll."

*   *   *

A PAIR OF VAMPIRES WITH CLIPBOARDS WALK INTO A BUTCH-
er's shop . . .

Actually, it's not a shop: it's a stall in the central hall at Smithfield
Market. It's a few minutes past four in the morning, and the wholesale market is already bustling with butchers, fishmongers, and res-
tauranteurs filling up crates and pallets with the day's meat produce.
This is London's main wholesale meat market—no longer a live cattle
market surrounded by abattoirs, but nevertheless a bustling hive of
early morning commerce. The vampires have swapped their suits for
jeans and suspiciously new white coats, purchased for the occasion
from a work outfitter's: they slip effortlessly through the crowd of
costermongers and their customers. But they have a dilemma.

"What exactly are we looking for?" asks Alex.

"Blood. Fresh blood."

Alex's sigh is intended to be withering but it's so much water off
Dick's duck's arse hairstyle. Dick is clearly in his element here: with
his protuberant eyes and green plaid jacket he fits right into place in
the meat market, in a way that makes Alex wonder if there isn't something to the old legend of Fae changelings. Despite being predestined
for a life as a butcher, the baby was swapped at birth to fill the empty
crib of a banker . . . "Pig's blood?" he asks. "Or sheep? Or cow juice?"

"Don't be daft, cow juice is milk—"

"Look, let's just fucking ask, okay? Excuse me, yes, you sir—"

"Eh, what d'you—" The balding middle-aged bloke in the white
coat and rubber boots turns a suspicious expression on Alex.

Alex stares into his eyes and grabs his attention. "We need blood,"
he says simply, holding out the aluminum drinking bottle from his
bicycle. "Fresh blood. Preferably from a cow. Can you sell it to us?"

"Wuh—Wuh—"

Dick raises a grubby finger: "No questions, mate."

They have discovered that there is an interesting drawback to the
mind control talent: it only works if you can supply a rationalization
that the victim can make sense of. Tell a banker to get lost after a hard
day's work and they'll tell themselves that it's about time they ditched
the high-stress job and went to live in a Buddhist monastery for a

year. Tell an aspiring model in a club that you're a rich investment banker and she wants to shag you, and her mind's eye will fill with Ferraris. But a blunt assault on the senses, with no wheedling wedge to crack the doors of cognition apart, will result in some fight-back. Alex realizes this, and sends a quelling glance in Dick's direction. "Heston Blumenthal sent us. We're with his TV production company, and we're sourcing material for a documentary on foods made with blood."

False enlightenment dawns on the victim's face: "*Oh*. Awright, mate. Come wiv me, I'll sortcha out!"

Fifteen minutes later, Dick and Alex stagger out of the market, lumbered down with the weight of sloshing gallon containers of the red stuff—pig, sheep, cow, and goat. Alex walks with one arm crooked protectively around his pocket, within which nestles a filched 20ml medical sample tube filled with the most exotic of sanguinary products—venous blue human blood. ("Mr. Blumenthal specifically wants to try a recipe for Tiết canh that the Viet Cong are rumored to have made using their own blood while besieged by the Americans . . . yes, I know it's disgusting: would a hundred quid help?")

"I can't believe you tried to force him with no explanation." Alex pauses to put down a gallon jug in order to wipe his forehead.

Dick looks around nervously. "Hurry up! We can't stop here; this is black pudding country!"

Alex raises his jug again. "After you."

"It was much easier in the club," Dick complains after a minute, as they round the street corner and head for where he's left his car.

"Did it occur to you that if you go to a club and chat someone up, there's a good chance that they're there to pull? Or to serve a minor reminder of their pull-ability on their boyfriend?" Alex has been thinking about this subject a lot lately.

"Bah." Dick raises his car key and pings the button to open the doors on his Porsche Boxster. "Hey, these won't fit under the bonnet . . ."

"So? Put 'em behind the seats." Alex walks around to the passenger side and begins to load his jugs into the back of the sports car.

"But if they leak—"

"You'll just get blood on the carpet. Right?"

"Ah, fuck it. Okay, next stop: the office."

Alex glances out of the windscreen nervously. There are still a couple of hours to go until sunrise, but this is London, and the traffic is capricious and potentially deadly to vampires. "Hit it. I can't wait to try this . . ."

LATER:

"Aaaugh."

"Jesus fuck, that was disgusting!"

"Gurrrrgh. Aaaugh." (Spitting sounds.)

"Have you finished there?"

"Gimme a minute, I need to floss my teeth. *Again*. That was *gross*."

"How are we scoring?"

"Nil for three. Pigs, don't make me puke. Cows, essence of fragrant bullshit. Sheep, well . . . I kind of *like* mutton, but not like that, you know?"

"And the black pudding . . ."

"Tastes a lot better deep-fried, doesn't it?"

"You are not shitting me. Um. That leaves the goat, and the control sample. Um. Oh dear."

"Are you thinking what I'm thinking?"

"I don't know. Are you thinking, goats are kind of like sheep with bad attitude? I'm not a fucking chupacabra, man. And maybe we should use the control sample just to be sure that, well, you know . . ."

"Blood works?"

"Something like that."

"That's what I'm thinking, too."

"Okay. Let's see, we get about two teaspoons each: human blood, two hours old."

"Oh."

"Oh *Jesus*."

"*Oh*." (Pause.) "Well, fuck me sideways."

"It just did, didn't it? Oh man, I've got to sit down. I feel weak at the knees."

"Wow."

"You know what this means, of course."

"We just ruled out the main vertebrates, haven't we? Of course, it might be because the donors are dead, but . . ."

"You want us to go find ourselves a farm and suck on a live sheep?"

"We *could*, but I'm not getting a good-idea vibe from that thought. Let's put it on the to-do list."

"You can if you want to, but I'm getting a feeling that it's got to be live human blood, all the way. How about you?"

(Sigh.) "Well, fuck."

"SUMMARY: THIS IS WHAT WE HAVE LEARNED."

Mhari has the baton (actually a chrome-plated blue laser pointer), the stopwatch, and the whiteboard: she's running this as a sprint review meeting for Oscar, who sits in the hemispheric Evil Overlord chair opposite the far end of the boardroom table.

"Evan. What did you and Alex learn from JESUS STUFF?"

Evan stands, glances down at his tablet. "We can enter churches. Crosses and religious symbols have no effect on us. I took holy communion without any ill effects. I was unable to acquire a sample of holy water, but I think we can reasonably expect it to have no effect. We tested a Church of England church, a Roman Catholic cathedral, a Reform Jewish synagogue, and a Jehovah's Witness meeting room. If you want us to continue, Alex and I have identified a mosque and a Sikh temple, but we'll need a pretext or disguise. Oh, and afterwards we ate out—Italian, with garlic bread as a starter."

He looks at Mhari expectantly. Mhari, for her part, takes a green Post-it note and plants it on the whiteboard, under the DONE column adjacent to the JESUS STUFF row. She smiles happily. "Strike one!" She turns to Janice. "What about BLOOD BANK?"

"This is going to take a while. Short version: Oh God, yes, *human blood*. Unfortunately getting it isn't going to be as easy as walking into a hematology lab and walking out with a six-pack. Blood is expensive enough that it's ordered centrally on a named-patient basis. On the other hand, it turns out we don't need much of it, and, oh my god, it's *lovely*. Let me see . . ."

Janice runs through her checklist and Mhari adds new Post-it notes in exciting shades of magenta and cyan to the whiteboard under the TO DO and TESTING columns. Finally Janice runs down, reserves of information sucked dry. Evan maintains a leathery silence throughout, punctuated by significant glances in the direction of Oscar, whose expression is one of distant longing, almost hunger. Mhari's expression, too, is fixed. They'd shared the final sample tube, enough to confirm its importance.

"Blood." Mhari nods to herself. "Thank you, Janice. So I guess this means we're back to hitting on the cleaning staff or getting creative with the, uh, mind control thing. John, Dick: did you get any endurance and scope metrics from your experiments?"

"I'll take this." John gives Dick a warning look, but Dick merely slouches in his chair, an expression of feline bliss on his saggy face. (He is clearly sleep-deprived and unshaven.) "Dick pulled," he announces. "Two nights running. In fact, on our first time out Dick walked straight past the bouncers at Vertigo 42 *dressed as he is now*"—a ripple of disbelief runs around the room—"then walked up to a Russian oligarch, out-stared his bodyguards, and asked the guy's mistress, quote, 'Hey, babe, how about we go and play Mr. Policeman Hides His Truncheon?' Unquote. Yes, he scored." John is visibly quivering with outrage at this affront to his imagination. "On the way out, he, um, he picked up an aspiring model *as well*."

Dick yawns, stretches his arms above his head, and shakes his head. "All it takes is imagining that I'm Austin Powers. Sheer animal magnetism. Hey, baby!" He looks smug. "They were looking for action: I just upped my visibility."

From brown dwarf to supernova by the look of it, Alex thinks. "Did you take them home?" he asks.

"Do I look stupid? I took them to Claridge's! On Mr. Petrov's dime." He grunts. "Bodyguards turning up on my doorstep the next morning: *do not want*."

Janice shakes her head. "It's the fucking end times," she husks. "*Dick* scoring."

"Anything else?" Mhari adds sharply.

"Yeah." John looks pensive. "I went back to check an hour later. They tried to keep it discreet, but there was a bit of a heated argument and the bouncers, the bodyguards, and Mr. Petrov all went home in ambulances. I don't know exactly what Dick told them to do to each other when they got in his face, but this mind control mojo needs a light touch."

"I got the blood samples by telling the duty hematologist to draw the samples from her own left arm and give them to me," Janice adds. "If I'd told her to cut her wrist, I'm not sure she wouldn't have done it."

Mhari adds another green Post-it to the board, against BRAIN-WASHING. She turns back to the table. "Dick?"

"Yeah?"

"Stand on your head, please. In the corner. Right now."

Dick sits where he is and stares at her quizzically. "Make me."

"Go and—" Mhari's eyes narrow. Then she glances at John.

"We seem to be immune. I *told* Dick not to do it but he wasn't listening . . ."

"You were right, though: they were too bony. And they didn't like each other *at all*. I could tell."

"Animal!"

"Dyke."

"That's enough, children!" Mhari raises her voice and Dick and Janice succumb to an aggrieved, resentful silence. But Mhari is watching Oscar: his displeasure is muted for now, but evident. Now he stands and clears his throat.

"Policy directive. We seem to have considerable scope for, ah, making friends and *influencing* people, people. And also for doing them damage. I don't think that's a good idea because, leaving all questions of morality aside, it's likely to draw attention to us. And as for questions of morality—" Janice stares daggers at Dick. "What you did is borderline indistinguishable from date rape. So—"

"Hey, they were on the pull!" Dick protests.

"Nevertheless, I'll thank you to *not do that*. Obviously there are exceptions—if someone tries to mug you on your way to work, for example, or starts asking questions about what the Scrum is doing this week—but you *will* avoid using this particular talent for trivial ends, or in public. Am I understood?" Everybody nods. Even Dick, although his expression is mutinous. "Are there any questions?"

Janice's hand goes up. "Blood," she says simply.

"We'll get to it when we loop back to planning, after the retrospective. Are you okay with that?" He stares at her.

"Copacetic," she mutters bitterly.

"Good." Oscar sits down. "Back to you, Mhari . . ."

"Okay!" Mhari beams at the Scrum. Her crimson lip gloss glistens beneath the spotlights. "Quickly, PROTECTIVE CLOTHING and LATEX MASKS. Direct sunlight burns us within seconds. I'm talking third-degree burns here, very nasty stuff. You do *not* want to shine a UV torch on your skin, either: we're photosensitive. We can see in the dark, and I notice everyone's got constricted pupils in office lighting conditions. On the other hand, we heal really fast. A one-millimeter deep cut in the skin actually heals in about an hour without scarring. Burns, similarly. That which does not kill us seems not to harm us too badly. And clothing—anything that blocks the sunlight—works fine."

Mhari takes a step back and raises her skirt to flash her left knee. "Look." She's wearing opaque black tights. "I stuck my leg in a sunbeam. After about a minute it was tingling and painful, but that's all. I exposed the back of my wrist to the same sunbeam and had a first-degree burn, with blistering, after two seconds. So it doesn't take much fabric." She smoothes down her skirt, then picks up a carrier bag from beside her chair. "So then I went looking for an emergency kit, and I came up with this." She reaches into the bag and pulls out a mass of black fabric. "This is a jilbab, with niqab—that's the face-veil—and gloves. The only skin it doesn't cover is the eyes." She rummages in the bottom of the bag and pulls out a pair of wrap-around shades: "And that's what these are for. It's not much fun, but I walked about for a quarter of an hour in daylight yesterday and I only got burned on the bridge of my nose. I recommend we all get two of these, and keep one by our desk and one at home as emergency escape kits. Sorry, gents, I know it doesn't go with your self-image, but look at it this way: blood-sucking bankers in burkhas could be next summer's hot new fashion!"

"What about the latex?" asks Oscar.

"I'm still working on it." Mhari makes a moue of concentration. "Turns out we're looking for theatrical special-effects cosmetics. I know where to buy it, but getting it right is another matter: we might need to hire a professional makeup artist." She scribbles a couple of Post-it notes: green for the DONE column, pink for the TO-DO list. "Anyway, that brings us to about the end of our current review. To sum up: we can move fast and heal fast, we're inflammable in daylight, and we can't see ourselves in mirrors (but we're still there and we show up on video). We still need to eat and we can eat garlic, crosses and holy water don't repel us, we have amazing powers of persuasion but we can't use them on each other, and, uh, human blood is *amazing*. Other species, not so much." Her eyes are wide as she looks down the meeting table, then makes contact with Oscar. "So, boss. Where do we go with this now?"

5.

HOT ZONE

IT'S ABOUT THREE IN THE MORNING AND WE'RE BOTH DEEPLY
asleep when the red telephone rings.

It's not a flashy electronic device with a scrambler; quite the opposite: it's a 1950s GPO-issue telephone. Which is to say it's made out
of bakelite on a pressed steel base, has a rotary dial, and the ringer is
a fucking church bell loud enough to wake the dead. It is connected
via a Victorian-era twisted pair line to an electromechanical Strowger
exchange in the Dansey House basement, all clicking relays and buzzing motors, guaranteed immune to EMP and other civilization-ending
disasters.*

The reason we have this archaic monstrosity in the house is that if
someone in Ops needs to declare a Code Blue emergency, the only
way to stop it from ringing is to hit it very hard with a sledgehammer.
Even popping a nuke over London might not be enough to stop it

---

* During the big Mexico City earthquake in the 1980s, a twelve-story concrete office building collapsed on the Strowger unit in its basement: the damn thing kept working under the
rubble for nearly two weeks, until its lead-acid batteries ran down.

ringing. Both Mo and I are on The List, under different headings; she's Agent CANDID, and I'm, well, among my other duties—we're big on matrix management here—I'm there as personal assistant and understudy to Angleton, the Eater of Souls.

Anyway: the phone rings. At the first bell, I awaken with a shudder but am confused and wonder if it's one of those curious auditory hallucinations sent to torment the somnolent by disturbing a good night's sleep with phantom dispatches from the Home Delivery Network. But with the second ring (it's the traditional British *ring-ring*, not the long-drawn-out American *riiiiing*) I'm halfway out of bed before I realize what's happening, and by the third ring I'm at the bottom of the stairs, swearing and fumbling for the receiver as Mo clatters around behind me, bare-arse naked and clutching her violin case.

"Howard speaking," I say, forcing the words through a sleep-congested larynx.

"Control here. This is a Code Blue call for Agent CANDID."

Oh fuck. I look round, see Mo looming over me with sleep-disordered hair, violin case in hand. "It's for you," I say, and pass her the phone. We squeeze past each other, and I go back up the hall staircase, shivering in the late-night chill as she takes the call.

"CANDID here," she says.

I go back to the bedroom and pull her go-bag from the closet. *What else? Ah, yes.* There's a spare toilet bag packed and ready to go in the bathroom: I fetch that, too, and carry it downstairs. She's still on the phone, listening intently, as I squeeze past her to the kitchen, plant the bags, then start prepping the coffee maker. Either she'll have time for a mug before they pick her up, or I can use it in a few hours' time: it all depends what kind of job it is.

This happens every month or two. Usually she's gone for a couple of days, sometimes only for a few hours, but on one notable occasion she disappeared for nearly a month. It's not her they need so much as her bone-white violin and its human attendant. (I *hate* that fucking thing.) It's an Erich Zahn original, one of a double-handful fabricated in Weimar Germany. You can't get the materials to make any more of them, and you wouldn't want to unless you were a particularly macabre serial killer. The reason the organization needs it is summed up in the now-tattered sticker Mo added to the case several years ago: THIS MACHINE KILLS DEMONS. But to do that, it needs a violinist. And she's very proficient. *Too* proficient: if she was less good at it they'd take the thing away from her and give it to some other poor bastard who I wasn't married to.

Presently I hear the clatter of her hanging up. "Got time for coffee?" I ask as her footsteps come closer.

"I think so," she says, and I flick the switch on the filter machine. "They've booked me onto a six o'clock flight out of London City, but there's plenty of time. Hand luggage only." It's dark in the kitchen, and she's as pale as a ghost in the twilight glow of the LEDs on the microwave oven. "Speaking of which."

"I got your bag," I say as the coffee begins to burble and spit.

"Oh, Bob." She puts the violin case down on the table, then comes towards me. We embrace awkwardly. She rests her chin on my shoulder. There's an unpleasant tension in the back of her neck. "I'd better get dressed soon." She makes no move to pull away.

"Can you say where you're going? Or how long you'll be?"

"No, except it's outside the Schengen Area, meaning I need a passport, and no, but probably not more than two nights. Maybe less. If you need to know more, you can yell at Danny White, or someone else in OpExec."

That tears it. OpExec don't deal with trivial stuff, paranormal parking tickets and the like: if she's working for them on this assignment, then she's probably going to come home with her heart—if not her sanity—in pieces. (Assuming she *does* come home, but that's a given in our line of work, for both of us: it's not a risk-free occupation.) Most likely she's on her way to one of the less-well-equipped countries—the UK has an unusually large and proficient OCCINT service—to help disinfect an ulcer in the skin of reality. There will be plenty of backup and support, but she's still going to have to do heartbreaking things to people who probably don't understand why the pale woman with the bone-white violin and blood dripping from her fingertips is coming for them. Innocent bystanders, collateral damage, victims the monsters just haven't gotten around to eating yet—and the monsters themselves. She has to deal with them all. And here she is, shivering naked in the kitchen at dead of night, and not just with the cold.

"When it's over, I want to schedule some quality time. A vacation, somewhere safe. A spa weekend, maybe. Would you like that?"

"Yes, Bob." I hear her, but her heart isn't in it. She's gazing inwards again, already thinking herself into the frame she's got to be in to do her job properly. "We can talk about it when I get back." I let my arms drop and she steps backwards, away from me. Closer to the kitchen table, so that her left hand is within reach of the violin case. It's instinctive, she always does that: like a hit man ensuring he knows where his pistol is, so that he can reach it without thinking, using muscle memory in the dark. "I'd better go and get dressed. Are you going to stay up?"

I nod. "I'll see you off."

It's not as if I'll be able to get back to sleep again.

ONCE MO'S TAXI COMES TO WHISK HER AWAY, THERE DOESN'T seem to be much point in sitting around the house brooding. Everything here serves to remind me of her absence, like a jaw from which a tooth has unexpectedly disappeared. So I force myself to make some breakfast, eat it in silence—it's too early for the *Today* program on Radio 4, my usual breakfast-time distraction—and I leave for the office around the time Mo's flight is pushing back for departure. Dawn is breaking as I reach the front door and let myself in. I go straight to my office, fire off a couple of terse, ill-tempered emails to various people (by way of pissing on the fire hydrant to let them know that I'm on the job even earlier than they are), and head to the coffee station for the first in-flight refueling of what promises to be a very long day.

Pete, bless his cotton socks, is either running late or has wangled a day off for pastoral duties. Consequently, I'm on my own in the office when Andy knocks on my door around ten o'clock. Obviously he's gotten the memo I sent out at oh dark o'clock. I let him in. "So, what do you think?" I ask expectantly.

Andy lowers himself gingerly into the guest chair and puts his feet up on the stack of dysfunctional laptops. "About your proposed methodology?"

"That, and the targets."

He purses his lips and inflates his cheeks like a gerbil, then allows the whistling exhalation to escape. "Let's see. Silver nitrate in styptic pencils, allergic reactions to. Hirsutism. Anemia and photophobia. A bunch of synonyms you dug out of a medical thesaurus. And you expect to find something?"

"I don't *expect*, Andy. But it'd be good to eliminate the obvious, wouldn't it? It's sound protocol to ensure we're not getting false positives, and it will hopefully conceal what we're really looking for."

"Which I was just getting to . . ."

"Krantzberg syndrome."

"Yes, that." He looks doubtful. "You think you can find it in the population at large?"

Krantzberg syndrome haunts me because it's a personal bête noire. Magic is a side effect of certain classes of mathematics, notably theorem proving. Sensible magicians—like me—use computers. But if you're smart and agile you *can* perform some types of invocation in your head. The trouble is, just as our symbol manipulating machines attract the attention of extradimensional agencies (demons, you might say), so do such DIY invocations. If you perform ritual magic regularly, some of the things you invoke will chew microscopic holes in your gray matter. At first it's not too bad, but the dizziness, numbness and tingling in the periphery, memory problems, and lack of coordination are irreversible and frequently progressive. The end result, Krantzberg syndrome, bears a rather unpleasant resemblance to Creutzfeldt-Jakob disease—not to mention that other happy fun prion disease, Kuru (which you can only contract by eating the brains of someone who had the condition).

Krantzberg syndrome is what people like me die of if the monsters don't get us first.

"There's a blood test for new variant CJD"—Mad Cow Disease,

to you—"so what I'm going to look for is cases of CJD diagnosed at post-mortem that test negative for nvCJD. Testing CJD cases for nvCJD is routine and gets reported to the Core Data Service as part of the program for tracking Mad Cow Disease; I'm going to see if I can pull out a geographical plot," I explain.

"What do you expect it to tell you?" Andy leans forward.

"It's too early to tell. For all I know, I'm going to draw a negative. Actually, I *hope* to draw a negative—finding a Krantzberg syndrome hotspot in the community wouldn't be good." (This is an understatement, to say the least: depending on how big a hotspot and where it was located, it could range in severity from a rain of boiling frogs to the End Of The World. File under Apocalypses and just hope it doesn't happen.) "It's got to be done. The vampire/werewolf cross-check is just a control, really." (Which is what Mo latched onto a month ago and wouldn't let me finish explaining, dammit.)

"How long do you think it'll take to get results?" he asks.

"Ah, well, that's a good question." I smirk unashamedly and fondle the shiny new smart card reader next to my keyboard. "Shall we see?"

"What, here and now?"

"When else?"

I start mousing around.

Now pay attention:

The NHS central data warehouse is one of those hideous, sprawling IT projects that aren't cleared for take-off until the stack of documentation exceeds the height of the Eiffel Tower. It stores tens of millions of patient records (hopefully in something resembling a valid XML schema) in a monstrous distributed database. There's a hideously ugly Windows application called the Standard Extract Mart which theoretically lets you run searches and pull reports out of the warehouse. In practice, it's sluggish and if you want to work on data covering more than about one month you're supposed to phone Mr. Jobsworth at BT and whine for help. And if you go dumpster diving for cabinet ministers or rock stars, you can expect the boys in blue to come knocking at your door toot sweet.

But we are the Laundry. We have almost as L33T hacking skillz as GCHQ. We also have access to some other data warehouses that I'm not allowed to talk about, even in classified internal documents such as this memoir, although if I mumble unpronounceable acronyms like CESG and GCHQ and MTI/CCDP and recommend that you speculate along such lines you probably wouldn't be too far off the mark. This *particular* database is run by a small and highly specialized group called the Home Office Demographic Profiling Group, which is sort of the twenty-first-century descendant of those nineteenth-century criminologists who thought you could infer the likelihood of someone's descent into criminality by measuring the bumps on their skull.

HO-DPG do not explicitly share their jealously guarded extracts of the SUS database with us. But they *do* make their source code repository available to other arms of the government, and I am more than happy to borrow the computer-assisted phrenology department's data mining toolkit and point it at the NHS data warehouse using my own login credentials. Which, as far as the NHS are concerned, belong to a very peculiar GP's surgery inside a silver-roofed toroidal office building in Cheltenham, whose inhabitants are allowed to snoop around the nation's medical records at will without any questions being asked—just in case spying turns out to be a notifiable disease.

It's taken me a few weeks to get the appropriate authorizations, and another few days to draw up the search queries I'm going to run, but now I've got an audience I can bash out a theatrical-looking arpeggio on the keyboard, grin maniacally at Andy, and say, "This is going to take a few minutes. How about we get some coffee?" Because I always grin like a loon when I'm wired on legal stimulants.

"I don't see why not . . ."

Ten minutes later, when we get back to my office, I find a new piece of email waiting in my inbox. It's from a software bot and it has an attachment—about 36Mb of Excel data. (It's formatted for a two-versions-obsolete version of the spreadsheet that has known bugs and everybody is trying to move on from, except that it has a couple of hundred million users going back nearly ten years. Consequently it's the file format from hell that refuses to die.)

"Okay, let's see what we can pull out of this," I say, and instead of firing up Microsoft Office I save the spreadsheet and feed it into a hairball of Python scripts I kluged together—because my programming skills are as obsolescent as Andy's, but a generation more recent.

"What are you looking for?"

"Severe early onset dementias. Sudden strokes. Neurological stuff, with or without hallucinations. We really need a doctor on the case"— I hesitate to suggest any of the staff from St. Hilda's—"to help us work out what questions we should be asking. But for now, I've got this dump of everything that's happened in the Greater London area in the past three months, and a script to suck it all into a bunch of MySQL tables. The patient data is supposed to be anonymized but I pulled in their postcodes so we can localize them to within about a hundred meters, pivoted the results on our Criminal Records Bureau and National Insurance database mirrors to get the place of work for everyone who's on the books, and the pre-processor is turning that into grid reference data so we can plot them on a map or query for areas where the rate of *that's* funny . . ."

"What's funny?" Andy stands up and tries to squint at the monitor: a good trick if he can manage it, given that I've got a privacy filter clipped to the front. I'm not paying attention to his contortions, though.

"There's something wrong with the data. Or I messed up the postcode-to-grid location mapping. This *can't* be right."

I scroll back through the logfile I had my script barf up in a terminal window. CJD, and it's cousin nvCJD—the cause of Bovine Spongiform Encephalopathy, aka Mad Cow Disease—is pretty rare; the UK, despite its positively suicidal attempt at ignoring the epidemic in the early '90s, still only generates about two cases per million people per year. The whole Greater London area, with fifteen million souls in its catchment area, should show about thirty cases a year, or two to three a month. And indeed, three months ago there were two cases.

Two months ago there was one case. But in the most recent month for which I have data—last month—I'm seeing twelve.

"What am I looking at?" Andy demands.

"This." I turn the monitor towards him, then pull off the privacy screen. "CJD detected at autopsy, a four hundred percent spike last month. Um. You know what? This has *got* to be a coincidence. Or a case of creeping data corruption. If the rate of CJD had rocketed like that earlier in the year we'd have been reading about it in the newspapers, there'd be questions in parliament. In fact—"

I hit up the map view. "Oh. Oh dear." A rash of red spots flicker across the map of London like a bad case of chickenpox. "Hmm, that's indexed by home address. But we can also look at their medical practice, or their place of work, see if anything jumps out at us—oh. Oh shit."

All but eight of the red spots vanish when I filter by workplace. But one of them is much, much bigger, flashing malignant crimson. "They all work for the same employer?"

Andy stares at the screen. "That's odd. Where is it?"

"Let me check." *Huh.* "It's an office cleaning agency in the East End." I frown. "Twelve cases in one month." Another seven outside it, sprinkled across the rest of London. "That tears it, doesn't it?"

"Yes, I should say so." Andy stares at the screen. He looks worried. "If it was evenly spread over the whole of London it'd only be a three-sigma spike, but just in one employer in the East End? I think you may be looking at five sigmas." He's thinking what I'm thinking: ten extra cases in a quarter million people in one month corresponds to about thirty *thousand* extra cases a year in the UK as a whole. That's not just a signal in the noise; it'd be fighting it out with lung cancer and heart attacks as a leading cause of death. "You need to pull those patients' records so we can double-check that it's not a database error. Then we need to get a neurology consultant on board who's cleared for K syndrome so we can rerun the post-mortem examinations." He falls silent.

"Then what?"

"If we're lucky, it's just Mad Cow Disease going nuclear under us. Or some hideous new epidemic getting started. If not, if it's actually K syndrome, the shit hits the fan." He reaches into his jacket pocket with a slightly shaky hand and pulls out an electronic cigarette case. "Looks like your ten-percenter just exploded, Bob." He raises the cigarette to his lips and takes a puff: the tip glows blue. Blue LEDs are the color of progress, the color of the twenty-first century. "Better find out where those cleaners were working, then pull an action plan together. I think you're about to come to the attention of important people."

I AM NOT A MEDICAL STATISTICIAN. I MEAN, I CAN SORT OF FOL-low a chi-squared regression and I know my standard deviation from my T-test, but I don't do that stuff for a living. Nor am I a medical informatics guy. For all I know, I fucked up big-time with my SUS trawl. So, first I swear Andy to silence (with an embargo time limit of forty-eight hours). Then I write a very anodyne memo that kinda-sorta explains what I've been doing, and send it to my HR admin person and all my various managers, tagged as low priority and with a not *entirely* misleading subject line. Hopefully that means they'll ignore it for a while. Finally, my ass covered, I shut my office door and do a quick change. Clark Kent uses telephone booths to ditch his suit in favor of the Superman underwear; I do it in reverse. These days I keep a set of office drag on a hangar on the back of my door, against those rare occasions when I have to go somewhere and look invisible in a suit-wearing managerial kind of way.

Like this afternoon. Because I need to visit a hospital and see a man about a brain.

The Laundry has an institutional aversion to loose ends—and especially to the existence of civilians who have, through whatever means, become aware of our work. For many years, if you had the misfortune to be a witness to the uncanny you'd inevitably end up working within the organization. However, since the 1980s the efflorescence of computational systems throughout our society has exposed so many people to the fringes of magic (I use the word cautiously, in the context of Arthur C. Clarke's famous aphorism, "any sufficiently advanced technology is indistinguishable from magic") that we simply *can't* stick them all in an office and have them keep tabs on one another. Nor would it even be a good idea to try. We need people on the outside, in every walk of life, bound to silence by a geas, but available when we need specialist consultancy—and also able to contact *us* if they stumble on something inexplicable. Butcher, baker, candlestick-maker . . . also, experts in biblical apocrypha and brain lesions.

(Other people, accidental witnesses who don't understand what they've seen, are bound to silence and then released—subject to monitoring. Or, if their services are no longer required by the admin side of the organization and they have no special skills, or are card-carrying members of the awkward squad, they can be bound to silence and allowed to quietly reenter civilian life. It's only the core staff—practitioners, executives, and agents like me—who have no exit options.)

I'm on my way out of the office today to visit a Dr. Wills at the National Hospital for Neurology and Neurosurgery, which is part of the sprawling complex of medical institutions around Great Ormond Street. Dr. Wills works with the National Prion Clinic and is part of a research group at University College's Department of Neurodegenerative Diseases, which is a long-winded way of saying that if *anyone* has spotted the spike and knows what's going on, Dr. Wills is probably your man. (Or woman, because all it says in our contact database is "Dr. F. P. Wills, UCLH, MRC Prion Research Unit—cleared per OSA(3).")

This person is our go-to expert on Krantzberg syndrome and I don't even get a recognition mugshot or a potted biography? *Great.*

LET ME TELL YOU A BIT MORE ABOUT K SYNDROME: BECAUSE *everything* is better with early-onset dementia.

Magic—the collection of practices that enable us to mess around with the computational ultrastructure of reality—has been around for thousands of years. We're not entirely sure how it works. One theory holds that computational processes involving observers can influence quantum systems up to the macroscopic level via entanglement. Or, from another angle, we reach out into an infinity of parallel universes and pull rabbits out of the hat—rabbits with too many tentacles, that do what we tell them to. Either way, thinking or cogitating or reasoning or singing or just plain *looking at stuff the wrong way* can make things happen in the physical universe.

So, yes, magic works—although the do-it-in-your-head variety is notoriously hard to master, like solving three-dimensional cryptic crosswords in multiple languages. But if magic has *always* worked, why are successful magicians so rare in the historical record? It turns out that the limiting factor is not just the difficulty of the job: it's the medical side effects.

Now for a brief diversion:

In the 1950s, Australian medics in Papua New Guinea discovered a perplexing new disease among the women and children of the Fore tribe. The victims would be overtaken by a sudden weakness and muscle pains: they'd succumb to violent shivering, lose the ability to stand up, and eventually die. The disease, known as Kuru, was infectious, although no actual agent was detected until the 1980s. The Fore practiced cannibalism as part of the funeral rites: the bereaved would consume parts of the body of the deceased to return their life force to the community. Men took the choice cuts, muscle from arms and legs: they mostly dodged the bullet. But the women and children ate the leftovers . . . including the brain. If you examined the brain of a Kuru victim with a microscope, you would see odd spongy holes scattered throughout the cerebral cortex; hence the term *spongiform encephalopathy*.

The disease agent in Kuru turns out to be a prion, a malformed version of a naturally occurring protein that catalyses conversion of normal protein molecules into the pathogenic state. It's a truly weird and scary corner of medical research, because the diseases caused by prions—such as Creutzfeldt-Jakob disease and Fatal Familial Insomnia—kill horribly, first taking the victim's mind and then their ability to move. Not to mention new variant CJD, also known as Mad Cow Disease.

Now, back to the subject on hand: ritual magicians who perform too many invocations in their head tend to develop a package of symptoms after a while which *eerily* resembles Kuru. It starts with tremors, unsteady gait, slurred speech, and confusion. Then they become unable to walk, suffer from ataxia and uncontrollable tremors, and show signs of emotional instability. They become depressed, but may suffer from fits of maniacal laughter. In the final stages, they lose all muscular control, can't sit, or swallow, or speak, become unresponsive to their surroundings . . . and from start to finish it can take between three months and three years.

Krantzberg syndrome is a horrible way to die.

Krantzberg syndrome is probably also the only spongiform encephalopathy that is *not* a prion disease. (I say "probably" because there are relatively few cases of it in the first place, which makes it very hard to investigate.) However, prion proteins appear to be absent in K syndrome, and extracts from K syndrome brains don't cause symptoms in other organisms that they've been tested on. (For obvious reasons, nobody's been able to perform the most important test—on other humans.)

The best theory to account for K syndrome is that ritual magic is intentionally designed to attract extradimensional critters—and not just big ones. There seems to be some variety of microscopically small, dumb eaters that materialize inside the gray matter of the practitioner while they are in the process of carrying out some sort of invocation, take a tiny bite, and disappear again. Brain parasites from beyond spacetime, in other words. The brain is a resilient piece of squishware, but if the K-parasites chew enough tiny holes in the headmeat, its owner will eventually succumb to a dementia-like illness. Furthermore, once the eaters have found a tasty lump of brains to chow down on they keep at it. So the disease is progressive, vile, and fatal if unchecked.

Unchecked? Well, yes: we *can* stop it progressing by putting the victim inside a locked-down protective ward. This is a huge step forward over, say, Kuru or CJD. What's more, if we isolate the patient for long enough the eaters lose interest and go away; but the victim isn't going to be casting any spells ever again. (If they're lucky they'll still be able to talk coherently and tie their own shoelaces.) It's a health and safety nightmare.

Especially for me, because when I'm wearing one of my more recently acquired hats (trainee necromancer) I'm *all* about the jamming-with-magic–in–my–head thing. My relationship with K syndrome is like that of a forty-a-day smoker with basal-cell carcinoma: not so much a matter of *if* as of *when*.

Which is why I am not looking forward to my visit with Dr. Wills.

"EXCUSE ME, IS THIS THE ENTRANCE TO THE DEPARTMENT OF Neurodegenerative Disease?"

"I have an appointment in the Prion Research Unit . . . ?"

"Hi, I'm here to see Dr. Wills?"

"How do I get to Dr. Wills's office . . . ?"

I'm lost in a twisty maze of whitewashed corridors, surrounded by glass-fronted cabinets stuffed full of photocopied notices on every side (not to mention a scattering of conference-surplus posters with excessively enlarged cross-sections of gruesomely diseased brains, just for variety). I've been wandering in circles for ten minutes now and I'm just beginning to despair of finding my destination. Trish booked me a slot with the doctor for 3:30 p.m., but I'm running a quarter of an hour late. I find myself flagging down an irritated-looking researcher who clearly thinks she has better things to do than give directions to visiting admin people.

"I'm not in," she snaps. "I'm running late for a meeting."

I do a double take. "Are you Dr. Wills?"

"Yes, and I'm running late." She begins to walk away. "If it's about the facilities audit it'll have to wait—"

I haul out my warrant card. "I'm not from admin."

Wills turns back towards me. "Hey, I'm supposed to be meeting you in room 2006. What are you doing *here*?"

"Nobody told me about a meeting room. Where's room 2006?"

"Oh for—" She stops. "Hmm." She has a way of tilting her head and narrowing her eyes as she assimilates new information that reminds me of Mo. The straw-blonde hair and slightly watery eyes behind thick lenses are very different, though. "Well, as you're here, would you rather use my office?"

I shrug. "If it's private." I put the warrant card away. "As I said, nobody mentioned a meeting room."

"Mack, our departmental receptionist, said he'd sorted it out."

"Well, it never got passed on to my end." Yet another detail that fell through the cracks. "Your office isn't shared, is it?"

"Yes, but Barry's teaching today." She eyes me cautiously. "Why?"

"What I want to talk about isn't for public consumption, I'm afraid." I shrug self-effacingly, trying to take the sting out of my brusque approach. "I need to pick your brain on the subject of a delicate matter."

Dr. Wills's office is surprisingly spacious. It's what we jokingly refer to as an Ark Special in the Laundry: it's actually sized for two people, with two desks, two workstations, two of everything. I take the visitor's seat across from her—one that is clearly accustomed to *regular* visitors, for it is free of clutter and situated in a clear patch of floor. She shuts the door behind us: I appreciate the gesture. "What can I do for the Laundry today?" she asks.

I take a deep breath. "You've worked with us before, I gather. On K syndrome."

"Krantzberg-Gödel Spongiform Encephalopathy. Yes?" She waits for me to nod.

"That's it. Um. Tell me, for epidemiological purposes, speaking hypothetically"—I'm making a hash of this; I force myself to get a grip—"suppose there was a significant outbreak of K syndrome in the UK, am I right in thinking that the first thing we'd know about it would be a spike in cases of CJD being diagnosed by post-mortem examination?"

"If there was a—" Her expression could not be more eloquent if I'd asked her how we'd know if there was a minor outbreak of the Black Death: a mixture of pungent disbelief, the barnyard stench of second-guessery, and a high note of *oh shit* all colliding simultaneously in the back of her mind. It's enough to freeze anyone's tongue, so I give her a few seconds before I grin and nod, trying to look like an idiot student in need of tuition. "Please tell me you're joking? No? Oh *fuck*." She slumps back in her chair. "Hang on." She straightens up again as second, and then third, thoughts line up in a disorderly queue. "This isn't a joke, is it?"

"I sincerely hope not. I don't want to waste your time or mine. Look, I know you'd be aware of actual referrals for treatment, patients with active disease and a diagnosis, right?"

"Yes, that's exactly right! So there can't be an epidemic without us knowing about it, because—" She stops dead.

"Because it's a progressive disease, and you'd be seeing them as referrals from wherever they were diagnosed?"

"Yes." She frowns, perplexed. "Your scenario doesn't make sense, I'm afraid."

"Okay. Let me try again. If coroners around the country began recording spongiform lesions in the brains of patients who had died suddenly in the past month, how long would it take you to hear about it?"

"The past *month*?" She shakes her head. "Then it can't be K syndrome, Mr. Howard. We get regular updates from the NHS epidemiological tracking database, part of the Secondary Usage Service. K syndrome is rather distinctive. Your typical patient exhibits the symptoms of nvCJD; it's a strikingly early onset dementia with nonstandard signs and presentation, and it's progressive. More to the point, the patients are also distinctive: mathematicians, philosophers, occultists. Also, they test negative for PrP variants. What you're talking about is something else—diagnosed only after death, which means the patients went downhill much too rapidly for K syndrome or any prion disease we know about. Do you have any more information about them?"

I finally get to open my briefcase. "This is the output of a query I ran on data extracted from the SUS data warehouse." I shove the screen shot I took of the geographical scatter plot across her desk. "Twelve cases were diagnosed at post-mortem, all in the past four weeks. The factor they've got in common—at least, what I've established so far—is that they all worked for an office cleaning agency in Tower Hamlets. I don't have the individual patient records, but I suspect the shit is going to hit the fan really soon, and I'd like to have some answers to send up the line." I shove the printout of the spreadsheet summary at her: ages, postcodes, other basic anonymized information.

Her eyes flicker across the papers. "This is—I—"

"It's crazy, isn't it?" I suggest.

"No! But it's something new. Hmm. How did you find this?"

I hesitate for a couple of seconds. "I don't think I can tell you," I finally say. "Not without prior authorization."

"Well, if it's not Krantzberg-Gödel syndrome that makes it even *worse*." She shakes her head in unconscious distress. "Mr. Howard, I'm going to have to go and do some digging in order to de-anonymize these patients and confirm that what you've found actually exists. Data warehouses tend to accumulate rubbish in the corners . . . I can't just go pulling these records without justification: there are issues of medical confidentiality here, and respect for the relatives, and so on. On the other hand, I can't write this off either. Um." She stares at me until I make eye contact. "I may need some arms discreetly twisted, and unlike you, I don't have one of those special badges."

I make a careful judgment call and decide to exceed my lawful authority. Just this once, in order to facilitate the speedy investigation of a major threat—that's what I'll tell the Auditors if they haul me onto the carpet. Doing it by the book, I should go and round up a committee or a herd of managers to agree with me first—diffusion of responsibility, it's called—but I honestly don't think there's time for that right now. Thirty thousand deaths a year corresponds to seven hundred a week. (Just sitting on it for the extra day it'd take to convince a committee could result in . . . let's not go there.) "Whose authorization do you need?" I ask.

"Professor Everett can sign off on the paperwork to pull the patient records, but I'll need to persuade him in turn that the Department of Health are happy about this." She bites her lip. "K syndrome is a special case, of course, but this, this is . . ."

"This is *suspected* K syndrome, or a K syndrome-related condition of, um, what's the right medical term?"

"Unknown etiology. Yes, that should do it. I need authorization to access medical records of deceased patients suffering from a spongiform encephalopathy of unknown etiology that is possibly associated with K syndrome. In writing. Preferably signed in blood. Can you get me that?" She does the tilt-shift thing again, like she's trying to view me as a miniature diorama.

"Yes. I'll email you a memo as soon as I get back to my office. Is there anything else?"

"Yes." She stands. "Better pray to whatever nameless horrors you believe in that you're wrong, Mr. Howard. If twelve people died of a new sudden-onset form of K syndrome in London in the last month, then you'd better hope it was just a group of cultists who got lucky. Because if it wasn't, we're in worse trouble than you can possibly imagine."

6.

RENFIELD PLC

THE THING ABOUT OSCAR MENENDEZ, IN MHARI'S OPINION, IS
that he is intelligent, charming, personable, manipulative, and *utterly*
ruthless. He is not a normal workplace sociopath: he is that much
more dangerous phenomenon, a not-quite-neurotypical person who
has worked among the regular sociopaths for so long that he can see
things from their point of view and manipulate them; a dolphin among
sharks. Sociopaths aren't good at impulse control or deferred gratifi-
cation. Oscar works out what they want, dangles it in front of them
like a shiny bauble in front of a kitten, and ensures that the shortest
route from predator to prize takes them right where he wants them to
go. Which is why the Bank gave him, if not carte blanche, then at least
a clean sheet and a low seven-digit budget with which to establish the
Scrum. It has been a pleasure to work with him, and to help steer the
Scrum around the worst obstacles in its path. And now she's going to
accompany him to a meeting with their overseers where he is going
to try and talk them into giving the Scrum a slightly larger pot to play
with.

He's assigned her the job of covering the exits, lest any of the
cattle try to flee.

It has been an *interesting* month since Alex's accidental flash of insight and their subsequent week-long scramble to research and define the potentials and pitfalls of their new condition. Mhari has been working eighty-hour weeks, and she's not alone—not that there's anyone waiting back home for her since Alan fucked off last year. (Or, if you want to be truthful, since she fired him for being an insufficiently supportive partner.) Oscar is similarly, if not single, then moderately unencumbered: his wife Pippa seems content to play the role of arm-candy on demand, keep their two children out of his hair, and look after the house in return for her annual Mercedes SLC and the Royal Opera House season ticket.

As the managerial side of the Scrum, they've barely been out of each other's presence for the past few weeks as they organized the office move, pushed their people through the planning and early execution stages of what they have come to call the Big Pivot, arranged the tiresome but entirely necessary in-house dental visits for the team, and attended to all the other necessary minutiae of the operation.

And now it's time for Oscar's big pitch.

"Good evening, Sam, Steph, Ari, and thank you for making time in your crowded schedule, Sir David." Oscar rolls into his warm-up while Mhari waits at one side of the table, within easy grabbing distance of the laptop and the projector, playing the glamorous assistant to Oscar's stage magician. "This isn't a routine report, you'll be pleased to hear. Five weeks ago one of our theoreticians made a conceptual breakthrough and I decided to put regular work on hold for a week while we explored its potential to revolutionize our operations. I don't use that word lightly, and I wouldn't have pulled my entire team off their normal workload if the value proposition represented by the new paradigm wasn't extreme, with a payback curve that will reach break-even within a single quarter. However, to continue in this new direction I need to confirm that all stakeholders are fully invested. Basically, gentlemen and lady, I need your consent to pivot the Scrum . . ."

Mhari strokes the remote lighting controller that she holds out of sight behind her back. She's been dimming the meeting room lights slowly since the four senior execs arrived, taking her cue from Oscar. She's got no idea how he managed to winkle Sir David out of his oak-paneled penthouse nest, but he's a prize—the Bank's director of quantitative trading. The others are all lower-level executives, from the head of the London Stock Exchange IT group to the Lord (or rather, Lady) High Executioner of the regulatory compliance team: but they're all critically important, because any one of them can spike Oscar's attempt to change his team's operation remit if they withhold their consent. Furthermore they're already beginning to look uneasy at what Oscar is telling them.

". . . We will be able to anticipate major trading strategy shifts among the quant-determined strategies of our rival institutions. This is medium-term stuff—a one to ten day lead—but with this fantastic new algorithmic approach we should be able to consistently anticipate the commodities markets. Ironically, the worst drawback is that it's so *good* it'll look eerily like front-running to an outsider—and we don't want to lay ourselves open to accusations of malfeasance. So we intend to bulletproof ourselves from a regulatory perspective before we go any further, which is why I invited you all here today—"

What Oscar and Mhari have in mind is not front-running. Front-running is the practice of executing your own trades on the basis of information about pending trades your clients have told you to perform on their behalf—a form of insider trading. But it's not insider trading if you gaze into the eyes of your opposite number from a rival brokerage or investment bank over an after-work cocktail, calmly *order* them to adopt a specific spread the next day, and then tell them to forget the conversation ever took place. It's almost certainly illegal, but vampiric mind control is much harder to prove than front-running. For their part, Oscar and Mhari are happy to leave the question of which laws (if any) have been broken to the eventual SFO investigation, because by the time it happens they intend to be over the horizon and far away.

Oscar's voice is intense but somehow mellow and pleasing to the ear: he's a hypnotic speaker, and Mhari is pleased to see that his small audience is nodding along with him in perfect harmony.

"I need access to a trading fund with an initial one hundred points of liquidity." (A point is a million pounds sterling.) "I'll need to liaise with you, Steph, about setting up appropriate accounting and oversight controls on the new fund, with full record-keeping so that it's clear that we're perfectly clean—that we're genuinely anticipating market movements. Ari, to minimize latency I need to move my group further into the bunker"—the basement levels below the Bank, windowless subterranean vaults full of servers and roaring air conditioning—"and, Sir David, I thought it would be best to keep you in the loop on this because the profits this pivot will generate will show up on the company-wide balance sheet by Q1 next year at the latest, and you'll want to be fully informed ahead of the next AGM." Oscar smiles, almost (but not quite) baring his new and very expensive dental work. Mhari runs her tongue around the inside of her upper jaw in unconscious sympathy: it's still sore and they're very tender, but at least her teeth won't raise any awkward questions if she's seen in public.

"Thank you, Oscar," says Sir David. "But you haven't told us exactly what this new breakthrough *is* yet. Would you like to elaborate?"

Sir David is a distinguished-looking gentleman in his mid-sixties, gray-haired and sober-looking—every inch a traditional British bank manager. That's one of the reasons the board keeps him on, to be wheeled out at press conferences when the unwashed proles need reassuring that everything is fine. Right now he looks, if not alarmed, then at least mildly perplexed. Mhari shivers and fixes her gaze on his collar, avoiding eye contact; also avoiding staring at the blood vessels in his neck, through which surges and hisses the stuff of . . . of . . .

"A fundamental new insight in probability theory," Oscar says smoothly. "Our existing strategies rely on Bayesian reasoning—which allows us to compute the probability of some event occurring in a given period on the basis of how frequently it has taken place in the past. That's all very well, but where no prior probabilities can be calculated, we can't predict future outcomes—or at least that's the way it's been in the past. Finding a way of reasoning under conditions of prior uncertainty has been the holy grail in one particular branch of mathematics for decades, like solving Fermat's last theorem. I'm pleased to say—" He smiles and shrugs. "Well, *that* would be telling."

Mhari flexes her fingers longingly. Then she startles, infinitesimally aware that one of the other audience members is in the process of noticing her staring, so she smiles, tight-lipped (very glad that English girls are taught not to bare their teeth like Americans: it's a sign of aggression), and glances around the room, registering that Sir David is gazing at Oscar as if hypnotized, his mouth slack. Oscar is laying the charisma on hard—perhaps too hard.

She intervenes. "We've verified the formal proof," she says smoothly; "that's what took us a no-holds-barred two-week hiatus in our normal workflow. I'd like to remind you that the Scrum has some of the best pure mathematics PhDs to come out of the Russell Group in the past decade. The lads are a little eccentric but basically sound—naturally they're a little miffed about not being able to publish and claim their Fields Medal right away, but they put the interests of the organization ahead of their own personal fame, which is why we're eager to give them the opportunity to earn a bonus that will put the Nobel Prize money to shame." The latter is strictly irrelevant—there's no Nobel Prize for mathematics—but she's not sure her audience have heard of the Fields Medal, and she wants to implant the idea: *seven-digit bonuses all round.*

Oscar nods, his expression pinched and intense, and relaxes his grip on Sir David's gray matter infinitesimally. Sir David twitches, then shuffles himself upright in his chair. "Capital idea!" he announces. "Yes. If you'd be so good as to forward me a copy of the presentation, along with a memo detailing your requirements, I'll push it forward. Stephanie, please give Mr. Menendez everything he wants, as a matter of urgency. You, too, Mr. McAndrew: if the Scrum requires hosting in the middle of the LSE interconnect, give it to them. Whatever it takes." He stands, implicitly bringing the meeting to an end. If smiles were luminous, his beaming approval could power a small solar farm.

The executives stagger out into the corridor, blinking and uncoordinated like excessively well-tailored zombies. "So." Oscar finally cracks a grin. "How did I do?"

Mhari takes his arm conspiratorially: "You did *brilliantly*." She swallows. "I thought you were laying it on a bit thick towards the end, which is why I jumped in, but it seems to have worked."

"Yes. I can barely believe it. It's not every day I ask for a hundred points on a plate. Much less get it, no questions asked. But I could *feel* them." He rubs his throat. "I'm really thirsty."

"Me, too." She lets go of his arm, intrigued by his carefully controlled non-reaction. "It's a quarter to six. How about we go for a drink after we shut up shop?"

"I'd like that." He grins again, this time catching her eye. "I'd like that a lot."

"DUDE, YOU JUST RENFIELDED OUR REPORTING CHAIN ALL THE way up to board level? Epic win! Achievement unlocked!"

"Piss off home, Evan," Mhari says wearily. She's been working since six in the morning and it's nearly seven at night. They've just moved into the Scrum's new office on the third subsurface floor of the Bank, and the rough edges still show: the ceiling isn't finished and a couple of missing floor tiles are surrounded by cones and yellow hazard tape to show where the trolls are still working on the wiring runs by day. There are fresh scars on the walls, and a cloying stench of fresh emulsion paint. But it's theirs, and it's *safe*. There are no windows, the doors lock on the inside, and there are other extras that make it a suitable bolt-hole for a nest of vampires. The specially installed fire escape opens directly into the garage, and there's a shiny black Mercedes van with mirrored windows parked next to the crash door.

Oscar bought it, and Evan promptly dubbed it the Mystery Machine: it's fueled and boasts features such as a minibar fully stocked with 20ml type "O" Scooby snacks and a couple of (discreetly hidden) sets of false number plates. The keys are in the ignition and the satnav is loaded with routes to a bolt-hole in the country. If a Van Helsing wannabe comes at them through the bank lobby, the Scrum can get clear in under thirty seconds.

"I'll go home after"—Evan is juggling a set of luminous green furry dice—"sunset, thanks."

"Ten minutes," Oscar warns. The office is already semi-empty. Alex has long since sloped away into the deep underground by tube train, Janice is molesting a server somewhere off-site, and the remaining pigs are oinking away happily in the old office upstairs, anticipating another shitfaced evening at a club where discreet activities involving syringes in toilet cubicles will raise no more eyebrows than usual.*

"I can tell when I'm not wanted," Evan snarks. He lets the dice fall as they will, then collects his briefcase and heads for the door. "Don't do anything I wouldn't do, 'kay?"

"Don't let the doorknob hit you on the way out," Oscar mouths silently as he leaves. Mhari glances at him. Oscar shares a guilty expression of complicity with her. "You didn't hear me think that, did you?"

"Think what?" Their eyes meet: a secret smile is exchanged. "I'm famished. How about you?"

"I could really do with a post-work drink." Oscar sounds as tired as she feels, Mhari realizes. He loosens the knot of his tie, then sits down in one of the pigs' chairs, slumps bonelessly, and turns to face the door.

Mhari picks up a phone terminal. "Janitorial, please . . . cleaning service for suite B314. Yes? Right now, thank you very much." She hangs up. "Cleaner's on her way."

"Thank you. You're brilliant."

---

* Obtaining a supply of cannulae and sample tubes was easy enough: there's a small chemist's in Stratford where the pharmacist is convinced that the supplies she's ordering for the phlebotomist at the local clinic are entirely legit. Teaching the pigs to use them properly was the hard part. Alex still feels faint at the sight of blood, although he's getting better; but it took actual threats of bodily violence—accompanied by a brisk lecture on hitherto unconsidered aspects of forensic dentistry—to convince Dick not to use his teeth.

Behind his head, out of his line of sight, Mhari smiles contentedly. *I know,* she thinks. *Story of my life: I'm brilliant, and nobody gives a shit.* Well, that isn't *entirely* true. She's here, working inside the most exciting in-house start-up this city has ever incubated, and she's *part* of it. One of the nighttime elite: one of the masters of the universe, if Oscar's plan comes to fruition. And it *will* work. Mhari knows this for a fact. She's been steering Oscar away from certain unfortunate ideas that might draw them to the attention of people she can't talk about. Through long force of habit Mhari's thoughts skitter away from that aspect of her prehistory, dead and buried and bound in any case to silence unto the grave.

Over the years it has become easy for her to avoid thinking about the people she used to work for, as a lowly admin body in a civil service niche role with no prospects. It's not hard to avoid the bad memories: crap housing, an infuriatingly obtuse boyfriend who couldn't get a clue if she whacked him between the eyes with it, not enough money. Not to mention the eventual bust-up, although frankly ditching him had been for the best in the long run. It's even easier to avoid recalling the embarrassing interview in which HR had carpeted her, suggesting more-in-sorrow-than-in-anger that perhaps in view of her personal relationships she would like to be released, might find life more fulfilling on the outside? But then there was the *other* interview they'd arranged with the Bank, which turned out far better than she could ever have imagined. *Oh yes, I'm brilliant. But soon They won't be able to ignore me anymore. So I'll have to be at least one step ahead of Them, won't I?* she adds.

There's a timid knock on the outside door—the security airlock and Faraday wallpaper aren't finished yet—then it opens to admit a cleaning cart and a person of no account. "Meals on wheels," Mhari murmurs, laying her hand on Oscar's shoulder: his muscles tense under her fingers.

"Ex-excuse?" The cleaner is middle-aged, a recent immigrant with poor English. She's a regular—they've had her before—but she's still surprised, as if it's her first time.

"Don't be afraid. There's nothing to worry about." Oscar stands and moves aside, gesturing at his just-vacated chair. "You're feeling tired. Why don't you sit down?"

"Excuse?" She shakily shuffles towards him, bovine puzzlement lending her an air of geriatric confusion.

"Sit. Down." Oscar points. Mhari steps out from behind the chair, keeping her expression calm and unthreatening. "You are very tired. You can relax here. You are among friends; you can sleep if you like." Oscar keeps his hands in motion, like small birds, fluttering delicately: he studied stagecraft when he was younger, NLP and other approaches to mind manipulation when he was older. It's magic, of a kind, although Mhari is aware of much more powerful varieties, types of magic that constitute a science rather than an art. She keeps a careful grip on her handbag. It's a neat black leather number that matches her suit. She keeps the medical supplies inside it.

"It's all right to close your eyes," Mhari assures the woman. "What's your name?"

"Sara."

"Sara, we know you've had a hard day. But you can close your eyes now. It's nearly over. You can go home soon. Why not take a nap?"

There are two of them, and one middle-aged woman of Somali origin, whose palsied hands twitch as they force their combined willpower down on her like warm, stifling pillows. They've used her before; there is no seduction here, just a brisk sixty-second interlude, at the end of which Sara slumps, snoring very quietly in the expensive office chair. Oscar bends over her and begins to roll up one of her sleeves. "Hang on, better use the right arm this time," Mhari suggests. "Otherwise we're going to leave tracks." *And it really wouldn't do to attract the wrong kind of attention. The Laundry kind . . .*

"Right." Oscar carefully rearranges her clothing and switches arms. "She doesn't seem well," he adds, mildly concerned. "Did you notice that?"

"The shaking? Yes." Mhari assembles the cannula, sample tubes, and tourniquet in silent concentration. "I don't see how it matters."

"That's the second one I've seen," Oscar says, almost absentmindedly.

"Second what?"

"The second subject. With the shakes."

"There's probably a bug doing the rounds," Mhari reassures him as she slides the needle in, searching for a vein.

She grits her teeth and suppresses a shudder of erotic longing as the first sample tube begins to fill with blue-tinged venous blood.

"Does it make you wet?" Oscar asks abruptly.

Mhari stares at him over their sleeping donor's head, then glances in the direction of his crotch. It's a moment she's been anticipating for weeks, the crossing of a delicious Rubicon. "Does it give you a hard-on?" she replies. She meets his gaze directly, then smiles and pulls back her lips so that he can see what they conceal. The pulse in his throat is fast. *What took you so long?* she wonders. "It's *better* than sex." She shivers.

"I wouldn't know," Oscar says slowly. "I haven't compared it directly to sex with one of our kind. Have you noticed that humans are less interesting these days?"

"Wait." Mhari forces herself to focus on the syringe. "Actually, yes I have. Take this." She swaps out the sample tube and passes him the full one. "Sorry. Where were we?" *Do you mean to follow through or are you going to chicken out?*

"We were discussing . . ."

He's married. Probably hasn't propositioned anyone in years. Scared of harassment lawsuits and the bill for the divorce settlement. Do I always have to do the heavy lifting? "My place or yours?"

"I was thinking in terms of a hotel? But first"—he raises the tube—"a toast. To health, life, and wealth!"

AFTER THEY RELIEVE SARA THE CLEANER OF APPROXIMATELY 100ml of blood—a third of a unit, so little that she'll barely notice it—Mhari and Oscar leave her sleeping soundly in Oscar's chair and head for the car park. Discreet decorum is observed until they're behind the tinted windows of Oscar's Panamera. Then they lean shoulder-to-shoulder and exchange a kiss tainted with a new and breathtaking scent that makes them both shudder. From which moment it runs forward as if on rails.

Oscar's self-restraint is superhuman. He imposes it on Mhari, even though she's shaking slightly with anticipation. He stays outwardly calm and collected as he drives into Mayfair, drops the keys in a valet's hand, walks up to the front desk at Claridge's, and says: "I'd like the best suite you've got for the night." Mhari tumbles along in his wake, trying to hold herself together. *I'm melting!* she thinks. Something in the blood has gotten to her. Then the door on one of the Linley Suites closes behind them and he turns to face her, and the frenzied animals come out.

About two hours later, tired and raw and sticky, Mhari comes to in the middle of the wreckage of a king-sized bed. She's almost but not entirely naked—Oscar turned out to be a stockings man. He's naked, too, lying on his back, snoring. She reaches out and wraps one hand possessively around his still-erect cock. She's been working towards this moment for weeks: happily, it turned out to be much more fun than she'd expected. The snore turns to a groan and as he pulls away she notices that his penis is redder than the rest of his skin. *Is that blood?* she wonders. *Or is he sore?* She, too, aches: but she enjoyed getting there. She's thirsty again, she realizes. "Hey, big boy." She punches him gently in the side. "Wake up."

"Um. Uh." He opens his eyes and stares at her. If she'd been dressed, his look would make her feel naked; as it is, it makes her feel stripped to the bone. It's a predator's expression, innocent and deadly. Then he spoils it by cracking a dazed schoolboy smile. "That was wild!" Mhari is about to glare at him in disappointment but he recovers his poise within a couple of seconds. "I would kill for a drink." He rolls on his side. "And I need a shower. How about you?"

"There are a couple of shots of blood in my bag. We can hit room service for food. Shower first?" She strips off her stockings and they move into the living room of the suite, ignore the dressing table set with a welcome bottle of Laurent-Perrier champagne, and head straight to the marble bathroom with its huge walk-in shower and whirlpool bath. There's room for two in the shower. "That was something else going on," she murmurs thoughtfully, as he rubs soapy water across her skin. She can feel every square millimeter; she's acutely, preternaturally sensitive.

"It's the smell of"—he kisses her shoulder—"the red stuff."

Mhari shudders and closes her eyes. It's true. If drinking blood is an erotic experience, then sex under the influence is like . . . She fails to think of a suitable simile. Coke doesn't even come close. The impulse to push him against the wall and fuck him in the shower is almost overpowering, despite the aches. "It's addictive," she says finally.

"Yes. Which is problematic." The icy chill of his intellect is returning. There isn't very much of the little boy left in Oscar; he didn't get to his position without being able to keep it under very tight control. He's not one for casual workplace flings, which makes her triumph all the sweeter. "Because, yes, we need it. Which is a weakness."

"You're thinking of the pawns." She leans against him.

"Yes. I'm not planning to ditch them," he adds carefully. "Not yet."

"Not unless they become a liability." She turns inside his arms and begins to massage his shoulders and spine with the soap. Their lips meet, briefly. "Am I a liability, Oscar?"

"You're not a pawn. A queen, maybe." His penis—*he's forty and he hasn't gone soft! Amazing!*—pushes gently against the side of her thigh. "You understand the value of keeping secrets." She wraps one hand around his balls, feeling them tighten as she strokes.

"I've had a lot of practice," she says, before she can think to censor herself. Then she realizes something else. "Oh, that's odd."

"What is?" He's instantly alert, sensitive to her perturbation.

"I'm not supposed to be able to talk about it." She leans against him and kisses him greedily to shut him up, covering her faux pas. But it's too much fun; one thing leads to another and she moans and bites his shoulder as he slides inside her again. *Blood.* But it tastes wrong. There's nothing sexy about Oscar's circulatory fluid. *He's biting her* now, then pulling away, disappointed. They continue to fuck, but the magic is leaking out of it, swirling down the shower drain with a thin red trail of soap suds. It's just ordinary mammalian humping, enjoyable but nothing to set her hair on fire and make her scream until the windows explode. And Oscar feels it, too, because after a minute he stops and slides away, slowly detumescing.

Back in the bedroom, Mhari rummages through the discarded bedding for her handbag. The four remaining sample tubes are fine: she pulls a couple and holds one out to Oscar. As he takes it she pops the lid on her own and raises it. "Your—hang on, this is skunked." Her nose wrinkles in disgust. She examines the tube closely: "It smells *wrong*."

Oscar unseals his and takes a sip. His expression of distaste speaks volumes. "Want to try the others?"

It takes Mhari less than a minute to determine that all the other sample tubes are spoiled. Not clotted or rotten: whatever previously made the contents so enticing has vanished, leaving only rancid red meat-juice behind. "This hasn't happened before," she observes.

"Well, we'll just have to hit room service, won't we?" Oscar towels himself dry. "For food *and* drink." He watches with detached amusement as Mhari collects her scattered clothes. "Unless you'd like to dine out?"

"I didn't bring my glad rags; room service will do just fine." She goes in search of the room service directory as Oscar begins to dress.

Later, over Kobe steaks flown in from Osaka that morning (with discreet tubes of blood donated by the bellhop as a digestif), Oscar asks her the question she's been worrying about. "What exactly aren't you supposed to talk about?" he asks.

"I"—*I can talk,* Mhari realizes, surprised—"before the Bank, I worked for a, a rather secret division of the civil service. I was"—*allowed to leave, classified as a liability*—"allowed to transition to the private sector, but they have these, uh, brainwashing-like capabilities that operate like our ability to, you know, that make it impossible to talk about what you did there without their permission, and I was, obviously, not able to talk about them . . . before." Her head's spinning. *I shouldn't be able to say this stuff,* she tells herself. *How* can *I say this stuff? The geas, does vampirism defeat it?*

"What?" Oscar looks puzzled. "What sort of stuff did they do?"

Her fork pauses, a blood-tinted slice of rare steak impaled upon the moment of the present. "They're the branch of the secret intelligence services that deals with occult threats. Like us."

"They're the—" Oscar stops. "No. I'm not going to say you're crazy." He chuckles briefly, then a dyspeptic frown steals all sign of amusement from his face. "We're fucking vampires, *of course* there's going to be a government department. It's in the rules." He peers at her intently. "What did *you* do for this agency?"

"Admin and management. HR dogsbody." She resumes eating, feeling her pulse slow towards normality again. "I saw, uh, something I shouldn't have. When I was at university. They've got a habit of picking up witnesses and finding make-work for them to keep them under observation for a while. Sometimes for life. I was there for three or four years. God it was tedious. Eventually they figured I wasn't a practitioner and they could let me go under a compulsion to keep my trap shut. They even sorted out a bunch of job interviews for me—there's a standard exit procedure."

"You said, practitioner. You mean we're muggles? Something like that?"

Oscar and Pippa have spawned, so they've clearly been exposed to the Harry Potter virus along the way. Mhari frowns minutely. "It doesn't work quite like that." She thinks for a moment. "There's not a huge gap between what their practitioners do and what our pigs get up to. They have a saying, magic is a branch of applied mathematics." Her eyes widen as she drops her fork. "Oh. Shit. Excuse me." She covers her mouth.

"Oh shit indeed." Oscar takes a deep breath. "Well, that changes a *lot* of things. Why didn't you tell me earlier?"

"Because I couldn't! I didn't know I could talk about it!" Her barely exaggerated distress is sufficiently obvious that Oscar feels compelled to do the gentlemanly thing, offering her a linen napkin to use as a tissue. She dabs at her eyes, then pushes her plate away. "I don't feel hungry. I feel *stupid*."

"Our ability to control ordinary people's minds doesn't affect one another," Oscar notes. "If this organization's grip on you works the same way—"

"That would explain everything." She reaches for her tube of *sang de sommelier* and knocks it back in a desperate shot. "*Oh!* This stuff helps me think. Isn't that stupid? It makes everything clearer." She stares at Oscar across the ruins of dinner. "I've been trying to steer you away from doing anything that I thought would attract their attention, but I'm pretty sure they're going to come for us sooner or later. I've been working on a plan, but being able to tell you about them will make things much easier." She takes a deep breath. "What we did with the board. Think of it as a dress rehearsal. The stakes next time will be much sharper . . ."

"Then we'll just have to be ready for them, won't we? At least we'll be forewarned and forearmed when your Men in Black pay us a call." Oscar very deliberately raises the other tube to his lips, uncaps it, and swallows. He shudders very slightly as he puts it down and focusses on her. "But first—"

They don't even make it to the bedroom this time.

SARA'S BODY RECLINES IN OSCAR'S CHAIR, SLOWLY COOLING, for nearly three hours after his and Mhari's departure. That's how long it takes for her supervisor, annoyed by her failure to report back, to go searching for her. Eva, the supervisor, is so wrapped up in her own timekeeping concerns that she angrily hectors Sara's body for nearly thirty seconds before she becomes concerned at the corpse's lack of response and tries to wake her.

The ambulance crew arrive to take her away at one in the morning. The cleaning services duty manager arrives to give the upset supervisor a talking-to half an hour after that, but he reluctantly concedes that there's more to this business than meets the eye. The cleaning services company has no alternative but to recognize that three employees have died on the job this month, in this particular client's office, working nights. And while once is happenstance, and twice might be coincidence, three times is sick building syndrome.

A memo is prepared for circulation the next day. And gears begin to turn . . .

7.

CODE BLUE

MO IS STILL AWAY ON BUSINESS THE NEXT MORNING. I GO IN TO work early and run into Pete, who has a list of questions three times as long as my left arm (the good one), mostly about what *I'd* do with MAGIC CIRCLE OF SAFETY if it was clogging up my to-do list.

"It's well past its sell-by date," he complains over his morning coffee. "I mean, it's *embarrassing*! They may be valuable cultural artifacts from the 1970s but there's no AM radio network to plug those sixteen rpm record players into anymore. The posters . . . no. And don't get me started on the pamphlet! It's straight out of the Jack Chick school of government communications—if I showed up at synod with a scheme to get bums on pews that relied on that type of paternalist nanny-knows-best approach, I'd, well, I'd be taken aside for tea, biscuits, and a serious talking-to about the history of marketing communications since the *Mad Men* era."

"Well fine," I say, interrupting him in full flow. "Can you write a report explaining what's wrong with it? Main conclusions on the first page, plus supplementary stuff and footnotes?"

"Um, I don't see why not! Why?"

"Because it'd be a good starting point." I take a sip of my coffee:

it's still too hot to drink, and I burn the roof of my mouth. "Do that *first*, then we can sit down and brainstorm what a public education campaign *ought* to look like in the era of WikiLeaks and Reddit. Oh, and Arsebook for the unwashed masses." (Like most other Laundry employees, I shun Facebook: their wheedling attempts to encourage personal disclosure are, shall we say, inimical to the core values of this organization.) "Stuff like, oh, adding 'how to tell if your neighbors are zombies' to the NHS Direct website, how to improvise a field-expedient basilisk gun from a pair of webcams, and so on. Disguised as background material for a role-playing game in case it leaks prematurely and we need plausible deniability—"

The phone rings. It's Dr. Wills, and she's very unhappy.

Unhappy?

No, she's livid.

"Mr. Howard!" she snaps. "I don't know what you're bloody playing with over there but I've just spent the past twelve hours digging through medical records and if this *is* your fault it's a disaster, and if it *isn't* your fault we've got a major-incident grade emergency on our hands—"

"Wait," I choke out, "we're talking about the, the report I brought round yesterday?"

"What *else* would we be talking about?"

My jaw flaps uselessly. See, it's the sudden cognitive whiplash that does it. One moment you're cruising along effortlessly at thirty thousand feet while the cabin crew slosh the whisky around in business class, the next you're in a screaming death-spiral with flames pouring from the hole where the starboard engine was meant to be before some toe-cheese puked a missile up its exhaust. It takes a little time to switch mode from business-as-usual to six-alarms-emergency if you're not primed to expect it, and so far this morning I've been trying to think my way into Pete's problem space, which is really just a training-wheels situation. Pete, for his part, is looking at me as if my head's begun spinning round spouting ectoplasm and he's wondering if an exorcism is called for. I wave a hand at him, then try to get a grip on myself. Dr. Wills is still talking when I finally get my voice back. "What exactly have you turned up?" I ask.

"Bodies. Are you people responsible for them?"

"No, I just went looking on a hunch." I take a deep breath. "How many of that cluster were false positives?"

"None of them. I think you'd better come round here right now, Mr. Howard. We're going to need to know everything you know if we're going to contain this outbreak."

I make a snap decision. "I'll be round within two hours. With backup. Please don't go public until we've spoken, for any reason at all."

Then I hang up, and quickly dial another number, the duty officer's desk line.

"Bob Howard speaking. As a result of information I have just received, I am declaring Code Blue, Code Blue, Code Blue. This is not a drill." I have *never* said those words before, in the decade-plus I've worked for the Laundry. "I need the emergency first response team to meet me in Briefing Room 201 in fifteen minutes. I'm heading up there right now, and I will be going off-site in an hour. Bye." I hang up.

"What does Code Blue mean?" Pete asks curiously.

"That the shit has just hit the fan." I twitch, then drain my coffee mug. "Nothing you can help with; sorry, you're on your own—I'm out of here."

And with that, I head for the stairs up to Mahogany Row.

NOT MANY PEOPLE KNOW THIS:

The Laundry is a government agency. It runs on rules: like all bureaucracies, it is designed to get the job done, regardless of the abilities of the individual human cogs in the machine.

However, once you get above a certain level, the practice of magic is somewhat idiosyncratic. Some people have a natural aptitude for it, perhaps for the same reason that abilities are not evenly distributed among computer programmers. Some folks can't handle abstract reasoning and formal logic, others thrive on it.

And so we have the everyday working stiffs, folks who in another age would have spent their days grinding out COBOL reports in a dinosaur pen somewhere. And we have the wizards, the people who write the COBOL compilers. In our case, they're literally wizards. We call them Mahogany Row—a little piece of misdirection, as most of the folks in the bureaucracy think that Mahogany Row is about management. The actual corridor with the plush offices and the decent carpet and the collection of paintings from the National Art Collection is usually deserted; the joke in the lower ranks is that our management have all sublimed or transsubstantiated or something. The truth is that they're *not* management—but they're scattered throughout the organization, given special privileges, and they can call on the full force of the agency to back them up as and when it becomes necessary. Once upon a time they were known as the Invisible College, presided over by John Dee at the behest of Sir Francis Walsingham, operating on the House of Lords black budget; today they're the powerful sorcerers at the heart of the organization.

For my part, I'm apprenticed to (and, it would seem, entangled with) a very nasty, very powerful entity who just happens to have thrown in his lot with the Laundry; I'm learning the principles of optimizing compiler design, so to speak. I'm at a high enough level to stick my head above the parapet and see what the non-bureaucracy portions of the organization get up to, while not actually being one of those movers and shakers (yet). So when I open the door to Briefing Room 201 I am extremely relieved to see Angleton sitting at one end of the table and staring at me as if he expects me to confess how I drunkenly broke into his office and threw up in his paper recycling bin last night.

(Because when you really need backup, even an Angleton who's pissed at you for disturbing his quiet Tuesday morning is better than no Angleton at all.)

"Hi, boss. Better cancel your lunch plans."

"This had better be serious, Mr. Howard." Angleton is gaunt and pale, his eyes slightly sunken: he has all the intensity and warmth of a public school mathematics teacher preparing to ream out a particularly delinquent schoolboy. I must confess to playing up to his expectations from time to time: I think he likes having a target who won't flee screaming every time he says "boo." But this is no time for games.

"I believe it is," I say soberly.

I take a seat just as the door opens again and Lockhart enters. He's another late-middle-aged ex-military alpha type. Most people in the organization think EA are in the business of tracking paper clips we've loaned to other government departments. This misunderstanding is highly convenient for EA. What they *actually* do is provide backup to external assets—high-level operatives working unaccountably and without official sanction, all very *Mission: Impossible.*

"What's this about, Mr. Howard?" he demands.

I glance at my watch. *Four minutes: not bad.* "I'm waiting for Andy, Jez, and Mona to show up. They're on rotation this week, right?"

"They'll be along, boy." Angleton leans forward. "What have you been doing?"

The door opens; it's Andy. "It's my ten-percenter project," I begin. "I'm investigating possible uses we can make of access to the NHS Spine's Secondary Usage Service—a data warehouse for clinical medical information, statistics on medical treatment, outcomes, and so forth. The original proposal from the suggestions box was to use it for advance warning of outbreaks of, well, anything relevant. Last week I began a run, and as a test case I went looking for cases of Krantzberg syndrome, expecting to find nothing at all because, let's face it, your average K syndrome case is an occultist who crawls into a hole and dies rather than clogging up the emergency room."

Andy is clearly one step ahead of my briefing because his muffled "Oh *shit*" is loud enough to draw a disapproving look from Lockhart, who is Old School about etiquette and bad language and so forth.

Angleton looks at me grimly. "I assume you called us here to tell us your assumption was mistaken?"

"Twelve cases in the last month," I say flatly. "Diagnosed at post-mortem, which is wrong for K syndrome. It normally presents like CJD, months before death, gives us plenty of time to treat it. It's up from a baseline of effectively two or three cases a year. I asked Dr. Wills at UCLH—she's one of ours—to investigate in case I'd made a mistake and she just got back in touch to confirm that it's for real. They all worked as office cleaners for an agency in the East End. I'm about to go round to the National Prion Unit and see what Dr. Wills has got, and will take it from there, but I declared Code Blue right now because"—I shrug—"do I need to draw you a diagram?"

"Oh *dear*," says Jez. She slipped in while I was talking, right behind Andy. She's management, subtype: sarcastic old IT hand, female, came out of Cambridge and has forgotten more about functional programming than I ever knew. I spot Mona as well. "Twelve cases, one month. How serious can it be?"

"Up from zero the month before that," I remind her. "The worst case, if I understood Dr. Wills properly, is we're watching the early stages of an epidemic's exponential take-off. There was another case this morning. Even if it's not going exponential, it's going to be very hard to sweep under the rug—it's a major spike in the national CJD mortality statistics. It all depends what we're looking at, but by the end of next month we could be into *Twelve Monkeys* territory. Or *28 Days Later*. Or Captain Trips."

Angleton looks at me blankly but Lockhart is suitably disturbed and Jez and Andy turn gray. Yay for pop-culture references. "Well bloody *get moving then*," grates Lockhart, his hairy caterpillar of a mustache bunching defensively along his upper lip.

"What resources do you need?" asks Angleton.

"Right now?" I look along the table. "Andy, do you have a couple of hours to come off-site with me?" I look back at Angleton. "I'm on first response. If you could prime OCCULUS, just in case I need backup? Andy can handle direct liaison with this committee and be my backup during initial enquiries. My first objective is to quantify the outbreak, identify its scope and geographical distribution, find out where the victims worked as opposed to where their head office is based, and identify what level of response is appropriate. Then I intend to shake the data and see if anything falls out—a pump handle for the cholera epidemic. Any comments?"

Angleton nods. "It's your show: get on the road, boy. Call if you need assets in the field, otherwise we should aim to reconvene here in four hours."

Jez looks at me. "Do you have any leads on the source? If this *is* K syndrome?"

"If it isn't, it's the world's fastest outbreak of Mad Cow Disease. Or something worse." I shove my hands in my pockets to keep from waving them around; it doesn't do to look agitated when you're trying to organize a measured response. "How we're going to keep the lid on this, I have no idea."

Medical scandals are a specialty of the British press, and with the government hell-bent on privatizing the NHS via the back door, they're sniffing around for anything that might make headline material. A dozen exotic deaths in one cleaning company will be all over the front pages if it gets out.

"I'll notify Public Affairs," says Jez. "Anything else?"

There is some more back-and-forth over things people present feel they can usefully take off my shoulders. Not because we've got the collegiate warm fuzzies for each other, but because they realize that the more balls I'm juggling the greater the chance that I'll drop one, or get myself killed, and then they'll have an even bigger mess to clean up. At least we're all grown-ups here: nobody is questioning the severity of the situation, or the need for calling a Code Blue emergency.

I glance at my watch again. Elapsed time: twenty-eight minutes since I made the call. *Good.* "Andy? We'd better blow."

"Ten-four, good buddy." And on that ironic note, we leave the hornets' nest I've just kicked over.

ELAPSED TIME: ONE HOUR AND FORTY-SIX MINUTES.

(I am keeping a written note of this in a little black book app on my current work smartphone, a bulky Android device from a dubious

South Korean chaebol that oozes more raw processing power than the Laundry's entire supercomputing dinosaur pen at the time I was recruited. The phablet lives in a pocket of my ScotteVest fleece, a garment consisting almost entirely of pockets held together with cable ducts that is marketed at geeks who have mistaken utility for elegance. In my case, I wear it because the other pockets are full of useful stuff, ranging from a couple of Hands of Glory (reprocessed from pigeon feet) to a battered digital camera (featuring some very dangerous firmware) and enough USB cables and rechargeable batteries to improvise a suicide belt if I'm feeling desperate. What the well-dressed agent is wearing about London today: a bulging fleece, faded Google tee shirt, combat pants, and Dutch army-surplus paratroop boots, with added occult firepower.)

In medical academia-land I am a lot more conspicuous than I was the day before, even accompanied by Andy (in his regular office weeds). I'm too old to pass for a student, too louche to be staff. However, in addition to warding off the zombies on the night shift, a raised Laundry warrant card can make eyes glaze over at twenty meters: non-compliance is not an issue I have to deal with. I march up to the reception desk in the Prion Research Unit and the secretary boggles in my general direction until I say, "I'm here to see Dr. Wills," at which point he points along a corridor I recognize and I head down it at a brisk march.

Dr. Wills is waiting for me, tapping her fingers; she does a double take at Andy. "He's with me," I announce. "Andy, this is Dr. Wills. Andy is here to liaise with my backup team."

Andy nods agreeably. "Where have we gotten to?" he asks.

"Bodies—" Dr. Wills sniffs. I get the feeling that she's looking for someone to blame for this, and I'm top of her list. Bringer of bad news, and so on. "There was another last night. She's downstairs, awaiting transfer to the mortuary in Poplar."

"Oh dear." Dead bodies, one of my favorite things. (Not.) "You've had a chance to look at her?"

"Yes." Her fingers whiten around the pen she's twirling. "I thought you might want to see what I found."

"Okay, let's go—what?"

"Sit *down*, Mr. Howard. We haven't confirmed this is K syndrome yet, rather than a new, *highly* contagious, *rapidly* progressive, and *extremely* fatal prion disease, so until we've done that, nobody's going anywhere near the cadaver without full protective gear. In the meantime, I've got her records." She eyeballs Andy. "Yes? You have something to contribute?"

"The other cases," Andy says diffidently. "They all worked for the same agency. Have you gotten anywhere with their actual work assignments? Other information that might help us narrow them down more accurately?"

"Yes." She shoves her monitor round towards us. "Move around here so you can both see this comfortably." Then she goes into full-on professorial mode. I'm used to it from living with Mo, but it's still impressive. "We have thirteen cases so far, all with underlying similarities. At autopsy, the first eleven brains were found to have the characteristic spongiform lesions of K syndrome or CJD. The two most recent cases were not subjected to post-mortem dissection but we used an MRI scanner to non-invasively obtain soft tissue images and they're consistent with the earlier ones. They test negative for nvCJD and other known prion diseases—classic CJD included. There is no family history. They were all flagged as dead on arrival, which implies extremely rapid progression, but ended up in different hospitals because most of them died at home. Upon doing some further research I determined that six of them had reported symptoms in the three days leading up to sudden death—ataxia, tremors, muscle weakness, one case that was misdiagnosed as migraine due to visual disturbances and nausea.

"You asked about geographical distribution. Here's where it gets odd. The agency they work for handles janitorial and cleaning arrangements for some of the large corporate offices in and around Canary Wharf. I can't confirm that they all covered the same building yet, but it's a striking lead—enough to raise suspicions in its own right. There were a couple of outliers. One is—was—a medical phlebotomist at UCH, which has got us extremely spooked, to be perfectly honest. And one worked for a wholesale meat supplier at Smithfield Market."

She pauses and clears her throat. "Then there was the other thing."

"The other"—Andy takes the bait—"thing?"

"All of them had recent needle-stick signs. But none of them have any of the usual indications of drug abuse, or recently gave blood samples. You'll want to check their police records, but they don't look like addicts: they had recent injections around the median cubital, but no regular tracks or collapsed veins."

What I *don't* say is, "Holy phlebotomists, Batman!" (Because that would be in excruciatingly bad taste, given that a baker's dozen families are mourning their dead right now.) But I'm shaken, and when I get shaken, my irreverent sense of humor comes out to play, and so I think it in the privacy of my own skull. Then I say the second thing that comes into my mind. "Is there any chance this could be some new street drug?"

"What kind?" Dr. Wills looks at me as if I'm a particularly slow-on-the-uptake student. "One shot and you're a downer? Mr. Howard, with all due respect, addicts don't *start* by injecting the hard stuff. They usually have a prior history, and work their way up to the overdose over a period of years. What we're looking at here is a cluster of relatively well-adjusted members of society, all of them working, albeit in low-paid jobs, all in decent health—well, the oldest was fifty-nine and had osteoarthritis that was going to cause trouble if she didn't get on the waiting list for a tin hip—but taken as a group, they're almost the exact opposite of the picture we'd get if this cluster was due to contaminated street drugs."

Andy scribbles something on his notepad—the old-fashioned paper variety. "So. I assume you think the needle-signs are significant?" She nods emphatically. "Therefore we're now looking for where they got them. That implies it's blood-born? And one of the victims was a medical phlebotomist?"

"Yes, from right here at this hospital. She phoned in sick one evening last month—she was on out-of-hours cover—and according to her husband she took to her sick bed. Self-diagnosed whatever it was as the flu: shivering, incoherent, not running an obvious fever . . . he went to work the next day, came back that evening to find her dead. That gives us a window from initial symptoms to mortality of around 36-48 hours, which is a bit worrying."

Worrying? From what I know of K syndrome it's unheard of for it to progress that fast. So I find myself reluctantly asking a question I've been dreading. "Can I have a look at the body that came in last night?"

She shakes her head. "I don't see what you could achieve, Mr. Howard—"

I glance at Andy. He nods, imperceptibly: best if she hears this from someone else. "Mr. Howard is a necromancer, Dr. Wills."

"A *what*?"

I sigh. "Ritual magician. Specialty"—*I'm the new trainee Eater of Souls*—"raising the dead as zombies, among other things. Actually I almost certainly *can't* raise a body that's been subjected to a post-mortem dissection, but I might be able to learn something from it." It's the lose-my-lunch approach to finding out what somebody died of. Some people aspire to necromancy; others have necromancy thrust upon them; me, I just didn't scream and run away fast enough when necromancy came and kicked down my office door. I'm slow that way. I rub the sore patch on my upper right arm and frown. "I need to be in physical proximity to the body before I can tell."

"That's—you'll pardon me for saying this, Mr. Howard—some-what problematic. As I said, until we can definitely rule out a highly contagious, rapidly lethal prion infection—yes, I agree it's unlikely, but you never know—we're keeping them in sealed biohazard stor-age. So you can't—"

"I don't need to touch it. I just have to get within a couple of me-ters. Even on the other side of a closed door. Can you manage that?"

"Oh, that's different. Let me make a call." She picks up her desk phone without waiting for a reply.

I'm used to seeing her odd combination of relief and queasy disgust from other people. Coughing to necromantic tendencies isn't quite as bad as admitting you're sexually attracted to six year olds, but it's not far removed (at least among people who are aware that it's not just a bad cliché). It's the equivalent of admitting at a swingers' party that you've got leprosy *and* AIDS, but they're both under control, honest. People get seven shades of funny around death and corpses, in my experience: death is one of the three big loci for taboos, along with sex and food.

"All right, I can take you down to the mortuary. You can look, but you can't touch—you'll have to do whatever it is that you do through a freezer door."

ANDY AND I FOLLOW DR. WILLS OUT OF HER OFFICE AND INTO THE maze that is UCLH.* It takes us about twenty minutes to wend our way between buildings, up floors, over connecting walkways, and down elevators until we reach the mortuary. Dr. Wills signs us in: not, I am sorry to say, without Andy and me having to make use of our warrant cards. It's a relatively small unit: this isn't a hospice. Bodies of people who died in hospital are generally only stored here until they can be sent to the district mortuary for post-mortem examination and subsequent transfer to the undertakers. There's a lobby area, then a room, one wall of which is given over to refrigerated storage, and another room with a pair of dissection tables. Dr. Wills has a brief conversation with the mortuary attendant, who lets us into the storage room and leads us to one of the drawers. "This is the one," Dr. Wills informs us. "Her name was Sara. Sara Siad. She was fifty-nine." Her hand lingers on the drawer handle, then she lets it drop. "I can't

---

* UCLH is a rare surviving example of old-time NHS architecture. It was founded in 1859, and extended continuously with total contempt for architectural consistency. The result is, to coin a neologism, Gormenghastly: a nineteenth-century workhouse with WWII-era Nissen huts tucked into corners at the bottom of Victorian gothic stairwells, 1960s Brutalist extensions clamped to the roof, and twenty-first-century high-tech side-bays shoe-horned into a First World War–era ward for Shell Shock patients. The porters drive electric buggies and there are signs inside the larger labs to keep the staff who work there from getting lost; they send out search parties for stranded patients on a daily basis.

let you get any closer, I'm afraid. She's double-bagged and not to be opened without contagious diseases precautions."

I take a deep breath. "Are her organs all present?"

"Yes." She frowns. "What are you going to—"

I breathe out, close my outer eyes, and, simultaneously, open the inner one—the one I first became aware of during a traumatic turn of events at Brookwood Cemetery in Surrey, where a gang of evil muppets tried to sacrifice me in order to bind the Eater of Souls, using my body as a container. (They hadn't realized that the said Eater of Souls was already incarnated in the shape of Angleton and working for the Laundry, thank you very much.) The trouble with botched summoning rituals is that you can never be sure what'll happen if there's a dangling pointer or a memory leak. In this case, they succeeded in summoning me back into my own body and binding me there, but not without side effects. In particular, I have inherited some of the aforementioned Eater of Souls' abilities. Which is a very mixed blessing, to say the least.

In the red-tinged darkness behind my eyelids, something stirs.

I look around. I can sense bodies around me, breathing, hearts pumping, minds churning. Two stand in close proximity. One of them is warded by a standard-issue self-protection device—that'll be Andy—the unwarded one is Dr. Wills. The third, on the far side of a partition wall, must be the mortuary attendant. Far more interesting to me are the other bodies, stacked floor to ceiling in a neat grid against one wall. They're not sleeping. They're *empty*, indeed, more than empty: they're filled with a peculiar kind of vacuum that seems to tug at my attention. There are no feeders of the night nearby, for which I am deeply grateful; nor am I about to call them. None of these bodies are suddenly going to fill with un-life and start banging at the doors, desperate to fill their ravening maws with the taint of humanity. There are no souls present save those of the living. All is as it should be.

But. *But.*

I turn my attention to the body Dr. Wills identified, and peer at it, and realize that there's something wrong here. I'm not sure what there is about it that feels abnormal at first, so I compare it with the husks in the drawers to either side of it. *Ah. That.* The adjacent bodies . . . they'd make good hosts. But this one might as well be made of ash and cardboard. It's not that it's unappetizing to that part of me that partakes of the Eater's nature, so much as that it's inedible: the necromantic equivalent of shit, fully digested matter containing no residual nutrients. Something or someone got here first.

I open my eyes. "This bod—sorry, Sara Siad's body. Was this one of the ones you examined by MRI?"

Dr. Wills nods. "We're not risking a dissection on possible prion sources these days, but we have an older scanner that we use for teaching and lab work on non-living samples."

"Right."

"What did you notice?" Andy asks.

"She's been eaten." I shiver, and not from the cold of the refrigeration system. "Her brain is so thoroughly chewed-up that you couldn't make a zombie out of her: if I summoned a feeder here and now I couldn't convince it to take up occupation. It's as if she's already been consumed. I'd guess the brain stem is mostly intact, but the cerebral cortex is like old lace."

Dr. Wills's expression is peculiarly intent. "K syndrome never gets that far," she says. "The patients usually die first. Whatever happened—you're right about her brain structure—happened very fast, and very thoroughly."

"Well then. We have needle-stick injuries. And we have something that eats neural networks. Presumably a relative of the feeders in the night, but different: more voracious, faster. If they haven't been injecting some crazy new street drug—"

Then it hits me.

"What if they weren't injecting something, but *removing samples?*" I look at Dr. Wills speculatively. "Are the injection sites consistent with blood donation?"

"Well yes, now that you mention it, but why—"

"Office cleaners. Blood samples. The two with bite marks. And now this." I close my eyes briefly, recalling Mo's dismissal: *Don't be silly, Bob, everybody knows vampires don't exist.* I open my eyes. Andy and Dr. Wills are both looking at me expectantly. "I want to know exactly which offices they were all cleaning. Then I'm going to pay a visit."

WE DON'T HAVE TO LOOK FAR; MRS. SIAD'S BODY WAS FOUND AT her place of work. But Andy still feels the need to angst at me.

"I see what you're saying, Bob, but don't you think we should take this a step at a time?"

I lean against the corridor wall. "Andy. Andy. What do all these deaths have in common?"

"Well, they're all K syndrome, or something like it? And they mostly have these needle marks? And you think someone's been taking blood samples and then they've been dying . . . ? Which somehow means you have to go rob a bank." He grins widely. "Simples!"

"You'd make a lousy meerkat. No, Andy. If you noticed the time of death, Mrs. Siad was found at two in the morning. And I happened to note a pronounced nocturnal association with the others in the spreadsheet, as well. And they've all lost blood."

"But there's no mechanism for—"

"Andy, I am thinking of the law of sympathy. As in, if you've got body tissues or fluids from someone, you've got an occult link back to their body. And I am thinking that it is just past noon, which means—if I'm right—now is the safest time to go break down the doors. But if we wait, it *won't* be. And at the rate this is increasing, we're going to have more dead bodies on our hands because if I take it to the oversight committee and they kick it upstairs we won't get an answer before tomorrow morning at the earliest, now."

"Hang on." He raises his hands. "Sympathetic links? Via the blood samples? So what you're saying is, someone is taking blood samples, and the donors are subsequently having their brains chowed down on by what, something related to the feeders?"

I nod tiredly. "I'm not talking about Dracula here, Andy. I know damn well there's not enough nutritional content in human blood to live off. But someone's taking these blood samples and I want to know *why*, and more importantly *what* they're doing with them. It looks like some kind of necromantic ritual to me. And the nocturnal fatality thing is, um, well. It doesn't give me the warm fuzzies. I'm thinking in terms of a cultist group who have fucked up by not spreading their net wide enough."

Andy straightens. "Oh, if you put it that way . . . okay, I'm convinced. We're going back to the ops room, right now."

"Hey! If we do that—"

"Bob." He puts a hand on my shoulder. "Do you want Mo to kill me?"

"Eh? No! What's Mo got to do with this?"

"Because she *will* kill me if I let you rush in without backup—especially when backup is available. See? I am aware that you are, to say the least, somewhat better able to handle yourself in field operations than I am. But you're not omnipotent and it wouldn't be the first time you've run into something you couldn't handle by yourself. Also, the good news is, if you're right and it's cultists then it is *not* some sort of contagious prion disease. So we're not looking at it exponentiating, going pandemic, and de-populating London. There's time for us to go back to the office to touch base, and then you can go and visit this cleaning agency or the bank or whatever with a full OCCULUS team* for backup."

I nod, reluctantly. "But time is critical—"

"Yes. Which is why we're going back to the office *right now*. Are you with me?"

"Shit."

"Good man."

---

* OCCULUS is short for Occult Control Coordination Unit Liaison, Unconventional Situations—the occult equivalent of a Nuclear Emergency Search Team. They're staffed by folks from 21/SAS or, these days, the Special Reconnaissance Regiment. Scary fuckers who you do not mess with, in other words.

8.

CONFRONTATION!

BY TWO O'CLOCK IN THE AFTERNOON, ANDY AND I HAVE RE-
turned to the New Annex briefing room, made our report, and learned
(by way of one of Jez's gophers) that the cleaning outfit is a subsidiary
of G4S and all the victims of the K syndrome outbreak were indeed
working in the same skyscraper, and, furthermore, were all on the night
shift. Which is excellent progress. Angleton has been called away to
deal with some other bush fire; Lockhart's in the driving seat. Unfortunately that's where the good news ends. The skyscraper in question—
well, at forty-five stories it's a skyscraper by British standards—is the
headquarters of a major British financial institution; indeed, a household name as prominent and honorable as Northern Rubble and Rat-
West. Unlike the aforementioned institutions, this one didn't end up in
public ownership in 2008. But it's not somewhere we can just go barg-
ing into mob-handed without attracting all sorts of unwelcome attention. Not to mention spooking the cultists. So we're going to have to
deploy our minions Stealth and Misdirection for this job.

"Can you handle a mop and bucket?" asks Lockhart.

"I don't know. Can you impersonate a bank manager?" I fire back
(which is unkind and unfair because he always dresses the part).

He looks at me with ill-concealed distaste. "We've sorted you out a way in," he says. "They're couriering a uniform over here right now. You're down on the roster as Sara Siad's replacement on this evening's shift; Sara's supervisor, Eva Kadir, can show you where Mrs. Siad's body was found. Just try not to mess things up."

"What else?" I ask.

"You'll be wearing a wire and the OCCULUS brick outside will be monitoring the feed from their truck. In event of trouble you'll have two extraction paths: one is via the police—we'll have our liaison in SCO1 ready to dispatch a team to 'arrest' you if you get into trouble, and they'll be pre-briefed that you're doing a black bag job for SIS. The other is the OCCULUS team themselves, but . . . we don't want to do that. Do you understand?"

I nod soberly. An OCCULUS extraction in Docklands would be visible all the way from six different TV studios and a couple of newspaper newsrooms. *Nobody* wants to be the subject matter of a COBRA briefing to the Prime Minister and cabinet, due to the tower of smoke rising to the east of Downing Street: that kind of thing can be a career-limiting move, especially if the existence of the organization you work for is a state secret the PM hasn't been cleared for. So the availability of a full OCCULUS team outside the bank HQ isn't about rescuing my sorry ass if I run into something I can't handle: it's about saving London if it turns out there's the thaumaturgic equivalent of a nuke in the basement.

"Okay, I'd better go visit Harry," I say. "Page me when the G4S package arrives."

Harry the Horse is our in-house armorer. One-eyed, with a manner he acquired from studying *The Long Good Friday*, he's an ex-cop or ex-soldier or ex-something that allowed him to acquire an alarming amount of expertise about killing people in the course of his profession. He hangs out in a cubbyhole in the basement, with a walk-in gun safe and a firing range.*

---

* Don't ask me how we crammed a hundred-meter-long underground firing range into the sixty-meter-long basement of the New Annex; it probably has something to do with ley lines and spatiotemporal distortion.

"'Ello, my son," he says as I stick my head round the door. "What brings you down here today?"

"A Code Blue," I say, which gets his attention instantly. "I've got to go poke my nose around an office this evening. Police and OCCU-LUS backup outside, but it's a low-key investigation: we don't want to attract attention. So I need arms and armor for self-defense, but nothing I can't conceal inside a cleaner's overall."

"Awright." He puts down the copy of *Grenade Fancier's Monthly* he's reading and unlocks the vault door. "Follow me."

Shortly thereafter I'm equipped with a new extra-shiny protective ward and an ultra-thin anti-stab vest—breastplate and back protector—suitable for wearing under outer layers. "Can I interest you in a little something for the weekend?" he wheedles. "Just a *little* one?"

"You know I don't like guns," I complain as Harry hauls out a Glock 17 in standard police spec. I rub my right upper arm. "I don't have the upper arm strength to hold a pistol one-handed for long." Not since that business when the Wandsworth Cell of the Brotherhood of the Black Pharaoh dined out on Bob sashimi, adding cannibalism to their charge sheet: the dent in my arm is a souvenir of the occasion. Also, in event of a police extraction, I really do *not* want them calling down SCO19 on my ass by mistake: those guys shoot first and ask questions later.

"Well then, let me see." Harry puts the Glock back and has a rummage in the drawers. "How about this?"

He pulls out something that looks at first glance like a silver knuckle duster, until I see that it's only got one ring, with some sort of crown on it—whatever it is, you're supposed to grip it in your fist. "What's that?" I ask.

"Stunner. You wrap your hand round the battery and capacitor and punch, like so. But it's also a wave guide: see these markings?" (I peer at the indicated runes.) "Class four banishment charge. If someone tries to summon a nasty on your ass, this'll send it right back where it came from."

"Okay, *that* I like." I pick up the taser-cum-banishment-charge. "I think we're about done here. I'll just make sure my camera's got a full charge." (It's a new one, a replacement for the one I totaled when we closed out Andy's office.) And with that, I head back to the briefing room, where a package containing one G4S cleaner's uniform has arrived.

MEANWHILE:

"Hello? This is Mhari Murphy checking in. I'd like to speak to Alison White in Human Resources. Yes, I'll hold."

Mhari reclines her chair and catches Oscar's eye. She nods minutely. He picks up the handset on his voice terminal and mutes it, then listens in.

"Hi, Alison? Long time no see! Yes I'm fine, how about you? How's Steve doing?" (She listens for a while, with appropriate verbal punctuation.) "The reason I'm calling is, I need a little favor. It's, um, yes, it's a Laundry problem. I've stumbled over something unusual and I need your help in tidying it up . . ."

IT'S SIX O'CLOCK, I'VE HAD A VERY LONG DAY ALREADY, AND I'M coming down in the world. That's the only reason I can think of why I'm standing here, keeping my mouth shut, while a middle-aged shift boss bitches at me.

"I don't believe this! I ask them for replacement cleaner who has corporate experience and they send me you! What are they thinking of in HR? You're useless!" She's pacing up and down in the breeze-block-walled janitorial room, pausing to periodically glare at me. "This is very exacting job! This customer is very critical! Why do they send me a man with no previous experience?"

We've got off to a great flying start, Eva and me.

"I can empty bins, vacuum, and dust," I offer. "What more do you want?"

"You have no security pass!" Eva rounds on me. "Why have you not got a CRB check? You can't clean bank offices without CRB! It say here you don't have CRB!" She brandishes a dog-eared stack of forms at me.

"Oh, *that*." Of *course* I haven't been checked by the Criminal Records Bureau prior to employment by G4S Cleaning. I'm subject to Developed Vetting as a regular, recurring part of the security clearance for my job; as far as the CRB is concerned I don't even exist. "Will this do?" I ask, hauling out my warrant card.

"What—" Eva stops in mid-flow.

"You will see that this warrant card identifies me as a plain-clothes detective inspector from the Metropolitan Police," I tell her, extemporizing on the spot. "I am here as part of an official investigation by the Serious Fraud Office. You will not ask me any questions about why I am here or what I am doing. You will take me around the offices that Sara Siad cleaned on her last shift. If anybody asks about me, I am a new trainee and you are showing me the ropes. Do you understand?"

"But—but"—she runs down after a few seconds—"we don't have trainees here!"

"Doesn't matter." They'll believe I'm a trainee if I tell them to: that's the beauty of the card, it's official ID with a class four geas attached, and as long as I'm using it on official business it will draw on the full authority of the organization to convince anyone I present it to that I'm on, shall we say, whatever official business it is in the best interests of the organization for them to believe I'm engaged in. The only people it won't fool are other Laundry staff and seriously powerful sorcerers. I don't like using it on civilians, but it's less hassle than calling the ops room to yell at her boss, and more merciful than the other options I have up my sleeve. "I need to see Sara's route. This is official police business."

"I'll take you there. (Never heard such a thing . . .)" She leads off, muttering to herself and periodically glancing back at me with angry-eyed suspicion, clearly disturbed by the impact my lack of office cleaning chops is going to have on her workload.

I follow Eva into the maze of twisty little corridors and open-plan cubicle areas that comprise the back-office IT support section of the bank. There are no windows—we're below ground level here—but there's an omnipresent dull roar of air conditioning that paradoxically makes everything sound muted: I guess it swamps other noises. Most of the offices are relatively spartan and cheaply furnished. Employees with the status to rate a window view don't generally work down here. And it's largely deserted. The market's closing bell has long since rung, and most of the staff have long since gone home or buggered off to the wine bar. With a sinking feeling I begin to wonder if I've left it too late—if the brain-eating phantasm I'm searching for comes and goes with the day shift. I have a smartphone loaded with our OFCUT suite and a suitably bluetoothy sensor, and I periodically check to see if it's picked up anything: but no, there's not so much as a haunted print server down here, much less a nest of don't-be-silly-Bob.

Eva leads me past a familiar-looking door that screams *server room* at me. It's secured by a keypad, with warning notices and a breeze blowing from around it. I spot a prominent red handle under a perspex cover, beside a notice warning of the risk of asphyxiation in event of a halon dump. I pause and check my OFCUT readout again. There's a very faint yellow warning, barely budging the needle: but that's enough to get my attention. "Why are you dawdling?" demands Eva, glaring at me. "We've got offices to clean!"

The server room's reading barely above background level. I follow Eva along a corridor that leads past it. There are signs of new construction here. I see raw sections of wall punctuated by open panels where new cable runs are being installed, converging on a cabinet with a patch panel. And then there's a door with a sign on it: **THE SCRUM**, subtitled: **KEEP OUT**. My thaumometer, needless to say, is pointing straight towards it.

Eva goes in.

I MAKE NO JUDGMENT UPON THE SCRUM AT THIS POINT, OTHER than to note that they clearly rate a much higher grade of office furniture than the janitorial and other staff who occupy the basement of the bank. The door opens on a room that looks like an outer office that's being turned into an access-control corridor. There's a door at either end of it, and something that looks like a half-assembled airport metal detector gate (or perhaps an excessively paranoid retailer's anti-shoplifting gizmo) standing between them, powered down and with neatly taped-up cables dangling beside an empty equipment rack. *Curious,* I think, and check my thaumometer again. This time it's reading amber: I'm definitely not in Kansas anymore. "Are you getting this?" I mutter into my lapel. "I'm in Basement Level B, office with a sign saying 'The Scrum' on the door, and I'm getting a three-sigma signal."

"Sara cleaned in here yesterday," Eva tells me. "She was in the next office along. I thought she was asleep at first and was very angry but she wasn't—"

"You'd better go away," I tell her. "You don't need to clean in here tonight."

"But I, but, you—"

"Leave this suite and finish your round," I repeat. She gets the message after a moment, nods jerkily, then turns and leaves, nearly stomping on my foot as she goes. She takes the cleaning cart with her.

There is the stench of the occult about this place. Something or someone is messing with the substrate of reality, and my magical mystery detector is picking up the overspill. It would be best to get some idea of what I'm up against before I open the next door. I take a deep breath then do the close-my-eyes-and-open-the-other-one thing, trying not to think how much I hate this. (A few months ago I had to do it in a hotel suite in Colorado Springs. Two men—well, they'd started out as men—paid for it with their lives using what was left of their souls as currency: I'm a necromancer, and the guy I'm apprenticed to isn't called the Eater of Souls for nothing.)

Against the dark background of my eyelids the world around me is tinted with faintly luminous green blobs. X-ray vision for the occult. One of them moves—

"Who are you and what do you think you're doing there? Who let you in?"

I open my eyes. A skinny guy in an ill-fitting but clearly expensive suit has just come through the door at the other end of the room and is staring at me with an oddly intent expression, like a ferret sizing up a rat for breakfast. He's not ugly but he can't be much past his early twenties and the skin around his jawline is cratered with the extinct volcanic debris of late adolescent acne. My inner eye pegs him for a practitioner the instant I clap eyes on him.

I hold up my warrant card and smile cynically. "Serious Fraud Office, my son. What's *your* story?"

"Oh God oh no oh God oh—" He starts off on a very promising meltdown: it's quite gratifying to watch, for about the first three seconds as he stumbles towards me. But then he trips over his own tongue and, as he comes forward, *focusses* on my ID, and does a double take.

"Wait. That's not a—" He straightens up and *I* do a double take as I realize he's way too close. He comes at me, raising one arm to grab the card. I pull it back out of reach, and we do a clumsy two-step for a moment, which ends with him grabbing my right arm. Despite looking like a weed, he grips like he's been taking arm-wrestling lessons from an industrial robot. Whether by design or by accident he's got hold of my bad bicep.

"Hey!" I squawk involuntarily, stick my left hand in my pocket, and pull out Harry's nasty little gadget. "Let go!"

"Are you a journalist?" he demands. "What are you doing here? What are you looking for?"

"Let go *now*," I warn him, and that's when he realizes I've got something in my left hand. "Identify yourself!"

He loosens his grip, as if it's dawning on him that it might be foolhardy to grab an intruder waving a warrant card and claiming to be a cop. I hold the zapper against his stomach but don't push the button. "You're not SFO," he accuses.

"I'm asking the questions. Who are you?"

"Alex Schwartz. That's Doctor Alex Schwartz to you. You're making a big mistake busting in here. We have security—"

"Jolly good, *Doctor* Schwartz. Is this your office suite?"

"You're making a—"

"Because if so, I think we ought to sit down, de-escalate this, and have a little heart-to-heart."

"But you're making a"—he backs up a few centimeters, then a few more, until he's moving towards the inner door—"mistake! We don't have anything to do with money here. We're the algorithm development support group for the quantitative trading desks, we don't actually have anything to do with—"

Picture a light bulb going on over my head, and make it a five million lumen floodlight.

"Blood," I say. Which is exactly the worst possible thing that could come out of my mouth at that moment.

Alex's pupils dilate and he grimaces, lips pulling back from his teeth. He begins to lean towards me and the ward on the silver chain I'm wearing under my shirt suddenly heats up painfully and begins to throb. "Freeze," he says, "be calm, everything is all right." Leaning closer, he reaches towards my shoulders: "Everything is— *Ouch!*"

Fifty thousand volts of happy juice throws him halfway across the room, flailing and twitching. I yank the camera out of my other pocket, whimpering slightly as I put too much effort into my right arm, and hit the power button. The rear screen lights up gratifyingly fast. I step over Alex while he's busy twitching and kick the inner door open, basilisk device raised and ready.

I get a moment to gawp at the Scrum's lair. There's a big open-plan office with glass-fronted smaller offices opening off it to all sides, and directly opposite me there's a huge whiteboard covered in multicolored Post-it notes. And that's *all* I get before a spike-haired woman in a black trouser suit leaps out from behind the door I just opened and does something extremely painful to my right wrist, at which point I drop the camera, scream, and reflexively try to eat her soul.

Ever got that sensation when you bit into a pitted olive and discovered a stone? Keep a grip on that feeling. Now imagine that instead of doing it with your teeth, you just did it with your brain.

While I'm staggering in sudden agony, Spikey the Wonder-Banker

yanks my arm round into a half-nelson and snarls, "Krav Maga, baby,
I *knew* that self-defense course would come in handy sooner or later!"
Then she gives me the bum's rush towards the boardroom at the
opposite end of the office. It's like she didn't even feel my attempt
at killing her. I'm still processing the *oh shit* moment and winding up
to kill her to death all over again (*Why didn't it work the first time?*
a little corner of me is gibbering) when my feet touch the ground
and I see what's in front of me and the bottom drops out of my
universe.

Two office workers, one male and one female, are sitting opposite
me at the far end of a boardroom table. The woman looks worryingly
familiar. "Bob?" she says, while her companion (an intense-looking
bald guy in heavy horn-rimmed spectacles) is working his way up to
a puzzled expression. "What on earth do you think you're doing
here? Put him *down*, Janice, how often do I have to tell you it's bad
manners to play with your food?" Then she gives me a familiar and
half-contemptuous smile that tells me in no uncertain terms that (a)
my fly is at half-mast, (b) she can see right through me, and (c) I'm
fucked.

"Mhari?" I ask.

Then Doctor Schwartz grabs me by the opposite arm with an inarticulate growl.

"*No*, Alex, do *not* rip his head off," Mhari says irritably. "Both of
you, back off! Sit him down at the table and give him a bottle of Per-
rier. We've got a lot of forms to fill out." She taps a pile of papers in
front of her suggestively and glances sidelong at Intensity Boy, who
nods, then stares at me with pursed lips. They're *all* staring at me. I'm
getting a horrible sinking feeling, because Intensity Boy is exchanging
knowing looks with Mhari in a manner suggestive of mutual understanding, while Janice and Alex are breathing down my neck and
sizing each other up like I'm the last slice of pizza in the Hunger
Games. *Well fuck me sideways with a wooden stake*, I realize dismally, *I've fallen in a wunch of vampires.*

My experience of Mhari, albeit a decade out of date, leads me to believe that anyone who can see eye to eye with her like that is quite possibly as batshit crazy as she is. Now her partner in crime opens his mouth.

"I'm sure you're wondering what this is all about," he says calmly. "Chair, Alex. Where are your good manners?" Janice is still holding me with a grip like a JCB. Alex grudgingly pulls a chair out from the table and shoves it under my arse while Janice pushes me down onto it until my knees buckle. Somewhere along the way the camera ends up on the table. *Ha ha, very funny.* It's like an anxiety dream. You know the kind where you find yourself sitting an exam in the school gym hall again, and you're naked? This is the other one, the adult workplace version where you're hauled up before a committee for a damning performance appraisal and it's chaired by your psycho ex from hell. And the rest of the committee are vampires or something. "Mhari, if you could explain? This is sufficiently unfamiliar that I do not want to risk misstating the situation."

"It may be unfamiliar but it's very simple, Oscar." Mhari glances at him again, almost fondly (which by itself almost makes me lose my lunch), then turns back to me. The past years have been good for her, insofar as she seems to have grown some kind of glossy high-powered captain-of-industry shell, with added stingers and venom glands. "Whatever fire drill you've called you can damn well call it off, Bob, because we're all colleagues here."

She hauls out a suspiciously shiny looking card wallet and flips it across the table at me. It's a warrant card. It's got her name and a rather out-of-date photograph on it. I pick it up and turn it over and it tingles just right, as indeed it should; in the small print the "Valid From" field contains today's date. I flick it back towards her. It stops halfway, then starts again, gradually picking up speed until it whizzes back into her hand. (That's a new feature, I note absently; mine doesn't do that.)

She pats the pile of paperwork by her elbow. "Actually, it's a *good* thing you turned up. Now you're here you can make yourself useful by helping me fill out their in-processing assessments for HR. Alison

White is expecting them on her desk at nine o'clock sharp to begin induction profiling."

"But, but"—I force myself to stop flapping—"you can't unilaterally recruit them! They're vampires! You're *all* vampires!"

Mhari looks at me pityingly. "Nonsense, Bob, *everybody* knows vampires don't exist. They're just extremely gifted mathematicians who have pioneered a new and fertile area of category theory that is undoubtedly of interest to the organization. I'd be the last to deny that there have been some odd side effects, but if you keep insisting your new co-workers are mythical monsters you'll have only yourself to blame when HR starts to question your sanity . . ."

WE ALL MAKE MISTAKES.

In our youth, if we survive them, they're called learning experiences or teachable moments or some-such. And that which does not maim or kill us usually makes us stronger, albeit sometimes also sadder and more cynical.

Mhari was one of *my* learning experiences.

(I'm not sure what I was, from her side of the looking glass: roadkill, perhaps. Or a useful idiot. Something like that. But let's not go there . . .)

Rewind to the late nineties/early noughties. There's me, Bob Howard, working on a postgrad CS degree. This means I'm putting in roughly eighty hours a week on the books and in front of the computer screen, in a field where the proportion of women is roughly what you'd expect of a sixteenth-century Benedictine monastery. I was, not to put too fine a point on it, single. I then managed to bring myself to the attention of the Laundry by means too embarrassing to relate. (Well, okay: I nearly landscaped Wolverhampton by accident, because that's what happens when your funky new realtime rendering algorithm that uses a *really* neat logical shortcut you can't believe nobody invented before turns out to be an open and ungrounded summoning grid. Which is the extradimensional equivalent of a fast food joint with a buzzing neon sign that says: GOOD EATS HERE. Can we move on, please?)

So, the organization made me a job offer I couldn't—wasn't allowed to—refuse. And then they stuck me behind a desk to rot for a few years, or at least until I'd been thoroughly studied and quantified and got sufficiently bored to ask for something more interesting to do instead. During which period I found myself working elbow-to-elbow with a whole raft of people I wouldn't otherwise have met, mostly in similar straits (they saw something uncanny, heard something go bump in the night, and got swept up in the dragnet when they were found to be useful), some of whom had no Y chromosomes and were also single.

Like I said, Mhari was a learning experience for me. Do you *really* want to hear about our doomed on-again/off-again car-crash relationship? The immediate nature of the teachable moment for little old twenty-something me was, as a drunken friend of mine questionably phrased it sometime later, "Do not stick your dick in the bad crazy." It took a lot longer, and a whole lot more perspective (not to mention being married for several years to someone who most certainly was *not* the "bad crazy") for me to work out what was actually going on in our dysfunctional relationship, which alternated between bouts of hot primal monkey sex and screaming pan-throwing arguments. What I *think* was happening was that the "me" that Mhari was alternately fucking and throwing things at was not *me*, but some sort of demented, revenge-rebound placeholder for a previous boyfriend of many years and some commitment. She'd split up with him acrimoniously less than six months before we first so much as snogged, and he'd done a beautiful gaslight number on her in the process. (Either that or she was bipolar with a topping of psycho special sauce: but resentful rebound relationships are a hell of a lot commoner, and I'll go with Occam's razor this time.) The net result was that she was a walking bomb, primed to take out all her existential resentment on whatever man she next took up with, because Bill (I think he was a Bill) had convinced her that all men were fundamentally untrustworthy bastards who would lie to her at the drop of a hat. And I, having recently emerged blinking into the light from a quasi-monastic existence, was simply a convenient cuddly punchbag.

Basically our relationship was doomed to be toxic from the get-go, if only I had possessed the experience to recognize it. Luckily . . . well, I got lucky: I met Mo, and then had a decade-long healing and maturation process because Mo was both older and smarter than me, and patient enough to wait for me to get my head out of my arse. As for Mhari, her instability got back to HR, who politely offered her an out-placement—sworn to secrecy on a permanent sabbatical, file marked DO NOT REACTIVATE EXCEPT IN CASE OF EMER-GENCY, and discreet help in building a new life that didn't press all her broken buttons on a daily basis by rubbing her nose in the tran-sience and irrationality of human life and the underlying horror of the things waiting for us at the bottom of the world.

So picture my joy at walking into that boardroom and being *smiled at* by my toxic ex from hell, in blonde highlights and a black suit with sharp shoulder pads, a pile of HR forms on hand for me to countersign, and the assurance that once again I'd be working with her.

No, time does *not* heal all wounds . . .

PHONE CALLS, EMAILS, AND PAPERWORK ENSUE. THE OCCULUS team is told to stand down, the ops room are sheepishly informed that there's nothing to see here, the Code Blue is cancelled, and I get a huge black mark for budget overspend on my departmental project matrix. There's even a post-mortem meeting scheduled for the day after tomorrow, to rub it in: INCIDENT 2911.1-A CODE BLUE/ MISIDENTIFICATION WALK-THROUGH pops up in my calendar.

The thing is, it *is* technically a misfire; very nearly a blue-on-blue incident. Mhari and her charismatically intense boss Oscar assure me that there is no ongoing campaign of exsanguination and hemophagia by the Scrum. Everything is copacetic with HR regarding their induc-tion as the Laundry's newest and most sparkly high-end formal logic brains trust. Even though her little playmates have developed super-strength and a disturbing tendency to burst into flames if they go outdoors in daylight, who am I to shout "vampire!" in a crowded graveyard?

Fuck it, she always *was* better than me at administrative/managerial maneuvering. As witness her success in leveraging the fallout from our out-falling to get herself semi-permanently out-placed to a company where she probably earns more in a month than I take home in a year.

I am certainly not stupid enough to *insist* on blowing the whistle on her little white lie about the V-word when a fang fucker—okay, a temporarily photophobic math PhD with the strength of a rabid grizzly bear—is resting his hands on my shoulder as I countersign the necessary paperwork to certify that said fang fucker is One Of Our People. For whatever value of "people" you choose to use. (In any case, in the Laundry we tend to take a rather looser definition of the word than is the norm elsewhere.)

Here's the situation, as I understand it at this point:

Mhari may have a history of periodically going off the deep end and throwing boots at my head, but she was never an idiot. She worked for the Laundry full-time on the admin side for two or three years before her sideways shift into investment banking. She knows exactly how the Laundry goes about dealing with outbreaks. And she knows that our three priorities are the three Cs: Containment, Confidentiality, and Capabilities. We contain outbreaks, maintain confidentiality, and enhance our capabilities. The Scrum's new and fascinating breakthrough is certainly an enhanced capability so she knew that as long as she could maintain confidentiality and do something to contain it, she could wrap it all up in a bow (with the right forms, filled out in triplicate and signed in blood) and hand them over to HR. And as soon as she realized she could talk about us to Oscar—the confidentiality geas apparently doesn't work too well on people who've contracted her unfortunate condition—she briefed him, called up her contacts in HR, and set all the wheels in motion to position her team on the inside of the tent pissing out, rather than vice versa. At which point the outbreak of K syndrome that sucked me into searching out the Scrum stopped being an external threat to be addressed and *turned into a fucking inside job*. Which neatly explains why my warrant card didn't work on Alex: as a barely-across-the-threshold new employee he was nevertheless permitted to see it for what it was: the geas on our ID cards doesn't affect our own people.

And yes, in case you were wondering, this *is* my angry-and-disgusted face with egg dripping down it . . .

9.

COMMITTEE PROCESSES

THERE ARE CLUBS, AND THEN THERE ARE CLUBS.

Back in the eighteenth century (and even earlier) London didn't have cafés, restaurants, or hotels, as such: it had coffee shops, and drinking dens, and a plethora of coaching houses and inns—but these were not places where gentlemen of quality might dine together in polite company, or drink, or sleep. To address the needs of the nobs (principally: somewhere to socialize, eat, drink, and sleep without being bothered by the raucous lower orders), some of their lordships established discreet clubs. They purchased buildings, hired staff, and acquired the habit of using them as a home from home in the big city.

Today, the gentleman's club is undergoing something of a revival. Over the years many of its functions were usurped by hotels and restaurants—and unlike a particularly exclusive club, you can find chain hotels and restaurants in every large city. But the club is by no means extinct, and London still harbors dozens of them, at least one of which has been in existence since the late seventeenth century.

One notable tradition, upheld by many of the stuffier clubs, is that discussions of a business or professional nature are strictly forbidden. So an astute observer might be intrigued to see Sir David Finch, director of quantitative trading at a prominent London-headquartered merchant bank, sitting down for dinner at a table for two in the great eating room at White's on St. James's Street. Sir David is not actually a member of the club—although he's eminently clubbable—but is here as a guest of his host, a fellow known to those of the current membership who pay attention to him as "Old George."

It's not immediately obvious why he might carry that nickname; Old George certainly doesn't look ancient. Perhaps he's a well-preserved sixty, or a mature-looking forty. If you asked the club's membership secretary at the right stage in the executive's life cycle he might reminisce about Old George's striking resemblance to an even older Old George, who had relinquished his membership the year that the New Old George was proposed. But you'd have to go back beyond living memory to find out whether Old Old George was in fact the successor to an even Older Old Old George. And who would ever bother to do that? Suffice to say that the club has, for nearly two centuries, quietly harbored a member called Old George who appears to be somewhere between forty and sixty years of age and who may or may not be the same person.

Sir David and Old George dine in subdued, if slightly tense silence—business must be deferred until stomachs have been filled, but Sir David is nevertheless curious as to the reason for this summons. So they chat quietly (Old George has an eye for the horses, and Sir David, despite not being a turf man, is well-briefed) and steadily work through soup and mains and a bottle of claret. Until finally Old George pushes back his plate (Sir David has already finished, but Old George eats slowly, cutting his salmon steak and vegetables into small portions and chewing them with bovine deliberation) and, leaning against the back of his chair, stares at Sir David with eyes slightly sunken beneath beetled and slightly unkempt eyebrows. "I gather there have been some exciting developments in your branch, Sir David. Can you tell me about them, or is it still super-hush-hush?"

"Well I, ah, that is to say—" Sir David stares back, then glances around. "I think." Another glance. "Are we in trustworthy company?"

Old George smiles thinly. "Nobody around here ever pays me any

attention. The truth flies from your lips to my ears, and no further."
He idly picks up the dessert fork—as yet unused—and raps it on the
table. Not a single head turns. "You see."

"Um." Sir David dabs at his lips with his napkin. "In that case,
well. As you know, nine months ago I authorized the formation of
a research group, operated by Oscar Menendez on an arms-reach
basis—it's established as a limited company, owned by the bank but
notionally separate—to investigate possible applications of the new
area of mathematics research you were kind enough to recommend
to me for quantitative trading analysis. A couple of weeks ago Oscar
reported that his team have made some sort of breakthrough in group
theory. This higher mathematics might as well be magic to me, I'm
afraid. If you want to know more, I can procure a copy of the research material for you. But in any case, they've established a new
technique for running ahead of the market without using inside information or doing anything else that might violate current exchange
regulations. In view of his report, we discussed and then authorized
the establishment of a modest investment fund for his group to operate for six months on a pilot basis—"

Old George nods to himself affably enough as Sir David rattles
along. Sir David, for his part, is increasingly confident that this is the
object of George's enquiry and that George is content to absorb the
offering put before him. Old George is, after all, if not a board member then at the very least a major investor, perhaps best described as
a sleeping partner: he, or his friends and proxies, control enough eq-
uity in the bank to light a fire under the feet of the board at the AGM
if they are displeased with the management of their assets. Sir David
is not *directly* accountable to Old George, but nobody to whom he *is*
accountable will find fault with his disclosure to this very important
shareholder. So as Sir David winds down he smiles hopefully as he
looks to Old George for a sign of absolution. "It's an absolute cer-
tainty that this is going to net us a bump in the first quarter bottom
line next year. Which can't be bad, eh?"

Old George nods once more. "Sir David, I am sure that our investment stance is safe in your hands. But, just to be sure, if I may make

a suggestion? I would like you to invite Mr. Menendez and his managers to an off-site meeting, somewhere outdoors, between the hours of ten a.m. and three o'clock in the afternoon. And I would appreciate it if you or your staff would immediately inform me of their response."

"Really? I—" Sir David's gaze is arrested by the intensity of Old George's stare. He dry-swallows. "Yes, sir. Of course. Is there anything else?"

"Not for now, I think." Old George looks around, attracting the attention of a waiter. "Perhaps I could interest you in a dessert . . . ?"

I SLINK BACK TO THE NEW ANNEX AT ABOUT 10 P.M. WITH MY tail between my legs, to check my various bits of hardware back into Harry the Horse's toy chest and deliver an accounting of myself to the irate managers on overtime who are waiting in Briefing Room 201.

Except, they're not there. The bastards have all gone home, leaving me a terse email instructing me to show up tomorrow at nine sharp for the inevitable circular firing squad that is the After-Action Debrief/Lessons Learned meeting, wherein we will play pass-the-parcel with a blame bomb until it explodes, spraying shit in the lap of whoever can most plausibly be credited with causing the fuck-up. Which, in this case, almost certainly means me.

How the fuck was I supposed to know that Mhari of all people was already in the loop and wrapping up the highly suspicious outbreak of algorithmically induced dementia? *What is this I don't even*, as they say on the planet Reddit. I thought we—okay, her colleagues in HR—fired her sorry ass a decade ago . . . well, reassigned her to the inactive list, bound her to silence, and gave her a pointed shove down the greasy out-placement playground slide.

But there's no getting around it. The key facts are:

• While furtling around with my data mining project I identified a heinous hotspot of horrible brain-eating nastiness located right on our doorstep

- One of our medical liaison experts confirmed that it wasn't your regular strain of Krantzberg syndrome . . .
- . . . But it wasn't CJD, Kuru, New Variant CJD (aka Mad Cow Disease), or any other known prion disorder
- I inspected the latest victim, confirmed that it was something *related* to K syndrome, and dropped in on her place of work . . .
- . . . Whereupon a pencil-necked maths nerd (not unlike my younger self) proved to be immune to some of my basic tools—including my junior league Eater of Souls mojo—bushwhacked me with some help from his dental hypertrophy support group, and dragged me into what looks like an external black op being orchestrated by my Ex–GF From Hell who doesn't work here anymore (except apparently when she wants to)

I mean, what the fuck? What the *fucking* fuck?

I check out and go home in a buzzing haze of exhaustion and cognitive dissonance, not to mention fear and loathing. I'm too tired to safely use the back way—a branch line of the old nineteenth-century Necropolitan Line, long since turned into a bike trail, that gives pedometers a nervous breakdown and lets me cover the six kilometers to home (according to Google maps) in about two klicks, as long as I don't mind an occasional haunting. Instead, I splash out on a taxi and slump in the back, trying my hardest to ignore the world.

Tomorrow's going to be a bad day. I can tell.

WE NOW INTERRUPT YOUR SCHEDULED VIEWING TO BRING YOU *an important public safety announcement:*

This is Bob speaking, in his capacity as your humble narrator. It's really a bad sign when you begin talking about yourself in the second person, isn't it? But I'm afraid I need to break in at this point and disrupt the continuity of my narrative by explaining some uncomfortable truths that only really became clear to me a few weeks after the dust settled from the events described in the RHESUS POSITIVE EPSILON file, which is to say, this document.

Luckily we live in the age of the word processor, which makes it trivially easy for me to go back and insert additional material that I have determined is not classified above your level (if you're reading this without scorching your eyebrows off) and that you will need to be aware of in order to make sense of this utter clusterfuck. And you really *do* need to understand what went wrong in RHESUS POSITIVE EPSILON, if only to ensure that it doesn't happen to *you*.

So wake up and pay attention now:

THE FIRST LAW OF VAMPIRISM IS THAT EVERYBODY KNOWS vampires don't exist.

It therefore follows that anyone who realizes that vampires exist is either a vampire, or dead. (Or is a member of staff with RHESUS POSITIVE EPSILON clearance, but that's another matter.)

Let me rewind:

Forget *Dracula*. Forget Anita Blake and Sookie Stackhouse and Varney the Vampire and Lestat and, oh, everything you think you know about vampires.

(Except for *Desmodus rotundus* and *Vampyroteuthis infernalis* and Goldman Sachs—they're all real.)

Almost everything in the pop culture lexicon of vampirism is basically fiction—and fiction is the art of telling entertaining lies for money. Whereas what we're discussing here is something else. Here in the real world of applied computational demonology and undead alien squid-gods without investment portfolios, we're totally down with walking corpses. (If you don't believe me, go argue the case with the Night Shift.) But vampires in the fictional mode—intelligent super-strong blood-sucking *walking corpses* who hang out in goth nightclubs and look incredibly sexy—don't exist.

Am I shattering your illusions yet?

Having said that much, what we do in the Laundry centers on the practice of setting up a sympathetic link between complex computational systems in this universe and another elsewhere in the multiverse, mediated via the platonic realm of pure mathematics. We invite useful entities to poke their pseudopodia through a hole in reality, then we grab them and set them to work.

Now, vampires:

They start out as ritual magicians, thinking furious blue soundscapes in their minds until they invoke *something*. Which sticks around and, shall we say, gives them certain powers. It's a symbiote, in other words, not a regular parasite. As long as they feed it, it stays happy and gives them a laundry list of handy tools. Super-strength: check. Good night-vision: check. Longevity: check. You-gotta-believe-me charisma: check. Good skin tone: check. A tendency to burst into flames if exposed to intense ultraviolet light . . . well, there are always drawbacks. But the important takeaway point is that they're *not* walking corpses. They're real live human beings, albeit immune to soul-eating (whether by me or by the feeders in the night), just like the people whose blood they get off on drinking . . .

. . . Although the hosts don't stay human for long, once the V syndrome symbiotes use the sympathetic link the blood meal provides to latch onto their gray matter and chew holes in it.

You can't catch vampirism from a vampire's bite: all you can catch from it is a horrible lingering death. It can sometimes take up to six months for a host to die of V syndrome. But if too many symbiotes snack from the same juice bar, the deterioration takes off like a forest fire. That's why the Scrum triggered the Tower Hamlets spike. If it was just *one* vampire, feeding on *one* victim, we might never have noticed. We might have mistaken it for part of the constant background rate of Creutzfeldt-Jakob disease.

Vampirism is, thankfully, extremely rare. Traditionally it took a ritual magician of some power, performing a major invocation that pushed back the frontier of the art, to attract the attention of the V syndrome symbiotes. And he or she would usually last until the first sunrise—either by accident or design. Most non-psychopathic practitioners who realize what they've become recognize the side effects and their likely fate immediately. They commit suicide rather than inflicting the cost of their survival on others, or pay the hideous price of abstinence.

Which is why most long-term surviving vampires are psychopaths. What are the traits of a *successful* vampire, a long-term survivor?

Well, they have to be a conscienceless killer, willing to accept the slow, cruel destruction of others' lives to fuel their own continual existence.* They'd have to be wealthy in order to finance the regular changes of identity necessary to conceal their longevity, and to buy the immunity from scrutiny that the eccentricity of their lifestyle demands. They'd have to be very intelligent and ruthlessly dedicated to keeping their existence a secret, because they are by definition a serial killer: one who can go no more than six months between victims. And they're a ritual magician of considerable power who is now immune to K syndrome parasites, the main brake on the ambitions of such practitioners.

(Speaking of victims, you can forget the night clubs and glamour. Real vampires prey on the lonely, the elderly, and the unloved. You might find poor ones working the night shift at a hospice, or befriending widows at a bingo hall. Rich ones are more likely to cruise homeless runaways, offering them a meal and cash in return for a night's sexual exploitation, only for the victim to wake up in a small bedroom with double glazing and a door that locks on the outside, fed by staff who never speak. Real vampires seek the ones who nobody will ever miss.)

Because of the vile secret of their long existence, if a vampire becomes aware of the existence of another vampire, their first response is to kill it with fire. (Consider: if *they* learned its nature, then *other people* might do so. And if the common people ever realize that vampires exist, it will be a very short time indeed before naked noonday identity parades are required by law.) Only if they fail to assassinate their rival and defuse the deadly existential threat of exposure will they even consider communicating with it as an equal—and even

---

* The noises you can hear in the distance are all my vegan friends giggling with shocked schadenfreude.

then, the only subject important enough to require joint action is the elimination of threats to their collective security.

Which is why everybody knows vampires don't exist.

Except for us. (And the Scrum, who didn't get the memo.)

So congratulations; you're now a target!

I MANAGE TO GET A VERY UNSOUND EIGHT HOURS OF SLEEP, punctuated by various anxiety dreams. You want anxiety dreams? I've got them all: if I could bottle 'em and sell 'em I could out-gross George Romero. There's the regular strain—at the office with no clothes, having to get home across rush-hour London in the buff— and the more recondite variety where I'm being stalked by zombie clowns because I misfiled an expense report. And then there's the extra special sauce variety.

In this recurring dream it's night, I'm at home in my own bedroom (yes, I'm in bed, dreaming I'm in bed, dreaming . . .) and Mo's awake next to me. And there's a crib. No, we don't have kids: given what's going to happen as the stars come into their unfortunately-too-damned-accurately-foretold alignment, it just seemed like a really bad idea. But in this dream, there's a bone-white cot in our bedroom, with bars around it and some kind of net curtain arrangement dangling around it. Talk about symbolism, right?

There's no baby in the nonexistent crib, but if there was it would be crying. And because the not-a-baby in the not-a-cot isn't crying, Mo is playing it a lullaby on her bone-white fiddle. All this is terribly *wrong*. At least I can't hear the music, which is a minor mercy. Probably my unconscious imagination doesn't have the cognitive horse-power to generate such a horror. Because Mo doesn't own her violin; she holds it in trust for the organization, and practices with it, and then operates it. It's bone-white because it's made from polished bones—human bones extracted from more than a dozen living donors without anesthesia in the predecessors of the medical laboratories at Birkenau and Belsen. It's an Erich Zahn original, with Hilbert-space pickups, and it plays the music of the hyperspheres until the audience bleed from ears, and eyes, and other orifices. I've seen it steal souls and lay the walking dead to rest. I've seen it whip up a storm and blast lightning across the floor of a megalomaniac's floating fortress. It is not a suitable instrument for lullabies and nursery rhymes and so it is a very good thing that we didn't have a child and the crib is empty . . .

Isn't it?

The point where I usually slam into shuddering wakefulness with my pulse hammering and the sheet clinging to the small of my back is the bit where I dream that I sit up and look towards the crib, with a choking sense of dread at what I'm going to see when I look through the hanging veil that shrouds the bars. But this time the dream is a doozie: it lets me sit up and look and *yes*, there in the crib *is* a baby, and look at its little metatarsals and vertebrae and the jawbone gaping in an eternal silent howl. And then I get to look round and see Mo playing the violin, but her face is skeletonized, eye sockets empty and glowing faintly in the light cast by the slowly turning wormlike feeders that possess her, and the violin—

I actually get to see the violin this time, in this particular dream. And that's when I wake up screaming to find that it's five in the morning and Mo is still away on whatever job they've sent her on this time, so I don't even have a shoulder to cling to. *Bad* dream: brrr! You want to know how bad it is? It's exactly bad enough that rather than trying to go back to sleep, I go downstairs to make coffee and try to work out what the hell I'm going to tell the committee in a few hours' time.

I GO INTO THE OFFICE AND HEAD FOR THE BRIEFING ROOM AT 9 a.m., clutching a mug of coffee as if it's the handle of an umbrella that can protect me from the incoming storm-front of blame. If you start out by expecting them to fire you, or at least ream you out for someone else's fuck-up, it's hard to see how the day can get any worse. Isn't it?

Bad mistake, Bob.

The five stages of bureaucratic grieving are: denial, anger, committee meetings, scapegoating, and cover-up. And we are now entering stage three.

The first meeting actually goes a lot better than I have any right to expect. First I give my version of events, while Jez scrawls it on the board at the front of the room, compiling a timeline. Lockhart is chairing. "You can sit down now, Bob," he says. Then he looks at Andy. "You got the file I asked for?"

"Yes, of course." Andy appears to have had no more sleep than me. He hauls up an ancient leather attaché file with a padlock and the EIIR crest branded into it: one of the secure wallets we use for shuffling paper files back and forth from the stacks. (The padlock is the least of the security measures attached to it: open it without permission—or try remote viewing the contents—and you'll be lucky if you don't spend the rest of your days drooling in a wheelchair.) "I see the privacy light is lit?"

"Witnessed," Jez echoes.

"Okay, by the authority vested in me I hereby declare this to be the designated committee with need-to-know clearance for BLUE DANDELION forty-six slash alpha, Bob's most recent Code Blue. And everyone here by definition has confidential keyword OPERA CAPE, which covers the nature of the, um, people Bob discovered. Everyone agree?"

Lockhart gives his assent, then sends me a quelling look. "Mr. Howard, if you'd be so good as to wait in the quiet corner?" he asks. It's an order disguised as a request. I stand up and shuffle over to the corner and stand facing the wall. All the sounds from behind me are abruptly muffled, as if a great distance away. Most of our meeting rooms are fitted with these cones of silence, for just this sort of situation: I may be part of this committee but I'm not, apparently, trusted to see the contents of Mhari's HR transcript. Which just goes to show that not everyone here is irredeemably stupid (or, alternatively, willing to let me compromise myself).

Standing in the corner like a naughty toddler gets old fast, but just as I'm contemplating tapping my toes and whistling something annoying to speed things along I faintly hear Lockhart call out: "Mr. Howard! You can come out now!"

I turn round and approach the table. The attaché case is zipped up and padlocked again, bulging like a snake that has just swallowed a rabbit. "What am I allowed to know?" I ask.

Jez gives Andy a significant look, then turns to face me. She's standing by the board again. "You're off the hook, Bob. Ms. Murphy was still on the permanent-inactive list for an hour *after* you called Code Blue. She didn't call in and ask to be reactivated until lunchtime yesterday. Off the record, I gather she might have tried to talk an old friend into backdating her activation a month or so—but HR aren't idiots. You very nearly caught her out."

"Whoa." I slump into my chair. "So you're saying whatever she was doing with that team of quants was *not* a deniable operation? She was actively up to something on the outside, and got a chill and decided to cover her ass at the last moment? That it's just pure bloody coincidence that I didn't catch her red-handed?"

Jez nods, very seriously. "It looks like they were waiting for you— or someone. We're going to find it hard to prove and harder to pin any culpability on her in view of her bringing it home before you caught up with them, but at the least it's going to go down as a big fat question mark on her record. The initial analysis suggests that whatever they stumbled on happened more than four weeks ago, and she should have reported it right away if she wanted to keep her nose clean."

Lockhart looks as if he's swallowed the proverbial early-morning frog; Andy isn't much happier either. As for me, I might be off the hook but I'm not doing the happy dance. Mhari has somehow reactivated herself and is fully aware that I'm on her case, which means she's either going to try and stab me or fuck me: possibly both, in no particular order. (And yes, the ambiguous use of the verb "to fuck" in the preceding sentence is intentional.)

"Maybe she fell into something and was too busy swimming to think about the big picture?" Andy proposes charitably. Uncharitably,

I decide that this is Andy's week for being charitable to fuck-ups (but I keep this opinion to myself).

It's a suggestion that has some merit, but Jez is shaking her head. "No, you saw the file. She's got form for contingency exercises. Even if her schemes didn't often pan out, she was capable of forward planning. I know Gilbert, and he wouldn't have written what he did on her annual review in '02 if she was just another mendacious bubblehead. Unstable and destructive, but also fast-thinking and potentially a high-flyer." (Lockhart rolls an eye at me: What's *that* supposed to mean?) "I think she worked out what she'd fallen into right at the outset. And she moved her plans forward just as we sent someone to round her up? That's not a coincidence. I think we were deliberately spoofed."

I'm shaking my head. "She's not smart enough to plan something like that," I explain. "I mean, she was mercurial and able to go from kiss to kill in about five seconds flat, but long-term planning wasn't her strong point."

However, Lockhart and Jez and Andy are nodding their heads at me like a row of bobbleheads, and I get an inkling that maybe I'm not privy to something.

"Bob, Bob." It's Andy. "You were close to her for a while, but you only had one angle on her. We've got full access to her file and she's more complex than that. Her private life and her actual work performance—at least, as of a decade ago—look like they belong to two different people. She's very good at performative compartmentalization. It's a major asset in an officer and she *should* have gone far within the organization, but, well. We—and by we, I mean we, the Laundry—clearly failed to get the best out of her, and in the end, *she* fired *us*. Gave us no sensible options other than to let her leave on more or less her own terms. And now she's reactivated herself—again, on her own terms. Do you really think she'd have ended up as a project manager in an elite rocket science team inside one of our biggest investment banks if she was an attention-deficit basket case?"

"But I—" I flap my jaw helplessly. "You're saying that as her boyfriend I only got to see the poor impulse control stuff she kept out of her work life?" I ask. Andy nods encouragingly. "And that she was venting at me because it provided an outlet for stuff she was keeping a lid on in the office?" This time it's Jez who nods. I can't tell whether her expression is sympathetic or patronizing. *Nerd with social deficit disorder: give him time to work it out for himself,* or some such. "She was just using me as a scratching post and chew-toy? Well, shit!"

"It's quite common," Lockhart says, his expression uncharacteristically distant and thoughtful. "It's why going native or falling in love with a source is such a big no-no on a HUMINT op. It blinds you to other aspects of their personality. You don't get to see their feet of clay when your head's in the clouds." I blink and do a double take: he sounds as if he's speaking from experience.

"Well, I'll grant you I had an unusual perspective on her. But what are we going to do now?" I ask.

Jez turns back to the whiteboard and sketches something that, after a moment, I recognize as a box. Then she writes a name on it: **MHARI**. "We put her in a box," she explains. An arrow points at the box: **INPUTS**. Another arrow leads out of the box: **OUTPUTS**. "Assuming she's trying to run something on us, we feed her a barium meal and see what leaks, yes? And for now we let her think her insertion phase succeeded."

"Hey, wait a—" I'm ahead of her, but only just.

"Bob, you're the sacrificial goat. We know she's got a low opinion of you, and has very little idea of what you're capable of. So we're going to work to reinforce that. The official minutes of this meeting will not record us discussing Mhari's timing. Nor will they mention your epidemiological research, the reason for the Code Blue, or your preparations. Instead they'll focus on us dumping on you for calling in a spurious Code Blue and wasting resources—" She stops and looks at Lockhart. "Yes?"

Lockhart shakes his head. "Nothing relevant. Forget I was here. Redact my name from the minutes."

We all turn to stare at him. "The Senior Auditor will sign off on everything if I advise him to," he says, and the temperature in the briefing room drops five degrees.

"Are you *sure*?" Jez asks tentatively. (Mentioning our overseers is about as welcome as mentioning Old Nick at a funeral.)

"Let's just say that I believe it would be unwise to attach my name to a document that Ms. Murphy might subsequently stumble across if she goes looking for it. She does not need to be aware that External Assets has an interest in this situation." He glowers at me. "She does not need to be aware that Bob is involved in External Assets, either."

"Well gee, thanks for the vote of confidence!"

"See me later, Bob," he grunts, then turns back to look at Jez. I notice that Andy is watching our exchange with the still, silent fascination of a fly on the wall that is canny enough to be aware of the existence of swatters.

"If you don't mind." There's a waspish edge to Jez's voice as she picks up her train of thought again: "Bob, we're going to whitewash this meeting's minutes, and unjustifiably blacken your name until such time as we have established exactly what Ms. Murphy and her worryingly powered-up quants are up to. At which time this committee will reconvene and correct the record. Meanwhile, we're going to conduct ourselves as if we have swallowed her bait. And then we're going to engineer a situation where she can't avoid interacting with you. Are you clear on why we're doing this? Can you cope?"

"What are you asking? Can I keep my lid on when dealing with my psycho ex from hell?"

"Essentially, yes." This from Andy, who has the decency to look slightly embarrassed in his characteristic hangdog way.

I shrug. "I've been married to someone else for years. I'm a grownup: I can cope."

"Good." Jez glances at Andy, then back to me. "Then the rest is up to you."

IT'S EASIER TO TAKE TIME OFF IN LIEU THAN TO FILL OUT THE overtime claim for a failed Code Blue. I go home early that afternoon, to lick my wounds and catch up on some non-classified reading. I'm expecting to spend another quiet night in with the computer, playing a cheesy MMO based in a Planescape spin-off, with maybe half a bottle of wine and a takeaway pizza for company. But at about six o'clock, just after dark, I hear the front door opening.

I'm not one to worry—our front door was reinforced a couple of years ago after I was doorstepped by a zombie from the KGB's occult successor organization, although it's sometimes amusing to let the Jehovah's Witlesses get far enough inside to see the security grid embedded in the porch floor—but I heave myself out of the buttock-eating living room sofa to go and check who's there, just in case. I needn't have bothered.

"Mo?" I ask, as she lets the door swing closed. She's wearing a long black dress and jacket with some kind of shawl over her shoulders, suitcase on the floor behind her and violin case in hand. She looks like she's been somewhere in the Middle East, and she's clearly exhausted.

"Bob, be a love and put the kettle on? Been a long day."

"Okay." I pad into the kitchen—I'm wearing bedroom slippers—and fill up the kettle again. She'll be wanting tea, at a guess. "Where've you been? Can you talk?"

"I—yes, I can talk." She doesn't sound happy, though. "Later. Some other time. For now I just need tea, then a shower and change and some company to keep me awake until bedtime. It's been a very long day."

"How long?" I ask, trying to keep her going.

"I was on a flight from Tehran to Istanbul at, let's see, five o'clock this morning? Which would be one-thirty over here. I've been up since before midnight, in other words." She comes in, pulls out a chair from the kitchen table, and drops into it like a sack of spuds. Her cheeks are jowly and loose with fatigue, her eyelids bruised by dehydration. "I hate this job."

I'm still processing. "You were in Tehran?" Adding a hearty *what the fuck?* is unnecessary: that's a bit far out of our usual stomping grounds to say the least.

She nods, begins to droop, then raises the violin case and plants it on the kitchen table right between the bowl with the browning fair trade bananas and the heatproof mat I was going to put the teapot on. "Usual guarantees apply."

Despite all the shouting about nuclear reprocessing, and the saber-rattling about aircraft carriers and the Strait of Hormuz, it turns out that almost *everyone* is on the same side with respect to the Axis of Ancient, Undying, and Truly Inhuman Evil. So from time to time the Laundry gets strangely phrased requests for assistance from a rather obscure corner of VEVAK, the Iranian Ministry of Intelligence and National Security. (They almost always ask too late, especially in view of the number of permits and authorizations required before we can agree to send someone, because they seem to think we're fiendish hyper-competent Svengalis of the Supernatural. They have always had an unrealistically high opinion of the British secret intelligence services. It's nice to be wanted, even if they'd die of shame rather than admit it in public.)

"So the thing on Monday, that was Iran?"

"Yes." She nods. The kettle comes to a rolling boil and switches itself off; I busy myself filling a pot with loose-leaf Darjeeling. "I need tea. And a bath. Then dinner. Then someone to keep me from falling asleep."

"Is the jet lag particularly bad?"

"No, but I'm going to have bad dreams." She shudders slightly and pulls her shawl tight around her shoulders. It's silk, and looks as if it's probably very fashionable, not to say expensive. She notices my gaze. "Isn't it nice? I bought it at the airport duty-free, on the way out. The VEVAK people I was working with kept trying to impress me with how Anglophile and welcoming they were, but going without a head covering there is like wandering around London topless, so I thought I should buy something I can use as a scarf when winter starts to bite." She lets it fall from her shoulders and shakes it out, then begins to carefully fold it. Her hands are shaking slightly, and I can see the veins and tendons through the pale, almost translucent skin behind her knuckles. They're more visible than when we first met: a side effect of growing older together.

"It's very nice," I say carefully. "What did VEVAK want?"

"They had a problem. I fixed it. Did anything interesting happen while I was away?" I noticed a faint tremor in her voice when she said *fixed*.

"Oh, I called in a Code Blue, but what I'd found turned out to be an internal op. Supposedly, anyway. It nearly turned into fratricide but we stopped in time." I grimace and try not to rub my right arm too obviously.

Mo sits up, looking almost interested. "Really?" She asks: "Can you tell me about it?"

A quick check with my internal censor reveals that I can, indeed, tell Mo everything about my ten-percenter project. Although I suddenly begin to wonder if it was wise to mention this at all, bearing in mind the Mhari angle. On the other hand, Mhari and I split up almost before I ever met Mo in the first place, and on the third hand, being caught later trying to conceal Mhari's sudden reappearance would be vastly more incriminating than coughing to the true situation right now. I make a snap decision that sometimes honesty really *is* the best policy—even between spies—but paranoia about the ex from hell can wait until Mo's a bit less stressed out.

So I stand up to pour the tea, and begin to explain what I've been up to for the past few weeks, with a focus on Andy's fucked-up summoning and subsequent search for a new office, and Pete's MAGIC CIRCLE OF SAFETY project. Who knows? Maybe it'll help her stay awake until she's over the jet lag. And maybe hearing about someone else's woes will distract her from whatever the bad thing is that happened in Iran that she's trying to avoid telling me about.

10.

DEATH CHAMBERS

THERE ARE SOME TRADITIONAL PROPRIETIES THAT MUST AL-
ways be upheld, except in the direst of emergencies. The current situation does not—yet—amount to such an emergency. And so it is that
when George decides to inform another of his ilk of Sir David's worrying news, he does so by invoking a protocol steeped in antiquity.

Not that Sir David himself realized that his news would be cause
for concern: he saw nothing wrong with directing a tenth of a billion
pounds into an untried research project, and indeed, that sum is only
a small fraction of the bank's asset reserve. But George's nostrils flare
and his lips involuntarily crease into something like a sneer at the
unwelcome memory dredged up by the miasma of meddling that Sir
David trailed into his club. Sir David has been touched by a will not
his own, and George cannot abide the stink of soiled goods, much less
the threat that it brings.

It's time for a parlay with a rival. On neutral ground and in the
absence of minions—of course—for this marks a diminuendo in the
century-long symphony of killing dictated by the law of vampires.

Exactly an hour after midnight, a cast-iron gate creaks open and
a man steps through it, onto the gravel path beyond. Old George is

shrouded against the chill of the night, his overcoat buttoned and hat brim drawn low to partly conceal his face. His driver and regular bodyguard close and lock the gate behind him, then wait in the car. His possession of the keys to this venerable institution does not surprise them, for they are far beyond such a mental state after so long in his service. They will await his return patiently, and they will bite off their tongues and drown in their own blood before they speak of this to any man or woman now alive.

Beyond the gate it is as dark as a London night ever gets in this electrified age. A ruddy sky-spattered glare deepens the shadows cast by woodland vegetation. The trees and bushes still sport autumnal leaves, but they rustle as drily as any crypt-bound bones. His heels crunch quietly on the path as he walks between lichen-stained monuments, corroded by decades of acidic soot before coal fires were banished from the capital. He remembers the choking, acrid fog as it once saturated the graveyard air around him, providing concealment and dampening sounds. It was a comfort, of sorts, rendering these approaches slightly less fraught. Now there's no night and mist to hide in if his contact has come adrift, hissing and snarling at the corrosive winds of time and determined to drag George down with him when he goes. He has only the trees and the overgrown tombs and mausoleums to hide amidst. Well, those and his own defensive preparations.

Even without consciously commanding the movement, his hand steals to his left pocket and pats it, outlining the slim black box within. It's a dead man's handle: if he does not press the button whenever the box vibrates, certain messages will be sent to trusted subordinates. The adversary will expect nothing less of him, and can be expected to conduct his affairs accordingly. He, too, probably carries a dead man's handle. It's just another step in the intricate and lethal waltz they've been dancing for decades.

George stalks the familiar, tree-shrouded avenues and paths of Highgate Cemetery, past so many people he vaguely knew (and in many cases despised) in life. He belongs here, and indeed his will once specified that this should be his final resting place, but they have long since closed his preferred section to new burials.

Coming to the impressive column-flanked entrance to Egyptian Avenue (its mouth pitch-dark to regular human eyes, although George's night vision is preternaturally good, as sensitive as any cat's), he pauses and waits for a few seconds, closing his eyes and clearing his mind. One of his kind has been this way, and recently. They took no pains to conceal themselves, which is a good sign. He opens his eyes again and straightens his back as he steps forward into the pool of night between the tree-shadowed lintel.

The older parts of Highgate Cemetery are preserved as woodland these days, overgrown with ivy-clad sycamore and ash trees, limestone and marble walls of gape-mouthed crypts gently aging into the landscape. Old George paces along a gravel-strewn path past a wall set in a gentle hillside, pierced by classical columns and open doorways. His nostrils flare once more as he nears his destination: a wealthy Victorian family's final resting place. Not all of their niches are occupied. Indeed, one remains empty for it is the one that had his name—an earlier name—earmarked for it. But it's not empty now. He pauses outside the entrance and speaks aloud, the words galling: "May we speak in peace?"

"Yes, subject to the usual caveats."

The other is male, and speaks with an old London accent tainted with mannerisms that strike George as modern affections—even though they predate the deplorable Americanisms that crept into everyday usage after the Second World War. George relaxes his facial musculature to an almost sheepish droop, carefully suppressing any expressive signatures.

"Very well. I shall speak from out here," he says carefully. "I will caution that I did not request this rendezvous without reason. If you try to kill me you will remain ignorant of a threat to your life. And mine, which is why I seek to make common cause."

The tomb's occupant is silent for almost a minute. Then: "You mentioned a threat. Please describe it. Then we can discuss the possibility of cooperation."

* * *

"LISTEN UP, PEEPS," SAYS MHARI. "THIS IS CRITICALLY IMPOR-
tant. There *will* be an exam, and if you fail, the consequences could
be, shall we say, worse than career-limiting."

A lot can happen in a couple of days. In this case, there has been
a drastic realignment of status among the Scrum. All the status mark-
ers are scrambled, for one thing, because a Casual Friday dress code
applies—today being Saturday, and the office theoretically being
closed. Mhari sits at the head of the table, in leggings and a little black
dress accessorized out of the spectrum of regular office-wear; Oscar
is off to one corner, kicked back in chinos and a polo shirt bearing the
bank's logo, one loafer crossed over an immaculately creased leg. The
others are variously attired in jeans and button-down shirts except
for Dick, who has accessorized his usual Oxfam-surplus tweed suit
with an ancient Cradle of Filth tee shirt, lovingly tie-dyed using his
own vomit. (This is Dick's unique interpretation of Office Casual.)

"You're doubtless wondering what the hell is going on and what
this bunch of government crap is about and what it's got to do with
you. So let me explain.

"Our power, talent, what-have-you does not exist in a vacuum.
The government got there first, back during the war. Apparently Alan
Turing had something to do with it. Anyway: there's a field of applied
mathematics that lets you contact extradimensional beings, and a
whole side-field called applied computational demonology—stop
picking your nose and pay attention, Dick, you *animal*—and during
the war a division of SOE, that's the Special Operations Executive,
was set up to perform Occult Operations. Turns out we live in a multiverse and there are things with too many tentacles—yes, Evan, I'm
talking about Cthulhu here. Yes, yes, I know. The Laundry (they were
originally headquartered above a Chinese laundry in the West End) is
the branch of the secret service for protecting the UK from the scum
of the multiverse. *And that means us.* Do you understand?"

Mhari glances around the motley gaggle of mathematicians, system administrators, and bankers. Out of pin-stripe uniform they could
be a bunch of Saturday-afternoon role players or canal-boating en-
thusiasts. Superficial appearances are misleading precisely because, so

much of the time, they're accurate. And it is a very good thing indeed that the Scrum's appearance is at odds with its nature.

"We can't go out in daylight, we're super-strong, we have a taste for blood, and we can make people do what we want. Oh, and we got there by way of Dick and Evan's sterling work in visualization and Alex's five-dimensional group isomorphism, which is, shall we say, Laundry territory. We are the sort of things they have nightmares about. And because it's their job to spot things like us, it was pretty much inevitable that sooner or later we would come to their attention. If we come to their attention in a bad way, that would be very bad—they play for keeps and they have kissing cousins in the military, never mind the police. The least-bad outcome would involve padded cells and a lot of intrusive medical tests. The worst . . . you don't want to know about the worst. Just think how every vampire movie you've ever seen ends, then imagine that instead of a handful of half-assed vampire-hunting heroes you're up against a Cold War–era government agency.

"However, there's an escape clause. If you're on the inside, pissing out, they will find a pigeonhole to put you in. Practitioners end up in very odd places all the time, and the Laundry has a habit of recruiting anyone with any remotely non-deniable exposure to the real no-shit occult. Fifteen years ago that was me; I spent a couple of years in there before convincing them to put me on permanent unpaid sabbatical with an employment placement thrown in. Which is why I had the contacts in place with Human Resources to get you all listed as new personnel acquisitions earlier this week, before our visitor dropped in for a chat."

She pauses to take a drink from the water glass on the table. This not being a meeting organized by their employer, the glass contains a liquid other than water: a Bloody Mary would be gauche but a G&T goes down fine.

"Unavoidable side effects: you will all have to accept that for the foreseeable future you are going to be inducted into an annoyingly sluggish and overstaffed part of the civil service, and they will expect to have first call on your time. You are going to have to sign a schedule to the Official Secrets Act that most people don't even know exists, and fill out a lot of paperwork. You will then spend *at least* a month on evaluation and training on their premises—indoctrination is more like it—while they assess your personality and aptitudes and make you jump through hoops, then give you a whistle-stop tour of the organization's divisional structure and a couple of training-wheels assignments. Luckily we are all classified as key workers because the bank is a strategic national asset, so they don't get to keep us forever; it's a bit like a Territorial Army enlistment. They can grab us for a month every year, but they have to square it with HR, and management won't be allowed to ask any irritating questions or fire us for being out of the office. If you do *precisely* what I tell you to do, say the right things, and refrain from scaring the crap out of them by showing what you're capable of, Oscar and I will do our best to get this organization recognized within the Laundry as a semi-autonomous research cell, part of a strategic national asset, hands-off, etcetera. Do you understand?"

Janice has been getting visibly spikier throughout the entire briefing, and now she sounds off. "You're talking Men in Black, the Van Helsing remix, aren't you? And you think you can make them take us in? Are you out of your fucking tree?"

"Now wait a—" Oscar starts up, but Mhari overrides him.

"I spent three years in human resources in the Laundry," Mhari says evenly. "*Yes*, secret government agencies have HR departments and Facilities and office management issues. It's not James Bond territory over there. *Yes*, there are autonomous research cells. I've handled payroll for them. *Yes*, there is a mandatory one-month induction course. *Yes*, you will be subjected to a Myers-Briggs test, an interview under polygraph—except it's not a skin galvanometer, they've got a tame sub-sentient class two emanation, a demon to you, that feeds on mendacity: if you knowingly tell a lie it *will* snitch on you—not to mention undergoing a graphologist's report, a medical, and a bunch of spurious make-work. You'll be given a mentor, another recent inductee, who will show you around the offices. But as long as you manage not to shit the bed by ripping your line manager's throat out and drinking their blood, you will very likely pass muster. And if you manage to look bumblingly useless, they'll get bored and let you go after a while. Are we clear?"

Evan raises his hand. "Why?" he asks, succinctly.

"What are the benefits?" Mhari glances at Oscar, who nods minutely. She begins counting off points on her fingers. "Firstly, they can't do the whole monster-hunting thing on our ass and kill us, because we're inside the magic circle. Or did you miss our visitor the other night?" (Her expression of disdain looks theatrically exaggerated to those of her audience who are unaware of her former relationship with Mr. Howard, aka your humble narrator.) "Secondly, we gain access to their resources and knowledge base. Thirdly, we are in a position, *once we all know what we're doing*, to leverage their connections to our collective advantage. Fourthly, Oscar is working on a Plan." She smiles tightly. "Oscar?"

Oscar nods and scoots his chair forward as Mhari pulls back. "I'm not going to tell you the details just yet," he says. "Hell, I haven't made my mind up yet—there's the polygraph test and loyalty oath stuff coming up: what you haven't decided to do yet you can deny planning. In any case, it's somewhat speculative at this point. But Mhari and I have been examining our options and we have identified a possible exit strategy from this scenario. If we can—if we *decide* to—develop it, we will generate a narrative and execute in due course. Those who decline to opt in will merely get left behind with a sinecure in the civil service or the bank, whichever you choose. I want to stress that we have not yet confirmed this is going to happen and if it does you don't have to join us. I believe if you *do* join us there will be sacrifices to be made. Plastic surgery, false identities, exile from the UK for the foreseeable future. But on the other hand, we won't execute unless the payoff is in excess of ten billion. And a billion-plus pounds for each of us should make up for a lot of inconvenience, shouldn't it?

"Anyway. Whether you want to join in the bust-out or not, we're all going to need to go through this Laundry organization's induction process in the next few weeks, and do so without incriminating ourselves. I've asked Mhari to develop a story list around the theme of setting up a successful presentation of the Scrum to the Laundry as an autonomous unit, and we're going to work through it and use the rest of this session to take our sprint assignments. During induction we'll meet each evening after work, to discuss progress and conduct back-log grooming. The Laundry has no need to be aware of this; I don't think it's a hanging offense, but it would certainly alarm any compe-tent counter-intelligence officer if they knew we were approaching our in-sourcing with systematic coordination. So: I'm calling a fifteen-minute break for refreshments, and then we begin. Item one: how to pull the wool over an intelligence agency's eyes . . ."

WORDS ARE EXCHANGED ACROSS THE THRESHOLD OF A CRYPT.

"A quantitative research group operating within one of the major investment banks appears to have transcended their humanity. Unfor-tunately, the outbreak was not confined to an individual. Worse, these people, who include a number of gifted mathematicians, are not prac-titioners of the art. They had no context within which to understand their new state, other than that provided by the mass media."

"Oh dear."

"I believe they may have drawn unwanted attention to themselves already."

"Unconscionable."

"I agree completely. It is interesting to speculate as to what might have prompted them to pursue such an unfortunate line of research."

". . . Yes, yes it is. What sort of scrutiny do you think they've attracted?"

"The heirs of the Invisible College have taken a direct interest. There was a visit. As our very own insider, that would make them very emphatically your problem."

There is a muffled thud from within the crypt, as of a fist striking a stone-hard palm in frustration. "Intolerable!"

"I quite agree."

"What is to be done? In your opinion."

"I am too closely associated with the source of this information to act without risk of coming to the attention of the investigators. The new data mining techniques . . ."

"Yes, I understand."

"Also, your connections . . ."

"That, too. What do you have for me?"

Old George unfastens the top two buttons of his overcoat. "One of my people in the bank provided my servant with the necessary passwords to connect his PC to the bank's network. I confess I don't fully understand such things, but it proved sufficient. I brought a summary of their personnel files for your edification." He withdraws a cardboard folder from his coat, then kneels and carefully places it before the tomb, then stands and buttons his coat up.

"How am I to know that this is not some trap?" the tomb's occupant asks, a trifle querulously.

"Don't be silly!" Old George finally snaps. "How long have we known each other?"

"Sixty-eight years too long, if you ask me." There is a pause in the conversation. "Never mind. If they're truly ascended but ignorant they will be easy prey. If they're not ignorant—well, we shall deal with that contingency if it arises. But mark my words, George, I *resent* this. Why can't you send your bloody-handed catspaw to take care of them?"

"Because she's about as subtle as a battalion of Cossacks and, as I intimated, they have already come to the attention of the people you hide among."

"Bah. So you decided to dump your problem in my lap."

"It's *our* problem, old enemy. We have the same stake in its speedy resolution."

"Be that as it may . . . there'll be a price. You're asking me to risk my own skin."

"D'you think I don't know that? Think of a price. Then name it. This lack of trust is unbecoming!"

There is silence, for a while. Then: "Your lady executioner. Lend her to me."

Old George tenses. "I think you misapprehend the degree of control I exert over her."

"Really? You created her, didn't you?" The other's tone is light, almost mocking.

"Yes, but she's not mine to command," George admits.

"What? She's not a minion? Did you turn—"

"Certainly not! But her utility depends upon her retaining the illusion of free will. And upon certain other delicate conditioning. She's like a very sharp Japanese sword with no guard—if your fingers slip—"

"Yes-yes, you'll cut yourself, I understand. Ahem. Why, may I ask, did you create such an uncontrollable and dangerous tool?"

"Because, like you, I am a creature out of time and a fish out of water. This is not our century. We live among strangers who have replaced the people we knew in our youth. For my first century, buried in my research, I barely noticed the changes—but after the Great War it became clear that I could no longer move unnoticed among the common herd. (Nor, I imagine, can you.) So I have made it a habit to forge a new tool every decade or two, taking the bright metal of youth and hardening and shaping it: she is merely my latest and deadliest."

"By tool, you mean predator."

"Yes, of course. And she is very good at it, isn't she?"

"You know I am immune to her particular methodology. Your black widow."

"Yes. But you are not the type of prey this hunter is trained for."

"Whereas our current irritant is, for the most part. So lend her to me!"

"Not unless you tell me why you want her. As I said, she's as subtle as a battalion of Cossacks."

"Yes. You did say that. That's *why* I want her."

"You need a decoy?"

(There is a pause.) "Yes."

"Very well, then. I shall send you her file. But I must caution you. Firstly, if you break her you *will* provide me with a suitable replacement. Secondly, I have installed a safety catch: you will not be able to use her against me. And finally . . . remember that this blade has no guard."

"I assure you I shall heed those warnings. Good-bye, George. May we not meet again for a very long time."

Old George freezes in place for a few seconds, staring at the doorway. Then he darts forward, limbs blurring in motion, and grabs something from behind the lintel before he ducks aside and rolls, presenting the Kevlar-lined back of his coat to the opening.

The explosion he half-expects fails to happen. After a few seconds he stands and dusts himself down, before examining the contents of his palm. Exposed wires and a compact speaker gleam in the bloody after-midnight glow reflecting from the clouds.

George nods at the empty tomb, acknowledging his old enemy's willingness to learn new tricks. A decade or two ago it would have been a bomb on a wire; now it's a remote speaker, doubtless on a line to a mobile phone buried in the bushes. He turns and strides back the way he came.

His rival is satisfyingly canny. Younger and weaker than George, but more flexible and willing to experiment with new techniques, he has once more declined to present his throat to his elder's knife. At the same time he has offered his cooperation. Which means there is a truce, at least for the now.

The law states that whenever two vampires meet, only one shall live. The youngsters in the bank are ignorant of the law; but ignorance is no defense. And soon they will learn about it the hard way.

I THINK I'M READY FOR IT—FOR THE USUAL AFTER-MISSION crash and subsequent messy, shaky, calm-down—when Mo awakens, screaming and choking for breath, in the middle of the night. But this time I couldn't be more wrong.

This is the pattern of our domestic life: that we keep each other sane. Mo and I both run errands for the Laundry.

I tend to be sent to investigate problems and work out what's going wrong: Why are there too many concrete cows in Milton Keynes, why a livery stable on a farm in Sussex is ordering fifty kilos of offal a day from the local abattoir, that sort of thing. Yes, these jobs sometimes blow up in my face and give me nightmares for years afterwards, but that's all part of the rich tapestry of life.

But Mo's job is different: she gets sent to troubleshoot problems that have *already* exploded.

Normally she divides her working week between lecturing in mathematics at one of London University's better-known colleges, and practicing with her violin. But once in a while she's called upon to pick up the violin, go somewhere, and fiddle until blood trickles from her fingertips. She does not play happy highland jigs. That damned instrument—and the word "damned" is an accurate description, not an expletive—is one of the organization's nastier assets. They placed it in her custody nearly a decade ago because she had an aptitude for the violin as an instrument (it used to be her hobby: when she was in her teens she briefly considered attending a music academy, but mathematics and philosophy won the toss), and she understands the eldritch mathematics used to describe the harmonics it is capable of achieving. Not many people can use an Erich Zahn instrument effectively. And even fewer can do it for any length of time without ending up in a padded cell.

So: after I get some food down her throat (not to mention half a bottle of wine) I run a bath for her, and make small-talk about office gossip. She's pretty tired so after she dries herself off and starts yawning I accompany her to the bedroom. She gets into bed and at first leans the violin case against her side of the mattress, but then rolls over and lifts the thing onto the duvet and curls around it, for all the world as if it's a teddy bear. I turn out the lights and wrap myself around her, spooning protectively, and within a couple of minutes she begins to snore.

I lie awake for a while. It's not that I'm not tired, but the violin is creeping me out. I can sense it, bony and hard-edged and hot. When I close my eyes I can't help seeing with that other, inner eye. With my eyes closed, I can see through Mo—human, warm, breathing softly, occasionally shifting against me—and through the case to the bony horror within. It's red and raw and pulses slowly, and I swear the thing is looking right back at me. It's not like sharing a bed with a teddy bear—more like a rabid attack dog who tolerates my presence only because the owner it is obsessively in thrall to is lying unconscious between us.

The violin doesn't like me. The violin has *never* liked me. I think the only reason it puts up with me is because of what I do for Mo. And if I ever stop doing it . . .

"Aaagh! Can't! Can't! . . ."

Mo sits bolt-upright in bed, making choking noises and wheezing.

Somehow, despite the presence of the instrument, I managed to drift off to sleep. As she wakes up in the grip of her night terror she yanks the bedding away from both of us, and I thrash around, turning away from her as I try to pull myself back from the edge of deep dream-sleep. I am naturally scared witless by the choking thing and I make a couple of grabs for the bedside light before I succeed in turning it on to push back the darkness. Then I sit up and put an arm round her shoulders. She's stopped choking but she's breathing frantically fast, and I can feel her pulse hammering.

"Mo?" I say inanely: "Are you all right? Mo!"

After a moment she manages to nod. I stroke her spine and upper back, shoulder blades and ribs: she's as tense as a tow-rope under load, still breathing too fast. I keep stroking and rubbing, and after a minute she suddenly twists her upper body and wraps her left arm around me, burying her face in the cleft between my shoulder and the side of my neck. Then the sobbing starts.

(I notice with distaste that she is still holding onto the violin case's handle with her right hand twisted behind her, but I don't dare try to detach it from her grip at this point.)

We sit there awkwardly for some time, holding each other while she sobs her heart out by dead of night. I feel helpless, and it's awful: I'm hugging my wife, vibrant, alive, and lovely; but she's in pain and I can do nothing to help relieve her agony except to be here, waiting for the memory abscess to burst and release whatever festering vileness has been poisoning her dreams. It feels *wrong*. And we're being watched all the time by the jealous attack dog on the bed behind her, chewing on the stump of its tail, thinking mad thoughts, waiting for me to let down my guard or for Mo to lose her temper with me.

Finally Mo sighs, then sniffs, then sniffs yet again. "It was an exorcism," she tells me.

I cautiously reach behind me for the bedside table, hunting with my fingertips for a box of tissues—I miss, and they go spilling across the floor. "Do you want to blow your nose?" I ask. Yes, it was an exorcism. Clearly the exorcism went badly. I realize with a sense of further foreboding that the Iranian secret police wouldn't have requested foreign assistance for anything they could deal with using their own resources, but I don't say that. She'll tell me when it's time.

"Kleenex." *Sniff.* Her death-grip on my back relaxes. "Do we still have that single malt I like, the special Glenmorangie one? Would you be a dear and fetch it?"

"Will you be all right?"

She nods. I get a good look at her: her eyes are red-rimmed and puffy and her nose is dripping like a three-year-old who's just been told that Santa doesn't exist. But she's awake, and getting a handle on whatever it was that woke her up. Which doesn't bode well for getting back to sleep.

ELSEWHERE IN LONDON ANOTHER WOMAN WAKES ALONE IN A cold and empty bed, to hear a telephone ringing elsewhere in her apartment.

She's a light sleeper, and the ringtone in question belongs to a land line that her employer provided. Its demands are never to be ignored. The bell rings: she salivates. And on this occasion finds herself already fully awake and halfway down the hall, pistol in hand, before the third ring.

The phone manages another ring before she gets to it, in the living room. "Speaking," she says tensely. Only one man has the number for this line, and a black box routes all random robocallers into a maze of twisty little voice mail boxes lest they annoy her; consequently, it only rings when her employer has a task for her.

"Marianne, your employer gave me your number."

The adrenalin spike triggered by these words makes her shudder from the tips of her toes to the ends of her blonde ponytail. She carefully places the pistol on the sideboard beside the phone base station, then clenches her fist. "Really?"

"Yes." The midnight caller sounds slightly amused. Going by the tone of voice, he's male—although there are devices for obscuring that. "George mentioned some instructions he gave you for this contingency."

The woman who calls herself Marianne shudders again, then repeats her long-memorized line: "What time of night do you call this?"

"The witching hour." Which is the correct counter-phrase.

"I'm not a witch." Which is a statement of fact, and not a password.

"I know. George told me all about you. How many vampires have you taken this year?"

Marianne raises her right hand to her mouth and bites the top joint of her thumb, quite hard. "Only one." Quiet frustration. "Are you a vampire? Are you looking for a date?" She lives in hope. Although any sane vampire who knows what she is will think twice before flirting with her.

"Let's just say I'm playing matchmaker." He sounds drily amused. She clutches the phone tightly, trying not to get her hopes up despite the thrill of anticipation. "I have a number of candidates in mind for you, if you'd like to meet them. At least five, possibly more."

"Oh! Yes." She almost goes weak at the knees. "Yes, of course!" It sounds better than she could possibly have imagined; what's the catch? "Why so many?"

"An, ah, nest has come to our attention. George is otherwise occupied, so . . ."

She puts two and two together. "You're his old playmate, aren't you? The one that got away!" She manages to suppress a girlish squeal of delight. "The one he keeps grumbling about!"

"He grumbles about me? I had no idea. I'm flattered! But that's as may be. George agreed to loan your services to me in pursuit of this, ah, common goal. You can confirm this, by the way. Call him up. Set your mind at ease."

"I'm always at ease!"

"I'm delighted to hear it. Anyway. To the task in hand: we will have to work closely together. I can assist you in isolating the targets, but the actual, ah—"

"Kiss."

"Yes, the *kiss* is entirely up to you. The first couple should be easy enough to steal, but thereafter we will have to make them come to us."

"You'll bring them to me," she says breathily, her heart pounding.

"I can't do that if you try to, ah, kiss me," he says. "But I am old and ugly and these are virile young bucks from the City . . ."

She takes a deep breath. "For five or six dates in a row I'll happily do what you want." *It's been so long,* she silently adds.

"Excellent." Her caller purrs. "I'll be in touch."

Click.

The line goes dead. She replaces the receiver, then stares at it wistfully. There's an unaccustomed warmth in her belly, a tremulous hope emerging. Whoever her caller is, Old George would not have lightly given him her number, which means this is certainly the real thing.

She is a fetishist of the type known to the very few people who study such recondite, occult perversions as a Fang Fucker. Old George found her and carefully trained and polished her; it is her delight and her pleasure to serve whenever he sends her on a date. But the past year has been a cold and lonely one, a famine of the flesh. She has been haunted by the nagging fear that her employer has tired of her, that she's doomed to the same future as an aging call girl whose clientele have dried up.

But now . . .

A nest. At least five! Be still my beating heart.

*   *   *

LEAVING MO SOBBING IN THE BEDROOM, I HEAD DOWNSTAIRS, grab a couple of tumblers, and rummage around the bottle rack for the single malt in question. (The bottle's still about half-full: neither of us is fond of drinking alone, which is a good thing.) I find a spare box of tissues on the kitchen worktop and hook it on a little finger, then take the stairs back up to the bedroom two at a time—but I needn't have bothered; Mo is moist but composed, if a bit fragile-looking.

"Here," I say, shaking the box of tissues loose over her lap: "I'll pour." I put the glasses down, uncork the bottle, and serve up a couple of uneven double-fingers of whisky. Mo gets the marginally taller tumbler once she finishes dabbing at her eyes—the bloody violin is leaning against her bedside table and she's let go of it, *hallelujah*—and I get back into bed beside her and plump up the pillows so we've got something to lean against. "You don't have to talk about it unless you want to."

She sips thoughtfully at the amber liquid. Her hair's a mess of twisted locks, almost in dreads: still coppery-red, although much of that comes from a bottle these days. Evidently wearing a head-scarf disagrees with it, and she hasn't had the time or energy to un-tangle it. "Maybe some good will come of it," she says quietly. "They'll have to stop the mass executions."

"The—" I bite my tongue. Then I take an incautiously large sip from my own glass. Gears crunch in my head: *she's back from Iran.* In the past few years, since the Arab Spring and the Green uprising that failed, the always-dependably-draconian regime has been going mad. So mad that our own Conservative government (catch phrase: hang 'em and flog 'em), who have hitherto been enthusiastically ren-dering all due assistance to the Iranian heroin traffic interdiction cops through the usual international police intelligence channels, have been backing away and muttering about not going too far, chaps. "What happened?" I ask, queasily curious.

"CASE NIGHTMARE GREEN strikes again." Mo sips at her whisky, clutching the tumbler in both hands to steady it. And my heart sinks.

CASE NIGHTMARE GREEN is the end of the world, more or less. Magic is a side effect of computation, and we're building too damn many microprocessors into too damn many toys these days— worse, we can't stop; civilization will fall apart if we don't have singing Christmas cards and intelligent gas meters, apparently. But there are other sources of computation. Human brains are computing machines *par excellence*, and the more of them there are, the more thaumaturgic processor cycles we produce. The whole thing is a runaway positive-feedback loop; while the demographic transition to a low birth/low death rate means we're near the top of the population roller coaster, it's going to take us a long time to get rid of all those surplus brains and the microprocessors they depend on, and in the meantime, the ultrastructure of reality is becoming extra-porous. Magic is getting easier to practice and more powerful, and the things that live behind the walls of the universe are becoming intrigued by the smell of thinking fodder that wafts its way towards them. The stars are coming right, reality is coming apart at the seams, and we'll all go together when we go.

Oh, and we can't even murder our way clear of it early. The deliberate killing of thinking beings (or thinking machines for that matter—there is a *reason* we really don't want to see any progress in AI) generates huge thaumic fields that can be used for, for want of a better word, necromancy. And if we don't use the power, someone— or something else—will.

"There's a prison near a city in the north of Iran called Mashad, I don't know where exactly, they put me up in an airport hotel overnight, then shipped me there in an Air Force helicopter—it's called Vakilabad, and it's near the border. They get a lot of drug traffickers there. Well, mules: illiterate, dirt-poor Afghan refugees who cross the border on foot with half a kilo of heroin in their pockets. There's no fence on the frontier, and no signs to tell them that the Islamic Republic of Iran has the death penalty for possession of twenty grams and that they won't get a defense lawyer."

Which is what gave our delightful Home Secretary cold feet about cooperation. See, here in the UK twenty grams of heroin is good for a slap on the wrist if you're an addict; maybe a six-month sentence if they think you're dealing. A mule caught entering the UK with half a kilo is going to get somewhere between a five- and eight-year sentence, with time off for good behavior and deportation at the end. Scragging them is seen as a bit of an overreaction. Especially as HMG is signatory to a whole bunch of treaties requiring us to work towards the abolition of the death penalty worldwide.

Mo takes a much bigger mouthful of whisky, closes her eyes, and swallows. Then she starts spluttering. I take her tumbler and refill it, wait for the coughing to subside, then offer it to her.

She continues, quietly and with remarkably little affect. "Vakilabad is a large prison, and there is a shed in the prison with a substantial roof beam running its length. They hang people from the beam; they make the prisoners stand on tall stools, then kick them away. It can take sixty bodies at one time, they told me, and although they seldom fill it up they use it every week. It's the world's largest gallows: they're very proud of it."

She puts her glass down. I hug her for a while, speechless with the horror of it.

"My contact was a man named Ahmad, from the VEVAK. What I thought I was getting into was a straightforward decontamination job—clearing up a battlefield from the Iran-Iraq War where there'd been a huge human wave attack, followed by a haunting. And that's what Ahmad seemed to think, too, when he met me. It was all fairly laid-back at first, until a bunch of Pasdaran special forces troops turned up, led by a lieutenant—that's the Revolutionary Guard. And they told Ahmad that the *real* problem was that the governor of Vakilabad prison had been unable to carry out any executions for nearly a month because a *Djinn*, an evil spirit, had . . . well." She's shaking. "I need another nip," she adds, pulling free and picking up her tumbler again.

"A *Djinn*?" I ask, then bite my tongue again: it's not my job to prompt her. She'll spill when she's good and ready.

"Well, there was a bit of an argument, and I nearly stamped my foot and told them it was a breach of protocol, but you don't want to get into a pissing match with the local equivalent of the Waffen-SS. Ahmad said later that he'd had a bad feeling about the assignment from the start, thought it was a whitewash for something, but he didn't like to say . . . So anyway, they piled us into a couple of Toyotas and drove us from the airport to the prison: a horrible place. It smelled of shit and despair. Once inside we were taken directly to this shed. The death chamber. I was . . . afraid. You know? You can never be quite certain what the revolutionary guards are planning because they are entirely rational, within the constraints of a belief system that is based on crazy and mutually contradictory axioms. But they gave me the VIP treatment, tea and refreshments, and they let me keep my instrument, so . . .

"We got to the death chamber. There were four bodies hanging there, and they were clearly dead, but not in the manner prescribed by law. The execution party had left in a hurry: three of the stools were still upright. The victims were levitating, Bob, hovering just below the beam the ropes were tied to, and their eyes were glowing— you know what I mean? The bioluminescence thing? Luminous worms in the darkness. They were all quite dead, and the smell was atrocious: they'd been floating there for a week, chanting: '*Aw der hal amedn aset, aw der hal amedn aset.*' Over and over again. Through dead men's throats."

She pauses for another suck at the water of life and I follow her example.

"I asked Ahmad. 'It means, *he is coming*,' he explained. Ahmad was clearly just inches away from crapping himself with fear. 'Now please would you banish the *Djinn* that is haunting gallows so these fine fellows will let us go?'"

She transfers her whisky glass to her left hand and reaches behind her with the right, to touch the violin case.

"I demanded some more background. Vakilabad has been busy for the past few years. He wouldn't tell me how many people they'd hanged there, but when I guessed over a thousand he didn't correct me downwards. Seems the execution parties had been troubled by odd sounds, emanations, chills and thumps and wails for some time;

they'd put it down to, well. You can guess. I checked, then, and the background thaum reading was off the scale. Executions are a form of human sacrifice, after all, and this was death magic on a huge scale."

She takes another sip. She's draining the glass steadily; I reckon she's only got ten or fifteen minutes left before she drinks herself into a stupor. What she's telling me suggests I ought to join in, lest I have some very bad dreams, so I knock back a burning mouthful of spirit. It's singularly disrespectful to a portwood finished single malt, but it's too late to go back to the bathroom cabinet to check if there's any Temazepam left—mixing drink and sedatives is dangerous.

"I had a dilemma, love." I feel her shoulders relax slightly. "If it had been a normal exorcism I'd have had no problem helping out. But they wanted the death chamber clearing down and neutralized so they could go back to hanging people. Nobody gave a shit about the thaum count until it got in the way of them strangling illiterate peasants. But then it was all, oh, INTERPOL will know someone who can help us out! Won't they?"

She falls silent for a moment. Then, fiercely: "I will *not* be complicit, an enabler for judicial mass-murder!"

"I—" I swallow. "You refused? But what—"

"I tried to refuse at first. The Pasdaran officer was really angry, although Ahmad said he understood. They had a big shouting match. I mentioned the European Convention on Human Rights and the recent EU Commission ruling on withdrawal of coordination of drug interdiction until they ceased executions and pointed out I'd be violating our own policy guidelines if I didn't obtain a legal waiver from the Home Office first.

"Then Firouz—the Pasdaran lieutenant—threatened to make me stay in the death chamber until I cooperated. With a Greek chorus of corpses chanting in the background and a thaum level off the scale. And he had his hand on his pistol—still holstered—and he was giving me the eye. You know? Well no, you probably don't: you're male. But anyway, I lost my temper. So I nodded and smiled and took out my violin and made the dead men dance.

"The cadavers dropped, one by one. And so did Firouz. He'd *threatened* me, so I used his soul as duct tape to paper over the crack that had opened under the gallows."

She takes a final sip, draining her tumbler. I nod along with her, not trusting myself to speak. This is a part of my work, you see. The organization puts Mo in situations where the only way to survive is to become one of the monsters, and it's part of my job to hold her together even when she does things that make me want to throw up.

"The Pasdaran soldiers were freaked out and scared, but I took enough from their souls that they didn't have the wits to realize I was responsible. I can be subtle when I need to. And Ahmad, he, he got it. I explained that this power doesn't come without a cost, and that if they began hanging people again—anywhere within the jail's walls—there'd almost certainly be a resumption. 'But what are we to do with the smugglers and criminals?' he asked. *Stop killing them,* I suggested. He said he thought it was a good idea and he'd pass it up the line, which means he'll write a report and they'll ignore it.

"Then the Pasdaran sergeant decided that waiting around in a haunted execution shed with a spook and a crazy foreign woman and a lieutenant who'd just died of causes unknown was a bad idea, so they shoved us all in the back of a truck and drove me back to the airport and here I am look at me I'm not shaking I'm not mad *I'm just so angry I could kill someone . . .*"

11.

BOARDROOMS AND BROKERS

A LOT CAN HAPPEN IN A MONTH.

A month ago I was back in the office, recovering from the avalanche of virtual paperwork generated by the aftermath of the GOD GAME RAINBOW mess (not to mention the still-unfolding headache of the COBWEB MAZE working group and BLOODY BARON process—our very own happy fun mole hunt), trying to get a handle on my new roles and responsibilities, having Pete's mentoring program dumped on my desk, and worrying about the doghouse Mo was making me sleep in.

Now I think things with Mo are patched up—at least insofar as they can be, when she's still having screaming gallows-chamber nightmares three times a week. Hell, *I'm* having nightmares about what she did, and we're both resorting to alcohol as a sleeping aid more often than is strictly healthy. I'd go and scream at her supervisory board if I thought it would do any good, but the problem is that *somebody* has to do these jobs, and if not Mo, then who? So I confine myself to writing a stiffly worded memo petitioning them to please fucking ease up on her for a while, because if she gets another assignment like Vakilabad there's a good chance it will break her. And then I pace her with the whisky bottle each evening.

Meanwhile, Andy is drifting from abandoned store room to temporarily vacant cubicle like a damned soul in exile, clutching his laptop; Pete is getting his teeth into the MAGIC CIRCLE OF SAFETY job, prototyping Facebook awareness campaigns and an official Laundry Twitter feed,* and I am attending too many committee meetings.

In addition to GOD GAME BLACK, GOD GAME RAINBOW, COBWEB MAZE, and BLOODY BARON, they have dropped another fucking committee process on my head. For my sins and because I discovered a wunch of bankers suffering from the syndrome to which we've assigned the keyword OPERA CAPE, I have been seconded to the shiny new exploration phase of DRESDEN RICE, and if you think that code name sounds like it has something to do with the V-word, have a cigar. It's a sign that not everybody in the bureaucracy is taking our new photophobic colleagues entirely seriously, because it's a *really* big security no-no to give a project a moniker that bears any relationship whatsoever to its subject matter. Breaches compartmentalization or something. But for some reason all you have to do is utter the word "vampire" and people around here pull out the pointy plastic choppers and the opera cape like they're some sort of joke.

It's not, actually, very funny. It's like turning up for work one morning at the Met Office and discovering that the earnest people who bring us the shipping forecast are all jovial Young Earth creationists who think Global Warming is a conspiracy by climatologists who are trying to use it to get rich. Or discovering that the Department for Trade and Industry is run by a Reiki practitioner whose special advisor is an astrologer. Or like finding out that the Ministry of Defense is lobbying for the urgent renewal of our strategic nuclear deterrent because it is vitally important to be able to nuke the capital of the So-

---

* His cover story: they're part of the viral marketing campaign promoting a not-yet-announced low budget horror movie.

viet Union at five minutes' notice.* For some reason we seem to have a screamingly huge organizational blind spot—a part of our remit that nobody even believes exists.

But be that as it may, I am jointly assigned as a humble junior manager in External Assets and as private secretary to DSS Angleton. And as a junior manager it is my fate to sit in on the committees my bosses can't be arsed attending. Consequently I don't have time to investigate our organizational case of macular degeneration right now because I'm up to my eyeballs in meetings. I don't even get to goof off from the boardroom antics—I have to summarize for them. It's like being forced to test a hideous new role-playing game in which you play at being gray-suited office minions trapped in a hellish world of paper-shuffling and boardroom presentations (mediated by frequent dice rolls) without meaning or magic. And because of the fucking DRESDEN RICE committee *other people are* laughing *at me*! Speaking as the former laugh-a-minute guy around here, I've got to say that it stings.

So, while I'm busy spending up to six hours in committees every day—yes, the beatings will continue until morale improves—let me give you a whistle-stop tour of the highlights of what's been going on in the New Annex since last month, in the shape of a clichéd movie montage.

KNOCK KNOCK.

Pete is not expecting anyone to come knocking on his office door. Or rather, the door of the temporarily vacant office to which he has been given a key and in which he has had installed a PC, a chair, a desk, and a bookshelf full of Aramaic concordances. When it comes, Pete is holed up inside, in jeans and a polo shirt, swearing mildly at a web design application as he hunts for typos and grammatical infe-

---

* Scratch that last: it's actually all because of BLUE HADES and DEEP SEVEN, which is arguably *our* fault. But that's another story.

licities in the copy he has spent the past weeks laboriously updating from the MAGIC CIRCLE OF SAFETY brochure.

Pete looks up. "Come in?" he calls.

The door opens. It's Andy, escorting a gawky late-teenage stranger on the usual office disorientation tour, wherein they meet loads of strangers and instantly forget their names, merely retaining a vague impression of organizational complexity gone to seed. *Intern,* Pete thinks instantly, then with a flash of mortification: *Am I going native already?* He's been here for five weeks; it feels like forever and he's itching to get back to his parish. However the bishop has clearly been nobbled, for he's sent a circuit priest to pick up the ropes without any complaints or queries; this is England, where the Church is notionally still part of the state, and there's probably an Office of Occult Coordination tucked away in Canterbury to handle embarrassments like this. At least Sandy is being understanding, and HR are fine with him taking time off work to accompany her to the antenatal clinic.

Pete is desperately aware of his lack of contact with the pastoral concerns of his people, like a nagging awareness that he's not getting enough vitamins in his diet; but the Laundry is more than capable of pandering to his guilty pleasure, offering glimpses deep into the fascinating patch of applied linguistics that he has tried to build an academic career in. (This Enochian metagrammar thing they've been working with demands to be contextualized with the variant proto-Aramaic dialects from which it strikes disturbing echoes.) But instead, they've given him this training-wheels web design assignment . . . it's a learning experience and it'll probably come in handy when he goes back to the parish newsletter, but it's not *work*.

"Pete? Hi, I'd like you to meet one of our newest recruits." Andy smiles warmly as he oozes into the office and somehow migrates into the ratty visitor's chair without disrupting the pile of yellowing government posters stacked precariously in front of it. "Alex, this is Dr. Peter Wilson, *also* a recent recruit. Pete, this is Alex Schwartz. Um. Alex is also a doctor, although his PhD is in theoretical mathematics, not Aramaic lexicography. Alex, Pete is a vicar by trade."

Alex, standing beside the door, attempts to fade into the wallpaper. He looks barely old enough to be out of school, much less to have earned a PhD. There is something, Pete realizes, that is not quite right about this picture. The body language is remarkably stand-offish. Maybe he's an atheist or something? Pete composes his face: "Right now I'm learning to be a web designer," he says as disarmingly as possible. "What brings you here?"

Andy clears his throat. "Alex is a member of a quantitative analysis research group who inadvertently stubbed their collective toe on something significant, so we're taking them through the usual in-processing and orientation while we work out what to do with them—basically, health and safety training. Then we and they can decide whether to release them back to what they were doing before, on inactive status, or find a more permanent role for them within the agency if they're so inclined. Bob told me you were working on MAGIC CIRCLE OF SAFETY, which is a rather low-hazard task, and I was thinking you might want to take on an assistant, for mentoring—"

Gosh, I've only been here a few weeks! If they're asking me to mentor someone, they must be really overloaded with new fish! Pete leans back and, while directing his eyes at Andy, tries to build up a picture of Alex using only his peripheral vision. The wallflower is braced against the side of the filing cabinet. Pallid skin, dark hair, the remains of what must have been a hideously embarrassing adolescent acne attack barely visible on his jawline. If he had better fashion sense he could make a pretty run-of-the-mill goth, but he's dressed head to toe in M&S office weeds, and hasn't even discovered the if-everything-you-wear-is-black-it-always-matches trick. He's seen the type before—they're all too common on Divinity degree courses: otherworldly, head stuck in a cloud of theory and trainer laces tangled together at ground level. Someone ought to take him in hand, but Pete is brutally aware that with a parish to get back to and the responsibilities of impending fatherhood he just doesn't have the spare energy for the job. "That's interesting," he says to Andy. "What does the mentoring job entail?"

"Well, you've been finding your way around the department for the past month but you're new enough that the frustrating and disorienting stuff is still fresh in your memory, so I was hoping you might be better able to build a rapport with Alex, here. You're still learning, too, so perhaps if you approach it as a team, with myself and Bob to fall back on . . ." Andy trails off, his pitch delivered, and waits expectantly.

Well, this might not be so bad. Pete looks directly at Alex. "What do you think, Alex? Are you happy to share a web design and public relations outreach job with a vicar?"

Alex stares at him for precisely three seconds, then says: "I'm a vampire."

As non sequiturs go Pete has heard worse. In parish work you periodically have to deal with young, slightly alienated gay teens whose overly concerned parents drag them in for a talking-to by the vicar—*there's something strange about Harry.* Part of Pete's job (as he sees it) is to talk them down from the ramparts of militant antiChristianism, explain that no, the entire Church does *not* hate them, and then point them at the nearest LGBT youth counseling service. With luck, in a few years' time they'll be happy and stable, and remember you when the last of the reactionary 'phobes have finally flounced out of the General Synod.

You get the really barking cases less often: they're usually paranoid schizophrenics who are convinced their meds are poisoning them or the radio is giving them orders from the gangster computer god on the dark side of the moon. When Jesus drops round for a chat in the day center, carrying a twelve-hundred-page printout of his new gospel in six-point type with no margins or paragraph breaks, you have to follow a slightly different script: one which involves discreetly checking for concealed carving knives, followed by a phone call to Social Services after he beams back up to the mothership.

Unfortunately there's no approved C of E standard script to handle *I'm a vampire.* So Pete improvises, and smiles brightly at Alex: "How long have you known you were a vampire?"

The lad relaxes slightly, which is unexpected. "It happened at twenty to seven in the evening, six weeks ago next Tuesday," he says. His eyes flicker sidelong in a saccade indicative of mild distraction, then he pulls out a gigantic slab of a smartphone and peers at it. "Although I didn't really confirm it was contagious until the next day at, um, six thirty-three? That's when I turned Evan. And the blood thing, well, um, ah, that is to say"—his cheeks redden: surely with blood vessels like that he was the victim of any number of cruel embarrassments during his school days!—"we didn't get to confirm that it actually worked for another couple of days, when management authorized us to take a one-week unscheduled diversionary sprint to provide inputs for the pivot narrative."

Pete blinks. There are words coming out of Alex's mouth, and they even sound like English, but—he catches Andy's eye. Andy nods, almost imperceptibly, but Alex spots it and tenses up again: "I'm not mad!" he says. "I'm not the only one of us, either."

Andy is clearly playing his cards close to his chest, and this leaves Pete feeling unaccountably annoyed. "I assume if Alex was mad he wouldn't be here," Pete points out. "So shall we take it as read that Alex really *is* a vampire?"

Andy muffles a cough with his fist. "The politically correct terminology is still a matter of some debate, but I am told it's hard to give offense by talking about, ah, Photogolic Hemophagic Anagathic, um, Neurotropic . . . um . . . what does the 'G' stand for, Alex?"

"I'm not sure; I think whoever invented it was just fishing for the world's ugliest medical backronym." Alex squirms, as if trying to shrug his way out of a straitjacket. "Anyway, it's PHANG syndrome. Or Persons of PHANG. Photogolic because we *really* don't get on with sunlight; hemophagic because, er, let's not go there? Anagathic because some of my older colleagues suddenly don't look a day over twenty. Neurotropic because it has some other interesting side effects, and the 'G' got tacked on the end because you can't call someone a PHANG Fucker without one, yes, ha ha, very droll, you'd better get it out of your system because you'll be meeting the rest of us in due course, and Janice *really* doesn't have a sense of humor about that kind of shit—"

His face is stony. For a moment Pete has a vision of an alternate universe where Alex is a stand-up comedian's straight man, or maybe earns his crust as one-half of a Proclaimers tribute band. Then the ineluctable truth begins to sink in. "You don't catch fire if exposed to garlic or holy water by any chance? Crosses or other religious symbols?" Alex shakes his head. (In the background, Andy stands and begins to slither doorwards.) "Jolly good. We don't have much to do with that stuff in the C of E anyway," he adds, "but it'd be kind of embarrassing to share an office with someone with a garlic bread allergy." He looks at Andy. "Will you please *stop that*? I know what you're trying to do, and so does Alex." To his relief Alex nods rapidly. "I'm sure this young man—"

"I'm twenty-four!"

"This young man has had a very trying few weeks, and you're not helping by making him wonder if you're using him as a crash test dummy for the departmental Dr. Van Helsing. Here's the deal, Alex: I'm in your shoes, just a month further down the line and I got roped into this, this *circus* because I can read Aramaic and a, an acquaintance needed a scriptural translation checking in a hurry. At least you're here for a reason, at least I *hope* you're here for a reason, and it's probably a better one than mine. So Andy here"—at this point the accused jerks and adopts a guiltily sycophantic expression—"wants to off-load you on me. And, you know what? That's *fine*. I promise not to try to hammer a stake through your heart or set you on fire, as long as you promise not to rip my throat out. Okay? We in the twenty-first century have this marvelous technical innovation, it's called *civilization*, and it means we don't have to make promises like that to everyone we meet because we can usually take it for granted. So, um"—Pete stands up, then offers his right hand—"welcome to my office. I've got this project that you might be able to help me with. Tell me"—Andy finally vanishes from his office like the memory of a foul smell, as Alex hesitantly takes Pete's hand and shakes it limply—"what, if anything, do you know about search engine optimization?"

*   *   *

KARMA'S A BITCH.

No, let me rephrase that:

Karma is your vengeful bunny-boiler ex, lurking in your darkened front hallway wearing an ice-hockey mask and carrying a baseball bat inscribed with BET YOU DIDN'T SEE THIS COMING.

(And, to over-stretch the metaphor, Karma *intends* to whack you upside the head so hard your cranium lands in the bleachers, but the hockey mask has slipped and she usually ends up hitting your blind next-door neighbor's guide dog by mistake, nine times out of ten, so that when the tenth strike lands true you *really* don't see it coming.)

But, as usual, I digress.

This is the Laundry. We are part of the secret side of the civil service, so naturally we do committees. Did I say we do committees? We probably invented the damned idea, sometime between the Roman invasion and King Canute's unfortunate intertidal dilemma. We're *good* at them, with the kind of polish and proficiency that only arrives after four hundred years of diligent practice. We use committees for all the ulterior purposes for which they might have been designed: diffusion of executive responsibility, plausible deniability, misdirection, providing the appearance of activity without the substance, and protecting the guilty. We also use them for fact-finding, pooling of knowledge about best working practices, and determining policy.

It's the latter wheeze that concerns me right now.

We're less than half an hour into the first meeting of the DRESDEN RICE committee, and I am already getting a very bad feeling about the direction we have been channeled in.

Firstly there's the *what*. From the moment it popped up on my Outlook calendar, flagged in red like an inflamed pimple full of infected bureaucratic pus, I realized there was something wrong with it. "Working group to produce recommendations on the employment requirements and retention of staff exhibiting PHANG syndrome characteristics," it said, and I've been trying desperately to get it shifted, but no, the remit is stuck like a king-sized dildo in a guinea pig.

Secondly, there's the *who*. Because it has been designed as a cuddly-wuddly touchy-feely care-and-feeding committee, fully half our membership consists of paired buttocks from Human Resources, Health and Safety, Building Services, and IT Support. I'm there *not* in my capacity as Bob Howard, Vampire Hunter Extraordinaire, or Bob Howard, Deputy Eater of Souls, but as Bob Howard, Technical Networking Manager (in other words, cable-crimper-in-chief for the New Annex). We are overstaffed (there are twelve bodies here), flabby (at least three each are from HR and H&S), and indecisive.

Finally, to make matters exponentially worse . . . nobody actually made it a requirement for membership of this committee that members have to be cleared for OPERA CAPE.

So:

"Don't be silly!" Doris Greene from Health and Safety announces: "Everybody knows vampires don't exist!"

She looks round the table, her stare challenging any of us to gainsay her. Middle-aged, plump, and gallus in twinset and pearls, Doris is one of the H&S types who seems to have had her sense of humor surgically shrunken and her perm prematurely grayed by exposure to one too many inquests into bizarre workplace accidents that involve cordless hammer drills, sex toys, and the phrase "Watch this!" Her broiler-hen impersonation would be met with fond affection in most situations where she didn't also have the authority to shut everything down on a whim or call on the Spanish Inquisition for fire support, but it loses some of its charm when there's actual work to be done.

"Everyone knows you catch vampirism by being bitten by a vampire," she explains. "So, they drink your blood—and then you rise as a vampire, don't you? But answer me this—if every vampire drinks blood, how come we aren't *all* vampires? It stands to reason! Vampire number one drinks from a victim. Then there's two of them. The next night they both drink from victims. That makes four." She subvocalizes for a few seconds, counting up powers of two on her fingers. "After a month, there are nearly a billion of them! And a week later, we're *all* vampires!" She twitches around triumphantly. "So they *can't* exist. Can they?"

"Nonsense!" announces Bill Heath. Bill is at least a decade north of the mandatory retirement watermark—unfortunately abolished some years back, under cover of the last government's campaign against ageism in the workplace. He clears his throat, making a disgusting gurgling noise reminiscent of a kitchen waste disposal unit chewing on a week-dead rat, then continues before I can get a word in: "If they don't exist, what are we doing here? It wasn't like this during the war. We 'ad no time to discuss nonsense and nightmares back then! Not with Jerry threatening to drop basilisks on us from V-1s. So this is either a waste of time or we should be stockpiling garlic-impregnated stakes. *Which ain't my department.* So can I go 'ome now?"

Sally Carlyle clears her throat loudly. "Not yet, Bill!" By virtue of age and duration of service Bill gets to sit near the head end of the table, but Sally is chairing the session and keeping minutes. She's a forty-ish, no-nonsense woman whose occasional impish smile predisposes me to like her, against my better judgment—for she is another denizen of the catacombs of Human Resources, and her usual specialty is mediating disciplinary hearings. Minor stuff—nothing involving the Auditors, much less the Black Assizes—but she's got the Administrative Procedure Manual and the Staff Ethics and Guidance Handbook memorized flat, so the effect is a little like being in a meeting chaired by an officer of the Gedanken-Geheimpolizei. "Doris, I'm afraid the, um, media portrayal of this condition is somewhat off-target. I am *informed*"—Sally's eyes narrow ever so slightly as she looks down the table, directly at yours truly—"that there is some truth behind the legend, although exactly how much may, shall we say, be a matter for debate." She grins. "What would you say, Mr. Howard?"

I take a deep breath. "Vampires exist," I begin. "I've met—"

Basil Northcote-Robinson, sitting at the opposite end of the boardroom table, fiddles with his hearing aid. It makes a hideous high-pitched whistling feedback noise, like fingernails on a blackboard shifted several octaves towards the ultrasonic. "Vampire blancmange!" he shouts, completely derailing my train of thought.

"Would you mind—" I begin.

"Vampire blancmange!"

Sally rolls her eyes. Basil has at least a decade on Bill. We're into hearing-trumpet and bath chair territory now. But he has an opinion, and he wants us to add it to the minutes. "The original Romanian vampire legend is *not what you think*, young feller-me-lad. Forget those walking corpses, rising from their graves and sucking the life out of the living! That's just a meta- meta- whatchewmacallit for tuberculosis. A refit. No, if you go back to the *old* days, vampirism was a *curse*. It's all over the archives, you know." (Basil works in the archives. He's a key part of the oral history project. Otherwise they'd have made him retire decades ago.) "You'd get this cursed gift, like an axe or a fiddle or a loaf of bread or something, and the nature of the curse was that it would *cause blood to be spilled* until it was passed on. That's all. You could catch it yourself—it'd turn you into a bloody-handed murderer—or it would stay on the axe blade—people would cut themselves on it, or murderers would use it—unless you pushed the curse onto *something else*. And literally *anything* could be a vampire. A monkey's paw. Or a blancmange, for instance. That's where the Pythons got the idea from, the Wimbledon sketch . . ." He looks around, bewildered. "Anyone else here a fan of Monty Python?"

"Vampire blancmange." Sally makes a note about something on her pad, then visibly suppresses a sigh. "Noted. You were saying, Mr. Howard?"

"Bananas!" says Bill. "We couldn't get bananas during the war for love nor money. Had to make do with blancmange instead!" He seems to find it all extraordinarily funny; he's chortling so hard I expect him to cough his dentures across the room.

This is more than Sally can reasonably take. "Committee will adjourn for five minutes," she announces. "Coffee and toilet break, not to mention sanity break. Bill, you can go home. In fact, please *do* go home. Your work here is done. I'll minute you as attending if you just go home and leave us in peace. Is that what you want? Are you happy now?"

"Bananas!" Bill says happily as those of us with any sanity left (not to mention full bladders) break for the meeting room door.

A few minutes later I'm back in the meeting room, a fresh mug of coffee cooling slowly on my blotter. I'm leaning my head against the even cooler surface of the wall when Sally clears her throat behind me. "Mr. Howard," she begins.

"Hi, Ms. Carlyle." I stand up and turn around.

"I expect you're wondering what this committee is all about," she says hesitantly, "and why you've been seconded to it."

"Yes, I was wondering that," I begin.

"Well, it's obviously a blind training scenario," she says. "And I think you're here as a counterweight for the ballast. I mean, Basil and Bill are not easy to handle, so the organizers wanted someone sensible to keep the process moving . . . Mr. Howard. What is it?"

I take a deep breath. "Sally, I am going to give you a keyword. Tell me, have you heard of OPERA CAPE?"

"What, you mean—that's an internal classification?"

"Yes."

"No, can't say I have." Her crow's-feet wrinkles deepen. "Is it relevant?"

I feel like groaning, but confine myself to a small nod. "Yes, it's relevant. Unfortunately I can't tell you why. So, um. You believe this is a blind training scenario, to test our business process for generating procedures for handling new classes of paranormally endowed personnel, am I reading you right?"

"Exactly!" She beams. "And as our go-to structured cabling guy you're clearly level-headed and approach things systematically. Anyway. As you can tell, we've been given a mish-mash of unsuitable personnel, not to say deadweight. Which means the rest of us are going to have to do a lot of the heavy lifting."

Oh dear. The committee chair isn't cleared for OPERA CAPE. *Which means I may be the only person on this committee who actually knows anything about vampires.* And if they're not cleared, I can't tell them.

"You're assembling a little subcommittee. Am I right?"

"You are indeed right. Clearly a man of hidden talents!"

"Jolly good. So I assume this means you want me to do something for you. Again, am I right?"

"Ye-e-s . . ."

Every instinct is telling me to run away, very fast. But I harbor a morbid curiosity, and something tells me it'll be useful and instructive to study the way unbriefed members of the unwashed masses deal with the idea of vampires, and in any case I'm the only person here who has any idea why this committee exists, so . . . I lean closer and say, "Tell me more."

She tells me. After which I want to set fire to my beard and flee, screaming. And I don't even *have* a beard.

HOMEWORK: I HAVE IT.

I have the angries, too.

"This is such bullshit!" I brandish a fistful of email printouts in the general direction of Lockhart's desk, carefully not pointing it at him directly—it's not his direct responsibility in any case. "The committee is overloaded with coffin dodgers. I mean, even Sally Carlyle couldn't get Basil to stay on-topic for more than thirteen consecutive seconds, and as for Bill . . ."

"Sit *down*, Mr. Howard!" booms Lockhart, in a stentorian tone that is familiar to sergeant-majors everywhere.

I sit, hastily, balancing on the edge of the visitor's chair in his office.

"Your point that nobody else on the DRESDEN RICE committee has been cleared to know about persons infected with OPERA CAPE is well-taken." Lockhart moderates his voice. "But has it occurred to you that there might be a reason for that?"

"I can think of several." I cross my legs. "Mostly ranging from the inane to the criminally irresponsible."

"Do enlighten me, then. What options do you see?" The hairy caterpillar balanced on his upper lip hunches its back in a sneer.

"Where should I begin? Sally thinks it's a training exercise, testing processes for developing procedures for handling fresh meat. That's a good blind, but it doesn't explain why none of them believe in vampires. Except for Basil, of course, good old Basil and his Romanian vampire blancmanges. Um. Someone decided to nobble the process so that the recommendations it comes up with bear no resemblance to actual reality on the ground, in furtherance of some hitherto-unimagined bureaucratic death-match designed to disgrace and discredit a rival? Or someone at the top, despite notionally being cleared for OPERA CAPE, didn't read the fricking daily pooled intel assessment and still doesn't believe in fang fuckers so they're treating it as a joke. Or. Or." I brandish my email again. "But they minuted it! They *set me homework*!"

"Do calm down, old boy. What's so bad about a spot of homework?"

"(Jesus Fuck)—" I subvocalize, rather than inflicting my Tourette's on Lockhart's unreliable and occasionally prissy ears. "They reached a consensus that the best way to go about working out the requirements of vampires was to do a literature survey. They then decided that a bunch of amateurs had obviously already done the legwork for them, so all that was necessary was for me to"—I take a deep breath—"read the complete works of Brian Lumley, Anne Rice, Jim Butcher, and Laurell K. Hamilton, and draw a fucking"—I can't help myself, it just slipped out, honest—"*entity-relationship diagram* of the hierarchy structures of all the vampires portrayed therein, while documenting their vulnerabilities, kill rate, dietary needs, and so on and so forth *as if they're not all works of fiction*."

I get louder towards the end, until I'm blaring. If Lockhart was of the feline persuasion his ears would be back and his eyes slitted. And as I wind down I half-expect him to deliver a royal bollocking: Lockhart's military background doesn't predispose him to handle insubordination delicately. But, for a miracle, he holds his tongue for a while and just looks at me speculatively. The hairy caterpillar is sleeping, or maybe paralyzed with indecision—

"That does indeed sound somewhat irregular, Mr. Howard. Would you mind passing me those papers?"

Lockhart takes the printed-out emails from my nerveless fingertips, then reaches into his desk tidy for a pair of half-moon reading glasses. He scans the pages, lips sagging slightly as if in the grip of the muscle-memory of long-ago readings-aloud in class; and then he shuffles the pages and reads some more, then refers back to the first page. Then he glances up at me. "Why are you still here, Mr. Howard?"

"Because I—" I stop. It's Lockhart. Of course. "Because you haven't told me to piss off, yet."

"Oh. Well, you can leave now. You were absolutely right to draw this to my attention, but the matter needs to be handled delicately. In particular, even *you* should comprehend the need to understand why the committee was so misconfigured before any remedial action is taken. So I suggest you suck it up and proceed as directed, until you hear otherwise. In the meantime, I shall make enquiries."

"What, you want me to—"

"Yes, Bob, I rather thought entity-relationship diagrams were your sort of thing. You're the expert in Visio, aren't you? Drawing up UML diagrams of fictional vampire brood hierarchies should keep you out of trouble for a while." His momentary grin is utterly lacking in human warmth. "I'll call you when I have something to pass on. Now do piss off; don't you have some in-placement recruits to be monitoring, or something?"

"GOOD EVENING, EMMA." OSCAR MENENDEZ IS EXPANSIVE BON-homie personified as he marches into Emma MacDougal's den and looks around. It's well after five, and HR are usually punctilious about observing core office hours and minimizing overtime, but he shows no sign of recognizing the special honor that he has been accorded. Addison Lee minivans with blacked-out windows might be normal in the City, but they raise eyebrows if sighted on a government expenses report without a good reason. Emma has signed off on them for Mhari's new recruits on grounds of medical necessity, but if Oscar thinks he can take her approval for granted he's in line for a nasty shock.

"Good day, Mr. Menendez." Emma MacDougal smiles from behind the armor of her Dior-framed specs, carefully not showing him her dental work. "Mhari has been filling me in on your people."

"Yes." Oscar sits down without being invited, taking the comfortable armchair opposite Emma's desk as his of right. "We've got a number of rather unusual requirements. And while I appreciate your organization's need to identify and evaluate new talent and find a pigeonhole to file everyone in, the trading arm of one of our nation's three largest financial institutions depends on the system my team is responsible for developing and supporting. So I hope you can agree that it would be in everybody's best interests to expedite our in-processing and let us get back to our critical roles as soon as—"

"Mr. Menendez." Emma's smile widens, revealing her teeth. They're not filed to points, but judging by Oscar's reaction they might as well be. Emma has switched from sanguine to sanguinary in a matter of seconds, and in Oscar's experience that's not supposed to happen; but then, Oscar is not as proficient at manipulating minds as his previous successes have led him to believe. And Oscar has never before tried to use his power of conviction to twist the thoughts of a woman who is wearing a discreet Laundry ward on a silver chain under her blouse. Much less a Laundry Human Resources manager to whom attempts at mind control are as routine as arbitration requests over gender or ethnic harassment allegations. *"Stop that at once!"*

"Stop what?"

The velvet-skinned smile slips, revealing a glimpse of the steely skull within: "You know *perfectly well* what you're doing, Mr. Menendez. You're new here but you should be aware that it is at a minimum a disciplinary offense, and at worst grounds for prosecution for common assault. We take a very dim view of using a glamour to obtain consent for unlawful activities, and furthermore we are prepared for and defended against it. So I advise you to drop it *right now* and refrain from doing it ever again in my presence. Do I make myself clear?"

Oscar's face is a perfect death mask of shock, every muscle hanging slack. "But you, I mean, I didn't—"

"Oscar," Emma hisses. "Drop it. I've got your number. You can't win this fight." Her ward is hot against her skin and she's having

to work hard to contain her anger. "You do not walk in here as a new recruit and try to roll your manager. Am I making myself understood?"

Oscar finally manages to nod, jerkily.

"Good. And in answer to your other point: we're the government, and we are engaged in a, a covert state of hostilities. If you would prefer me not to mince words, *we're at war*. This country abolished military conscription for the conventional services in 1960, but an exemption clause in the Act authorizes us to co-opt without limitation individuals who meet certain criteria, set by ourselves but principally defined by their awareness of and ability to program or control metaphysical phenomena.

"Now, the healthy functioning of the organization for which you *used* to work"—Emma does not miss the startled microexpression that flickers across Oscar's face—"is clearly aligned with the interests of the State, but as I mentioned, *we are at war*. It's a secret conflict, a wizard war if you like, but we are under threat of invasion by entities and agencies from beyond spacetime, ancient horrors that would make your toes curl and your hair turn gray overnight if you met them and were lucky enough to survive the experience. And not losing that war is *vastly* more important to the nation than ensuring the bottom line of an investment bank. Even if your annual bonus is at stake. Am I making myself clear?"

"But I—" Oscar swallows it. "I see," he says slowly, "that you believe there's a war on. And you have emergency regulations out of the 1940s to help you fight it. But is all this strictly *necessary*?" He hand-waves around the office, as if to encapsulate the dusty warrens and cubicle farms of the New Annex beyond. "Has anyone tried talking to these, ah, ancient horrors? Investigated what, if anything, they are after and looked for a compromise solution that would allow us to get on with business as usual? Your organization is—"

"Stop right there, Mr. Menendez, it's *your* organization now. You're subject to its lawful authority and subordinate to its goals. *If* we decide to let you go, you can go back to your bank. Until then, it's my job—one of my jobs—to evaluate the extent of the contribution you can make to the defense of the realm. As to your question, we're several steps ahead of you. Now, I will admit"—she pats the cardboard folder, so fresh it's barely dog-eared, that sits beside her monitor—"I'm a little perplexed. Some of my colleagues opine that your team, um, ruck, um—"

"Scrum?"

"*Scrum*—I'm afraid rugby was never my strong point—contains individuals who exhibit highly useful abilities in the areas of higher mathematics and necromancy, but the medical side effects of your condition present us with something of a conundrum. And then there's an irritatingly large community of our co-workers who refuse to believe that people like you can possibly exist in the first place. I'm afraid decades of being the go-to monster for second-rate Hammer Horror movies and the like have not predisposed the public to be accepting of persons of hemophagy. So for the time being you and your friends"—(Emma's deliberate mischaracterization of Oscar's relationship with his staff causes him to bristle satisfactorily)—"are going to have to pretend to a slightly different status. We have a cover story: you've been infected by a virus transmitted by an annoyingly biocompatible extradimensional intrusion which causes you to be photophobic and to succumb to sunburn and skin cancer in daylight. Your actual status is classified as confidential, and you should not discuss it with people who do not have the codeword clearance OPERA CAPE unless there's an emergency, such as needing to evacuate a burning building during hours of daylight. Do you understand?"

"Oh for—" Oscar's exasperation boils over. "What do you expect me to *do*?" he snaps. "I thought this induction was a formality! Over in two weeks and we could all get back to work. Instead we're stuck in a bad 1960s situation comedy, while my line managers will be expecting a report on the first week trading results of our new investment account, which is currently completely adrift. It could be in the hole for *millions*, for all I know, and I'll be held responsible!"

"You won't be." Emma MacDougal speaks with complete assurance. "Your head of quantitative trading is Sir David Finch. One of our people will have a quiet word with him. The bank may have bought back most of the shares that HMG acquired during the distressed trading a few years ago, but the Treasury is still into them for a sum that can be offset against any reasonable losses that your unit's experimental trading account can run up in a few weeks.

"As for how we're going to use you—well, that depends. You're familiar with the Territorial Army, or the Army Reserves as they're being renamed? In all probability, once we've assessed your capabilities and come up with a tailored action plan and general orientation package, you'll be conditionally discharged back into civilian life. You will remain liable for activation at short notice and will be expected to spend a month a year operating for us whatever else happens, but as far as the bank is concerned . . . you'll all be in the TA. It's a serious criminal offense to dismiss an employee for taking time out for TA service, and we can take steps to stagger your duty cycle so that there is minimal disruption to your business unit's operations. But all of this depends on your willing cooperation. If it isn't forthcoming, I'm afraid we may have to deal with you severely, Mr. Menendez. Do you understand?"

"I understand that this is blackmail."

"No, Mr. Menendez, this is *war*. It's a shame we had to have this conversation, and so soon in our relationship, but I think it's best that we know where we stand, don't you?"

Oscar inclines his head, not meeting her eyes.

"Well then." Emma smiles again. "Reading your file I notice that among other things, you've had some dealings with commercial intelligence services; at least, you've been paying STRATFOR an awful lot of money if all you were getting for it was their weekly newsletter. So. Why don't you tell me about it?"

"GOOD MORNING, MR. SCHWARTZ!" SAYS THE TRAINER. "I haven't seen you around before. I assume that means this is all new to you, and probably a bit confusing. So what are you expecting?"

Alex shuffles his feet uneasily. "I don't know. I was just told to come to room 118B after lunch for some sort of evaluation. This *is* room 118B, right?" Somehow he resists the urge to add, *Is this the room for an argument?* While there is something Pythonesque about the terribly old-fashioned British ambiance of this organization, something tells him that displaying inappropriate and irreverent humor could get him misfiled, drastically and permanently.

He is, truth be told, confused and apprehensive about the whole secret government agency thing that Mhari and Oscar pulled on the Scrum with no advance warning to speak of. At first it seemed to make sense, after a fashion: once you've swallowed one unpalatable fact before your metaphorical breakfast—vampires exist, oh, and by the way, *tag you're it*—then it is a short hop, skip, and a jump to accept that *of course* the government is aware of this inconvenient truthiness and has a secret agency for keeping it under wraps.

That Mhari used to work for this agency in her pre-banking days is perhaps an anomalous coincidence, but the revelation that magic is a branch of higher dimensional algebraic group theory is just plausible enough to explain why she ended up in Oscar's circle, and why the PHANG syndrome emerged from the particular algorithms Alex and the pigs had been told to work on, like an exotic poisonous spider tumbling from a box of bananas on a supermarket shelf.

The past several days have been a trial and an ordeal for Alex, even though the institutional feel of the organization he's been drafted into gives him persistent déjà vu flashbacks to encounters with the more arcane nooks and crannies of university administration.

"I'm Donald Paulson, and I'm part of our in-house professional skills development wing—staff training, if you like, or perhaps more accurately in-house higher education." Paulson has an indefinable air about him that instantly puts Alex in mind of staff common rooms and polite but distant quizzing by his dissertation supervisor's sanity monitors. Paulson smiles, apparently in an attempt to put Alex at his ease, but Alex finds the pulsing of his carotid artery too distracting. "I asked you here because as part of all staff induction processing we're required to administer a set of aptitude tests."

"Oh? What for?" Alex asks, leaning forward slightly, interested despite himself. "I mean, what traits are you examining?"

Paulson coughs into his fist. "Well, as an agency tasked with providing intelligence and countermeasures against paranormal threats, obviously we take a keen interest in computational demonology, inductive oneiromantic ontology, and the geometry of Riemannian manifolds, to say nothing of the applications of Kolmogorov complexity theory to topological . . ."

Alex realizes that Paulson is closely watching his expression while he reels off a list of everyday topics of discussion over the Scrum's coffee machine. So Alex nods, encouragingly. "And?"

"Well, I need to ask you to take a couple of multiple-choice tests. To see if you have an aptitude for the necessary abstract reasoning skills that we'd need to develop in order to train you up as an, ah, magician."

"Oh, that's all right then!" Alex says brightly. Alex *likes* puzzle challenges. "Out of curiosity, if your tests show I've got what it takes, what happens then?"

"Well, then we send you on a six-week training course. It's actually fun, if you're into that kind of thing; it's a boot camp for higher mathematics, taught by some of our brightest people. They start with an introduction to set theory and first order predicate calculus, then tackle the lambda calculus and the halting problem. I don't know if you've heard of them—"

Alex blinks. Words are coming out, but they don't make sense. This is training-wheels stuff, taken for granted at his level. "You're talking about a first-year undergraduate curriculum, yes?"

Paulson focusses on him. "Really?"

Alex blinks again. He said *the necessary abstract reasoning skills for magic*, he realizes. *Kid's stuff.* The flash of insight is devastating: *All I need is an entrypoint and I can probably figure this stuff out for myself* . . . "Yes, of course." He rubs his hands together. They're very cold, and he's been feeling hungry pretty much continuously ever since that Howard guy zapped him with the taser, but for the first time in days he barely notices the discomfort. "I'm ready for the tests, Mr. Paulson. Bring them on."

*   *   *

"I CAN'T *BELIEVE* WHAT THAT BITCH DID!"

"Which bitch? Or witch bitch? Are we still talking about Emma Dearest?"

Oscar fumes quietly in one corner of the black leather sofa in the living room of the hotel suite. "*Fucking* bitch."

"You're the one who's always telling everyone to quantify." Mhari is coolly unsympathetic. She walks over to the sideboard and twists off the cap of the complimentary bottle of pinot noir, pours two generous glasses, and carries them across to the sofa. Her heels sink into the thick carpet; she hands one of the glasses to Oscar, then carefully kicks off her shoes. "What are your losses?"

"Which ones?" He laughs bitterly for a moment. "Nine point two million down on trading as of close today. We can probably still make it up this quarter if I can get us up and running again by the end of next month, but that all depends on having a full hand of pigs sniffing for truffles, doesn't it? And that bitch intends to keep us on a tight leash, I'm sure of it." He looks morose. "There goes my end-of-year target. I'll be lucky to get a bent paper clip and a shirt button for a bonus. You, too, for that matter."

Mhari sits down next to him, smoothing her pencil skirt. She sips at the wine, pulls a face: it tastes *flat*, lifeless and flavorless even though it's nearly the color of venous blood. "Remember why we're doing it."

"Remind me again?"

"You need one of these." She puts her glass down on the coffee table, then pops her clutch open and pulls out a slim wallet. Flips it open and shows him a photo-ID card within. "A warrant card. This is mine."

"But that's—" Oscar pauses thoughtfully. "A warrant card?"

"You tried to tell Emma Dearest what to do, didn't you?" Mhari smiles sympathetically. "I'm surprised she didn't shoot you. Oscar, you don't *do* that to Laundry personnel. They're all warded, anyway.

But when—if—you've got one of these, it's like the you-gotta-believe-me thing, only better. You can tell someone you work for the government, any department at all, and they'll simply believe you. I've seen their people march into police crime scenes and tell the detectives they work for the Home Office and be believed. Or into military bases. You could tell people you work for the SFO and, well, you saw Mr. Howard, didn't you?"

"Huh. Didn't think much of him."

Mhari leans against Oscar; he raises his arm to make room for her. She compares her memories to the warm and dynamic presence beside her: the idiot ex comes off infinitely worse. "Neither do I, frankly. I don't know what I saw in him. But he's going to come in useful along the way, I think. The point is, once the Laundry have us pegged as working for them they're not going to consider the other possibilities until it's much too late. They place too much trust in trust—they assume their people are loyal, or at least rendered incapable of rebelling by their coercive geases. You know, the binding oath they made you swear. Do you feel any different?"

Oscar tenses for a moment. "Loyalty has always seemed to be a two-way street to me," he murmurs, which is music to her ears because it's exactly what he *ought* to be saying at this point, even though she's pretty sure that he doesn't mean it. Oscar sometimes seems blind to his own mildly suppressed sociopathic tendencies. "By my estimate they owe me at least ten million. If they really wanted my loyalty . . ."

"Exactly." She turns and nibbles on his earlobe, extracting a sharp intake of breath. "How are Pippa and the kids doing, anyway?"

"How are—? I don't know and don't care, frankly. She took them off to the Bahamas for a couple of weeks, something about seeing they spent some time with their grandfather. He refuses to set foot in the UK until it leaves the EU for some reason." She feels his free hand working its way around her shoulder, outlining her bra strap. "So I'm free for a while. Listen, I'm thirsty and this grape piss simply isn't cutting the mustard. How about you?"

"I could kill for a drink," she says wistfully. They've been dry for over a week at this point.

"Well then, why don't we? There are plenty of homeless people out round the back of the hotel who won't miss a couple of tubes full."

"I think that's a great idea. Okay, let's nip out for a midnight snack. And then . . ."

He stands, rising smoothly to his feet, and offers her a hand. "And then?" He raises an eyebrow.

"Mammals, Discovery Channel, you know the Bloodhound Gang song." Mhari grins, alive with anticipation, and slides her stockinged feet back into her heels. There's nothing like a bit of glam to make people let you get close enough to strike, she thinks. That goes for institutions as well as individuals.

"And then," Oscar slides an arm around her waist as they head towards the door, "we should talk exit strategies."

12.

GREEN LIME

LIFE GOES ON.

Over the next week, Mo gradually recovers some of her usual humor and level-headedness: a couple of visits to the security-cleared therapist are approved, and a discreet prescription or two. I try to do the supportive husband thing, with mixed results: I also request my own visits with the security-cleared therapist. Meanwhile, back in the office, I throw myself into the mundane administrivia of life: mentoring Pete (who in turn is mentoring Alex), minuting meetings of COBWEB MAZE and BLOODY BARON, helping Andy fill out the forms necessary to justify assigning him a permanent new office, writing up critical reports on the proposed network infrastructure of the Dansey House redevelopment,* and trying to find time to schedule my annual training workload in the middle of all this.

---

* The proposal to flood-fill the building with dark fiber and light it up on demand would be great if it didn't run headfirst up against the equally high-priority proposal to make the entire place an airtight Faraday-caged box with optical, as well as e/m spectrum, emission control . . .

I'm also taking extended lunch breaks, because unfortunately Sally Carlyle made her little make-work (it was clearly—let's be honest about this—a "get Bob out of my hair" gambit) stick to the minutes. So I'm spending a not insignificant portion of my time reading vampire novels. There's a stack a meter deep in the corner of my office, expensed from Waterstones.

I argued for a Kindle but they pointed out that if it could be associated with me, then the information bleed—Amazon logging every page turn and annotation—was a potential security hazard. Not to mention the darker esoteric potential of spending too much time staring at a device controlled by a secretive billionaire in Seattle. The void stares also, and so on.

The giant hairball of nodes, names, and lines in different colors (labelled "drinks," "fucks," "turns," "fights," and "author is confused") is growing into a mammoth file on my computer. I must confess it's mildly distracting, and not too onerous a chore, but *oy!* the misconceptions. Ancient solitary predatory creatures of the night, my ass. Fashion sense, my ass. (I've had Dick in my office. When he's not trying to cause maximum eyeball trauma while staying just within the envelope defined by the bank's dress code, he looks like a hipster. A *trailing edge* hipster, if such a thing is possible; as deliberately uncool as an experimental fusion reactor.)

But at least the project means that whenever Sally sends me a needling email asking for an ETA on my report, I'm able to say: "2,891 pages down and graphed, 3,385 to go." And when she says, "Why can't you automate it?" I can point to the memo forbidding us from selling our personally identifying data to the Big River Corporation, whose terms and conditions of service are incompatible with our security policy. Check *mate*.

The next Wednesday I make my way into the office on foot, as usual. I take the shortcut along the ley line. It's late enough in the autumn that there's a distinct chill in the air; so close to the BST/GMT clock change that I approach the side door in the wan, predawn gloom. Wrapped up in worries about the upcoming weekly DRES-

DEN RICE meeting this afternoon, I barely notice at first when my ward—worn on a cord around my neck—throbs. Once for a warning: someone or something is watching me.

Then it throbs again. *That* gets my attention. I spin round, scanning for threats, and open my inner eye and feel *hunger*. Then I look down. "Oh. You again. Go away." It's the cat that's been hanging around the dumpsters for the past couple of weeks. At least, I think it's the same one. Small and black, it's looking rather damp and miserable right now. It gazes up at me and chirps like a bird. "No, really, you don't want to follow me in here. The night staff would eat you."

I look away—eye contact only encourages them—and punch in the keycode. But as I step inside the darkened lobby I feel something brush against my leg. Stupid animal! The door slams behind me and I pull out my torch and head towards the stairs, then a pang of conscience prompts me to hesitate.

I hear shuffling footsteps approaching from beyond the nearest fire doors. "Here, puss. Puss?" It'll be the night staff, coming to eat the intruders. I fumble my warrant card out of an inside pocket, transfer it to the hand holding the torch. "Cat? Puss? Here—"

"Grraaaah . . ."

I look around, inner eye wide open. *Hunger and fear.* A body limned in balefire hunches towards me, arms outstretched, as the fuzzy nexus of deprivation that got my ward's attention hurtles away from it with a startled hiss and runs up my leg.

"Fuuuck!"

That's me, screaming. I am not a fan of impromptu body piercings, and the stupid little hairball is *sharp*. Luckily I'm wearing jeans and a padded coat against the cold, so once the self-propelled barbed wire makes it past my belt line it's just a weight. It gloms onto my chest, shivering, and I wrap an arm around it as I raise my warrant card and tell the night watchman to piss off. Starving, cold, and the cat's just met a zombie: I resign myself to an inevitable trip to the Battersea Cats and Dogs Home at lunchtime. Maybe I can delegate it to someone . . .

"Ooh, isn't she *cute*?" I blink at Trish as I pass the reception area.

She's in work uncharacteristically early. "I didn't know you had a pet, Mr. Howard!"

"I don't," I tell her, and feel like a shit as her face falls. "It just followed me inside."

"Oh, that's a shame." Trish blinks a couple of times. "Do you think she's a stray?"

"Might be, it's been haunting the dumpsters out back for the past few weeks. I think it's feral. I was going to take her to the Cat and Dog Home at lunchtime . . ."

"But it's October! And look, she's all black." Trish looks alarmed. "Don't you know what the bad kids do to black cats at Hallowe'en?"

I can live without this. "Listen, I've got a meeting later this morning. I'll put her—him, it, whatever—in my office for now. Do you think you could scare up a bowl and fill it with water? And a file box and an old tee shirt or blanket or something. She—it's—pretty damp."

"Yes! I'll see what I can do."

I head for my office. My passenger is still clinging to my coat, breathing fast. When I close the door I notice there's an odd buzzing noise coming from somewhere in my office. It takes me a while to work out that the electrics are just fine and it's the cat. So I sit down at my desk to check the email and figure out what to do about this added minor complication, and that's when my calendar pops up a reminder. The DRESDEN RICE meeting time has changed: it's been brought right forward and starts in half an hour.

What a way to begin the day!

LEAVING THE HAIRY GRIFTER TO TRISH'S TENDER MERCIES, I gather up the necessary file folders and shuffle off to the meeting by way of the nearest coffee station. I am sub-optimally prepared to face two hours of vacuous inanity, senile discursive rants, passive-aggressive office politics, and jokes in questionable taste; but at least I've resisted the temptation to borrow Harry the Horse's AA-12 assault shotgun and a couple of fragmentation grenades. I *am* carrying a vampire novel with malice in mind, in case it should become necessary to telegraph extreme boredom and disdain in the middle of the meeting. (I have a theory that they can't reasonably censure you for pointedly doing something they tasked you with.) But my main goal for this morning's session is simply to come away from it with my sanity intact and no additional make-work tasks. And I'll count it as a bonus if, when I get back to it, my office doesn't smell of cat piss . . .

I'm a minute or two early and it's a Wednesday morning, so I'm not surprised to find myself the second person present. Sally has beaten me to it—this committee is her little red wagon—but if her face was any longer she'd need a handcart to hold it off the floor. "So you've come to gloat, have you?" she asks, before I even have a chance to put my coffee mug and papers down. "I hope you're pleased with yourself!"

"Um, what?"

"Going behind my back, playing politics, *that's* what, Mr. Howard. You've got your way, but don't think this is the end of it!" She gives me the evil eye, then goes back to shuffling together printed hardcopies of the minutes from the last meeting, the agenda of the coming one, and some other random crap that she obviously thinks is too important to trust to the secure email system.

I pull out my chair, sit down heavily, and say: "I have no idea what you're talking about."

Sally rounds on me: "Oh yes you do! If not you, who else went to Mahogany Row whining to have me replaced as chair?" *Now* her anger is palpable: I recoil, and it takes me a second or two to realize that she might actually be right. The door opens: other people begin filtering in. Bill, Basil, Doris, Katie from Facilities . . . *If Lockhart delivered,* I think hopefully, *then the new chair will at least have clearance for OPERA CAPE, and we can start work on a reality-based policy—* "Here she is," Sally says quietly (and more than a trifle bitterly): "Meet our latest greasy pole dance—er, climber."

"Hello, everybody!" says our new member. "I've been assigned the chair of this committee!" Her teeth gleam as she looks around the room, making eye contact with everybody except me. "I'd like to thank Sally for her sterling work in getting the process started, but her talents are in too much demand to waste on a peripheral planning exercise like this, so I've been parachuted in to hold the fort for her while she focusses on higher priorities! So"—she briskly taps her papers into shape in front of her, looking as terrifyingly efficient as a front bench government minister—"I'd like to start by going once around the room clockwise, asking everybody to introduce themselves and give a thirty-second rundown of what they've achieved since the last session. I'll begin as I've nothing to report other than my name: Mhari Murphy! And I'm looking forward to working with you all. Now you, Ms. Greene? I believe you hold the Health and Safety brief on this working group. What deliverables have you achieved since last Wednesday . . . ?"

I STUMBLE BACK TO MY OFFICE IN A HAZE OF CONFUSION AND mild misery, tempered only by the mild schadenfreude I feel at seeing Sally get her just desserts.

Watching Mhari run the meeting was . . . well, it was enlightening. She's sharper than when I knew her a decade ago, and also more mature, more in control, more . . . everything, really. Authoritative. Charismatic. She's blossomed into a truly formidable committee warrior, and if I didn't know better, if I'd met her for the first time today, I'd assess her as a very promising hotshot who is destined for executive-level advancement in the very near term. She didn't just run it on wheels, she ran it like a TGV: blasting through the minutes of the previous meeting, then switching track seamlessly onto an any-other-business siding that pared away at the dead wood, soothing egos as she dismissed the chair-fillers and time-servers back to their regular duties, thanking them and relieving them of the need to attend future sessions.

Sally would have taken most of two hours and barely gotten anything done. Mhari, in contrast, rips through the agenda in under forty minutes.

In the end we are down to four people: Mhari, Katie from Facilities, Sally from HR, and me. And then she lays her cards on the table.

"Katie, Sally, I'd like to thank you for your work so far. However, as you probably know, this committee is a false flag operation and whoever set the terms of reference failed to require a certain code-word clearance from everybody concerned. So I'd like to ask you to go back to your offices and request clearance for OPERA CAPE before the next meeting. It's a limited-confidential clearance, not secret or higher, so you'll probably get it—but until you're on the distribution list I can't discuss our business further. The only people who're currently cleared for it are myself and Mr. Howard, so this concludes the non-confidential part of our meeting for today. If you'd like to go? No, not you, Bob."

There is shuffling of papers, and dark muttering, and a little bit of *well I never*, but even without the vampire mind control thing Mhari is good at getting her way. Two minutes later we're alone in the meeting room, sizing each other up like strange cats.

"You stage-managed that coup remarkably well," I admit.

I am, let's face it, a little bit uncomfortable. Mhari has—*had*—my number, or my younger alter-ego's number, or something like that. But I'm ten years older and a lot wiser these days. And on the other hand, she shows every sign of having done a lot of growing up, too.

"I've spent a decade managing boardrooms full of would-be sharks, Bob. You learn to lead them by the nose or they eat you. '3,385 pages to go,'" Mhari mimics, then smiles. "I can't *believe* you let Sally dump that on you!"

I shrug. "It's quite relaxing, actually."

"Makes a change from laying cables?"

"Something like that."

"So you've spent the past decade managing servers, laying cables, and being a doormat." I can tell she doesn't believe this—office tech support drones don't get sent to probe nests of vampires—but she's on a fishing expedition and I have no intention of giving her any ammunition.

"You could say that." I smile, but I don't show her my teeth because I'm using them to hold my tongue in place. "Working my way towards retirement one day at a time, that's what I'm doing." (By lying to ex-girlfriends. Don't you feel proud of yourself, Bob?) "But that's not important. Mhari, what are you trying to achieve here?"

"I'd have thought it was perfectly obvious." She gives me a wide-eyed look, emphasized by the subtly applied eye shadow—not something the old Mhari would have bothered with. (She may have matured and gained depth along the way, but she's lost something as well.) "I'm just a girl trying to make ends meet and get by in a harsh, uncaring world."

"By working with blood-sucking fiends who drain the life out of people. Also, vampires."

A flicker of anger, instantly suppressed. "If you had *any* idea how much shit I've had to put up with—" She slams on the brakes. "Listen, I know we had some bad misunderstandings in the past. But that's over, isn't it? We're both grown-ups now, aren't we?" I nod. She continues: "Well *good*, because we have to work together on this. These—*idiots*—who don't believe in vampires—"

"'Vampires don't exist.'" I finger-quote as I say it.

"No, listen to me, Bob, this is not the time for your passive-aggressive denial thing. I said yes to taking on this committee because, let's just say, *Dracula* was a novel about syphilis, right? I'm not Lucy Westenra. Or Mina Harker, for that matter. And having a policy based on works of fiction is worse than having no policy at all.

"You know, and I know, that my condition—that of me and my colleagues—is both a threat and an opportunity for this organization. I'd vastly prefer it to show up on the opportunity side of the balance sheet, because I know how the Laundry deals with liabilities. From my point of view it's a simple utilitarian calculus. I need this committee to emit a set of sample guidelines for the care, feeding, and employment of PHANGs, and I don't care whether most of the dead wood on the board have that ridiculous OPERA CAPE clearance—who comes up with these codewords anyway?—or not, as long as I'm safe from sunlight, don't starve to death, and nobody wants to hunt me down and stick a cricket stump through my ribs. I'm not going to let you, or anybody else, get in the way of that."

She stares at me, level-headed, with such chilly self-assurance that

I find myself nodding almost in spite of myself. "Also, I'd like to put it to you that the value proposition to this organization of having a team of vampires on call is not insignificant; I'm just surprised nobody's thought of it already."

"Are you sure they haven't?" I look right back at her with all three eyes. "If it wasn't for this ubiquitous, um, conviction that people like you don't exist, I'm sure they would have, by now . . ." I trail off.

Seen through my regular ocular appendages, Mhari looks like a fine specimen of Modern Management Woman. She's neatly groomed, somewhere on the handsome/striking scale rather than the pretty/ beautiful one: a couple of notches below "jaw-dropper," but still a head-turner (especially if you're me). But, seen through my third eye—she *glows*. She's an occult powerhouse. Not worm-riddled, but strong and healthy and full of a strange vitality that simply does not belong inside the body of a human being.

She notices me staring—"Bob, what are you . . . ?"—then she meets my gaze with eyes that are clearly seeing more than light: "*Bob?* What *have* you done to yourself?"

Well, trying to conceal the changes from her was always going to be a losing battle.

I shrug. "You remember Angleton, don't you?" She nods; a flicker of fear crosses her face. "These days I'm his personal assistant." (Her sharp intake of breath is gratifying, but it comes at a high price. She's a lot less likely to underestimate me now.) "I also work part-time for a couple of other departments. And along the way I got married."

"Oh, really?" She says lightly, but a little shakily: "Congratulations! So are there any little Bobs running around?"

"Not exactly." I flash on the memory of the recurring bad dream: an empty crib and a violinist with hollow eyes. "But enough social chitchat. You didn't stay late after school just to catch up on the gossip, did you?"

"No." She shrugs, fetchingly—I can't help my male gaze, dammit— and continues. "I'm going to write the findings, you're going to help me, and we're going to get everyone to sign off on a shiny new PHANG Integration Protocol. It's going to run like clockwork and at the end of the day I get what I want and the organization acquires a protocol for dealing with a new type of asset." A smile, a flash of teeth, an impish callback to long-ago intimacy. "You're here because I wanted to make sure that you understand that you're going to help me if you know what's good for you, because I will not tolerate passive-aggressive resistance, let alone active subversion. If you don't like it"—another shrug, and this time I'm *certain* she's vamping deliberately to draw my attention to her boobs—"I'll find a way to make you sorry. Are we clear?"

"Clear," I say. Then—I'm not too proud to admit it—I run like hell.

Her mocking laughter follows me out the door.

THERE IS A CERTAIN DRAB CORRIDOR IN THE NEW ANNEX.

Most of the doors opening off it are small, windowless rooms used for document storage. At the far end from civilization there is a fire door, beyond which there is an emergency stairwell with whitewashed brick walls, illuminated by grimy tungsten bulbs like something out of a 1960s noir movie. Halfway down the stairs there is a landing with an unmarked door. Casual explorers usually assume it's where the night shift rest up during daylight hours and give it a miss; there are few regular visitors.

After blowing out of the DRESDEN RICE meeting with Mhari's threat fresh in mind I go straight there and knock three times.

"Enter, boy!"

Boy. I've lately concluded that in Angleton's public schoolmaster usage it reflects a certain distant affection. In any case it's better than some of the other things he could call me. (Dinner, for instance.) So I place my hand on the doorknob, which is stuffed full of so many lethal defensive wards that it positively hums, and push.

If the corridor was '60s noir then Angleton's windowless den is '40s pulp horror, if the mad scientist's lab was designed to accommodate a mad library science professor. The walls are lined from floor-to-ceiling with oak index card drawers, varnished so heavily they are almost black; the floor is dominated by a hulking green-topped metal table, topped by something that looks like a microfilm reader engaging in intimate congress with a stenotypist. It's actually a 1940s Memex, an opto-mechanical hypertext information storage machine. When it was new it cost about as much as a strategic bomber. This is the only working example I am aware of, and it has been so heavily customized by the enchantments applied to it by its long-term user that it is certainly unique.

Angleton sits behind the Memex, a gaunt figure with pale, almost translucent skin and deep-set, burning eyes. He's speed-reading something on screen, a set of vernier dials pinched between thumb and forefinger as he taps out Baudot code with his other hand. I wait for a minute. Finally he pauses, shoves the huge viewing apparatus back on its hydraulic arm, and looks at me. "Well?"

"Well what?"

"You didn't come here to ask if I take one lump or two in my tea, boy. Something's come up. Spill it, or go away: I have things to do and important people to brief."

I pull out the visitor's chair (wooden, with a leather seat that's as hard as a board) and sit. "It's the DRESDEN RICE committee. Someone, quite possibly Lockhart, is using it to fuck with me."

Angleton looks at me. This feels a lot like being a bug on a microscope slide, pinned under searchlights for scrutiny by a vast, inhuman intelligence. "Inhuman" is actually quite accurate, because Angleton *isn't* entirely human: for one thing his current body is at least a century old, and for another thing, the mind occupying it isn't the one it came with. There exists a class of entity that have been known since antiquity as hungry ghosts. One of them—the being known as the Eater of Souls—has a rep for being able to take over bodies and go walkabout, among other things. Several decades ago some of my less scrupulous predecessors deliberately summoned it and bound it into a human body; luckily for them, the aforementioned hungry ghost decided that its long-term interests aligned with those of the organization. (He *went native*. In a boarding-school staff room.) Which is why these days he can be found lurking in a basement office, reading dusty microfilm records and monstering former interns like me.

"Boy," the Eater of Souls asks, "what makes you think it's about you?"

"But I—" I stop. "Let's see." I force myself to rewind to the beginning. "I started poking into data mining epidemiology stats under the pretext of running a ten-percenter. You know Lockhart's been steering me towards running my own operations? I don't *think* anyone prodded me in that particular direction, but one thing leads to another and before you know it, there's a Code Blue. At the other end of which I run into a rather dubious off-site operation being stage-managed by, er, Ms. Murphy—"

"I know about your history." Angleton looks bored, rather than disapproving: he probably puts it down to human foibles. "Continue."

"Are you cleared for BLUE DANDELION and OPERA CAPE?" I ask. It never hurts to check.

"Don't be silly, Bob, *everyone* knows vampires don't exist." Angleton snarks like no other person I've ever met.

I do a double take. "You don't think—ah, ignore me. Okay, I got seconded to OPERA CAPE because someone needs to keep an eye on it and it might be a good way of getting . . . oh."

"Yes, Bob. Perhaps you should have asked Gerald?"

"You mean he's behind Mhari taking over the committee. This is the BLUE DANDELION thing, isn't it? Forcing her to interact with me so that I can bait her?"

"Well, you didn't think she could hijack it all by herself, did you?"

"Oh. Sorry. I feel thick; I'm slow on the uptake sometimes."

"It's true, though," Angleton says, in portentous tones, "that everyone *knows* vampires don't exist."

"Yes, but—" I stop.

"Yes, indeed." Angleton grins cadaverously.

I look at him. "Some people would say . . ."

"Don't be silly, boy. *I'm* not a vampire: I don't drink blood and combust in sunlight. And neither do you!"

"But there's more than one origin to the myth, isn't there?"

"Yes." Angleton briefly touches his Memex. "If I've been trying to teach you anything it's to always look for the gaps, boy. The blind spots. The nightmares that lurk in the holes nobody peers into."

My mind's spinning. "Are you suggesting that there is a *reason* why everybody around here knows vampires don't exist? Like, perhaps, a person infected with PHANG who, shall we say, is thoroughly embedded within the organization and makes a point of suppressing knowledge of their existence?"

"I couldn't possibly say." Angleton leans back and contemplates the cobwebs in the corners of the ceiling. "What do *you* think?"

"Well, let's see. If such a person exists, they're obviously very secretive and a very powerful ritual magician. It's not you or me, obviously, or we wouldn't be having this conversation. Presumably they've been working here for a long time to get their geas bedded in so deeply. Long enough that you can't identify them directly." (I suddenly realize something.) "And, um. The arrival of a bunch of newbie vamps– sorry, PHANG cases, with no sense of secrecy, would presumably put their nose out of joint because it would risk blowing their cover. Whatever the reason for maintaining it might be. Um. The K syndrome analog? If they *have* to feed periodically, then, um, that would imply killing people. On an ongoing basis. Obviously if they're official then Mahogany Row would have something to do with keeping them supplied"—I really don't like where this train of thought is leading me, but Angleton is nodding along from time to time, listening silently, which leads me to believe I'm on the right trail, however gruesome and body-strewn it might be—"with victims."

"Not that common, actually," Angleton volunteers at last. "The frequency of vampirism has historically been low. The sane ones usually kill themselves as soon as the implications sink in, and the *in*sane ones are, shall we say, not well adapted for survival in the human society they are dependent on."

"So they *do* exist! Officially."

"We may be on the verge of an unprecedented outbreak, Bob. A side effect of CASE NIGHTMARE GREEN: with the stars in alignment and the potentiation of all magical powers, it's becoming increasingly easy for the V-parasites to break through and acquire new hosts."

"Jesus."

"Yeshua ben Yusuf won't save you, boy, for that you need to be fast and smart and move in daylight. Vampirism may be contagious, but it is memetically so, rather than genetic: before you can acquire it you need to be a practiced logician, if not a practitioner in your own rights. You and I are, of course, immune to that particular cognitive parasite—we have our own abnormality. But I assume you are aware of the Black pre-prints? Areas of research that are discouraged due to the high frequency of spontaneous human combustion among people who think too hard about certain questions? One might wonder *why* a group of quantitative analysts were pointed in the direction of those particular algorithms, and by whom. If someone was considering the possibility of raising an army of vampirism-augmented sorcerers, perhaps they might start by conducting experiments on a limited scale . . . It is in any event a complex jigsaw and if you wish to assemble it fully you will first need to locate the source of that troublesome and ubiquitous disbelief that pervades our organization."

"You're telling me that the Scrum are probably pawns in a game of vamp versus vamp?"

"No, Bob, you deduced that for yourself. You may or may not be correct. *I do not know.* However, I would strongly advise you to investigate further."

"So, er . . . who is he?"

Angleton crosses his arms. He looks annoyed. "I don't know."

"*You* don't know?" I stare at him in disbelief.

"I am not omnipotent, boy. Or omniscient. We are discussing the possible existence of a *very* powerful sorcerer, immune from K syndrome and probably more than a century old, who has encrusted our organizational premises with an obfuscatory geas going back decades. They predate my arrival and probably know enough about me to stay out of my way." His expression of irritation deepens.

"Okay, so let's say there *is* a long-term PHANG in the Laundry, and you don't know who he is—surely at least you have a suspect in mind?" (Yes, *he*. If we're talking about someone older than Angleton, we're talking about a prewar sorcerer. Pre–*First* World War.)

Angleton shakes his head. "I have suspicions. But I don't want to share them with you; they might lead you down a blind alley."

"If you insist." I pause. "So we have this invisible blood-sucking mole within the organization. But there's also another long-term PHANG outside the big tent, and he's lately set up the Scrum to, to, start a fight with our PHANG?" Angleton nods. "But they must have been doing this on and off for decades!"

"Correct, Bob. We are discussing some of the world's deadliest magician-assassins; if you meet our in-house monster you should be at pains not to underestimate him, however meek and mild he might seem. They play their vicious games using a range of proxies. The Scrum are proxies. *You* or *I* might be proxies, without ever knowing it. You might consider investigating where the suggestion to look for K syndrome clusters using the NHS data warehouse originated—but I expect he's covered his traces well.

"The key facts are that he works with what he knows, and because he is embedded in the Laundry, what he knows is *us*. So: let us suppose that our in-house monster became aware that his long-term adversary was beginning a series of experiments intended to eventually give him an army of tractable vampire minions. (My understanding is that such attempts have hitherto always failed, because viable vampires are anything but tractable.) In response, our man inserted Ms. Murphy into the adversary's experiment, and arranged for you to find her: a stroke of pure genius. One might even speculate that he planned it as a move to steal his rival's toy-box, the baby PHANGs. But now the adversary can't help but realize he's being played—and sooner or later he'll retaliate. Either by throwing his toys on the floor, or by upsetting the game board."

"Wait, what—" My head's spinning.

Angleton turns back to his Memex. "Get out of here, boy, I've got a job to do. Call me if you need my help, but not until you're in over your head."

I stand up. "Be like that!" I vent. The Eater of Souls doesn't dignify my tantrum with his attention. I leave.

IT IS ONLY AS I PUT MY HAND ON MY OFFICE DOOR'S HANDLE that I realize I've forgotten something, and I'm too late to cancel the arm movement that pushes down and shoves the door partway open before I complete it.

Someone—presumably Trish—has installed feline conveniences.

There is an object on the floor that resembles an animal carrier at first, except it's got a plastic swing-door on the front. After a moment I realize it's a covered litter tray. There are a couple of plastic bowls at the other side of the room, one containing water and the other half-full with dry brown kibble. It looks like breakfast cereal but smells revolting. Or maybe (a horrible thought) the smell's coming from the litter tray. I head for my desk and see a receipt on my computer keyboard as I sit down—

"WAAAOW!"

An air raid siren goes off under my arse. I jackknife forward, and a bolt of black furry lightning hurtles out from under me and lands in the corner by the door, its back arched and tail fluffed out like a bog-brush. It gives me the evil eye as I hyperventilate, then slowly lower myself back down onto my chair seat.

"That's all right, pay no attention to me, just make yourself at home," I tell the self-propelled whoopee cushion, then audit the itemized receipt with a sinking heart. Judging from the bottom line, cats fall somewhere between a new Porsche and a used Lamborghini in running costs, and I've got a nasty suspicion that I'm not going to be able to expense this claim. I mean, I might be able to concoct an experimental protocol that involves hosting one all-black specimen of *Felis catus* in the lap of luxury before sacrificing it on a summoning grid—but I suspect that would annoy Trish, and one should always avoid pissing off the departmental secretary.

The potential sacrifice-to-be stares at me mistrustfully, then sits down and begins to wash its left hind leg, which it stretches out in front of it. I examine it from a safe distance. It's a generic short-haired black cat, slightly tattered about the edges and a bit skinny. There's a kink in its tail as if it was broken once. Gradually the blob of darkness works its tongue into the gaps between its claws, and I realize there's something odd about its paw. Cats don't have opposable thumbs, do they? Unless there's some medical condition . . .

I shake my head, unlock the computer, and haul down a shiny new VM from our classified information repository. (It seems a bit excessive to create and download a whole new Windows Vista guest instance in order to open a new notepad document and type a few notes, but that's how we're supposed to roll these days.) I'm partway through typing up some notes on the DRESDEN RICE mess and Angleton's advice pertaining thereto when there's a knock on the door. "Come in!" I call. As the door opens, the cat looks up in sudden alarm and scrambles for cover under my desk. *Oh great.* It's Andy. "Well?" he asks, with the expression of a friend who can't quite bring himself to ask how the blind date he fixed up on a dare went.

"Come in and sit down," I suggest, "but watch your feet."

"Watch for"—Andy spots the litter tray—"what?"

"It's the stray that was hanging around the dumpsters; it followed me in." Andy sits down. "I was going to take it to the Cat and Dog Home at lunchtime but Trish has unilaterally decided I'm adopting it."

"She probably thought you needed the humanizing touch," Andy agrees as he sits down. There's another knock on the door.

"Yes?" I call.

"Hello, Bob. Got a minute?" It's Pete. He spots Andy: "Oh, hello."

I give up any thought of getting any actual work done, shut down and save the VM, and push my keyboard away. "You might as well both make yourselves at home. Pay no attention to the hairy squatter, it's going to the Cat and Dog—"

"Oh *hello*," says Pete, kneeling and peering under my desk. "Aren't *you* a fine one?"

He is answered by a curious chirrup. I glance at Andy.

"Has it been positively vetted?" he asks.

"Very droll." The vicar is allowing his index finger to be sniffed from the shadows.

"I'm serious," Andy adds. "Strange animals, lurking around our back door, waiting to be taken in—could it be bugged?"

"What, you mean like the crazy CIA project from the sixties? Electric Kitty? No, Acoustic Kitty?"

Andy shrugs. "Or like our paper clips. Destiny-entangle it with a littermate, keep littermate in a summoning grid, anything one cat hears the other cat hears also. You just have to figure out a way of making it sing."

"Well *that's* a—"

Pete stands up, holding a buzzing black furball. He looks at me accusingly. "You are not going to take Spooky here to a cat shelter! You are going to take—er—*her* home and give her the love and affection she so obviously deserves." He scritches the little monster under its chin: it buzzes like a badly grounded transformer.

I close my eyes for a moment and open my inner eye. I stare at Pete, and the thing in his arms. Human. Cat. Human. Cat. No doubled vision: it's a cat, singular. A solitary diurnal ambush hunter with good hearing and binocular vision and a predilection for biting the neck of its prey in half while disemboweling it with the scythe-like claws on its hind legs. Basically it's a velociraptor with a fur coat and an outsize sense of entitlement. Right now it has convinced Pete that it is harmless, but I know better: just give them thumbs and in no time at all they'll have us working in the tuna mines, delivering cans from now until eternity. (*Hey, wait a minute, doesn't this one* have *thumbs?*)

I open my eyes again. "Andy, it's just a cat, not a Black Chamber spy wearing a furry suit. Pete, we can talk about what to do with Spooky later." (I can tell the name's going to stick: What else do you call a stray cat that decides to adopt a secret intelligence agency?) "Drag up a pew and I'll give you an update on the meeting." Pete, despite his extremely probationary status, has got clearance for OPERA CAPE by default, if only because it would be impossible for him to mentor Alex without it, and Andy was in on the original Code Blue.

"The DRESDEN RICE committee is supposed to formulate policy for dealing with, ah, PHANG syndrome as they're calling it. From a human resources and health and safety perspective. First it was nobbled from the top down—the only person on it with OPERA CAPE clearance was yours truly, and it was over-endowed with WOMBATs." (A WOMBAT is a Waste Of Money, Brains, And Time: the non-IT equivalent of a PEBCAK. (A PEBCAK is a Problem that Exists Between Chair And Keyboard. (You get the picture: it's parenthesized despair all the way down.))) "So I complained to Lockhart"—Andy looks at me sharply, but Pete, bless his little cotton socks, shows no sign of awareness, being focussed entirely on fulfilling the hedonistic whims of a furry egomaniac with a brain the size of a walnut—"who said he'd investigate. Anyway, the upshot is that the DRESDEN RICE chair was replaced by someone who does indeed have OPERA CAPE clearance . . . Mhari."

"Mhari." Andy frowns: it was a long time ago. "Wasn't she your—"

"Never mind that," I say hastily, "the point is, they just handed Dracula the keys to the blood bank."

"Why would they do that?" Pete looks up, interested, to the apparent displeasure of his lap fungus. "For that matter, who are the 'they' you speak of?"

"Management," I say hastily, just as Andy says "Mahogany Row." I send him a dark look.

"What's Mahogany Row?" asks Pete.

"*Management,*" I say firmly. Andy looks as if he's about to contradict me, then gets the message and shuts up. "So-called because back in Dansey House—which is currently a hole in the ground, thanks to the public-private partnership that's years behind schedule on the refurbishment—the floor the executive offices were on had plush carpet and mahogany-paneled walls. Very old-school, high-end civil service."

This is actually only about 25 percent falsehood: Mahogany Row (the office floor) *did* have tropical hardwood paneling, and if the bastards from Ove Arup or Foster Associates or Wimpey or whoever have vandalized it some of us will be very annoyed. But describing

Mahogany Row (the people) as "management" is a bit like calling a B-52 bomber an "air freight delivery vehicle." They manage problems, yes. The rest of the organization exists to support them, certainly. But the *way* they manage problems resembles normal management practice the way a B-52's cargo of free-fall thousand-pound bombs resembles a Post Office sorting room.

Pete points a questioning index finger at the ceiling and makes a circling motion while raising an eyebrow.

"What?" asks Andy.

"You make it sound like the House of Bishops. Somewhat political and hands-off."

"They are, usually," I explain. If they weren't, there'd be glowing craters all over the landscape. "But in this case it really looks like a case of hands-on management, with some deliberate meddling."

"This Mary—"

"Mhari."

"Mhari. What's wrong with her? Apart from . . ."

I shrug. "Apart from her being my long-ago psycho ex? She's one of *them*, Pete. A PHANG, a Person of Hemophagic Autocombusting Nocturnal Glamour, or whatever the fuck the politically correct acronym stands for this morning. She's a stakeholder in the whole process and she's been given *carte blanche* to control the outcome of a committee process tasked with defining policy for Human Resources with specific reference to Workplace Health and Safety, employee special needs subject to the Equalities Act (2010), and other relevant legislation. What DRESDEN RICE comes up with has the potential to be set in stone—"

"Stop!" I stop, startled by Pete's interruption. He raises a hand. "Can you tell me what's wrong with that? Because what I'm hearing is, if you had an equivalent committee looking into the needs of, say, an Orthodox Jew or a paraplegic in a wheelchair, you'd object to the group in question being represented on the committee—"

Andy shakes his head, for which I'm profoundly grateful, because I seem to have stepped on a landmine in the fraught field of discrimination awareness, and it's only a matter of time before someone unmasks me as a running dog of the oligoheteropatriarchy. (Which I will cop to, but it's a hell of a handicap to play under when you're participating in a game of privilege bingo.) "There's a fundamental difference between a vampire and a regular human minority, Pete: normal people don't have super-strength, mind control powers, and a thirst for blood."

"Also," I add, "the committee seems to have been weighted from the outset with the aforementioned WOMBATs. Whose defining characteristic seems to be that *they don't believe in vampires.* So someone upstairs put a vampire with rad mind control skillz in charge of a ship of fools who are blind to the problem this presents. Like, oh, the whole new variant K syndrome thing that led me to them in the first place."

"New variant *what*?"

"K syndrome; it's a kind of dementia that ritual magicians are prone to," Andy explains. "What Bob found was a new one, let's call it *V* syndrome. It doesn't affect the PHANGs themselves: it affects their victims. Looks a lot like Kuru or Mad Cow Disease, only it kills within weeks."

"Oh dear"—Pete's hand moves instinctively to his throat—"God."

"They still eat and drink normal food," I add. "I've seen them in the staff canteen, complaining about the mac and cheese just like everyone else. So it seems to be more like the transitive-hemophagic-curse model of vampirism than the blood-drinking-zombie story. The trouble is, we don't know yet if everyone they feed on develops V syndrome. And we don't know whether they can live without human blood, or use some acceptable substitute, or whatever. Or how often they need to feed. If it turns out to be optional, well, that'd be like the question of celibacy in the priesthood, wouldn't it?" Pete nods thoughtfully. Sandy, his wife, is due to pop in about two months' time. "But if they have to feed or die, and the victims *also* die, what the hell are we going to do with them?"

"That's a sharp dilemma." Pete pauses. "Maybe find donors who are terminally ill . . ." He shakes his head, looking pained.

"*Now* do you see why putting a PHANG in charge of OPERA

CAPE is a bad idea?" I ask. "Someone—I *really* hope it's not me—is going to have to make some hard decisions sooner or later. Value judgments that factor in who does the dying and who does the living, and whether the moral calculus makes maintaining vampires worthwhile to the organization.

"But there's something worse." I self-censor the obvious next sentence: that Angleton as good as told me that Mhari got shoved onto the committee to expose her. Neither Andy nor Pete need to know that. I continue: "It occurs to me that there is something very smelly about the number of people who have been telling me that vampires don't exist—here, in an agency *devoted* to the occult."

Andy's eyes widen. "You're wondering if we've been infiltrated." I can tell he's rattled: he instinctively reaches for his e-cigarette.

"Yes." I try to smile reassuringly, but the twitching tic in my cheek probably undermines the effect. "I might be jumping at shadows"—I really don't want to tell him what Angleton told me, because that kind of knowledge is dangerous—"but it's good to be sure, isn't it? So I'm officially declaring this the first meeting of the, um . . . Let's find an unassigned codeword." *Clickety-click.* "Ah, GREEN LIME is free, so we'll use that. Yes, this is the GREEN LIME committee. Circulation: restricted, no reporting. Budget: bill to Bob Howard, discretionary funding authorization pending approval. Initial membership: Bob Howard, Andy Newstrom, Peter Wilson, and, uh, Spooky the Office Cat. Remit: to examine archival resources for evidence supporting the hypothesis that one or more PHANGs have been operating within the Laundry and working to conceal signs of their own existence, and if so, to identify the blood-sucking mole. Hopefully we'll draw a blank, but if not, it'll give me some ammunition when I escalate it to the next level.

"You're drafted. So how about we work up a plan of action, then hit the archives?"

13.

VAMPIRIC MANEUVERS IN THE DARK

"HI, HONEY, I'M HOME!"

I needn't have bothered calling: the house is dark and cold, the heating turned down. I pick up the two crates and trudge inside. One of them complains vocally, the other reeks silently. *That* one can live under the stairs. The loud one I carry into the kitchen, where it moans like a particularly deranged ghost as I hang my coat and gloves up in the hall. Then I turn the lights on, fiddle with the thermostat, and let Spooky out of her carrier.

"Waaow?"

I remember to close the kitchen door just before the little fuzzball wanders out into the hall, then set my backpack down and start unloading supplies: food bowl, water bowl, kibble. There's a thudding sound behind me: I whip round in a hurry and am confronted by a mad, black-eyed stare from atop the kitchen table. "Hey, cat, what are you doing there? Get down—"

Spooky levitates as if a poltergeist has just grabbed her. She comes down on top of the kitchen unit, a good two meters away, then leaps again, for the precarious gap between the top of the storage unit and the ceiling.

"Oh for fuck's sake—" I pause. *Why the hell am I talking to a cat?* I wonder, resolving to ignore her. She'll come down when she's hungry or needs the litter tray or something. It's been a long day and I do not find it relaxing to chase an antigravity-enabled predator with a butterfly net. So I finish unpacking provisions instead, listen to the radiators gurgling away as our ancient central heating system struggles to emit a trickle of hot water, then haul out my battered netbook to spend some quality time anonymously stalking my relatives on Facebook.

After about half an hour I realize there's an unaccustomed warmth on my lap. And it's *buzzing.* This perplexes me for a few seconds, until I realize what it is. Dammit, I've caught lap fungus! I carefully reach down with a fingertip, which Spooky sniffs, then attempts to pick her nose on. Then, while I'm trying to work out how to make a dash for the kitchen sink without being lacerated, I hear the front door opening.

"Hi, honey, I'm home?"

It's Mo, of course. The joke may be threadbare but it's not *entirely* worn out yet. But I instinctively move to stand up, at which point Spooky startles and emulates a rapidly deflating party balloon in terms of high-speed movement and random three-dimensional handbrake turns. She ends up crouched on top of the smoke extractor over the cooker, glowering at me as if I'm to blame.

"In here," I call, standing and walking over to switch the kettle on. The kitchen door opens.

"What a day—" Mo freezes, violin case in hand. "What's *that?*" she demands, bristling.

Oh dear. "Mo, meet Spooky. She's the stray who's been hanging out around the dumpsters at work; she followed me indoors today, and I was going to take her to the Cat and Dog Home but—"

"Oh for—" Mo plants her violin case on the kitchen table, removes her glasses, and rubs her eyes tiredly. (No eye shadow, I note, just old-fashioned exhaustion.) "It can't stay here, it's probably got fleas."

"Not anymore." Spooky has a shiny new flea collar. "Anyway, she doesn't have to stay, but I couldn't leave her in the New Annex overnight—the cleaners would eat her."

"You didn't think to put her back outside?"

"The forecast said frost tonight." The kettle boils right then, so I busy my hands with the making of a pot of tea, leaving my brain free to chew over whether I'm simply making excuses or, or, or.

"Well, *you're* on litter tray duty. Not my problem. And if it craps in my shoes it can look forward to a promising future as a violin string."

Spooky stares at Mo with enormous black eyes, pupils fully dilated. She looks as if she understands *exactly* what Mo is saying, and likes none of it. "Well okay," I say. "But if you're so worried, how about we just spread a tarp or one of those gigantic plastic IKEA shopping bags over your precious footwear?"

"Feh. It's *my* house, the lodgers are the ones who should go out of their way not to make waves." She sits down and I suppress a sigh of relief.

"Bad day?" I ask.

"*Terrible.* First, I had two hours of instrument practice cancelled because of a problem with the anechoic damping in Practice Room Two—there was too much leakage. Turns out a dripping pipe in the ceiling had soaked some of the panels. Then I had another shitty committee meeting I shouldn't really talk about, all to do with the fallout from Vakilabad. Our people in the FO are going to deliver a strongly worded complaint, threaten to withhold cooperation if they don't promise to tell us the entire truth when they ask for assistance in future. There might even be some finger-wagging." (Which seems only reasonable to me.) "Seems that what's gotten up certain people's collective nose isn't what the Pasdaran wanted me to do, but the way they went about it. I'm afraid I had a little snit."

Her eyes *are* puffy, I realize. And she usually spends a few minutes on cosmetic basics before interdepartmental sessions, suggesting— "Oh, Mo."

She waves it off. "I didn't break down or get excessively emotional—in the meeting. I *did* raise my voice a little. Had to remind them I'm not a fucking human waste disposal machine. Crashed and burned afterwards."

I pivot silently from teapot to drinks cupboard, wherein I locate the remains of the bottle of Glenmorangie from the other night. There are still a couple of fingers left in it so I pour them all into a tumbler and shove it in front of her. "Sun's over the yardarm. Drink."

"If I must." She looks morose. I turn back to the pot, add loose-leaf tea and hot water, and set it aside to brew. "There is a distinct lack of contact with the hard edges of reality in some parts of the organization these days."

"Alternatively, you spend too much time poking around corners of the envelope that sensible people stay away from," I propose.

"*Somebody's* got to do it." She stares at me.

"I had an interesting interview with Angleton today," I say, "between meetings. Well, after one meeting. Then I sort of called another." I look guilty. "I created a new committee."

"Oh. Really?"

"I think someone inside the organization is trying to gaslight us."

"Well, *that'd* be a first." She knocks back a startlingly large gulp of water-of-life then puts the tumbler down and fans herself. "Nobody, in the history of the Laundry, has *ever* tried to pull the wool over anyone else's eyes—"

"Planet Earth calling?"

"Yes?" She pays attention but she looks worried. My heart goes out to her but I'm not sure how to break through the icy sheen of cynicism she's wrapping around herself.

"'There's no such thing as vampires,'" I finger-quote at her. "I keep *hearing* that. Even from people who know better."

"But that's—" She peers at me. "Bob?"

I peer back at her, confused. "Didn't I tell you?"

"Tell me what?"

I shake my head. I'm feeling distinctly fuzzed. "I *found* them. Genuine no-shit vampires." I motor on, anticipating her resistance and not wanting this to turn into another argument: "As in, they're super-strong, can project at least a level three glamour, are predisposed for the practice of ritual magic, and they need factor-one-million sun-block to go outside in daylight. Oh, they also drink blood. Unfortunately I didn't find them fast enough; Mhari got there first and reactivated herself and now HR are running in circles trying to draw up a policy for handling their Special Needs."

"What? Mary who, hang on, wasn't she your . . ."

"Yes, *her*. Mhari Murphy. Back from the land of the merchant bankers and even crazier and more ambitious, in a blonde-executive-with-sharp-shoulder-pads-and-sharper-fangs kind of way."

Mo stares at me for a moment, clearly wondering if I've taken leave of my senses. Then she takes another sip of whisky and sits back, the gears visibly beginning to mesh. "You've verified this, I take it."

"Oh *hell* yes." I count off points on my fingers. "Epidemiological factors—we've got a whole new thaumodegenerative neuropathy to deal with, tentatively called V syndrome. Andy can vouch for my research on the data mining side. That's all logged confidential OPERA CAPE. Then we've got the HR briefing and the DRESDEN RICE committee, currently sitting. The clusterfuck when I confronted them, well, you can find it filed under BLUE DANDELION. And I just set up another one, GREEN LIME, although we haven't got very far yet. *That* one is investigating the possibility that for some time now we've been infested with fang fuckers telling everyone to shut up and look the other way because *there's no such thing as vampires.*"

There's an odd double-thud. I look round: Spooky has teleported from the extractor hood to the worktop and is now sniffing the electric kettle suspiciously.

"Vampires? You're sure? That can't be right . . ."

"They're not fucking Dracula but they're close enough for government work. It's fallout from an algorithm research group supporting the quantitative trading desks at one of our larger banks. Turns out a rather rare combination of a multidimensional visualization system and a particular area of group theory makes mild-mannered mathematicians grow fangs. Anyway, the first of them only turned about five or six weeks ago. He turned his colleagues, and they went all agile on it, exploring the parameters, which triggered the V syndrome spike in Tower Hamlets which led me to them."

"Where does Mhari come into all this?" Mo asks, still sounding confused. "I thought she got shown the door, years ago?"

"Too right. She was on the permanent sabbatical list. Trouble is, they showed her the door by way of an entrance interview with an investment bank. She's been management track ever since and ended up as second in command on this team. So they turned *her*. And *she* knew about *us*, so she phoned it in and, as an ex-HR body, she knew exactly how to induct her little bat-buddies into the Laundry. Did it in the nick of time, too, just before I turned up with an OCCULUS truck and half of Special Branch in tow."

"Oh good god." Mo doesn't believe in any gods other than the ones I believe in, but the expostulation comes instinctively.

"I know it's not a bunch of bloody-handed lunatics from the Middle East, love, but I have had my hands *ever so slightly full* this past week . . ."

"Vampires." She takes another sip of whisky. Her shoulders are shaking with suppressed laughter or anger or something. "Blood-sucking fiends." More shaking. I can't tell whether it's mirth or hysteria, which worries me. "Poor Bob!"

"Maaaaow?"

I ignore the cat. "It's not funny," I say stiffly. "They drink blood. Not much, but the donors die of something like Krantzberg syndrome."

"*A-HAHAhaha—*" It's like a sneeze, and it passes just as fast. "What?"

"I said, their victims *die*. I'm guessing there's a sympathetic connection. Whatever gives them their vampiric superpowers is like the K syndrome parasite, but instead of chewing down on their own gray matter, it uses them as a vector—to take blood meals that allow them to sample many more victims."

"Oh. Oh shit." She drains the glass. "What are you going to do about it?"

"What *can* I do?" The tea's brewed; I pour myself a mug. "Right now we don't even know if they have to drink blood to survive, or if it's optional. Right now we're still gathering data. *Right now* I suspect we've had a fang fucker in the organization all along, telling us they don't exist. The intensity of collective denial has been, shall we say, anomalous." Spooky, tired of being ignored, starts gently bumping her head against my ankle. "But if you could keep your eyes open, I'd be very grateful. Coordinate with Gerry and Angleton and Andy. I've got a bad feeling about this . . ."

IT IS TRADITIONAL, AT THIS JUNCTURE IN THE NARRATIVE, TO insert yet another Hollywood-style montage of diligent bureaucrats sleeplessly combing the archives in search of clues to the identity of the enemy mole within their organization. (Optional: one of them is stabbed in the jugular by said mole while working late. They use their last five minutes not to call for an ambulance, but to compose an amusing cryptogram naming their assailant, and to finger-paint it on the underside of their desk using their own blood as ink. Where it is found the next morning by Facilities and promptly cleaned up before anyone with a clue gets to see it.)

Well *fuck that shit.*

What actually happens is called Division of Labor, with a nod and a wink to security protocols. Andy and I send Pete away to draw up a questionnaire about vampires and why people think they don't exist, emphasis on the "why." We want to find out if vampire denialism is a statistical anomaly, so we plan to use his church as a control cohort. If anyone asks he can soft-soap it as an enquiry into the level of belief in supernatural phenomena among his parishioners. (We remind him to keep this away from Alex for the time being.)

Andy has a whole bunch of clearances for keyword access to confidential files. *I* have a whole bunch of clearances for etcetera. We're not going to search secret sources at this point—the flaming hoops we'd have to jump through would leave us seriously scorched. As it is, our confidential clearances overlap but are disjoint sets, so we go to the Security Coordination desk and ask the blue-suiter on duty to generate lists specific to each of us and a shared list we can split down the middle. We both have blanket permission for archive searches on anything over a century old, and for newer stuff that's classified but has passed its expiration date. (This being the Laundry we don't publish our declassified archives for the general public, but employees *can* get access more or less at will once it has expired.) Most of this material is available from our computerized document retrieval system these days, so it's a lot like doing a university library literature search, except grubbier and more esoteric.

> Search keyword: vampire.
> *Searching.*
> 19,260 results. Listing page 1 of 771 . . .

Did you know that if you search for "vampire" in books on amazon.com you will get approximately 33,770 results?

We don't have quite that many documents on the topic—a lot of our search hits are duplicates—but it looks as if, for a long period (from about 1792 through 1969), *every single vampire novel* published in the United Kingdom was read and synopsized by our Occult Entities Monitoring Desk, or the Zoological Enquiry Bureau, or the Linnean Anomalies Committee. (It got renamed every couple of decades, like clockwork.) I am absolutely gobsmacked to discover this. I already knew that we had far more information about unicorns on file than seems strictly necessary to anyone without EQUESTRIAN RED SIRLOIN clearance, but vampires? You can't even write it off as the work of a single demented fan; not when it ran for 177 years. (Well, 153 years. We have synopses going back to 1792, but the first folios didn't get compiled until 1816.)

But wait, there's more! There is a once-classified (Top Secret, fifty-year rule) file on one Abraham Stoker of London (d. April 20th, 1912). It's quite thick and appears to contain a bunch of PV interview records with his friends and family, for pre–First World War values of positive vetting. (Full of comments along the lines of, "Jolly good chap, eminently clubbable for an Irishman.") I checked with HR, and there's no record that we ever employed him.

There's a report of an investigation, circa 1899, into the book

Dracula, which appears to have investigated the possibility that it was based on fact (and drew a blank). A much more urgent investigation into *The Lair of the White Worm* followed in 1912, but Mr. Stoker was indisposed to answer questions in person, and the investigator hinted darkly that "excited delirium due to an unspeakable ailment" had more to do with the phantasmagoric (not to say misogynistic) visions in that book than any supernatural experience.

There are all sorts of other things, investigations into silent movies and TV serials (I pulled the file on "Quatermass" for shits and giggles—strictly speaking not germane to the project in hand, but I'd hit burn-out by that point and badly needed some relief reading that wasn't the eleventh Harry Dresden novel). As I implied earlier, the frequency of reports tailed off after the late 1950s, until there were only a couple a year coming in. And then everything stopped dead, as if guillotined, on April 5, 1969.

April 5th. You know what that means to me? That means the budget for the project expired at the end of financial year 1968 and was not renewed. (Yes, British government budgets—and the tax year—start on April 6th. Why are you looking at me like that? Don't *your* tax years start and stop on a random date in April?)

I finally save the spreadsheet I've been using to keep track of this shit, mutter "bingo" quietly, and email Pete and Andy, inviting them to an impromptu team-building exercise in the Turk's Head round the corner. Trebles all round: I've found what I'm looking for.

MEANWHILE, IN ANOTHER OFFICE, A MEETING IS TAKING PLACE. And I haven't been invited to it, or even informed of it. Even though I'm the subject.

Mahogany Row in the New Annex lacks the plush nineteenth-century gentleman's club ambiance of the original, but it's still a step up from our regular offices (both figuratively and literally: it's on the top floor). It has thicker carpets and nicer bathrooms. There are no cubicles, and some of the offices have outer vestibules for the executive PAs. However, the New Annex was built in the 1970s, so it lacks a whole bunch of modern conveniences we grunts take for granted. Who'd spec out a desk with a blotter and a rotary-dial telephone but no power and network points for laptops, or even electric typewriters?

Nevertheless. Sometimes it's a good idea to have an office that is discreetly shielded—no outside windows, no electrical appliances except the carefully checked overhead lights, and Faraday shielding hidden behind the Laura Ashley wallpaper. And it's in one of these offices that a conclave of old monsters are having an informal chat.

"Are we secure?" asks Lockhart.

"Yes." Angleton laces his fingers together and looks at the third man present, who nods mildly. This worthy is the Senior Auditor, and the mere idea that he might be taking an interest in my affairs—well, it's a good thing I have no idea about this meeting, or I'd be hiding under Spooky's litter tray and gibbering instead of dragging Pete and Andy off for a wee celebratory bevvy down the pub. Ignorance, as they say, is bliss. Neither the Auditor nor Lockhart bother to ask just how Angleton knows they are secure: some capabilities are simply trusted to exist.

"What's the latest news, then?" asks the Senior Auditor. With his silver hair, gray suit, and half-moon reading glasses he could pass for a distinguished partner in a law or accountancy firm. But even the likes of Angleton and Lockhart are slightly on edge in his presence.

"Hmm." Lockhart glances sidelong at Angleton.

"Well." Angleton grins—an expression strangely at home on his sallow face, but rarely seen by the likes of me. "I had to give the lad a nudge, Gerry. But I think he's probably working along the right lines now." The grin vanishes abruptly. "He appeared to be distracted."

"Hmm." Lockhart glances down at the day planner in his lap. "Well, that's not surprising. Unfortunately Agent CANDID may be becoming a stability issue, and he'd be the first to know. That business out east: shocking."

The Senior Auditor nods. "But there is clearly a matter of priorities for us to discuss here," he says smoothly. "We have benefited from two excellent assets meshing frictionlessly for too long. Or at least, providing each other with mutual support."

"But the current enquiry . . ." Lockhart's mustache twitches.

"It was inevitable, I'm afraid. As with all such phenomena, the closer the great alignment comes, the more frequently we'll have to deal with outbreaks like this. Especially when inside meddling is implicated. Sooner or later one of our night-crawling friends was bound to make a power play: or perhaps it's just another of their interminable duels. It's just unfortunate for us that the nexus in question involves Agent CANDID's partner's former lover: the threat surface is wider than usual . . ." The Senior Auditor trails off into a thoughtful silence. "Agent CANDID, in combination with her instrument, is a major offensive asset. We can't permit trivial insults to jeopardize her efficiency."

Angleton's expression is stony, but he holds his counsel.

"That may be true," Lockhart ventures, "but what about Agent HOWARD? He's on the tier below, but coming along nicely. In the long term"—he glances sidelong at Angleton—"he may be an even more important asset."

"I am aware of that," says the Senior Auditor. A slight stiffening of his spine and a glint of light from his glasses causes Lockhart to purse his lips. "Now tell me about Ms. Murphy. And Mr. Menendez."

Lockhart flicks through a few pages. "Oscar Menendez: nothing special. He's your usual managerial overachiever, very bright, *organizationally* highly competent, and about as untrustworthy as—well, I wouldn't have chosen to bring him in, let's put it that way. He might be useful if he manages to avoid making any fatal errors of judgment in the short term, but for the time being I'd be inclined to put him in a padded box and throw away the key. He doesn't really understand that we're not playing by the rules he's used to."

"And Ms. Murphy?"

Lockhart's mustache thins. "She's much more interesting, if you ask me. We originally recruited her straight out of university, in more innocent days—the 'if someone sees something' dragnet was still practical back then. She was badly mishandled by her original managerial oversight people, let go, given a discharge placement in the bank, *then* turned out not to be a waste of space after all."

"And now she's back, as a vampire. And she actually kept her coven alive and survived as such for nearly six weeks. That's quite an achievement." The Auditor nods to himself.

"What *is* the life expectancy of a vampire in this day and age, anyway?" asks Lockhart.

"Ninety-six hours," Angleton says drily. "It's been shortening progressively ever since the 1960s. Although most of the initial die-off is down to the sane ones working out their likely fate and killing themselves to avoid it. If they survive longer than a year—vanishingly rare, these days—there's no obvious upper limit."

"Except for the ceilings imposed by epidemiology."

"And fratricidal predation, yes." Angleton meets the Senior Auditor's gaze with his own unblinking expression. "Bob knows it is his duty to keep Ms. Murphy alive, for the sake of the organization. He's a clever boy and he'll work out the angles for himself. The risks, I believe, are that Ms. Murphy will underestimate and try to manipulate him, or that Agent CANDID will prove to be an insurmountable distraction rather than a pillar of strength."

"Human relationships are so painfully messy." The Senior Auditor looks away; he carefully removes his glasses and starts to polish their lenses with the end of his tie. "But for the greater good . . ."

"If Agent HOWARD expresses concern about Agent CANDID, I believe he will come to me in the first instance," says Angleton. "So we will have sufficient warning. It would be expedient to have an urgent assignment ready for her, though."

"A wild goose chase?" asks Lockhart.

"No, that would potentially make things worse, if she can see through it. But . . . don't over-stress her. The business out east—"

"Vile, I know." Lockhart looks at the Senior Auditor. "She should really be on sick leave, you know."

"I am aware of that." The Senior Auditor replaces his spectacles. "But she is dangerously close to indispensable."

"We should find a plausible task that is important enough to demand her full attention while being unlikely to generate additional stress in the Howard/O'Brien household. And which takes her away from home while not placing her at such a remove that we can't call her back in a hurry if we need her."

"Yes." The Auditor falls silent for a moment. "She's cleared for BLUE HADES, isn't she? The upcoming treaty renewal negotiations . . ."

"That'll do it. Come to think of it, *they* know *her*, which gives it even more plausibility." Angleton is nodding now. "It doesn't do to show them a weak front. It makes perfect sense for us to send her along with the delegation."

Lockhart interrupts: "But if she's on a disused gas platform in the North Sea—"

"That's what helicopters are for." The Auditor looks at him. "We need to clear the stage for the next act of this little drama, so that the reluctant star can be tempted into the floodlights to deliver his soliloquy.

"See to it."

THERE IS A BOOTH AT THE BACK OF THE TURK'S HEAD AND I plant Andy and Pete in it before I go to the bar to retrieve two pints of Adnams, a Diet Coke, and a bowl of olives. Having done my duty as honorary barmaid, I amble around the public rooms, sliding my way between knots of chattering post-work imbibers and idly patrolling past the various other booths and the former smoking room and lounge. The new and thoroughly tested ward I wear on a thong under my tee shirt stays cold and inert, which is good. This one isn't only sensitive to sympathetic entanglement and glamours, it's also supposed to pick up most electronic proxies for human malice. Sweeping for bugs in a public space like this is a fool's errand in the age of the cellphone (all of which, by definition, contain sensitive microphones and radio transmitters), but I can be reasonably certain that nobody in here means to do me harm.

By the time I get back to the booth, Pete is a couple of centimeters down his Diet Coke and Andy is looking at me curiously. "Is this what I think it is?" he asks, tapping his e-cig on the table.

"Could be." I slide into my seat. "I found the photographic negative of a smoking gun. Trouble is, an absence isn't proof positive. Even if it's a highly suggestive absence. How about you?"

"I got nothing." Andy pauses. "Was it inside?" He glances sidelong at Pete, who is focussing on his glass but clearly paying quiet attention.

I address my next words to Pete. "If you think something's smelly in the house, you talk about it outside. And vice versa. What Andy is asking is, do we have an internal problem. You may have noticed me walking around earlier. I was checking for listeners. Didn't find any, by the way." I look at Andy. "We had a very thorough monitoring program running for a very long time indeed. But it seems to have been de-prioritized in the late sixties, and cut off in '69."

"Oh, really?" Andy taps his cigarette again. The blue LED in the tip flickers on briefly: he fumbles with it for a moment, hunting the on/off switch, then gives up and takes a furtive hit, shielding it inside his cupped hand like an old lag. "Who do we know who's been with the organization since 1969? Or earlier?"

"It's not Angleton," I say dismissively. Angleton may be unaging and extremely scary but he's not a vampire: I've seen him in daylight. Besides, I probably know more about the Eater of Souls than anyone else in the Laundry. Certainly enough to rule him out as a suspect.

"Really?"

"I can vouch for him." I glance at Pete, minutely, and Andy nods, getting the picture. "Unless Angleton had some other reason to squelch the old vampire monitoring program, it's not him. And as he's on . . ." Andy nods again. Pete has no need to know about BLUE DANDE-LION. So I change the subject away from sensitive topics. "Pete, what have you discovered so far?"

"Oh, that's easy!" He looks up. "Would you believe that, of forty-six parishioners informally polled, thirty-six of them believe in the existence of evil incarnate, in the person of the Devil?" He sighs. "Well, their average age was somewhere north of sixty, and they're self-selected for being frequent attendees at religious services, so there was bound to be an element of literal-mindedness to them. But, taking the Devil as a baseline, the really interesting thing is that forty of them believe in vampires. Over 85 percent! Vampires are out-polling Satan in the bogeyman charts this decade."

He takes a mouthful of fizz. "Mind you, I added a couple of control questions. I said they were a self-selected sample? 52 percent of them think gays are going to hell, and 39 percent think the Earth was created late one Saturday night in October of 4004 BC." He looks pained. "I can see I have some sermons to write on the subject of metaphor and creation myths. And tolerance."

"What about the office?" I ask.

"Well, um, I had a problem there. I emailed the same questionnaire to the entire department and Jack from the Security Office came round to have a little chat about *asking questions*—"

"Oh shit," Andy and I say, nearly simultaneously.

"No, no, it was quite all right!" Pete looks startled at our reaction. "I explained that I was sending out the poll because you'd asked me to." I tense. "Then I asked if he really believed in vampires or Satan? So we had a good chuckle and he went away. Answer was 'no' and 'no,' by the way."

The cold sweat that began to spring up the instant Pete mentioned Jack from Security is drying. I share a knowing look with Andy. Mentally I'm kicking myself. Tasking Pete with asking questions of his church parishioners? That's totally fine. Pete asking questions of random passers-by in a secret government security organization is another matter entirely. I should have seen this coming—by nature he's an organizer, so of course he'd mailbomb the entire department, and of course Security would prick up their ears the instant someone not on their radar began asking questions. Even innocent-sounding ones. Demarcation and Chinese Walls and OPSEC and need-to-know rule our procedures. Those of us who are on the ladder and have worked together for over a decade sometimes cut corners to get things done, but a new inductee is another matter entirely.

Luckily, everyone in the Laundry knows that Satan doesn't exist. (We have worse nightmares to keep us awake in the dark.)

"Pete," Andy says, calmly enough, "I don't think you should get into the habit of asking questions on unclassified mailing lists. In fact, before you do that again, just make a point of checking if it's okay with me or Bob, right? We wouldn't want you to get into trouble."

"Oh. Um. I see." Pete is subdued, perhaps a little surprised at how scared we both looked for a moment. Not realizing that we're not scared for *us*, we're scared for *him*.

"Did you get any results?" I ask, leaning forward.

"Um, yes!" Pete brightens. "Mostly from junior staff and new inductees—I included a time-of-service question and the median was fifteen months. It turns out that of the eighteen responses I got, *nobody at all* believes in Satan and only two believe in vampires. Those two were recent inductees, by the way, time of service less than twelve months. Age is much more representative than the church survey, averaging thirty-two, outliers as young as twenty-one and as old as, well, one joker wrote in that they were two hundred and thirty-one and what was my blood group, please?"

Pete stops and stares at me. Then at Andy. "That was a joke, right?" he asks uncertainly. "Wasn't it?"

"Do you still have the responses?" I ask, trying to keep my voice level and even and unfrightening.

"Sure: they're in a mail archive I created for them . . ."

"What do you think?" I ask Andy.

"I think"—Andy looks as worried as I feel—"it's probably a joke. *Probably.*"

"Well, then," I say, pushing my mostly undrunk pint glass away: "Let's go and find out, shall we?" I stand up.

"What, right now?" asks Pete.

"When better?"

BUT WHEN WE GET BACK TO PETE'S OFFICE HE CAN'T FIND HIS mailbox full of survey responses.

I spend a fruitless and frustrating hour digging around with some forensics tools and groveling over logfiles. And finally I work out what happened. Pete did indeed save all his survey responses to a mail archive. But he stashed it on the local drive of the PC he was working on. Which is, of course, connected to our NAS. And for some reason when he logged out the VM image he was working on didn't get uploaded back to the storage array. So when we came storming back into the office and Pete logged himself in for me, he downloaded a stale copy of the VM he'd been working with, which scribbled all over the local copy with the mail archive. And because we are the Laundry and we are hip to the whole INFOSEC thing, these days our desktop PCs store everything local in a rather expensive PCIe RAM disk card (not even Flash—Flash memory retains data when you pull the plug) with whole disk encryption. And it's soldered to the PC's chassis, *precisely* because we don't want random interlopers to be able to trivially retrieve erased files.

Somewhere in the guts of the departmental mail server there's a logfile recording the origin and destination of every email message that was delivered to Pete's desktop client. (Or anybody else's, for that matter.) But somehow I don't expect to find Pete's joker listed in it.

In the process of confirming that belief in vampires is bizarrely, implausibly low within the organization, and that an active surveillance program was discontinued more than forty years ago, we've blundered into a tripwire.

And now they know we know.

14.

THE HUNT IS ON

DESPITE MY DEEP FOREBODING OVER THE ENTIRE FANG FUCKER fiasco, life goes on.

Work: I attend committee meetings, write reports, and continue to grind on the bid acceptance process for the networking infrastructure in Dansey House (which is running eight months behind schedule already, and losing ground by approximately forty days per elapsed month of calendar time). I also get to go off-site a couple of times because I am supposed to be taking a self-defense course. Not that I've ever been much into unarmed martial arts—my general response to people trying to kill me is to scream and run away as fast as I can: I *don't like pain*—but some REMF in HR has expressed concern about my ability to look after myself without a basilisk gun and a Hand of Glory. And after my run-in with Alex and Janice, I have to admit that they have a point. So it's off to the dojo I go-go, dammit. (Where I am signed off as somewhere between "cannon fodder" and "zombie bait," but that's another story.)

Play: at the weekend, Mo and I visit my parents again. They've stopped taking every available opportunity to ask when they can expect to hear the patter of tiny feet, which is a minor blessing, but our inability to talk about work and their inability to talk about work (because Dad's recently retired and his idea of a hobby is watching *EastEnders*) are leading to increasingly uncomfortable gaps in the conversation. Mum *insists* on baking cakes, and Dad discovered one of the secrets of a happy marriage early on (never criticize your spouse's culinary skills) and applies it as a religious observance. So, let's just say Mum's cakes are sub-optimal and leave it at that, shall we?

Despite the lack of children there is a new and exciting presence in our life. When we get home, we discover that Spooky has expressed her displeasure at being left all alone in the dark in typical feline fashion, right in the middle of the front hall. Mo waits outside in the cold while I deal with it, and it takes considerable effort to persuade her that she doesn't actually want a new fiddle *right now*. In other news from the Fur Kids Department, the expensive new cat-tree goes unused, the living room sofa receives the Spooky imprimatur of best scratching post *ever*, and every open cardboard box in the house receives a mysterious lining of shed hairs. Spooky is a graduate of the "if I fits, I sits" school of feline furnishings. (If Mo ever gets serious about getting rid of the cat, all she needs to do is to leave an open FedEx shipping box on the kitchen table.)

Spooky has also developed a bad habit of waking up in the middle of the night and screaming that she's being attacked by an axe murderer ("Help! I'm all alone in the dark! Where are you?"), then haughtily ignoring me when I go downstairs to see what all the fuss is about.

And don't get me started on vet bills. Let's just say that civil service salaries and pet ownership are two lifestyle flavors that really do *not* go well together.

The following Monday I get up at my accustomed time to find Mo is in the kitchen, suited and booted and double-checking her go-bag. "Jesus, what is it *now*?" I ask. "I thought we were supposed to be looking for a spa break?"

"Got an email this morning," she tells me. "Actually Gerry Lockhart forwarded it on Friday evening but we'd already left the office

and Facilities were taking the mail server down for maintenance." I
startle guiltily: that was probably me, going through the server logs
with fire and the sword in search of Pete's joker. "Calm *down*, Bob,
it's not OpExec this time. Turns out the negotiation team for BLUE
HADES—it's the once-a-decade Benthic Treaty renewal fish-fest—are
down one sorcerer: Julie Warren's got pneumonia, so Gerry asked me
if I could go along to bulk up the front-facing team. You know how
They get if They think we aren't taking Them seriously."

They are the Deep Ones, the ancient alien water-world types who
own about 70 percent of the planet's usable surface area (the bits that
are below the crush depth of our nuclear-powered submarines). We
have an agreement with them: we agree not to piss them off (by, for
example, building the Underwater City of Tomorrow! or otherwise
intruding on their territory without prior arrangement) and they
agree not to exterminate us. The bilateral agreements need to be renewed regularly by just about every nation with a coastline and a
submarine, and BLUE HADES tend to get stroppy if they think we're
taking the piss or getting blasé about them. So every decade a bunch
of our more powerful occult offensive operatives get to hole up on a
disused North Sea accommodation rig and play bodyguard to the
folks from the Foreign Office (Non-human Affairs Department).

"How long are you going to be gone this time?" I ask, relaxing
slightly.

"I have to be on a chopper out of RAF Lossiemouth at about six
o'clock tomorrow morning, which means catching the morning flight
to Aberdeen, then an onward flight this afternoon. Then I'll be with
the negotiating team for, hopefully, a day or two, and back home
again. Don't worry, love, I just have to hang around and look professionally formidable."

"But if things go wrong—"

"I said *don't worry*, dear. *Nothing* is going to go wrong." She
smiles at me, a trifle sadly.

"But—" I shut up.

What she *actually* means is that everything will be all right unless
someone on our team fucks up and offends BLUE HADES so badly

that no conceivable apology is acceptable. In which case, the first we'll know about it is when the Storegga Shelf and Cumbre Vieja simultaneously collapse. You won't be reading about it in the newspapers because the combined hundred-meter super-tsunamis will wash the British Isles clean (killing everybody who lives within a hundred kilometers of the coast on both sides of the North Atlantic, just for an encore). The devastation will make a strategic nuclear war look like a lovers' quarrel.

"Well, good luck, or break a leg, or whatever." I stand up and she walks towards me and we hug. "And say 'hi' to you-know-who if you see her."

"Unlikely." She hugs me again, then lets go. "Be good while I'm gone, okay? And stroke the cat for me."

Then she leaves.

"DUDES, THIS IS *NOT* WHAT I SIGNED UP FOR! WHERE'S MY TUXedo? Where is my license to kill? Where are the hot Bond Babes? This *sucks*!"

Evan juggles his furry dice while he complains before an audience of one: Alex. Evan used to be able to keep three or four in the air for a couple of minutes before he dropped them. Now he's casually keeping eight at a time airborne without even tracking them with his eyes. There's a fat ring-bound training manual on the chipped utilitarian desk, and every ten seconds or so his left hand zips sideways to flip a page as he speed-reads, swinging back in time to catch a falling die.

Alex hunches in on himself, hugging his stomach. "She warned us," he points out. "I wish this hunger would go away. I'm *starving*." He's mildly feverish: the pangs and the hot chills running through him won't let up no matter how much he eats. A stack of wrappers from all-day breakfast sandwiches litter the floor under his desk.

"It's not fucking James Bond; who knew? I bet Oscar and Mhari aren't being handled like this."

"What, shoved off into an office with a bunch of health and safety manuals to memorize?" Alex considers for a moment: "I very much suspect that they *are*. This isn't an accident, Evan. They're—"

"They're trying to bore us to death." Evan gives up on his juggling, guides the stack of dice down to a safe landing in an eight-cube tower.

A couple of weeks ago it had been an impressive trick; now it strikes Alex as a distraction. He fingers the small, sealed locket they've given him to hang around his neck. The thing itches pretty much all the time now. "They don't work the same way as an investment bank. Boredom is part of the process, at least at first: they're trying to see if we act up. Didn't you read section two?"

"What, the induction training process? They're going to give us a sodding *aptitude test* to see if we have a predisposition towards formal logic? Then send us on a ten-week residential circle jerk that's going to teach us the basics we need to embark on the study of applied computational demonology? Stuff like binary arithmetic, basic set theory, and predicate calculus?" Evan doesn't try to keep the offended pride out of his voice. "Before assigning us trainee roles?"

Evan chews the inside of his cheek. "You can do that in your sleep," he points out. "If you want out badly enough, you can fake incompetence. They'll let you go."

"Yes, but then I won't *learn* anything. Anything new."

"So." Alex shrugs. He's half-enjoying watching Evan climb the walls. Admittedly the training course is a bit of a joke; he or Evan could teach it themselves, in their sleep, except for the exotic and recondite bits relating to the actual praxis of summoning—the core elements of magic. They're ready to leap on that topic and get their fangs into it, given the opportunity. But clearly nobody in this organization is prepared for such enthusiastic and talented inductees; or perhaps they have other reasons for taking things slowly. A bureaucracy is all about standardization, so that necessary tasks can be accomplished regardless of the abilities of the human resources assigned to it. And the Laundry is impressing Alex as being a remarkably mundane and plodding organization, given the nature of the adversaries it is required to deal with.

"Why don't you relax? You've got an all-expenses-paid month-long vacation from the Scrum, even if you decide to blow off the training. And nobody's going to say boo to us when we go back to work." The novelty of having a guilt-free working holiday from work has gone right to Alex's head: even having a vicar for a mentor strikes him as funny, now he's over his reflexive fear of holy water.

"I'm hungry, too, dick-weed." Evan gathers up his dice and sweeps them into his briefcase. Beside them it contains a couple of energy bars, his iPad, and a water bottle. (The iPad caused some trouble with building security until Mr. Howard intervened and explained the ground rules, and now it sports a hideous asset tag that proclaims UNSEC PRIVATE NOCLASS inside a disturbingly eye-warping silver star. The mere thought of trying to put secret information on it makes Alex feel ill.) "I am so out of here," Evan adds.

"But it's only six thirty! And it's Tuesday!"

"Not a banker." Evan grabs a jacket from the back of the office door. "I need some R&R time. Call me if you get bored."

EVAN SLIPS OUT OF THE SIDE DOOR OF THE BUILDING, OUT PAST the battered row of dumpsters and into the twilight of an alleyway. The van with blacked-out windows is waiting to whisk him to his apartment in Docklands. He leans back in the padded, comfortably dark capsule and closes his eyes, opening them only when the driver offers him a form to sign. Then he gets out and goes in through the front door to get changed for a night out on the town. He doesn't notice the car parked with its lights turned off across the street from the building.

Alex, Evan thinks, is not merely a nerd—nerddom, and even a degree of Asperger's syndrome, is entirely forgivable in the hothouse conditions of the Scrum—but a coward. He's hungry, probably as hungry as Evan, but he won't act. He'll just sit there in a blue funk, shivering and complaining as the hunger gives him ulcers.

Evan happily embraces his inner geek, but harbors the conceit that he is an actor, a doer, not a sitter. He's hungry. They are all—those he's spoken to—hungry, having taken Mhari's caution about feeding to heart. But there are limits, and this goes past anything that's reasonable. They've told their HR contacts that they're starving. And they've all received responses ranging from blank incomprehension to bovine fright and a promise to refer it to some sort of internal committee as soon as next month. Who will presumably look into the logistics of ordering blood donations from expired stock in the transfusion service and get around to it sometime in the next year, by which point the Scrum will resemble refugees from a death camp.

Evan's been with the Bank nearly two years longer than Alex; long enough to climb the pay ladder a couple of increments, even if he hasn't qualified for a major bonus yet. He's got a very nice flat in a former Seaman's Mission, and his eye on a Porsche Boxster after the bonus season. Evan pays a cleaning service to handle his clothing, along with his everyday mess: every day he gets home to find the laundry basket empty and the bed neatly turned back. It's a lot like living in a gigantic hotel suite. Since the turn to the night side, he's made special arrangements: had motorized blackout blinds installed inside all his windows, converted a cleaning closet into a panic room with a reinforced door frame and a futon on the floor.

When he gets home, Evan ditches his work kit (including the annoying necklace-gizmo), then undresses and showers briskly. Afterwards he sorts through his wardrobe for an outfit. He would normally inspect himself in the wardrobe's floor-to-ceiling glass mirror, checking for imperfections, but that's impossible now; instead, he has to use his computer's webcam to show him a suitably rotated view of himself. He's aiming for a blandly anonymous clubbable hipster look, just distinctively different enough from every other aspiring Silicon Roundabout wannabe to be hard to describe from memory: skinny sixties mad men go after-work casual with big horn-rimmed glasses. (Never mind the optically neutral lenses.) He nods to himself, smiles, and inspects his dental work. Then he opens the locked medicine cupboard in the bathroom and removes his works.

It's time to go hunting.

* * *

AT ABOUT THE SAME TIME THAT EVAN DECIDES TO NIP OUT FOR a nighttime snack, I am working late in the office. Mo's en route to Lossiemouth—she texted from Aberdeen to reassure me, bless her— and if I go home there's nothing to do but read or watch TV. Spooky will shout at me, I guess, but it's hard to have a meaningful heart-to-heart with a cat. So: I have a stack of novels to finish for my book club report (continuing what I now realize is a long-standing tradition in this organization, even though it was discontinued a little over forty years ago), some more work to do on the cabling bid, and more logfiles to search. In a moment of anomie I glance around my office and spot the portable computer that time forgot. *Hmm.*

A sneaky thought suddenly occurs to me. *If you can't decommission it properly because it has no hard disk to shred, then it needs a hard disk.* There's no rule saying the hard disk has to work with the laptop, is there? As long as I'm not *removing* a disk from it, then I don't have to jump through the decommissioning-a-disk hoops. Adding a disk is easy: I just need to order one. Say, a cheap 300Gb external USB drive. Never mind that the luggable in question predates the USB interface by more than a decade. I just need to nail the hard disk to the side of the computer, and then, hey presto! It meets our decommissioning checklist because it's got a drive I can feed to the shredder!

Problem solved. I hunt through our intranet looking for the requisition form ("portable direct access storage device for backup, unsecured") and start filling out the PDF. Then there's a knock on the door.

"Come in—"

The door opens. "Bob, we need to talk."

Jaw flaps, words flee: it's my least favorite blonde. Finally I haul my scattered thoughts back into line, kicking and screaming. "Talk?"

"Yes, Bob. You know, that thing we do with our mouths? When we're not eating and breathing?"

"Oh for—" I wave at my visitor's seat.

"No, not here." For a moment she looks uncertain, a flicker back to a ten years' younger state of affairs for both of us. She's wearing a sharp black suit and heels, with a hairdo that can't be cheap; but it suddenly occurs to me that maybe she's dressing up because she feels exposed. Office dress codes for women are more ambiguous and less forgiving than for men, and sometimes status signifiers can mean the exact opposite of what one might naively expect. "It's nearly seven. Did you have any plans for this evening?"

"Wait, what?" I shake my head. "I have to go home and feed the cat. Eventually. Other than that, no, no actual plans." I glance instinctively at the pile of dysfunctional laptops. "As you can see, all work and no play makes Bob a sour boy."

I think maybe I'm babbling a little because she gives me a strange look, appraising and cautious at the same time. And she's still standing, despite the chair, looking a lot more subdued than the other day, after the meeting. "I was thinking there's a wine bar I know about five minutes from here? They do food as well, if you're hungry." An unreadable expression flickers across her face for a moment, then vanishes, airbrushed out of her muscles. She's wearing makeup, I realize, expertly applied to look natural. Then I look closer. No, what made me think there was eye-liner and lipstick? What made—

"You want a drink?" I say. "Okay, we can do that. But, please. Drop the glamour? It doesn't work on me." *You're not a patch on Ramona,* I think. *Or Raymond Schiller.* I smile in an attempt to defuse the jab.

"I'm not *trying*," she says tensely, "it just *is*." She glances away, breaking eye contact. "Can you will yourself to stop breathing?"

"No, but—" I stop. "You're telling me you're walking around in a level two glamour and you can't turn it off?"

"Would I lie to you?" She sniffs. "Don't answer that." The lacquered mask of cool detachment is back in place. "Look, Bob, we got off on the wrong foot. Hell, we *left* off on the wrong foot, ages ago. But we don't need to be enemies now. It's . . . it's childish and silly. Dangerous, too. So I was hoping we could, um, have a chat. Catch up on gossip. Bury the hatchet, if it still needs burying."

"Oh." I pull myself together. "Well, if you put it like that. Hmm." I glance at my screen. There's nothing here of pressing importance; I can requisition a scratch hard drive tomorrow. "One second." I swipe my thumb across the reader, drop into the hypervisor, and kill the guest session, then tell the PC to switch off. When it's done, I stand up. "Yes, let's do that. Meet you in the lobby in ten minutes?"

"Okay." She smiles momentarily, then pivots on a sharp black heel and sashays away. My gaze follows her as if my eyeballs are magnetized. Mhari used to have a hotline to my libido, and an older, more sophisticated, more powerful version of the Mhari I knew when I was younger is impossible to ignore when she wants to be watched. But I am disturbingly aware that I can't tell whether she's deliberately making a play in my direction, or whether I'm just falling victim to the vampire glamour even though I know I ought to know better. (Not to mention needing to pinch my arm and remind myself that I'm a married grown-up who shouldn't be looking around and who *especially* shouldn't be doing so in the vicinity of a crazy ex.)

More proof, if you needed it, that even a grown-up and self-aware Bob still harbors an inner eighteen-year-old who knows he ought to know better but just can't help himself. But grown-up Bob will just have to arm-wrestle his inner eighteen-year-old into submission, because grown-up Bob needs to know what she wants, and there's only one way to find out.

EVAN'S HUNTING PLANS ARE SIMPLE ENOUGH. WITH NIGHTFALL complete, he uses his smartphone to conjure up a pre-booked hire car. He tells the driver to take him to Great Eastern Street in Shoreditch, locus of far too many night clubs and restaurants and pubs, overspill from Hoxton and the whole Silicon Roundabout thing—the perfect happy hunting ground for a carnivorous hipster. There's a cluster near the corner with Old Street, social venues for happy young people with brass in pocket who're looking for food, drink, and merriment. Or in Evan's case, food and a drink.

He's thirsty and food won't touch that, but he's not immune to the lure of food. So first of all he hits a gastropub for a light bite, a stir-fry with tiger prawns and a cocktail on the side—a Bloody Mary. A Mary will do nicely tonight, he thinks, amused at his own impertinence. To tell the truth Mhari's been getting up his nose a lot lately, cracking the whip and brandishing the chair at the Scrum as if they're a mangy pride of performing circus lions. Fuck her and her little red wagon; there's going to bed hungry once in a while and then there's this awful gnawing emptiness, as if starvation is sucking the life out of his bones even though he can eat as much as he wants in the staff canteen.

Evan moves on to the East Village, where they're having a Chicago club night. It's still a bit early and the dance floor's two-thirds empty, but that just gives him an opportunity to chill in the shadows near the bar, wrapped around another Bloody Mary as he checks out the talent. He can keep track of people better than he ever managed before Alex pointed him at that screen. He follows their gyrations and perambulations and holds them in his head, a cat's cradle graph of which dancers spin into the personal space of others, a map of who's comfortable and who's stand-offish.

There are lots of groups here, gaggles of men and women and smaller numbers of single-sex groups, bros and girl couples out looking for a pickup or just some dance action. He can smell it on them: he barely has to look to see who's on the prowl and who just wants to have fun. Which makes his own hunt almost ridiculously easy. He amuses himself by keeping score of their intersections, making silent side-bets on who's going to trap off with whom—and so he's taken completely by surprise when a blonde in a silver sequined mini-dress gooses him on the right thigh and giggles in his face. "Hi!"

Evan spins round but manages to block his instinctive reaction before he punches her in the face. A split second later he's very glad that he did so. So what if she just tried to grab his balls? Her pupils are wide and she's beaming delightedly at him and she is, indeed, exactly what he would have been looking for: large breasts plumped up beneath a plunging neckline that supports a fancy eye of Horus pendant on a silver chain, accessorized by bangles and war paint and a matching sequined bag slung over one arm. She's dressed in silver from head to toe: silver dress and hose, silver evening gloves, silver glitter in her eyelashes. His nostrils flare: they tell him that she's very female and very hungry. (Possibly in estrous, he thinks, although he's not entirely certain, not sufficiently confident in his new senses.)

Her expression slips slightly as his face slides into view. "Oh man, I'm sorry, I thought you were someone—"

"No, that's all right." Evan reflects her smile right back at her and puts the full force of his will behind it, shoving at her inhibitions: "You're beautiful and happy and that forgives all. What's your name, love?"

"I'm Marianne," she says automatically, and maybe she's not an actual Mary but she's close enough for Evan.

"Kiss me and make up, Marianne?" he asks theatrically. And to his not-quite disbelief Marianne leans forward and plants her lips on his face and her breasts against his chest, then wraps her arms around him with startling enthusiasm.

"Oh wow," she breathlessly whispers in his ear, "I was so embarrassed! I thought you were—" Evan silences her by turning his head, until her breath steams his spectacles and she moans quietly as she melts against him. His chest is tingling where she leans against him. Marianne is a slick gelatinous mess of emotion stretched around his focussed will; he feels as if he can make her do anything.

"Did you come here with friends?" he asks quietly.

"Tracy and Debs, but they won't—" Her breath catches. "This isn't right."

"Don't worry, my intentions are nothing but honorable," Evan tells her, mugging sincerity. And despite her expression of uncertainty her arms around his waist are solid. Using vampire mind control to pick up a clubber who's already popped an E and who was halfway looking for a playmate isn't so much easy as spurious. He eases up the pressure, afraid that if he doesn't she might go down on him right there and then on the dance floor, which would be totally counterproductive and uncool.

"How about we go somewhere more intimate and get to know each other better?"

"Oh yes. Yes. What's your name?"

"Evan. I'm—"

"Oh, Evan. Yes, let's go."

Marianne is passably hot and she is wildly overexcited with Evan, which he finds flattering. Dick had to fucking zombify his pickups to get them to go with him, in Evan's opinion. Marianne grabbed Evan's ass and he's actually back-pedaling on the willpower to stop her trying to drag him down an alleyway. Evan is, if not inexperienced, nevertheless very happy indeed to meet a lady who with barely any nudging at all wants to jump his bones. And so he decides that there's no harm in playing with his food first: "I can call a cab," he says, "if you want to come home with me?"

Evan and Marianne tumble into a taxi together. He gives the driver his address while she plasters herself against his flank and buries her face between his neck and shoulder. Her tongue is hot and moist in the secret spaces of his ear, and he finds himself sprouting wood. He explores her stockinged thighs by touch in the sodium-limned shadows of the cab. Things are burning too fast, nearly out of control: he's past second base and in danger of outraging the driver when the taxi finally pulls into his street. The cabbie is silenced by a couple of purple drinking vouchers, a tip of investment banking proportions; he disappears into the night, leaving Evan with his arm around Marianne's waist. "This is your pad?" she asks.

"One of the flats, yes." She giggles.

He punches in the keycode and the door opens. They stumble upstairs hand in hand like giddy teenagers. Then Evan is at his front door and pulls out his key.

As the door closes behind them she drags Evan towards the living room, the great big bean-bag leather sofa. "Wow, this is great!" she exclaims. There's a click as she opens her clutch. Then they're sitting down, making out, and she's massaging his cock through his skinny-fit trousers. Cunning gloved hands in lycra work magic at his fly. "Listen, I want you to wear this," she says, holding up a ribbed condom.

"I have no trouble with *that*—" His voice catches as she unrolls it over his cock, squeezing it; then she rolls sideways and straddles him, tumbling down onto him with a sigh of delight. *Crotchless panties for the win*, Evan registers excitedly: *my, she's hungry!* They fuck enthusiastically, if somewhat haphazardly, rolling across the sofa until they come to rest again with Marianne straddling him, leaning against his chest and gripping his wrists in her gloved hands.

"I want to try something," she breathes in his ear. "It's a surprise: relax a little and close your eyes . . ."

Evan does as he's told, lost in the glorious sensation of getting his end away, and doesn't think anything of it until he hears a faint *click* and feels something close around his wrists. "What—" He opens his eyes.

"Nothing to worry about." Her smile is secretive as she thrusts her hips down upon him again. "Just a little surprise."

He tries to pull his wrists apart. "Hey, I didn't say handcuffs were—"

She leans close again and kisses him, grinding down again. Her lip gloss tastes of plastic. "Kiss-kiss!" she says as she wraps her gloved hands around his head and twists. "Oh, and I'm not called Marianne," she gasps excitedly. He tries to say something, but no words can make it past the tear in his spinal cord that has paralyzed him from the neck down. All he can do is blink at her, as the muscles of his face freeze in a final expression of horrified understanding. A few seconds later his nerveless body twitches and begins to ejaculate—and that's when she comes.

SO MHARI WANTS A DATE; I'LL GIVE HER A DATE. SHE'S dressed, if not to the nines, then at least to the sevens or eights. Luckily I keep my emergency meeting kit hanging in its carrier on the inside of my office door. It's the work of a couple of minutes to swap jeans and trainers for a not entirely unfashionable suit (Mo made sure of that) and respectable shoes: I don't bother with a tie, though. No need to go overboard. Especially as this isn't a *date* date: more like a sorry-I-haven't-fucked-with-your-head-in-ten-years, how-about-we-try-again date.

I get downstairs just in time. Ten seconds later Mhari arrives from the opposite direction. She pauses and looks approvingly at me: "Oh my, that's very grown-up! You've been working on your Clark Kent act, haven't you?"

I can't keep from rising to the bait. "It's a uniform, Mhari. I sometimes have to go places where it's useful to blend in." Then I hold the door open for her. "Where do you have in mind?"

"Somewhere"—she takes my arm, surprising me—"where I wasn't going to take you thirty seconds ago. Because, doormen."

Which is why we end up in the Gordon Ramsay restaurant in the lobby of a dauntingly expensive (and famous) hotel.

Mhari seems to have spent the past decade acquiring wallet-humpingly expensive tastes, and I have no idea how I'm going to justify the particular credit card bill to Mo, but the surroundings are striking, the food and wine are memorable, and I'm sitting at the other side of a starched linen tablecloth from my own personal femme fatale, exchanging gossip about times gone by. And we get along fine: we always liked each other, if you can ignore the screaming tantrums, the venomous sulking, and the outbreaks of boot-throwing followed by startling eruptions of hot monkey-sex in lieu of actually working out what was wrong with our relationship.

"So that's me," she says over the *amuse-bouche*. "Dedicated corporate foot soldier, married to the job." She shrugs, smiles, eyes twinkling. "Except once you're in the . . . our organization, you never leave, do you? Not really. Hence the business with HR and your unfortunate misapprehension."

"Yes." It's my turn to smile. We could play smile ping-pong all evening, table tennis diplomacy, and not get anywhere. "And your new trick. Tricks. Tell me, did someone in the organization put you up to it, or was it an accident?"

"That"—she raises an incredibly over-engineered canapé to her crimson-glossed lips—"would be telling." *Crunch.* Some delicate chewing ensues as she watches me speculatively. "Mm. Tell you what. How about. We trade?"

"What?"

"Question for question, Bob." The smile is back. Wicked or impish? I can't tell: it's in some kind of superposition of states, Schröding-
er's wildcat.

"Work or play?"

"That's a *question*. Tell you what, I'll answer yours first. Then I'll
ask you one. How about it?"

I can tell she's trying to play some kind of head game on me, but I
have an edgy feeling that I need her information . . . and besides, she
hasn't made me promise to tell the truth, has she? Mhari remembers
me from over a decade ago. I have grown old and cynical and devious
in her absence. *Let's see where this leads,* I decide. "All right, within
limits: I can't discuss confidential or secret material."

"I can live with that. Okay, answer to your first question: I don't
know." She holds up a finger. "There are back channels, Bob. Nobody
came up to me and said, 'the Laundry wants you to get your program-
mers to have a look at this area.' In fact, nobody from the Laundry
has made overt, official contact with me in *years*. On the other hand,
the area of group theory Alex was focussing on, and the multidimensional visualizer Evan was tweaking . . . they didn't come out of
nowhere. And it would amount to gross negligence if someone in HR
wasn't keeping track of which inactive assets were working for which
employers. If you wanted to steer us into going that way you could
have done it with a nudge, by having someone on one of the trading
desks raise a requirement for . . ." She trails off, looking at me.

"*I* didn't do it!"

"I didn't ask," she says drily. "And that wasn't a question. So
to complete my answer, I am not aware that the Scrum was set up to
deniably explore a dangerous area—but the fact that a former Laundry HR body just happened to be in an executive role in the team is
one hell of a suggestive coincidence, isn't it?"

"Mm-hm." I nod. "So you think someone else in the bank may
have been acting as a conduit? Who might it be?"

"That's another question. My turn first!"

"Okay." My buttocks tense. I can't help it.

"Let's see . . ." She raises her wine glass. "What have you been doing, career-wise, since I left?"

"I can't discuss that." I think for a moment, then add: "However, you already know that I was sent to drop in on you a few weeks ago. If you think about it, that should tell you something."

"Oh." A minute furrow appears between her eyebrows. "Well, then. If you can't answer that . . . what's your domestic life like? You said you were married. Who to?" She puts her wine glass down. "*Don't* tell me to check your Facebook profile, Bob."

I shrug. She's got me bang to rights. (Like everyone in the organization above a certain level, my Facebook profile is maintained by the disinformation office. *Not* having an FB account is suspicious these days, but we can't afford to risk folks maintaining their own—the potential for inadvertent leaks is horrible, especially on a social network designed to promote self-disclosure.) "I've been married for eight years. She works for the Laundry, too, and I can't tell you what she does. No kids, as I said before." I shrug again. "We live in a safe house, we're both on call, and we're boringly vanilla. Perfect little organization homebodies, you could say."

The furrow between her eyebrows deepens. "Really?"

Really? No, not really. Things *aren't* perfect. We're clinging on to the precipice-edge of normality by our fingernails, with rocks and small boulders bouncing off our backs. Sometimes we argue, but I'm damned if I'll tell Mhari that. I smile. "Really."

"Good for you," she says under her breath. A waitress appears from nowhere and makes the soiled plates disappear; another waiter dances past and vanishes, while bowls of exquisite-smelling soup appear in front of us. I blink, wondering if they're using some kind of gate invocation—but no, it's entirely sleight of hand. "This will be good," she warns me. "Respect the food."

We give the soup the silent appreciation it deserves. For myself, it also serves as cover for analysis. Mhari wants to know about my personal life? That's suggestive, but there are multiple possible explanations. I wait until we're most of the way through the course, then clear my throat. "Ready for another question?" I ask. She nods. "Okay, my question is the same as your last one. Married, divorced, single, kids, and so on. How about it?"

She puts her soup spoon down. "As subtle as ever." She manages a wry smile. "Married for three years. Divorced. Had boyfriends since then. Currently single."

My ward stings me, hard, just above my solar plexus. "Oof."

"What?"

I close my eyes. "Mhari."

"Yes—"

"Lying to me is not a good idea." I open my eyes and she flinches. It's a brief reflexive motion, rapidly controlled, but her pupils dilate. "'Currently single' isn't the whole story, is it?"

"What—" She breaks eye contact, looks away with an expression of distaste. "Dammit, Bob. Are you clear on the concept of plausible deniability?"

I roll my eyes. "It's not important. I don't honestly need to know if you don't want to talk—"

"Oh, I'll tell." She rolls the stem of her wine glass between forefinger and thumb. "He's a banking executive and he's married. It's a status thing: trophy wife, two kids, famous in-laws, officially all stable and happy. So we've been having a fling on the side, but it's strictly casual. He's not going to divorce her in order to whisk me away to live happily ever after, and anyway, I'm not interested in life as Executive Wife 2.0." *This* time my ward remains quiescent: she's telling the unvarnished truth as she sees it, although there's a slightly bitter edge to her voice. She looks at me speculatively: "I give it two weeks to run, plus or minus.

"Now. My next question. What are you hoping to get out of this conversation?"

I roll my eyes. "Who wants you dead?"

"No, it's not your turn—"

"You misunderstand, that wasn't a question. That was my answer."

"What?" She looks perplexed.

"Mhari." I look at my soup bowl. It's empty. Time to lay my cards on the table: "Until forty years ago, the Laundry had an elaborate early warning program looking for v—for cases of a certain syndrome. It got de-funded. More recently, *everybody knows* that this syndrome doesn't exist. If you challenge them on this point they will go to elaborate lengths to confabulate a rationalization for why this is so. More recently still, *your* Scrum shows up on *my* radar precisely as and when I go looking for you-know-what. And you know what else? You developed this condition about *one month* before I undertook the first systematic search for you-know-what by anyone in the Laundry in more than half a century." I meet her gaze. "I don't think that's a coincidence. Someone with access to HR personnel records set you up. I suspect they anticipated that our history would predispose me to shut you down with extreme prejudice."

Her pupils dilate. "You couldn't do that—"

Something is pressing on my mind, like a warm, damp pillow. I shove back, hard, and she squeaks in surprise. "Mhari. The Bob you knew is—" I was about to say *dead*, but that's over-dramatizing things a little, and in any case, I dodged on a technicality. "I'm not the same. Put it this way. If you were in OpExec, would you send the Bob you used to know to look into a nest of vampires?"

She must already have guessed, but she's pinching the edge of the table with each hand. Gripping it, actually, as if she's afraid of being blown away. Her eyes are wide: Did I push back too hard? "What *are* you?"

"I'm the person who's trying to *save your life*, because right now you're treading water in the dark and there's something very nasty circling underneath. Tell me, do you know what happens to the people you feed on afterwards?"

"The—what do you mean?"

I close my eyes again. "You don't know?"

"Know *what*? Bob, you aren't making any sense!"

Waiters appear, disappear: our soup bowls vanish, replaced by artistic compositions in salmon. "I think someone decided to run a very dangerous experiment," I tell her. "With total deniability. Set it up, then shut it down again, with nobody any the wiser. Only someone else, a rival, decided to hijack the project and that is why you're still alive and we're sitting here happily having dinner as I put the pieces together." I pick up my fork. "You weren't meant to live this long, and now you're a problem for them."

"Who *are* they?"

"I don't *know*." It's my turn to be frustrated. "Whoever caused the Scrum to be set up. Not necessarily the person in the organization who knows about V syndrome and arranged for you to be part of it as their unwitting catspaw. Presumably they're both, ah, people like you, only older. Ancients. But they're going to have to shut you down, permanently, and soon."

"Why?"

I've lost track of our little Q and A game. It doesn't matter anymore: I push a morsel of salmon onto my fork and raise it. "Because every time you drink, you set up a sympathetic link between the V-parasites and a new victim, on whose brain the parasites then feed until the victim dies. Looks a lot like Krantzberg syndrome, or Mad Cow Disease," I add in response to her horrified expression. "And the more vampires who hit on one donor, the faster it progresses." I focus on the once-living thing on the end of my fork. "Just by feeding, you infect people. And I've got a suspicion that if you *don't* feed the V-parasites, if you try to fast, they'll eat you instead."

Mhari pushes back her chair, stands, and marches towards the lobby of the restaurant. Her expression is set, her face pale, but she's left her handbag. Halfway to the front desk she breaks into a trot and heads towards the discreet archway leading to the toilets. I can feel the waves of nausea coming off her from halfway across the restaurant. *Yes, she's hungry.* I wonder if she's been trying to starve the parasite? This could turn ugly, very ugly.

I spend the next five minutes eating slowly, trying to work out what to say and do next, all the while desperately trying not to admit that she's my most important ex-significant other—before the woman I'm married to—and I've just told her that she's contracted a fatal condition where the cure may be worse than the disease.

I feel like shit.

* * *

AFTERWARDS, THE ASSASSIN FINDS IT REMARKABLY EASY TO tidy up the scene. She returns the handcuffs to her evening clutch; the condom goes into a baggie before it joins them.

A typical human body sheds perhaps five million skin particles per day. The woman who is not called Marianne has been in Evan's company for only an hour, in gloves and tights and with lip gloss and sealer over freshly exfoliated facial skin. It will take painstaking forensic work to recover any DNA traces from his body, and just to make it all the harder, she retrieves a small baggie of gray powder from her clutch and squirts the contents across the sofa. It's dust hoovered from the crevices of a booth in a night club, dust containing hundreds of thousands of fragments of skin from sweaty excited dancers.

Before she leaves, she pushes and shoves the sofa until Evan's paralyzed body is positioned in front of the living room window. Then she touches the button to withdraw the curtains. She turns and leaves, exits the building, and gets into the car that has been parked across the street from Evan's apartment since before he left the office. She walks with a spring in her step, tingling and happy from the mingled contact high of sex and death.

Shortly after she drives away, her phone rings. She pushes the button to accept the call. "Yay?"

"How did it go?" The voice at the other end of the connection is male, unaccented.

"It went just fine." A smile, very different from the one she treated Evan to, tugs at the edges of her lips. "Just *fine*, thank you for asking." An involuntary shiver tightens her grip on the steering wheel.

"You took care of the mop-up?"

"Yes, and as long as you took care of the cameras we should be clear."

"The cameras are in hand."

"You'll be mine, one day," she assures the voice at the other end of the phone.

"I look forward to it." He sounds amused. "But first, I have more work for you."

"Good." She pauses, biting her lip, then looks both ways before driving onto a feeder road to the Blackwall Tunnel.

"I told you I would be a more dynamic patron than your creator."

The woman shudders. "That's good, too."

"Are you up to the next job?" asks her caller. "It's a little soon, I know, but it needs doing soon."

"I'll be fine," she reassures him. "This one was charmingly naive, if a little pushy. But he was basically lightweight: an appetizer. From your briefing, this next one sounds slightly more substantial."

"Yes, so don't underestimate him. I'll check in with you tomorrow. I have a joint operation I'd like to bring you in on, if that's of interest."

"More baby vamps?"

"Yes."

"I haven't had this much fun in *years*!"

"If you can refrain from killing me on sight, I can promise you many more."

"I think I like working with you." She pauses. "You don't have to worry about me. Just keep them coming and I'm all yours."

"Talk to me tomorrow and we'll discuss it. Meanwhile, I've got a few loose ends of my own to tie up first."

"I look forward to hearing from you," she says. "This burner is now going away." And she ends the call.

A few minutes later, the steep descent into the tunnel under the Thames cuts off the phone. When the car emerges at the other end, the phone is inactive, battery removed, SIM transferred to her purse for disposal along with the other evidence—and the e-ink number plate identifies the car as a different vehicle of the same make and model from the one parked outside the Seaman's Mission earlier in the evening.

All in all, it's a good start to an excellent night's work for the woman who is not called Marianne, and her new patron. But the best is yet to come.

15.

CLUB DEAD

"AH, MR. SMITH! HOW GOOD TO SEE YOU! CAN I OFFER YOU
something to drink?" asks the banker.

"I don't think so." George sits down, uninvited, in the visitor's
chair opposite Sir David Finch's desk. He wears an overcoat and
leather gloves over a sober suit. Sir David is clearly unnerved by Old
George's unheralded appearance in his inner office—his PA didn't put
informal visit by major investor anywhere in his daily schedule, and
it is in any case late enough that he was about to leave for home. "I'd
just like to keep this quick, Sir David. My request the other week—
did you act on it?"

"Your request? Oh, the off-site meeting? Hmm." Sir David frowns,
and taps his fingers. "I'll have to ask Sandra what happened to it. I
don't recall attending . . . no." He pauses, about to touch the intercom
on his desk. "Do you mind?"

"Be my guest." It's delivered with an ironic half smile, but something about Old George's manner gives Sir David the very peculiar
feeling that perhaps he *is* here in this office by George's grace and
favor.

"Thank you." Sir David pushes the intercom button. "Sandra?"

A couple of seconds pass. "Sir?" His PA's response is tardy, annoying. She's new on the job this past week while his regular, Andrea, is off sick.

"The off-site meeting I asked for with Oscar Menendez and his team . . . what happened to it?"

"Let me check? Oh I'm sorry, Sir David, there seems to have been some sort of scheduling problem. I've been trying to arrange a mutually convenient time for everyone, but there's a logjam in the calendar system: Mr. Menendez is on some sort of secondment right now, and his team are either off sick, on vacation, or also on secondments. All of them! It's most irregular and I'm trying to get to the bottom of it but HR say it's entirely . . ."

Sir David meets Old George's quizzical stare. "Thank you, Sandra," he says. "That will be all." He hesitates for a moment. "I won't be needing you anymore this evening, you can go home now." He releases the call button. "Well?"

Old George nods to himself, but holds his counsel.

"What's going on?" asks Sir David.

"I really don't think you want to ask that question."

Sweat beads on Sir David's forehead. "I in-insist." He takes a deep breath. "I'm su-supposed to keep the board informed of all developments. How did you get in here? What's going on? Why are you asking about Oscar's team?"

"Fancy that." George stares at the banker. "An intelligent question at last. What a shame."

"What? What's going on?"

George looks away. "Imagine what it's like to be more than two hundred years old and not to have seen the sun rise once in all those years. Imagine what it's like to be an adept at the peak of one's powers, immune to the depredations of K syndrome, but utterly alone— the carrier of a parasite so disgusting that every man's hand will be raised against you should they learn of it. Imagine yourself locked in a duel to the death with the only other one of your kind in London, a duel that has been in progress for nearly a century with no victory in sight. Imagine what it is like to wake one morning and discover that your enemy has placed a catspaw inside your finest experimental project, where their pawn has taken control of a nest of ignorant and deadly children who will inevitably bring the full power of the secret state down on their necks and, in all probability, yours. Imagine furthermore that the enemy has cozened you, concealing their intervention, portraying themselves as your ally, cajoling you to lend them your most powerful weapon when in fact the enemy plans to steal your work and then to expose you, to bring your centuries of secret labor to a premature end at the hands of the modern-day witch finders. Imagine, Sir David, the end of all you ever wanted brought about because *an idiot banker did not prioritize highly enough a simple request from their master . . .*"

George rises and walks over to the curtains that cover the floor-to-ceiling office windows. He parts them carefully and looks out across the glittering nightscape of the East End. The view from thirty stories up is breathtaking; the dust and pollution rendered invisible by distance, the glory of the lights magnified in contrast. He opens the curtains fully and turns to stand with his back to the city. "Forget you asked."

"What was the question again?" Sir David's expression is vague, like a dreamer prematurely awakened.

Old George stares hard at Sir David, who freezes, his mouth ajar. A string of spittle begins to slide from one side of a paralyzed lip.

George pauses. "How annoying." He peers at Sir David. "I do believe you are developing some degree of resistance." Two strides take him across the room and back to the table—Sir David has barely had time to stand up. "Sit *down*," he snarls, putting the full force of his will behind the command.

"But—"

"*Down.*" Old George stands over the banker and places his hands on the man's shoulders, pushing gently. Skin contact reinforces compulsion. Sir David sinks back into his chair, confused.

"I think you were just telling me how depressed you are feeling. Pressure of work and all that. Despondent and low. Positively suicidal in fact. Isn't that so, Sir David?"

"G-g-gug. Ugh." Sir David shudders.

"Sir David, why don't you write a note? Something brief and touching, explaining how guilty you feel about the manner in which Oscar Menendez manipulated you into giving him unsupervised control of a hundred-million-pound trading fund. Or perhaps you could confess to your sleepless nights worrying about the millions of pensioners and orphans starving to death for want of the money your enterprise looted from their retirement funds." George grimaces. "I think that might be over-egging the pudding, on second thoughts. But write it anyway. It'll make you feel so much better, won't it?"

Sir David picks up a pen from his desk set, and retrieves a leather-bound planner from one drawer. His motions are jerky, almost robotic. He begins to write rapidly, scrawling spiky glyphs across a page as Old George walks back to the window unit. He uses a compact tool to loosen the bolts that secure one of the corner window units in place. Sir David has almost filled a page with a rambling confessional of his inner turmoil by the time Old George peels away the gasket around the glazing unit.

"Jolly good. Sir David, if you could step over here, please?"

Sir David shuffles towards the window. Old George is ready for him: holding the waist-high railing with one hand, he pushes hard against the glazing unit with the other. It resists for a few seconds, then pops free, tumbling away into the night. A gust of chilly air rushes in, and Sir David takes half a step back. "No—"

"You are depressed, Sir David. Mortally tired. You really need a break." George takes him by the shoulder and propels him into the void. "It's only traditional," he adds. There is a faint scream, abruptly cut off.

His informant disposed of, Old George glances around the office incuriously. There's a minor gale blowing through the hole in the glass wall; he walks over to the desk, locates the suicide note, and places the multitool atop it as a macabre paperweight. Then he picks up Sir David's telephone handset in one gloved hand and dials an outside line. He waits for a minute as the call connects through to a voice mail number, punches in four digits, and replaces the receiver.

Then he leaves the office, merging with the homebound employees as they trickle out into the sheltering night.

He will deal with the rest of the loose ends tomorrow.

"YOU'RE A COMPLETE BASTARD, BOB."

"Yes."

"You—no, wait. You make me feel dirty. Like you've been cheating on me."

I can't be bothered to remind Mhari that we have not, in fact, been in a meaningful interpersonal relationship this decade—or that last time we were, she was the one who was sleeping around. (Mostly in an attempt to get my attention, I think. Or maybe to punish me for something I hadn't done. I'm slow on the uptake, but I can figure it out eventually.) "You're feeling dirty because you've just discovered that this isn't a game. Congratulations, Mhari. Are you feeling thirsty?"

She glares at me, and for a moment I think I've gone too far. Her eyes are still cornflower blue but my inner vision shows me red-rimmed holes in a wall fronting a nightmare, glowing red worms writhing in a shimmering furnace . . . I blink. "You *bastard*, Bob. Of course I'm thirsty! It's eating me up. Burning away at me, a constant ache. But now I've got anorexia. Thanks to you."

"Well." The wreckage of a very expensive meal sits strewn across the table between us. "We have a problem to solve, don't we?"

"What problem?" Her blank-faced stare is even more worrying than her anger.

"How to keep you alive!" I snap. She recoils.

"What?"

"Listen. This is London. Eight million people, give or take: a hundred thousand deaths a year, on average. Twenty thousand terminal cancers. Ten thousand strokes. And so on. You need blood to establish a sympathetic link that allows the V-parasite to feed: you can probably make do with a tiny amount. And you don't need to feed very often. If it's taken from a donor who's waiting for the transplant surgeons to break them up for spares, if it's used immediately, that's not going to shorten their life appreciably. Taken from someone dying of advanced metastatic cancer who's on so much morphine they think it's next Friday already, ditto. We'll need to find a cooperative hospice, or a hospital with terminal care facilities. And a cooperative consultant or two. We can arrange for blood samples to be taken from patients who're within forty-eight hours of death and have them couriered over to where you and the other PHANGs are waiting to consume it immediately. We can make this work, Mhari, but it's not going to happen unless you can give the organization a reason to want to keep you alive. Do you understand?"

She nods—reluctantly, I think. I can't tell if I've gotten through her layer of defensive self-loathing or not. I try again. "I keep hearing, *everybody knows vampires don't exist*. And you know what? That phrase, that conviction, will kill you if you can't overcome it. And it'll kill Alex, and, uh, Evan, and Mr. Menendez, and what's-her-name-with-the-spikey-hairdo-and-bad-attitude—"

"Janice."

"Janice. It'll kill you all if we can't work out where it's coming from. And even if we get past it, we've then got to justify why we're going to take elaborate and dangerous measures to keep you alive, measures which are frankly repulsive to most right-thinking people— think of the newspaper headlines if it got out; it'd look worse than the hospital that was saving up organs from autopsies on dead children— we need a *justification*. Just being powerful ritual practitioners who are immune to K syndrome isn't going to be enough: you need to bring some added value to the organization. This is not office politics as usual. This is deadly serious: if not now, then in twenty years' time. Or weren't you planning on being around in another couple of decades?" I meet her eye. "Oh hell, Mhari, don't be *stupid*."

She shakes her head. "It's awful," she says. "This can't be happening."

"Tomorrow. The next DRESDEN RICE meeting is two o'clock, isn't it? I'll see you there. We need to shock the other attendees out of the whole denial thing, and propose a, a liaison with the Blood and

Transplant Service to procure essential supplies from terminal cases. And also to come up with a list of things PHANGs can do that will justify the expense of keeping you alive. Hmm: why don't you look into areas of occult research that are currently off-limits due to K syndrome? It'd give you a unique edge." I pause. "That's not what you were planning, is it."

"No, I—I don't know." She shakes her head. "Oscar had other ideas."

"Your boss Mr. Menendez is a charismatic corporate sociopath who did just fine in banking, Mhari. His problem is that the Laundry is not a merchant bank. If he tries to play us like fools he'll end up like Bridget and Harriet. Or worse."

"Like—what? Oh." Word gets around: what happened to Bridget and Harriet is legendary, and not in a good way. Evidently it even got as far as Mhari. She stares at me, wide-eyed. "You really think the organization would make arrangements for us? In spite of, of what you just told me?"

Spare me the baby-vamp naiveté. "I see no reason why not: we've done deals with worse beings before. But you'll have to work at justifying it, not just plan a—whatever." There is no point in mentioning what I think this was about. Mhari didn't drag her old ex out to a posh dinner just to pump him for gossip. She had some sort of scheme in mind, probably involving making me an offer I couldn't refuse: at a guess it involved immortality, super-strength, photophobia, and a taste for Rhesus Positive. Only it went out of the window almost immediately. Probably when she worked out that I'm pretty much immune to her glamour, and not entirely natural myself. (Score: hungry ghosts one, vampires nil.) It was definitely off the cards by the time I got around to telling her the truth and she finished throwing up in self-loathing. "Go into the meeting with a laundry list of useful things PHANGs can do. I'll tag-team with you on the support arrangements. And together we can try and work them around to believing that there's actually a problem in need of a solution."

"Huh." Mhari puts her fork down. At last. I relax infinitesimally. When she was getting worked up a few minutes ago I was half-convinced she was going to stab me in the eye. "You've changed more than I thought, Bob."

I resist the urge to roll my eyes. "Haven't we both?"

"Well." She looks at me speculatively. I notice that her pupils are dilated: I seem to have got her attention.

"There are a couple of other angles to cover," I add.

"Such as?"

"Firstly. That fucking reading assignment. I want it off the agenda."

"The reading—" She pauses. Sighs dramatically, miming disappointment, as she pulls the tattered shreds of normality back together. "Spoilsport."

"You're the chair. I do *not* want a teacher's black mark for failing a homework assignment. But if you want me to help save your ass I don't need the distraction."

"Well, if you put it that way . . . What was the other thing?"

"Oh, nothing significant." I glance away from her face for a moment. "Just, I'm fairly sure someone is going to try to kill you. I mean, kill all the PHANGs. It's the only explanation for what's going on. Trouble is, I'm not sure who's going to do it, or why. So, um, I'm going to have to keep an eye on you. I don't expect them to try anything violent at first; using the committee to starve you into going rogue would be a much better tool . . . But we need to keep up appearances. I don't want to spook whoever it is before I can identify them. So if you could avoid mentioning this to the others just yet?" I reach into my pocket and pull out a small jewelry box and pass it across the table to her.

"What—"

"Open it." She opens the box. Normally I like watching pretty women open boxes containing rings I've just given them. It's not something I get to do very often, truth be told. But this is business not pleasure, and I catch Mhari's frown as she stares at it. "Yes, that's a sympathetic link you can feel. Go on, put it on." She slides it onto her right middle finger, an unadorned loop of silver. I haul out the matching ring and try and work it onto my admittedly thicker digit. "This is the other one. Pinch it—ouch! Yes, like that."

"What's it for?" she asks.

I shove a form across the table towards her. "Sign here, twice. Yes, against the Xs. It's so that if someone tries to kill you, you can contact me. In fact, if someone tries to kill you it'll let me know even if you're unconscious." *Or dying,* I don't add. "And it'll let me find you."

"What's wrong with the phone?"

"A fearless vampire hunter is chasing you with a stake and you've got time to phone me? This is simpler, is all. Also, it doesn't rely on batteries and it works in mobile phone black spots and on the underground."

"Okay." She passes me the paperwork and slides the box into her handbag. A curious expression crosses her face. "I can't believe you just gave me a ring and I put it on."

"Would it have changed anything if I'd done it ten years ago?" I ask.

"Probably not." She stares into some inner distance, then calls for the bill. "But who knows?"

I'M IN A HUDDLE/INFORMAL CONCLAVE/MEETING WITH ANDY AND Pete when the phone rings.

It's late afternoon, the day after my questionable date. I spent the morning, as threatened, dealing with various bits of paperwork and then trying to work out a possible protocol for how we might organize necessary blood bank supplies for a small cell of PHANGs with minimum risk of public exposure, minimum risk of private embarrassment—we are going to have to run this past the Auditors with an eye to legality and compliance with the operations code, for starters, and don't get me going on how feeding blood from terminal patients to vampires is going to play out in terms of Quality Adjusted Life Years on the medical ethics side—and minimum risk of being derailed by any idiots with axes to grind and an unreasoning prejudice against bloodsucking creatures of the night. Then I broke for lunch (don't get me started on the spaghetti bolognese, either), and then an efficiently run session chaired by an unusually subdued Mhari.

I played nice. *She* played nice. I wish the same could be said of the other delegates. Old what's-his-name, Basil Northcote-Robinson from Archives, seems determined to make a big joke of the whole thing. Every time Mhari or I tried to convince him that PHANGs are a serious subject, he found an excuse to turn it into a reminiscence about his time in the army right after the Second World War, doing something dodgy with SIGINT in Romania. Or to talk about the time he got to shake hands with Boris Karloff. And the others on the committee kept playing along. I'm coming to the conclusion that whatever causes the disbelief is a powerful but very low-key, persistent geas. If it was splattered all over Dansey House as part of that annoying contamination problem they're dealing with, that would explain why I can't pick up any signs of it in the New Annex. It would also explain why the oldsters are so damned intransigent: they've been picking up subliminal nudges for forty-five years.

In the end, during a particularly hysterical (not) digression (during which Doris Greene from H&S tiresomely explains that vampires really *don't* exist and if they did it would be Too Bad, because they'd have to wear surgical masks, gowns, and eye shields at all times because of the risk of blood-born contamination; I think she's mistaking them for Hep-C patients or something), I manage to catch Mhari's gaze. Which is difficult when her eyes are rolling. But we make eye contact nonetheless, and she nods, and I can tell she gets it because at the end of the session she stays behind. "I know what you're thinking," she says, as the coffin-dodgers shuffle through the door, leaving us alone.

"Yeah. Listen, your list looks good to me. There are a couple of things I'd like to add to it, but it's a good start."

"Oh I am *so* relieved." She winces and clutches her forehead theatrically. "And?"

"My protocol. Do you think it could work?"

"I think there's an element of 'and now a miracle happens' in the process for extracting samples, somewhere between organizing a hospital liaison and sorting out a regular courier run. But I want to believe."

"So. Wanna take it to email?"

Mhari finally smiles. "I like it when you talk dirty."

"Listen, you're the chair. Co-opt me as secretary and we can kick it around until we both agree to it. Then we hold another meeting, feed the peanut gallery the edited highlights, let them spin some more war stories, then get everyone to sign off on it."

"I think that's a great idea." She narrows her eyes and stares at me. "Why are you being so proactively helpful all of a sudden?"

"Because it's necessary. For the organization."

"No, I mean why are you. Being so, um, cooperative?"

I blink. *She still thinks it's personal . . . ?* "Would you rather I nursed grudges?"

"I was afraid of it. I guess." She gives a little self-deprecating laugh. "Well, got to be going. I have minutes to write up. And then another meeting. They're keeping me busy, bringing me up to speed on changes to management appeals processes."

"I've got to go, too," I say. "Take care. And if you see something . . ."

"Say something. Right." She smiles, and reveals her teeth. The canines are gleaming again: I guess the cosmetic dentistry doesn't last forever. (Maybe they're like rodents? Continuously growing?) "I'm a grown-up, Bob. Of course I'll call you."

"Bob?" says Pete. I snap back to the here-and-now.

"Yeah?" I say.

"What happened?" he asks.

"What? Um. Well." I gather my thoughts. "Nobody believes in vampires. Our monitoring program that keeps an eye open for them was shut down forty-plus years ago. Then around four to eight weeks ago three things happen simultaneously: a whole bunch of vampires appear *ab initio* in an external organization. One of our former HR people *just happens* to be in a senior-ish position in the Scrum. And I *somehow* end up pulling a part-time data mining project that is designed to flag early warning signs of vampirism. I emphasize: all of this happens at *the same time*.

"Let me speculate. Someone in the organization has been aware of vampires all along. Probably because they are one. Quite possibly, being infested with the V-symbiont confers immunity to K syndrome— in which case, becoming a vampire might be an occupational hazard for ritual practitioners. One with an upside to balance the downside, if they're sufficiently ruthless.

"So, let's posit a very old, very ruthless sorcerer embedded within the Laundry. For a long time they've been running a very low-level geas, probably the source of the contamination under Dansey House. We can construct a number of narratives that start this way. For example: recently they decided it was a good idea to do some research into their condition, and the best way to do this was by, well. We know it's a memetic parasite. Think the wrong thoughts and you, too, could grow fangs and catch fire in sunlight. So they looked around for a suitable petri dish to culture vampires in. And of course you don't mess around with lethally dangerous infections without keeping a means of sterilizing it to hand. I was, I guess, intended both to deliver a report on the experiment and to, uh, recycle the petri dish? Someone with access to my long-ago HR file would know about me and Mhari getting along like a house on fire, complete with the screaming and smoke inhalation." Andy looks at me. "Yes?"

"You're still here and they're still here," he points out.

"Yup. So let's spin another yarn. A different vam—sorcerer, outside the Laundry, experiments with minions. They decide to generate a bunch of baby vamps as enforcers for some reason. Our vamp, inside the Laundry, decides to take their toys away from them, by inserting Mhari into it and drawing the side effect of their feeding to my attention."

Pete looks at me. "Isn't this a bit far-fetched?"

"Normally I'd say so," I agree. "But it all lines up, and it's much too *neat*. And there are too many tight links in the chain. It's almost as if it was designed as a plausible cover story for something else—"

That's when the phone rings.

I pick it up. "Bob speaking."

"Bob." It's Angleton. "BLUE DANDELION is open again. Are you alone?"

I glance around. "I'm with Andy and Pete. I can have them leave—"

"Not necessary. Is Alex Schwartz around? Mhari Murphy? Any of the PHANGs?"

"No." Suddenly I'm hunched over. Andy watches me, eyes narrow; Pete merely looks resigned, as if he thinks this is just another case of bad telephonic etiquette cutting a casual conversation dead.

"All right. Meet me in the lobby immediately. I need you to come with me to make an identification."

Oh *fuck*. That does not sound good. "Right." I pause. "Anything for Andy or Pete?"

"Ask them not to go home until we're back. We should not be long."

"Okay. Bye." I hang up. "That was Angleton. I have to go off-site for a while. Not long. He says you should both stay here until I get back—I think he intends to rope you in on whatever this is later."

"What does that mean?" Pete complains.

"Hope he's wrong and you don't find out," Andy says darkly. "Good luck, Bob."

"Hope I don't need it," I say. Then I grab my jacket and smartphone and run for the stairs.

I MEET ANGLETON IN THE LOBBY. "WHAT'S UP?" I ASK.

He strides towards the front door, trench coat flapping around his knees. "You'll see." The usual expression of arch amusement is missing from his gaunt face right now. He looks—old? Tired? Ill-at-ease? All of these things, I decide. Which is bad for my stomach, but not as bad as the crimson police BMW with the yellow stripes and the flashing blue lights that's waiting for us with a heavy from SCO19 leaning against it beside the open door.

"You Angleton and Howard?" asks the cop. He doesn't look terribly amused.

I pull out my warrant card, carefully not moving too fast. Unlike most British cops this one has a holstered pistol to go with his bulletproof vest, and there's undoubtedly an exciting collection of things that go bang in the locked safe in the car boot. "I'm Angleton," says Angleton. "He's Howard. I gather we're needed at . . ." He gives an address, somewhere in the East End.

"Okay, hop in." The officer passes my warrant card back and looks at me, checking my face against the photograph. "We'll have you there in no time."

That's when I realize how serious this is: the Met charge top dollar for their services as a taxi firm, especially when automatic weapons are along for the ride. Also, there's a dress code for the back of this limo—uniform or handcuffs—and we're breaking it. Our interlocutor climbs in the front next to the driver, and we barely have time to shut the doors before he switches on the disco lights and sound system and floors it. It's not a terribly comfortable way to travel, but it's the third fastest way to get around London—after helicopters and motorbikes—and it's astonishing how the buses and taxis get out of your way when you've got lights, sirens, and submachine guns on your side.

Barely fifteen minutes later we pull up in a very tidy residential street, outside an imposing chunk of Victorian masonry that's clearly been converted into posh apartments. They're not so upmarket right now, with police incident tape strung around the railings and doorways. A couple of constables are on hand, bitching into their wallyphones as they stand by to check IDs for the upset residents who will be coming home from work to find their des res is a crime scene. Angleton strides over to the nearest PC. "Which flat is it?" he asks briskly.

"Can I see your—oh, it's *you* guys." The cop gives me the hairy eyeball. "Him, too?" I pull out my warrant card. "Okay, it's Flat Four. Go on in, the front door's locked open. Don't mess with the crime scene unless you want the inspector to shout at you." He turns away.

I follow Angleton up the front steps. "What was that about?" I ask.

"None of your business, boy." He seems amused about something. I shrug and follow him up the stairs, pausing to stand aside as a couple of SOCOs in bunny suits shuffle downstairs, almost doubled over under the weight of their cameras and bashed gear bags.

"What *is* this? A murder investigation?" I ask.

"Perhaps." Angleton arrives at the entrance to Flat Four, which is indeed wedged open. The white door is smeared with fingerprint powder all around the handle. (Very old-school; maybe the door surface doesn't play nice with cyanoacrylate?) "Anyone there?" he calls.

"Wait one!" There is a loud rustling noise, then a boil-in-the-bag cop appears. Her Tetra radio is crackling excitedly. (It's digital: I suspect they add the fake interference because it confuses the users if the quality is too good.) "Who are you?"

"Angleton and Howard, to ID the victim." *Oh, now he tells me.*

"Okay, come on in. You don't need to suit up but you should avoid touching anything." She backs into the apartment. "We left him in situ, in the living room."

I get my first premonition from the greasy, mouth-watering smell. It's faint but noticeable: last night's Chinese char siu takeaway, or something worse? (Or was it last night's? Could it be even older?) "Wait one. There's a corpse? Do you know what he died of?"

Our guide stops, her bunny suit rustling. "You're *definitely* Howard?" I nod. "You're here to ID the victim?"

Angleton buts in: "He is."

"Well, thanks for briefing me," I say sarcastically. In context, the smell is nauseating. And my ward is itching—it's not under attack, but something very bad happened here not long ago, and it's picking up the aftershocks. "How bad is it?"

"Breathe deeply," she suggests. "If you're feeling faint, it's okay to go back into the hall. Or sit on one of the dining chairs. But don't throw up on the evidence."

Oh, that *bad*. We move on, doing the pantomime horse thing, into a big open-plan dining-kitchen-living area. Kitchen and breakfast bar at one end, then a dining table, then thick shag-pile carpet and sofa and living stuff opposite a picture window. Someone's sitting on the sofa—

Oh, right.

I wander over to the window, turn round, then squat on my heels facing the corpse. The victim is badly burned, but the sofa's made of thick cowhide over fire-retardant padding, and the carpet didn't catch. Like many burn victims the corpse's arms and legs are drawn in, its back arched by contracting muscles—so why is his charcoal briquette of a head lolling to one side? I close my eyes and anchor myself, then look. Yes, I've seen him before. In the Scrum's office, then a couple of times on induction courses around the New Annex crèche. There's still a faint crimson glow inside his skull, but it's not human; there's not enough life there for me to reanimate, just the quiet crunching and munching of the V-parasites chowing down on a host who can no longer deliver the goods.

I open my eyes. "It's Evan," I say. "Evan Elliott. Teamed with Alex for pair programming, specialist in Hilbert-space visualization interfaces." I look at Angleton. "Neck's broken, and there's some residual V-parasite activity. But nothing I can reanimate." The SOCO sergeant is giving me a glassy-eyed stare. "If I had to speculate, I'd say someone broke his neck. Then, while he was paralyzed"—(looks like vampires are tougher than merely mortal humans)—"they positioned him in front of the window and opened the curtains, leaving him for the daylight. Which implies they knew who and what he was." Evan has clearly participated in his final burn-down. I stand up and look at Angleton. "When did we hear about it? How long has he been dead?"

"You knew the deceased?" asks the cop. "Do you know how he was set on fire? We haven't been able to find an ignition source or an accelerant."

I keep a straight face. "Everyone knows vampires don't exist," I say. "So if I was to tell you he was a blood-sucking fiend—"

"You have got to be kidding." For a moment I wonder if I've gone too far: cops take a very dim view of people messing with their heads. But she's seen the warrant card; I'm not sure who she thinks we are, but as long as she thinks we're authority figures she can trust, we should be okay.

I shrug. "Have it your way. It'd explain everything very neatly, though, wouldn't it? Otherwise how else would Vampy Vicious here break his neck sitting down, then spontaneously combust?"

"There are signs of abrasions around his wrists, inflicted pre-mortem. And if you examine his crotch—"

Hmm. "Abrasions? You think someone cuffed him? What about his crotch?"

The sergeant walks over, points at a carbonized mess where the legs join the torso. "Looks like Mr. Polyester Pants suffered a bit of a meltdown in the wedding tackle department. Which was unzipped, privates on parade." Angleton is watching me with arch amusement. "Hm. Your V—theory. Would Edward Cullen here be very strong, by any chance?"

"Yes," I admit. "So, um. Hypothesis: the killer seduced him in order to get close enough to cuff him, then broke his neck and left him to face the rising sun. Which would destroy most of the other evidence, wouldn't it? DNA, skin samples, and so on." *Yummy! Self-cremating murder victims.* "How long ago did it happen?"

"We're not certain yet but the body's cold enough he could have been dead for—"

"It happened yesterday," says Angleton.

"What?" I ask, just as the cop says, "How do you know?"

"He left the office yesterday around 4 p.m. and missed work today." Angleton looks annoyed—and rightly so. Someone in HR was asleep on the job if we didn't learn about it until after the police. "How did you find him?"

"The housekeeper has a key, came in to make the bed, got the fright of her life." The sergeant shakes her head. "Am I looking for a female or male?"

I shrug. "I have no idea. We could ask his co-workers which way they think he swings—swung—but he could have been closeted or have some other reason to lie."

"Well. Perhaps you could introduce me to these co-workers?"

Angleton spares me a quelling look, then slides into gear: "I'm afraid not, Sergeant. Mr. Elliott was engaged in secret work for the government, as are his colleagues, and I must remind you at this point of the terms of the Official Secrets Act. Although, having said that, we entirely understand your desire to bring the perpetrator of this, this—"

"Crime," I suggest.

"*Crime* to justice, and we will immediately notify you if we develop any leads, identify any witnesses, or find any evidence that will further your investigation." Angleton straightens up. "Come *on*, Mr. Howard. We have a briefing room to inform."

"Hey! Now stop right there, you can't just—"

Angleton smiles at her, and she freezes. I sympathize with her predicament: being smiled at by Angleton is a bit like getting a glimpse through the gates of hell. Or seeing an atom bomb go off over your hometown and getting to watch all your pets and lovers and children and parents die simultaneously. "We will leave now," he says, and steps past her. I follow him, and try to ignore the solitary tear overflowing her left eyelid and trickling under her surgical mask.

IT'S AFTER SIX. I'M IN THE BACK OF THE POLICE CAR, SHOULDER to shoulder with Angleton as we ride back to the office, when it hits me and the shakes begin.

I'm no stranger to death. I'm in a profession where people die by accident—there is a *reason* we have such a strong emphasis on health and safety at work. In my particular role, I am sometimes responsible for killing people. It's a horrible, sordid business and I try to avoid it by any means possible—but a chunk of my business is carried out in graveyards and mortuaries. (*What band does the necromancer dance to? Boney M.*) I'm usually blasé about this stuff; after all, you don't get to graduate from Trainee Eater of Souls to Journeyman Scoffer of Spectres without chewing some ectoplasm.

But every once in a while it gets to me.

I didn't know Evan well; in fact I barely knew him at all, and I certainly didn't kill him myself. But that puts him in a particularly odd space, sort of like a friendzone for collateral damage. If he'd been a real friend, ally, or close co-worker I'd be angry and bitter right now, and justifiably so. If he'd been a complete stranger I'd be, well, not indifferent, but not personally invested either. I'd be professionally engaged, and nothing more.

The trouble is, I knew Evan just well enough that he's not a total stranger, but not well enough for mourning and anger. So I feel acutely uncomfortable and edgy and introspective and worried that I'm not responding normally to this kind of shit, or that perhaps I'm losing it and overreacting to the death of a near stranger, and chasing my mind's tail in circles—

"Stop it, boy," says Angleton, and I startle, just as the police car crashes over a speed pillow so hard I crunch my tailbone and clack my teeth together. "I can't hear myself think while you emote like that."

I turn my head to glare at him, but he's already looking away, staring into the distance—not the queue of buses and taxis ahead, but some inner vista of desolation and horror. "It could have been Mhari," I say quietly.

"What if it was?" Angleton murmurs.

"If someone is stalking the PHANGs—"

"Isn't that a bit of a leap?"

I look straight ahead, at the back of the head restraint on the front passenger seat, where a pair of police ears are undoubtedly pricking up and paying attention. "Yes, it *is* a leap, but don't tell me you haven't been half-expecting it. I believe we have a duty of care and should arrange to move them to a place of safety before we continue—"

A throat is very loudly cleared in the front of the car. "'Scuse *me*, folks, but I couldn't help overhearing. And I have to advise you that if you are aware of a threat to life then *we're* the experts in—"

"Ahem," says Angleton, in a tone of voice that comes pre-chilled in liquid helium. "Are you gentlemen qualified for vampire protection duty?"

"For *what*?" says the first cop. Then the driver chips in: "Don't be silly, vampires don't—"

"*Correct,*" Angleton cuts him dead. "Therefore vampire hunters don't exist either. Also: who exactly do you think you'd be protecting from whom?"

"Hang on," says the first cop. "Vampires. Are we talking, like, blood-sucking undead walking corpses? Or people with some sort of disease? Because the first kind, if they've been declared dead, then they're not people. Stands to reason, dunnit?"

"But you can't stake them or set them on fire," interrupts the driver (who has slowed down slightly to join in the conversation). "That'd be Interfering with the Proper Disposal of a Corpse, which is an offense subject to, um, I'd have to look it up. Also, wouldn't it be Interfering with the Work of a Coroner? That's heavy."

"But if they're just a sick human, then the Human Rights Act applies," says the first cop. "So our normal rules of engagement would apply, and we'd have to meet the minimum criteria for deploying lethal force. And the vampire hunters would be up for GBH or attempted murder if they did anything, right? Common Assault at the very least, possibly criminal harassment. Stalking, maybe. If they tweeted or texted the vampire first we could do them for an s.43 under the Malicious Communications Act . . ."

I glance sidelong at Angleton. He glances back at me. "This is *your* fault, boy," he mouths. What, it's my fault we're stuck in traffic while Constable Savage lectures us about how to arrest a vampire for wearing a loud opera cape in a built-up area? Angleton turns his head and makes eye contact with our driver in the rearview mirror. "Kindly shut up and drive, there's a fine chappie," he says; "we're in a hurry. Oh, and don't *ever* talk about this conversation to *anyone*. On pain of extreme pain." He doesn't even bother to pull his warrant card: his words have the weight of stones. And, for a miracle, the officers of the law stop speculating above their pay grade and mash the pedal to the metal.

16.

CODE BLUE

THE BRIEFING ROOM IS WAITING. IT'S CROWDED: JEZ, LOCK-
hart, and Andy are there, obviously. Less obviously needed are the
other heads at the back of the room, who bracket just about everyone
from the DRESDEN RICE committee, including Mhari—and also
Pete and Alex. Neither of whom are remotely cleared for this kind of
shit, so I view their presence here as either a sign of desperation or of
leaking stovepipes and prolapsed security. "Who invited *them*?" I ask
Andy as I join him at the top table.

"Why don't you ask the ring-wraiths?" Andy murmurs back, swiveling his eyes in the direction of a side-door which is just opening to
admit a familiar figure whose mere presence makes my blood run
cold and my ward tingle: it is the Senior Auditor, followed by another
of his cabal—middle-aged, female, kind-faced as death in her twinset
and pearls.

"Good evening, all," announces the Senior Auditor, looking round
the assembled crowd. A quick smile; light flashes from the gold frames
of his half-moon reading glasses. "Mr. Schwartz, I'm pleased to meet
you." Alex jerks, doing his best guilty schoolboy impression. "Our
Patient Zero. I've heard a lot about you."

"Charmed," says the female Auditor, a twinkle as of ice in her eye.

"What is this?" Alex squeaks, sounding as intimidated as a mouse that has just woken up in the middle of a cattery.

"One moment." The Senior Auditor raises his left hand, extends a couple of fingers—reminding me, incongruously, of a death-metal star messing with his audience's head—and utters a word. I don't hear it so much as I feel it, ricocheting back and forth inside my skull like a *really* angry hornet getting ready to sting someone repeatedly. "I declare this meeting room sealed by the authority vested in my office. What is spoken here may not be discussed with those elsewhere, on pain of execution of your oath of office."

I spot Pete huddling in a chair with his arms wrapped around him, looking most unhappy. He's a modern enlightened vicar of the variety who has a PhD in Aramaic Studies. He probably thinks of the whole Bible thing as a fascinating abstract historical puzzle (which he has read in the original tongue—at least those bits that survive via the Dead Sea Scrolls). Of *course* he's unhappy! He's trapped in a committee with a bunch of demonologists and necromancers, the Eater of Souls, two vampires, and a kindly-looking old gent in half-moon specs who scares them all shitless. He must feel like an atheist at a revival meeting.

"I'd like to open this session by announcing that it's a Code Blue emergency briefing. You are all involved, to some extent. Is anybody unclear as to why they're here?"

Hands go up all round the room. "Yes!" It's Doris from Health and Safety. (My heart sinks: old Basil the coffin dodger is sitting right beside her, sucking on his dentures and rocking slowly.) "What's this about?"

"Ah, Mrs. Greene!" The SA smiles, apparently in genuine pleasure. "You're here because you're the Health and Safety monitor on the DRESDEN RICE committee. And I see you brought Mr. Northcote-Robinson from Archives along, too? How charming. (Basil, we really must get together one of these days, it's been too long.) The reason for this meeting is somewhat less happy, I'm afraid to say. This lunchtime we became aware that one of our vampires was missing. I believe James and Mr. Howard are just back from investigating . . . ?"

Angleton clears his throat. "Evan Elliott is confirmed dead. Bob identified him. Cause of death was hemogolic incineration followed by V-parasite autophagosis. His neck was broken, immobilizing him; the killer then positioned him in front of a window."

He falls silent. "It was a professional hit," I add. "Whoever did it knew exactly what they were doing and left no forensic traces. There may be CCTV footage from the lobby and the cameras nearby, but I expect the assassin took care to avoid standing too close." CSI's magic image enhancement software doesn't actually work on real-world CCTV footage: a blurry low-resolution image saved at eight frames a second won't tell us anything useful about a careful professional who never came within fifty meters of a camera.

I'm interrupted by a retching sound. It's Alex, with his head between his knees; Pete is leaning over him, clearly concerned. From across the room, Mhari catches my eye: she's clearly upset.

"Would someone care to explain what this means in plain English?" complains Doris Greene. "As the incident didn't occur on our premises I don't see how we can possibly be blamed—"

"What—what?" chirps Basil Northcote-Robinson. He looks puzzled.

"Please leave your questions for later," says the SA. He's still smiling, but there are wrinkles in his forehead and crow's-feet at the sides of his eyes. "I see that Oscar Menendez is not present." Mhari startles. "That could be significant. I have further bad news. In addition to Mr. Elliott's death, last night Sir David Finch wrote a suicide note, then unscrewed one of the window units in his office and jumped to his death." Alex seems to have got his rebellious stomach under control, but Mhari turns white as a sheet: she looks as if she might start with the head-spinning pea-soup spraying thing at any moment. "Which is extremely convenient. Ms. Murphy, do you have any reason to believe that Mr. Menendez might have wanted to kill Sir David?"

"Bu-buh—" Mhari's jaw flaps for a few seconds. "No! It's too early!" *Now* she looks ashen. "He's not ready for the, uh, the bust-out. Nowhere near."

"Thank you, that will be all," the SA says, not unkindly. She flops back in her seat, gasping as if she's just swallowed a toad. "We will discuss his plans further during your next enhanced vetting."

"Pale" doesn't really describe her right now: "ashen" would be a better word. She's shaking, either from fear or anger. I'm not sure whether she's pissed at (or afraid of) the Senior Auditor, or freaked because he thinks Oscar might be a murderer. But the SA rolls sub-limely on, leaving the rest of us floundering in a sea of uncertainties.

"If Mr. Menendez is not responsible for Sir David's death, then we must assume that he is in immediate danger. Gerald, if you'd be so good as to take care of matters? You may leave the room."

"I'll get onto it right away," Lockhart says as he heads for the door. I suspect he's relieved to be out of the firing line, with a straight-forward task to accomplish. "Resource level?"

"This is a Code Blue," interjects the female Auditor. "Do whatever is necessary to locate Mr. Menendez and move him to a place of safety."

Mhari sticks up her hand. "There is a Mercedes van," she says hesitantly. "Kitted out with food, fuel, and a full bug-out kit. Oscar called it his Mystery Machine; it's parked in the Bank's basement car park on level B." She rattles off registration, make, and model details. "He was prepping a bolt-hole somewhere in the countryside. I don't know where exactly, he refused to say."

The Auditor beams at her. "Thank you, Ms. Murphy!" She glances at Lockhart. "Proceed as authorized."

And then Gerry Lockhart is gone, and I suppress a shudder. Did I just hear an Auditor tell one of the heavy hitters in External Assets to *do whatever is necessary*? Then I look at Mhari. She's wearing a pro-foundly guilty expression. Is it putting two plus two together if I infer that the senior executive she mentioned over dinner was . . . *oh*. Well, it's none of my business, I suppose. Especially now.

"I have called this meeting because it has become apparent that

someone is attempting to liquidate our OPERA CAPE employees,"
says the Senior Auditor, taking over from his colleague. "This working group therefore has three tasks. The first item on the agenda is to
place all personnel with PHANG syndrome who are not members of
this committee in protective detention for the duration. The second
item is to identify the threat—"

"Oh *no*," groans Alex. (The SA chooses to ignore his interruption.)

"—by establishing a decoy protocol whereby two assets will be
exposed, albeit with protection—"

"Now wait a minute!" starts Mhari.

"—and the third action item is to neutralize the threat," the SA
adds, ignoring her, too. "Which means identifying, characterizing, and
preventing it. Ahem. There is some reason to believe that it may have
resulted from an inadvertent contact with our own organization. This
cannot be confirmed at present, but you should be aware that this is
why I have established a Code Blue working group and bound you
all to silence. Colonel Lockhart is, incidentally, already privy to this
plan."

Colonel Lockhart? Well, I already knew he was ex-army, but that's
some heavy stuff. I look around the room. Everybody is looking as
grim as a tax audit, except for Mhari and Alex (who look petrified),
Pete (who is appalled), and the DRESDEN RICE dead wood (who
appear to be wondering what time dinner is served in this nursing
home).

"Working groups: Greene, Northcote-Robinson, you are working
under Jez Wilson on task alpha, securing our human resources. You
will coordinate with Colonel Lockhart once he has secured Mr.
Menendez. Angleton, Howard, Murphy, Wilson, Newstrom: you are
on tasks beta and gamma, threat identification and neutralization.
Which is to say, you have to identify, track, and intercept a dedicated
assassin who has successfully killed at least one PHANG and quite
possibly a senior banking executive." Everyone looks duly grave.
"You will now form breakout groups in, ah, this briefing room and
next door, room 203, and conduct a task breakdown exercise and

develop proposals for taking the operation forward. Judith and I will coordinate from here. Are there any further questions? No? Very well, let's get to work."

I END UP TAKING MHARI HOME—*MY* HOME. BECAUSE . . .

"It's a safe house. No, really: class one secured, and tested the hard way."

I do not tell her that the testing involved me being doorstepped by KGB zombies. Or articulate just how little faith I put in the DRESDEN RICE coffin-dodgers who are half of team alpha. For now, it's enough for her to know that "home" is a Victorian mid-terrace owned by the Crown Estates and leased to approved personnel at a rent affordable on a civil service salary (otherwise we wouldn't be able to staff our offices in central London). With additional security and wards provided by our own Facilities Management Unit, just in case work comes calling, or we need to take files home that must be protected from the depredations of random burglars.

"We've got a spare bedroom you can use." (Actually, we've got two spare bedrooms: it's a family-sized house with no family to fill it.) "And if our Mr. X is trying to rub you out, the last place they'll look is under the roof of the guy they set up to kill you. Now, your own apartment is another matter . . ."

I don't need to remind her about Evan. She swallows, and nods. "Are you sure your wife won't mind?"

"She'll mind any number of things," I tell her. "She'll mind if you smoke in the bathroom, she'll mind tripping over your suitcase in the front hall, and she'll mind if you don't buy your own groceries or keep clogging up the washing machine—but she won't mind *you*, if you follow? As long as you're a co-worker and it's just for a day or two. Until we neutralize the threat."

If the threat is an insider, it's quite likely that they've got access to the PHANGs' personnel files. It'd explain how they got to Evan. The alpha group worked this out. So they offered the PHANGs a choice of the duty officer's accommodation (a lumpy bunk bed in an office next to the staff canteen), a cheap room in a Travelodge, or relocation to the Village Formerly Known as Dunwich (where we maintain a whole bunch of training facilities, and which has rather good security against intruders).

However. I have a nasty, sneaky, suspicious mind, and I am aware of the possibility that our PHANG-killer might not only be an insider, but that they might be on the inside of the Senior Auditor's tent, pissing in the communal punch. And "under Bob's roof" is the very last place that anyone with access to her personnel file will expect to find her lurking. So I am minded to conduct a controlled experiment. I don't think Mhari is suicidally inclined, so during a coffee break an hour into proceedings I propose this arrangement to her. And because she's neither suicidally inclined nor any less paranoid than I am, she agrees . . . on condition she can tell the Senior Auditor where she'll be bunking, first.

Which is fine by me, as long as the SA is the only person she tells. If we can't trust the SA, we are so comprehensively fucked that we might as well wind up the organization and chow down on the poison pills right now.

Before heading home I spend another hour with the beta group, working out our plan for the morrow. I have some misgivings about it, largely because it relies heavily on Alex and Pete, both of whom are (in my opinion) undertrained newbies. On the other hand they'll have me riding shotgun, along with a small battle group of specialists (who will be briefed at the last possible hour, to reduce the risk of leaks). And it's all going to be supervised from the New Annex by Angleton himself. I'd ask for JOHNNY PRINCE and BASHFUL INCENDIARY if they were available, but most of our heavy hitters are out of the office this week, presumably hitting heavy things a very long way from home. The BLUE HADES negotiations had to come up at the worst possible time. I suspect the SA is taking steps to recall the delegates, but even so they won't be back in town for at least twenty-four hours. So, in the meantime, we've got to work with what we've got.

Eventually it turns nine o'clock, and people are yawning. "Let's call it a day," I suggest, and nobody—not even Angleton—demurs.

I walk out into the corridor and, a few seconds later, Mhari follows me. "What now?" she asks.

"Taxi." I don't like the expense (London taxis are not cheap) but there are two of us, and I don't like the exposure of walking.

"Okay," she says. "Do you have a spare key? What about dinner?"

"Spare key's at home. I was thinking of Chinese takeaway . . ."

She rolls her eyes. "Oh you. You haven't changed a bit, have you?"

We hail a taxi, and after a brief ride (and a cabbie-administered walletectomy) I lead Mhari up the garden path, all two wheelie-bin-lined meters of it. "Watch out for the wards," I tell her as I apply key to lock.

"You don't have to warn me. Brr! What did you do, bury an electrical substation under the front step?"

The door opens. "Come on in." I step inside and turn on the hall lights. "We had a problem with unwelcome visitors a couple of years ago and they really beefed up the security afterwards." I don't tell her about the additional precautions we're taking tonight: the basilisk camera in my left jacket pocket, or the Glock 17 loaded with banishment rounds in a quick-draw holster in my right. Mhari might be back in HR but I still don't think she's got the full picture about what I actually do these days.

"What caused the problem? Jehovah's Witnesses?"

"Nah, they were easy enough to get rid of: I just made an appointment to discuss the Bible later, then invited Pete round. We've been blacklisted ever since. It was the Brotherhood of the Black Pharaoh." I rub my right upper arm instinctively. Everything is better with cannibalism and necromancy.

She closes the front door and I relax as the defensive ward reactivates itself. For a moment we had a break in the secure perimeter. But now . . . we're okay. I begin to shrug out of my overloaded jacket, planning to hang it in the hall, as Mhari squeezes past in the direction of the kitchen.

"*Wrrraow?*"

"Waugh!" Mhari almost levitates out of her Louboutins. "You didn't say you had a cat!"

I look round. The cat is lurking on the staircase that runs up one side of the hall, roughly at eye level, staring out at her from between the baluster poles with an expression of concentrated, black-eyed malevolence. One paw flops between the rails, over the side of the stairs. "Er. I have a cat. Mhari, meet Spooky. Spooky—ah, what the hell. You don't have a problem with cats, do you?"

"No." She eyes Spooky warily from just out of paw's reach. I can guess what happened. Darkened hall, dark brown carpet, black-furred ambush hunter. "Did she go for you?"

"She nearly gave me a nasal piercing!" Spooky, detecting that she is the subject of attention, rolls on her back and squirms, purring and exposing her rib cage like a hairy mantrap. Mhari glares, then walks through into the kitchen, leaving the cat to enjoy her control of the commanding heights. "Huh. This doesn't say 'Bob' to me."

"That's because it says 'Bob and Mo,'" I point out. "Tea and coffee's in that cupboard, milk's in the fridge, bread bin's over there, recycling's under that worktop by the back door." She hasn't put her bag down yet. And now that I'm paying attention, I realize that all she's got is what she's wearing and what's in her handbag. Nobody was planning a sleepover when they woke up this morning. "Hmm. We've got some spare toiletries and a dressing gown you can use, and if you give me a list of necessities I can pick them up tomorrow and drop them round before plan beta kicks off. But first I need to check the spare bed's made up and the blackout curtains are adequate. Let me show you around . . ."

"If you don't mind." She smiles, uncharacteristically diffident. "I'll try not to be any trouble."

WHAT AROUSES OSCAR IS THE DEGREE TO WHICH HIS KIDNAPper reminds him of a younger version of his wife, Pippa. They're both skinny blonde chicks with that brittle finishing-school lacquer, cheekbones sharp enough to hone knives on, firm, rounded breasts just about bursting out of the top of her cocktail dress, long, stockinged legs that go on forever, arms sheathed in black satin gloves. She has natural-blonde hair up in a ponytail, bee-stung lips, glistening like . . . don't think about it. Pippa's gone slightly to seed in the past few years, rosy-cheeked from the vino, saggy skin and stretch marks from dropping the crotch-fruit, skin showing the first wrinkles from over-exposure to sea and sun. But this girl could be Pippa's mad-eyed party-animal jailbait younger sibling, from back in the day. Except that Pippa's an only child.

Being kidnapped by someone who looks like your wife's demented younger sister in a party frock is a very strange experience, but he's enjoying it so far. Yes, she's got a gun and she's obviously unstable. But since he became a PHANG his senses have become acute. He can smell waves of lust rising off her like steam: if there isn't a puddle in her panties with his name on it, his name isn't Oscar Menendez. And if that minx Mhari isn't putting out for him right now, beggars can't be choosers, can they? (Even if they're really millionaires, soon to be billionaires.)

It's all a bit of a joke, really . . .

It had started at eight o'clock, when his cellphone rang. It was the car alarm monitoring service. "I'm sorry to bother you, sir, but did you know your car alarm is going off? According to out tracking system it's not moving, but someone's opened the door."

"Which car?" he asked.

"It's the, ah, the Mercedes Vito, sir." The getaway van. He blinked, taking a moment to remember, relieved that it wasn't the Porsche. "It's still in the car park at—"

"I'll sort it out," he said, mildly irritated. "That's a secure pound under my office; it's probably a false alarm. Can you call me again if it moves? It'll take me a while to get there and reset the alarm." Hanging up, he took the elevator down to the hotel lobby and hailed a cab to the bank. Going to his long-lost place of work for the first time in what felt like years (even though it was only a few weeks) was alienating. It felt even weirder to be making the trip in home-casual rather than office uniform. Like a dream, complete with the same sense of something-not-quite-right. Not for the first time he found himself wondering if buying the van hadn't been a mistake right from the start.

The van was an indulgence; also, an obligation; and finally, a precaution. He'd bought it as soon as he began to grasp the scope of the opportunity that brilliant fool Alex had presented him with, but before Mhari had told him about the Laundry. It wasn't his true getaway option, but it was a good-enough decoy to convince the rest of the Scrum that he was planning to take them with him, and it also served a secondary function. His *real* getaway option lived in an anonymous wallet in a bottom drawer in his second guest bedroom at home: a genuine Canadian passport with genuine biometrics matching him, in a name nobody he worked or lived with knew about. Along with the matching birth certificate and the diamond Visa and Mastercard—both genuine—the wallet's contents had cost him ten times as much as the van, and would carry one tenth as many passengers to safety. But the van would do in an emergency, if the bug-out wallet was compromised by an Interpol Red Alert: Oscar had not got where he was today by skimping on preparations.

The Scrum were also blissfully unaware of the special fixtures and fittings he'd installed in the Mystery Machine to support its secondary function. The illegal pistol hidden behind the plastic trim on the front passenger-side door. The false number plates and the phlebotomy kit and the body bag folded under the floor of the rear compartment. It behooved Oscar to keep an eye on the van, hence the expensive anti-theft tracking system.

Oscar had taken the lift down from the lobby to the underground car park, expecting to find nothing much. Most likely an inconsiderate ass who'd exceeded his recommended daily dose of intra-nasally delivered Vitamin C had backed his Chelsea Tractor into the front bumper before screeching off home. Nevertheless, he inspected the van from a distance, then close-up, before approaching: everything seemed to be in order. But as he walked around the driver's side he noticed an anomaly. The door lock button was raised.

Frowning, he opened the door.

"Hi!" said the woman in the passenger seat. "You must be Oscar. Please don't move."

Oscar had blinked. One moment she wasn't there; the next, he opened the door and she was beaming at him over the barrel of his own—

No, it wasn't his pistol. His was an ancient, battered, and very illegal revolver: the best he'd been able to get, given his shortage of low-life acquaintances. This was an automatic, dull and black, with a suppressor protruding from the barrel, like something out of a James Bond movie. Her black opera gloves made it look like a bizarre extension of her arms.

"For your safety and comfort," she said in a sing-song voice, "you should be aware that this gun can shoot *straight through* the side of this vehicle. Mm-hmm! Now I want you to open the rear passenger door and climb in, then sit down in the right-hand seat and fasten your seat belt. It's going to be a fun ride!"

Bemused, Oscar did as he was told. Then, because he had to try: "Please point that gun somewhere else?" he asked, putting just a bit of mental push behind the words.

"I don't think so." She was still smiling, a fey, secretive expression as if it was a great big joke they shared. "Doesn't work on me, lover-boy. Is your seat belt tight?"

Oscar swallowed. *Is she a vampire?* he wondered. "What is this?"

"Put these on." She produced a pair of handcuffs. "Then we're going for a drive. A magical mystery tour! Isn't that wild?"

The handcuffs featured a fake leopard-skin lining. Still bemused, Oscar clipped them around his right wrist.

"And the left, dear," she said. He put his left wrist in the cuff, leaving it loose. Then something happens. A blur. He blinks and she's standing next to him in the open doorway, gun out of reach and her left hand on his wrist, the cuffs closed and locked. They're the modern kind, with a rigid steel bridge. The door slides shut and slam-locks, and he peers out through the dark-tinted glass as she walks forward and climbs into the driver's seat. "No one outside can see anyone in here except the driver," she says.

Oscar shakes his head, but the glamour she's hit him with over-powers his skepticism. He's sprouting an erection, as if being kid-napped at gunpoint and handcuffed in the back of his own engine of abduction is a turn-on. The knife-edge between sex and death is very sharp.

She slides the keys into the ignition—somehow she's taken them from him—then starts the engine and carefully pulls out of the park-ing bay. As the van climbs the exit ramp, she starts to sing, in a pass-ably good voice: "*I think we're alone now . . .*"

She drives for a long time, out into the back roads of Hertford-shire, until she finds a suitable place to park: the north gateway lead-ing to a field, at the end of a lane half a mile from the nearest bus stop. Then she climbs into the back of the van and has her way with Oscar. He disappoints her by ejaculating almost immediately; she frowns in distaste. "Kiss-*kiss!*" she chides him as she breaks his neck. Then she rides him until she comes repeatedly, eyes squeezed shut, shuddering in triumphant dominion.

Afterwards she cleans up the crime scene as usual. The last thing she does is to turn Oscar's paralyzed head to face the open passenger door. It's facing east, and the sky is black and cloudless, sprinkled with stars. She kisses him on lips that still sense and move, trying breathlessly to form words even though he has no control over his lungs. Then she walks away towards the bus stop, leaving him para-lyzed and alone to face the dawn.

She wonders what her new patron wants her to do next. She hasn't had this much fun in years.

NOW PAY ATTENTION! WE HAVE A PLAN. AND THE PLAN IS SIM-ple enough:

Someone is stalking and killing our hemophagously inclined em-ployees.

We believe there is an inside connection, and they know where the PHANGs live. (More speculatively: the inside connection may be a very old, very sneaky PHANG who doesn't like the competition, or the attention they're drawing, or who manipulated them into existence as an experiment and who has now decided they are surplus to requirements, or who has stolen them from some other very old, sneaky PHANG with some other scheme in mind . . .)

Obviously, we want to protect our people, hemophagous or otherwise. After all, if we can't even protect our people, what does it say about our ability to meet our operational targets? (Also: if you ever want to see a self-kicking conga line, tell a security organization that for the past forty years someone has been manipulating its information flow from the inside.)

Anyway: we intend to place all but one of our PHANGs out of reach, then build an ambush for whoever or whatever goes after the only available target. Who will look like an easy kill because, normally, they would be. However, anyone who goes for Alex is going to have to come at him across a prepared killing ground guarded by me and an entire OCCULUS team, including a couple of "bricks" from the Special Reconnaissance Regiment, and through a security cordon controlled by SO15, the Met's Counter Terrorism Command, who are there to ensure that the SRR and SAS heavies get to do their stuff without drawing undue attention.

That's the theory—the easy part. The hard bit is how to go about exposing our tethered goat, without actually tipping off the adversary that it's a trap. As my archival enquiries have almost certainly activated a tripwire, that's going to be hard. As all the surviving PHANGs (except Oscar, who, as of my departure from the office, is still missing) are under cover or locked down, we've effectively served notice on our adversary that we know they're out there. It's hard to see how we could have avoided it, in view of their very public disposal of Evan and Sir David. So our exposure of the bellwether has to look like some kind of accident, and we have to present an easy enough target to tempt the killer out of hiding, but not such a juicy one that their suspicions are aroused.

Even if our adversary is an insider and takes the bait, I give it only about a 25 percent probability of working. And once it fails, we're going to be in a world of hurt—at that point, we run out of options other than a plonkingly obvious inquisition and witch hunt. Witch hunts are a reliable way of devastating organization morale, squandering human capital, and uncovering lots of trivial stuff that we didn't want to have to officially pay attention to. They generate a boom in business for circular firing squads, but don't achieve anything useful—and will ensure we render ourselves operationally incompetent for the next six months. We can't afford to lose six months. Time is money that comes out of one particular purse we can't afford to spend, even if we succeed in winkling out the PHANG-killer in the shadows. We are in CASE NIGHTMARE GREEN days, and the next threat we have to deal with might be one of the existential anthropic kind, which is to say, the variety where you have to get it right the first time because there is no second chance."

Which is why the Senior Auditor, bless his heartless, twinkly eyed smile, chose the Pete'n'Alex Show as the main draw for our vampire hunter carnival.

As he points out with inexorable logic: "Mr. Menendez is unavailable. Ms. Murphy may be presumed to be a hard target, due to her prior experience within the organization and, ah, incompatibility with the *modus operandi* that was used on Evan. This goes for Janice Hill, too." Mhari suppresses a snigger. "So our candidates are Dick, John, and Alex. Alex is fully briefed and seconded to this working group because he was available; the principle of minimizing operational exposure suggests we should use him." The SA smiles brightly at Alex, who cringes beneath his gaze. "Don't worry. Your utility to us as bait will be severely impaired if we allow any harm to befall you! So that's not going to be allowed to happen."

"Hang on a moment," I interrupt. "Isn't this several notches above Alex's competence? He hasn't even been assessed for active operational service. And Reverend Wilson"—it feels really odd to be using Pete's official day job title—"is almost certainly not equipped to deal with . . ."

I trail off. The Senior Auditor is *looking* at me. It feels a bit like being an amoeba on a microscope slide, pinpointed by million-watt searchlights and observed by a vast, unsympathetic, alien intellect.

"The adversary will make no attempt to take the bait on organization premises," the SA points out with complete self-assurance. "He will wait until his prey is off-site. I believe"—the SA glances sidelong at Pete, and I take a shuddering breath of relief—"you have a work assignment that takes you to the KGB.2.YA archive in Watford on a regular basis. And that Dr. Schwartz is assisting you. Is that correct?"

"What, you mean the MAGIC CIRCLE OF SAFETY stuff?" Pete looks momentarily confused. "Yes, that's right. Why?"

"Tomorrow afternoon, after dark, you will take Dr. Schwartz for a ride out to the warehouse," the Senior Auditor tells us. "Mr. Angleton will take control of the security cordon around the New Annex prior to your departure. You will be provided with a covert escort, under Mr. Howard's control, and the target area will be adequately prepared for our ambush team to move into position upon your arrival." He smiles reassuringly. "We will ensure that your movements are well-trailed, but no more than three hours in advance. If the bait is *not* taken, you will simply retrieve the items Reverend Wilson needs to continue his project, then return to the New Annex. And if the bait *is* taken, we'll be waiting."

He looks straight at me. "The rest is up to you, Mr. Howard."

A PHONE RINGS, AND A VOICE ANSWERS: "HELLO?"

"George, it's me."

"What is the—" (A pause.) "Yes?"

"The wheels have come off, I'm afraid."

"The—tell me. Speak. Now. I command you."

"Marianne has dispatched two of the new brood, and she and I are going to take care of two of the others in the next day. However, a problem has arisen. The Laundry are now officially aware that someone or something is stalking their new intake. And when I say the Laundry, I mean the Invisible College—word has travelled all the way up the ladder."

(Another pause.) "Well, *that* tears it."

"There's still time to cauterize the canker before it putrefies, George. But I can't do this on my own. You'll have to move, and move fast. Marianne and I are luring our next targets away from the security cordon, and we have dragged a lot of their guards along for the ride—it's an ambush, in case it isn't obvious. But we can only keep them away from the New Annex for about two hours. Then the entire house of cards will collapse."

"Bastard! You planned this! You set me up!"

"Not well enough, I'm afraid. The best laid plans of mice and men, etcetera. It's all very unfortunate. Someone needs to go into the New Annex office building and liquidate the control team that the Laundry has established to stalk us. For obvious reasons, it cannot be me."

(Tightly.) "What can I expect to find?"

"Two Auditors. One DSS who I know nothing about—he's not in the declassified archives. A bunch of chair-warmers. And the site security I outlined in the briefing document."

"You'll owe me for this."

"Yes-yes, of course. But can you do it? Or have the decades of sitting on your arse in your nice warm club rotted the sinews, old chap?"

"You'll owe me blood."

Click.

AT PRECISELY HALF PAST FIVE THE NEXT AFTERNOON, TWO helmeted figures slip out of the side entrance of the New Annex, slink down an alleyway, then unchain and climb aboard a tricked-out Vespa. The rider—Pete—seems no more or less suspicious than is to be expected, but the passenger—Alex—is clearly as twitchy as a TWOCer who suspects a police stakeout. It's not surprising (Pete, after all, isn't the tethered goat in this scenario, he's just the driver) but it's worrying.

I watch them via a battery-powered wireless webcam glued to the shutters on the betting shop opposite the alley entrance. I'm sitting in front of a laptop in the cramped back of a bright crimson box on wheels that proclaims itself to be a City of London Fire Brigade Major Incident Command Vehicle. It's not; it's an OCCULUS truck. Fire Incident Command Vehicles don't carry wiry-looking taciturn guys in black webbing and urban/nighttime camo uniforms, or an unfeasibly large number of guns. "Decoy is moving," I announce. I'm wearing a headset and mike and a webbing/camo outfit of my own, albeit lighter on the guns and heavier on the occult accessories. "Turning left left left into the high street—"

"On it. Moving out." The narrator is "Scary" Spice, who I've worked with on other occasions, and who currently doesn't have any army rank I understand—he's some sort of "civilian contractor," having graduated from being a sergeant in the territorial SAS a couple of years ago. "Eyes up, guys."

There's a loud rumbling noise from somewhere in front as our driver guns the engine, then a distant wail of air horns as he switches on the blues and twos.

(I had to warn Pete: "Do not be tempted to shoot amber lights or exceed the speed limit. Remember you're leading a twelve-ton truck full of men with guns who will be very annoyed if they lose track of you. But not as annoyed as Alex will be if they lose track of *him*, and our adversary doesn't.")

("Spoilsport." The vicar snorted. "As if I'd do that . . .")

We drive for about fifty minutes, heading north and then east until we hit the North Circular at rush hour. The North Circular moves for no man, even if he's got flashing blue lights and enough firepower to start World War Z. Inevitably we lose Pete and Alex for a while. But then I get a call from the traffic ops control room for North London, where our friends in blue are keeping a special eye open for a vicar and a vampire on a Vespa. (They're also keeping an eye on the warehouse via CCTV, but we don't want any obvious watchers on-site before we arrive, lest they spook the target.) The North Circular is okay for this sort of long-distance tail—it has more traffic cameras than Spooky the cat had fleas. I relay to the cab: "He's about a kilometer ahead of us, still on the A406 westbound. Due to turn right onto Neasden Lane North . . ."

My phone rings. It's Pete; he's got a hands-free helmet. "Hi, Bob—I seem to have lost you. Where are you? I'm going to pull over—"

"No, don't do that. We've got you on camera; you're about a kilometer ahead of us. We're stuck in that tailback on the North Circular you passed a couple of minutes ago. You should on no account stop moving. If necessary, if we haven't gotten free of this, you should ride on past the Watford turnoff, join the M25 anti-clockwise at junction 21A, then leave it again at 1A and take Western Avenue back in until you hit the North Circular again. But *don't stop moving*. If you stop you become a target. Do you copy?"

"Don't stop, loop around the M25 and North Circular if you can't shake the traffic." I feel a sudden lurch as the big truck begins to move again. "Got it."

He disconnects. I don't cross my fingers or clutch my nonexistent rabbit's foot, but I check my ward (a heavy-duty item I checked out this morning), pat the belt holster with my G17, and take a deep breath. Mo will kill me if I let anything happen to Pete. (Hell, she nearly killed me already, just for asking him to read a dubious Bible translation.)

Someone nudges my shoulder. "You okay, Bob?" asks my neighbor. It's Warrant Officer Howe, and if he's sounding concerned rather than ripping my lungs out through my left ear I must be a pretty picture. (Either that or he's afraid I'll go nonlinear, like the way things turned out that time at Brookwood.) I dredge up a reassuring smile from somewhere. "Pre-op nerves," I say. "I'll be okay once it shakes down."

More juddering and acceleration and braking as we roll along, doing the lights and siren thing. My phone rings again. "Bob?" It's Pete. "I have you in my rearview mirror so I'm proceeding to the warehouse. Bye."

"Decoy has us in sight and is proceeding to target location," I announce over the intercom.

"Wait one," says Scary. "Please repeat."

"Decoy confirmed he has us in rearview mirror and is accordingly proceeding to target location," I repeat.

"Negative, Howard, decoy is out of sight."

"What!" I stop. Obviously there's more than one fire engine out and about tonight. "I'll check with traffic control." I start poking at the airwave radio, trying to remember my cop-speak. Why didn't we slap a GPS transponder on the bike? *Don't be silly, Bob, it takes time to requisition those things and if everyone does their job properly it won't be necessary . . .*

"Scooter registration LB59KPT is on the A411 London Road, northbound towards Watford," the dispatcher tells me.

Well *shit.* That puts Pete well ahead of us. He'll be there almost five minutes before we catch up. "Is there any way to make this thing go faster?" I ask Scary. Meanwhile I speed dial Pete on my phone. And that's where Murphy's Law takes over, because he picks up the phone, and the call drops immediately. I dial again. And again. The third time it goes straight through to voice mail. "Hello, you have reached the voice mail of the Reverend Peter Wilson. I'm sorry I'm not able to speak right now; if you leave a message I'll get back to you as soon as possible. In the meantime, you may find these parish numbers helpful . . ."

"Decoy's phone not responding," I tell everyone. "We've lost contact."

"Okay, hang on to your 'nads," says Scary. "Hit it," he adds, possibly forgetting that he has a hot mike. The driver floors the accelerator and tries to bounce my brain out of my skull. I just hope we haven't left it too late.

PETE PULLS INTO THE SMALL CAR PARK BEHIND THE KGB.2.YA warehouse and switches off the ignition. He looks around. It's dark and the industrial estate is nearly deserted, dimly lit by sodium lights that cast long shadows across the concrete and tarmac. The metal-clad buildings hunch like the shells of long-dead giant tortoises. There's a single cheap hatchback car parked out in front, and a cheerful light glows from the office window beside the front door. Pete climbs off the scooter, then holds the handlebars while Alex disentangles himself and fumbles with his helmet strap. "Is this it?" he asks anxiously. "Where *is* everyone?"

"It's always like this, apparently," Pete replies, looking round. "And don't worry about the others. Bob'd let us know if they were delayed again."

"Well, I don't like it." Alex shivers. He's been doing a lot of that lately, and not because he's cold—as a regular cyclist, even in winter, he's used to it: his hoodie and trousers are up to the job of keeping him warm on the back of a bike. But he's still suffering from the culture shock of having migrated from academia into the pressure-cooker intensity of the Scrum, and the Laundry is even worse in some ways, combining the dingy institutional conservativism of a particularly stuffy Oxbridge college with the stuff of nightmares. It seems to be staffed by a curious mixture of battle-axe civil servants, slightly demented CS/math geeks like Howard, and scary old men who *smile* at you in a way that is simultaneously friendly and horrifying, like a hangman sizing you up for a noose. And then they explain that some lunatic is trying to *kill* you, has in fact already murdered Evan quite horribly, and that they expect you to quietly walk in front of a bus to see if the driver hits the brakes in time—

—And you can't seem to think of a reason to say "fuck! no!" before your hands are fumbling with a motorcycle helmet and you're sitting on a scooter behind a vicar, and then facing a locked door on an industrial estate with who-knows-what beyond it—

—Alex makes a complex gesture with the fingers of his left hand, in the privacy of his jacket pocket. Then he pulls out his hulking great tablet of a phone and discreetly fires up an app he flung together in a frenzy of focussed hacking overnight. And which he hasn't told anybody about. Because, well, if they won't take him into their confidence, why should he take them into his?

"Let's go in," suggests Pete. He steps forward and pulls out a bunch of keys. Then he pauses and pushes the intercom button. Pushes it again. There's a brief crackle. "Wilson and Schwartz from Capital Laundry Services," he says. The lock buzzes and he pushes the door open, pocketing his keys again. He glances over his shoulder just once. "That's funny," he says. "I wonder where they are? It's jolly hard to hide a truck that size—"

Alex follows, pushing the door wide open and steps across the threshold. At once he feels a pricking in his fingertips and a buzzing like angry wasps in the small leather fetish-bag they made him wear on a thong around his neck. His pupils dilate. "Something's *wrong*—" he begins to say.

Everything seems to take forever.

There is a desk and a chair in the office behind the door, and the chair is occupied by a dead man, head lolling, eyes staring vacantly at the ceiling.

The man in the chair is not alone.

A tall, slim woman stands over him. Blonde hair, black leather jacket, black leggings—this is what Alex notices before he gets as far as the pistol she's holding in one blue-plastic-gloved hand.

"Kiss-kiss, boys." She smiles, sweet as rat poison. "Over there, please." She makes a minute gesture with the gun. "You"—to Pete—"kick the door shut." Alex knows very little about guns (beyond the basics: that they're machines for making holes in people, and being shot apparently hurts a *lot*) but it looks very black and there's a fat cylinder sticking out in front, which can't be good.

"Are you going to kill us?" asks Alex, unable to keep a quaver out of his voice.

"No." Her smile turns sour. "Not that I don't want to, you understand, but . . . orders."

"Don't provoke her," murmurs Pete.

"Oh, I'm unprovokable." Her hearing is acute, too. "It's my vocation to cleanse the world of things like you." Another smile, teeth aggressively bared. "Of bloodsuckers and their enablers."

"Why?" Alex asks, voice rising. "I haven't done anything to you!"

"If sheep had guns, would they tolerate the farmer just because he hasn't done anything to them *yet*?" She motions with the pistol, in the direction of the closed inner door. "Open the door. Go inside. Close the door. Don't make me impatient."

"What if I say no?" asks Alex, just as Pete tries to say, "You don't have to do this, truly—"

"*Open* the door, *go inside*, and *close* the door! Or I will shoot you in the kneecaps and drag you through the doorway myself!" Her sudden vehemence makes Alex jump.

Pete reaches for the door handle. "What's on the other side?" he asks.

"Fucking *do* it." She raises the gun, holding it two-handed, her eyes burning.

"I'm going! I'm going!" Pete opens the door and shuffles through. Alex twitches, then cringes after him when he sees her expression. It's the hunger of a tiger on a choke chain, in sight of its next meal but not permitted to approach. A moment later the door closes with a click.

The woman (who is not called Marianne) relaxes slightly. She crosses the room and hurriedly turns a key in the lock on the inner door. She returns her pistol to an inner pocket. Then she sits down on the edge of the desk to wait for the next victims to show up, shivering with joyful anticipation. Her new patron has promised her his leftovers.

IF THERE IS ONE THING WORSE THAN VAMPIRES, IT WOULD HAVE to be vampire hunters.

Consider: vampires are obligate predators. If they try not to feed, eventually the V-parasites get hungry and chow down on the host. Prudent vampires do not feed indiscriminately, and try to minimize their chances of being caught by picking one victim at a time, and fasting as long between victims as possible. But they are, of necessity, serial killers.

Vampire *hunters*, on the other hand . . .

A vampire hunter is *a serial killer who hunts serial killers*. Not only that: the serial killers they hunt are supernaturally strong ritual magicians with mind-control chops and an aptitude for occult magic.

So I think it's reasonable to say that vampire hunters either have an extremely short life expectancy, or constitute one of the most deadly threats you are ever likely to encounter. They are invariably howling-at-the-moon stark raving bonkers, and not in a good way. Nobody who wasn't several screws short of a full set would ever consider hunting vampires for business or pleasure. (Especially because vampires don't exist. Right? Right.) We are not talking Buffy here. *Paging Dexter, Dexter to the white courtesy telephone* . . . Both Buffy and Dexter are fictional characters, and kind of cute, because their creators want to entertain you, not scare you to death. The real thing is something else.

Having established that vampire hunters are a whole bundle of no fun at all, it's also important to bear in mind that vampire hunters can sometimes be *a vampire's best friend.*

Consider that the first law of the vampire club is that, if I can see you, I *will* kill you. But killing in person is messy, dangerous, and can backfire horribly: the risk of overexposure is very real. So smart, experienced, ancient vampires collect vampire hunters wherever possible— cherish them, feed them, keep them in a cotton-wool lined box, and only take them out when it's time to point them at a rival and pull the trigger.

Do I need to draw you a diagram to show the relationship between Old George, the fang fucker who is not called Marianne, and our mysterious adversary inside the Laundry (not to mention inside a crypt not far from the tomb of Karl Marx)? Yes? Well, it gets complex, like one of those optical-illusion 3D triangles that tries to turn your eyeballs inside out if you stare at it for too long. Let's just say that right now they are all using each other for their own ends. George created Marianne as a proxy to kill rivals for him. The Rival has gaslighted him into loaning her to him. Marianne is happy because the Rival is feeding her play dates. The Rival, for his part, is using Marianne and George for his own ends in turn . . . and if any of them *ever* slip up in one another's presence, they will die.

Which brings us back to the scenario I am describing. Not-Marianne is working for a new employer, who has asked her to guard a warehouse door. She has just herded a newbie vampire (and a vicar, by way of innocent bystanders) through it, into the presence of our internal adversary, who has secured her cooperation by promising them to her when he's finished. Which is to say, he's neatly detached her from Old George, who will now have to run his own bloody-handed errands. And he's maneuvered Old George into a position where the only way to safety lies through the New Annex.

Things are about to get very messy indeed, for blood-on-the-walls values of messy.

17.

CODE RED

"GOOD EVENING, VICAR! AND YOU MUST BE ALEX, WHAT-WHAT? It's a little cold in here: I'm afraid I couldn't get the heaters to work. Would you like a cup of tea? I've made a pot."

Alex looks around the darkened warehouse. It's not totally pitch-black: a couple of underpowered bulbs glimmer in the twilight, dangling on wires from the cross-beams. There's enough light to see rows of shelving receding into the distance, rising to just below the ceiling, stacked with boxes and tubes and piles of paper on pallets. There are some work tables at the front of the space, and behind them stacks of enormous billboard-sized posters—

The old man gestures at a teapot, surrounded by a neat cluster of mugs and an open half-pint carton of milk. His loose-skinned hand shakes quite noticeably as he picks up the teapot and begins to pour. "I come out here quite regularly. I find that creature comforts always make it slightly more bearable. Don't you agree?"

Alex nods, unable to break the sudden conviction that this is all a horrible dream.

"Yes, that's certainly true," says Pete. To Alex's surprise he seems to have relaxed somewhat. "We've met, haven't we? In, um, Archives? You're Basil, um, I'm sorry, Bob didn't introduce us properly—"

"No, no, that's quite all right," says the ancient archivist. "How do you take your tea? Milk and sugar?"

"Milk, no sugar," says Pete. He nudges Alex.

"Oh! No milk, one sugar." Alex looks at the door they entered through, then back at the elderly Basil. Woman with gun, or elderly man with teapot. Nostrils flare. "You're a vampire!" he exclaims, then bites his tongue.

"Don't be silly, vampires don't exist," Basil retorts, then sniffs. He finishes pouring the tea. "Unless we're talking about the sanguinary curse that adheres to inanimate objects, of course, the organization has several of *those* in inventory; but that's another story. I could have said it takes one to know one, but then we would be tacitly admitting that vampires *do* exist, and then we'd have to do what vampires always do when they meet." His hands shake, Alex notices, but his voice is steady and his speech is clear and unhesitating.

"What do—*would*—vampires do when they meet?" asks Alex.

"You've seen *Highlander*—there can be only one." An expression, hard to read in the twilight, crosses Basil's face. "No? You haven't seen *Highlander*? I must confess, the talkies are my one vice—I picked it up in the early 1920s and can't seem to shake it. Vampires kill, lad. It's in their nature. They can't help it; if they don't kill, they die horribly. It is common lore among their kind that the public, were they aware of vampires, would mandate naked noonday parades and shoot everyone who didn't turn up. Or something like that. So a vampire who allows himself to be recognized as such is a clear and present danger to all other vampires. More tea, Vicar?"

Alex stares at Basil. The gears in his head are whirring as they mesh at high speed, building a Babbage-engine picture of a proposition in predicate calculus. "Why are you breaking the rules?" he finally asks, taking the mug.

A wry smile creeps across Basil's face.

"If you don't need me, I'll just be leaving," Pete suggests, sidling sideways towards the door. Evidently he's decided that he'd rather take his chances with the serial killer outside.

"No, I think you should stay," Basil says, affably enough, and Pete lurches to a stop, as if his feet are rooted to the stained concrete floor. "We don't *always* kill each other. If we're evenly matched, we may even leave one another alone: there's no victor in a fight where everybody dies. To each, his territory. I'm not the only ancient in London, Alex, or even the strongest. But that's a long story. If I arranged for you to be made, why do you think I would kill you?"

"But the woman outside—but, but Evan's dead—"

"Evan was your colleague, wasn't he? The, ahum, hipster?"

Alex nods.

"He went hunting," Basil explains. "If he hadn't gone hunting, he'd still be alive."

"Hunting, for—"

"Hunting for a blood meal. Because he was *hungry*. Can you feel the hunger, Alex? Can you feel it eating you?" Alex nods, convulsively. "I've been reading up on you, you know. Almost everyone's file ends up in the Archives eventually. I read your Miss Murphy's folder years ago, and the reports on her progress: saw she'd make an excellent client. If I ever need to dispose of her, I can shut her down with a single anonymous phone call. Mr. Menendez is, shall we say, surplus to requirements, and I have arranged for him to be let go as part of the downsizing. He's another solitary hunter. We can't permit that. The others—you, for instance—are promising. If you can follow instructions to the letter, we can work together. I can feed you, you know—safely. It has been a long time since I have had slaves, but I think a Praetorian bodyguard of vampires will suit me nicely during the troubled times to come: CASE NIGHTMARE GREEN and all that. Drink your tea, lad, it's getting cold."

"But—but—" Alex looks at Pete. The vicar is clearly frightened, and is making the most peculiar hunching/crouching motions. After a few seconds Alex realizes that Pete really *does* think his feet are glued to the floor: it's as if he's stuck in a tar pit. "Why am I here?" he finally asks. "If you didn't bring me here to kill me." He blinks.

"You were in on the Senior Auditor's meeting. On the inside of his scheme to unearth the vampire in the Laundry . . ."

Basil nods and puts his mug down. (Alex reads the logo and message on its side: MAGIC CIRCLE OF SAFETY.) "It was inevitable that sooner or later somebody would notice. I could feel the questions beginning, the skepticism slipping. Once everyone moved out of Dansey House it was only a matter of time before the geas I worked into the very stones began to lose its grip on their minds. So I planned for this contingency. There will be a small downsizing in an obscure government department, and the individuals who are most credulous and inclined to believe in the existence of vampires will cease to trouble me. At the same time, a particular thorn in my side—the most dangerously psychotic sorcerer in London, who coincidentally created the lady who greeted you—will be drawn out, removed. I've stripped him of his best defenses and maneuvered him into a position where he thinks he has no alternative but to attempt to execute the threat presented by the Laundry. I do not expect him to survive. You're in the safest place you could possibly be right now, Alex, drinking tea in this warehouse with an ancient and powerful vampire while a vampire hunter stands guard on the door. All you have to do is obey me and you'll be fine." Basil peers at Alex. "You are thirsty. Yes?"

Alex nods again. There is something soothing and reassuring about Basil's presence, about the knowledge that Alex is in the presence of an ancient and benevolent elder who wishes him only good— if only the ward he wears on the thong around his neck would stop buzzing like an angry wasp.

"There is lifeblood here," says Basil. He turns and shuffles slowly towards the far end of the work table; Alex follows him, on the other side. "The MAGIC CIRCLE OF SAFETY public information posters, such as this one here, show how to create a basic protective ward. They were for distribution to the herd, in event of an incursion. However, they are also easily modified with a conductive pencil. Add a simple circuit and they can be activated. Like this one, nearly six feet in diameter. The warded zone is cut off from space and time outside:

but you can also use it to stop time from passing inside. There are some, ahem, drawbacks, but if one wants to store something . . . like a packed lunch, to be consumed later . . ."

And indeed there is a perfect hemisphere of darkness rising from the floor beside the end of the large table, atop a sheet of heavy paper that flops across the concrete: its darkness is so complete that in the twilight, it is almost invisible. Basil gestures at it. "I use this warehouse to store my meals. While they're in stasis the progressive deterioration caused by the parasite is kept in check. I need to take them out of stasis while I'm drinking, so that they can feed the parasite and the parasite feeds me in turn . . . but it reduces the frequency with which one needs to kill. Reduces the risk of exposure, too. Would you care for a glass? I have a passable O Rhesus Negative on tap, stored in this chart."

Alex's stomach rumbles. Then, as if in sympathy, his phone vibrates.

"Give that to me." Basil holds out his hand. As if in a dream, Alex watches himself hand his phablet over. The old man looks at it in distaste. "I see," he says. "A primitive ward, without the standard organization backdoor. How annoying! How does one—ah." Alex's stomach lurches again as Basil removes the back cover and pulls the battery, then tosses the disemboweled phone along the work table. "No interruptions, if you please. Now attend."

He bends down, then extends a finger towards a tracery of silver script that circles the base of the stasis field, and smudges out a single character. The dome of darkness disappears. In its place, there is a small wooden chair. A young boy, aged perhaps eight, sits in the chair—or rather, is strapped to it with duct tape at wrists and thighs and ankles. He's cheaply dressed, in scuffed trainers and sweatpants and a hoodie that don't fit properly, and his head lolls: he doesn't seem to be aware of his environment. The green head-end of a cannula pokes from the top of his right hand, held in place by surgical tape; a box of syringes sits beneath the chair.

"He's sedated, but if he could talk he would tell you that perhaps eighty minutes have passed while he's been sitting on this chair. His mother sold him to me for two hundred pounds and an ounce of heroin a couple of years ago. She's dead now, of an overdose. I think I got the better deal." Basil picks up a 20ml syringe and bends over the boy's wrist. His extraction is fast and practiced. "Here. *Drink.* The more time he spends out of stasis, the faster he'll deteriorate."

Alex takes the syringe with nerveless fingers. Behind him, across the warehouse, he can hear Pete retching, but it doesn't matter. *Nothing* matters next to the thirst that has been eating away at his guts. The ward around his neck has stopped buzzing and lies quiescent against his skin, burning hot. He raises the syringe to his lips and squeezes the plunger, overcome by a sense of desire that is erotic in its intensity, turning his knees to jelly as the first drops touch his tongue.

Blackness. Orgasm. Total loss of control.

A few seconds pass. Alex realizes he's lying on the floor. He opens his eyes. He's fallen over but he feels *great*. For the first time in weeks he isn't half-starved, on the edge of perpetual mild nausea. Someone is standing over him.

"Alex. This is important. Are you awake? Can you hear me, Alex?"

He tries to nod, then tries to say *yes*, but what comes out is: "Oh wow."

"Good lad! Stand up."

Alex rolls over, then pushes himself to his knees.

"You, Vicar: over here, yes, go to the young boy in the chair. Stand behind him. Bend over, I'm going to reactivate the ward . . ."

Something out of sight changes, some texture in the background noise, which tells Alex the dome is back in place. And of a sudden, the hunger pangs are back, albeit muted.

"Alex, ah, good. Stand up straight." He can feel the force of Basil's will wrapped around him like a warm blanket, and he feels so grateful he can barely find words to express himself. "Stop trying to think, there's a good boy. I want you to go and stand by the door. Facing it."

"Wh-what?"

"The *door*, Alex." (Dammit, you're half-starved into idiocy.) "That door. The one you came in through, do you remember?"

Alex nods.

"Good. Go and stand by it. If anyone comes through the door, I want you to kill them. It is very important that you kill them."

"*Must* I?"

"Yes, Alex, you must. Otherwise *they* will kill *you.*"

"But I've never—" He shakes. "Need my phone."

"Never mind your—wait, your phone? Is there something on it? A weapon?" Alex nods. "All right, you may collect your phone. Then go and stand by the door and kill anybody who comes through it."

Alex, full of energy for the first time in days, jumps to obey.

BASIL NORTHCOTE-ROBINSON, STRIPPED OF HIS COFFIN-DODGER cover story, stands revealed as an ancient and powerful vampire, who has been working his insidious will on the organization for half a century without detection.

But Basil is not omniscient. He has forgotten something. In fact, he has forgotten several somethings, the combined effect of which will undermine his fiendish scheme to use the organization to destroy his greatest rival, while using his greatest rival to snuff out everybody in the organization who knows the truth about vampires.

For the past century, Basil has lived in England, in the heart of a country riven by two world wars and a grudging retreat from empire. But the retreat from empire ended nearly three decades ago, with the handover of Hong Kong to China.

Basil does not, for the most part, deal with young people. He experiences them as most pensioners do: as shadowy presences in menacing hoodies who dart and mock from the pavements and slums, fearful images touched up by *Daily Mail* headline writers and *Telegraph* editorials. He experiences them mediated through the distorting lens of the silver screen, the nightly drama of the television news broadcast. He is unmarried and has no living relatives that he is aware of. He does *not* experience them as the larval form of his co-workers. He was born so long ago that he has forgotten what it was like to be a teenager or a young adult male. Metrosexuality is something he reads about in newspaper op-ed rants but doesn't actually *know.* And as for geek culture . . .

Most of the young men of Alex's age who Basil has known over the past century had undergone military service. If they haven't carried a gun, they've lived through bombing raids. Grew up playing Cowboys and Indians (or Provos and Army). Took a keen interest in things martial.

Basil is applying these sepia-toned benchmarks of young and virile manhood to Alex, and basing his assumptions of his capabilities upon them. But Alex is a child of the late 1980s, of helicopter parenting and stranger danger and school rides and the Snowdrop Campaign and a blanket ban on handguns. Alex is a brilliant mathematician and promising (if embryonic) applied computational demonologist. But Alex is also a geek who suffers from impostor syndrome and hypochondria to boot, and whose knowledge of handguns was acquired from movies where the stars hold their pistols the wrong way up and obey the laws of Hollywood physics. He is, in short, not exactly the ideal vampire bodyguard.

He is also prone to overthinking things.

WE ARE DELAYED IN TRAFFIC AGAIN. WHICH MEANS WE ARE now twelve minutes behind our bellwether.

(I know the arguments for and against having a brick waiting outside the warehouse; let's just say, the arguments against won. If there's one thing worse than going up against an ancient and powerful vampire sorcerer with mind-control skills, it's going up against an ancient and powerful vampire sorcerer with mind-control skills who has noticed you and taken over your eight-man squad of elite special forces soldiers before you arrive.)

"Orders, Mr. Howard?"

I rub my forehead. "Wait one." I call up the police CCTV operations room again. They've got a constable monitoring the cameras around the warehouse in real time. "No change notified. One car arrived ninety minutes ago; a woman got out and went inside. Hasn't left. Then our decoys arrived nine minutes ago and went inside. Monitoring commenced three hours ago; nothing before then, although presumably the security guard showed up for work this morning. So we're looking at four souls inside: security chap, unidentified female, our two." I pause.

"My working assumption is the female is hostile until proven otherwise. She may be a PHANG, or she may be a lamplighter for the adversary. We're all warded but you should not assume that your wards will work normally around the adversary. Treat with extreme caution; put her down if she presents a threat."

I pause again. "Scary, do you prefer to go in through the front door, or use the loading dock and the fire exits? You have tactical control."

My ward vibrates briefly, then stops. I glance down at my smartphone, and see the particular app it's running. (Burning goat's skull—don't ask: it's part of our special occult countermeasures suite.) "Alex's ward just overloaded and fried. We have contact."

"Team alpha, plan two," announces Scary. (That's the fire exit.) "Team bravo, plan three." (That's the loading bay.) I feel the truck lean forward on its suspension and sway as it takes a bend, then bounce twice, very hard, on speed pillows. "We're going to park in front of the office door, on top of the bike and the car: stand by for a bumpy landing. Action in thirty seconds."

There's a click in my headphones. "Mr. Howard, if you'd please *stay behind us* this time—"

"Thank you, Sergeant, your advice is noted." I grit my teeth and close my eyes, forcing my inner eye to open. I can see surprisingly well this way, although *what* I see is nothing very nice: I have nightmares about using this talent. "You'll need me to handle the adversary. Once you've cleared the way."

"Yes, sir." A hand pats me on the shoulder. Then there's a violent crunching sound and I'm hurled against my seat belt. Poor bloody Pete, if he gets out of this alive, is going to have one *hell* of an insurance claim form to fill out. I'll have to see if I can get the SA to sign off on buying him a replacement scooter, citing necessity . . .

I pull off my headphones and yank on my helmet in the moment of silence that follows. A gust of cold air hits me in the face as the doors slam. I pull my visor down, release my seat belt, and wait ten seconds as the heavies bail out, then I follow them through the nearest exit, opposite the entrance to the office.

So I'm standing right behind Sergeant Howe when the door explodes.

That's why I survive.

I register it as a bright flash and a simultaneous ringing in my ears, then I realize I'm lying on my back looking up at the side of the OCCULUS truck. *What happened?* I wonder as I flail around and try to sit up, then slip on something warm and moist. I can smell shit. Something buzzes in my ears, and then my ward goes off like a hive of bees. I can't hear properly. I roll to my knees and realize numbly I'm rolling in what's left of Steve, which means *enemy action*, so I keep rolling and roll under the OCCULUS truck as I reach for my pistol and realize I can't find the holster and my bad right arm is stinging like crazy so I open my inner eye fully and the confusion and darkness light up.

(I will note that Steve Howe wasn't visible from the office window and wasn't yet trying to open the door: it just went *bang*.)

Walls dissolve. There's a smoking hole in the front of the warehouse, and a body inside, and another body—live, with a gun, and there's an unhealthy bluish sheen to it like an oil slick or toxic waste or something. I hear faint shouts, the harsh metallic crack of gunfire. There are more people standing farther inside the building, but the one in the office is advancing and raising a pistol—

I grunt, and reach out for them with imaginary fangs and claws. I'm about five meters away but I've done this before, through a door even. I can feel their mind squirming like a toad, and there's something sick about it. It tastes *foul*. No, *she* tastes foul. I bite and bite and chew and spit and then I find myself wishing for a psychic glass of water: the trouble with this Eater-of-Souls talent or curse or what-have-you is that there are some people whose souls you'd want to scrape off the underside of your shoe if you trod in them, and you *really* don't want them giving you gastric symptoms.

I rewind her rage and her joy as the door blows, taking down the first attacker, and catch an echo of earlier memories: the memory of sex, the memory of her white-lightning orgasm as she broke Evan's neck while sitting astride his lap, in a moment of total exultant control over everything she hated. I squeal and try to shove her out of my head but it's too late, because she's lying halfway through the doorway with bloody tears trickling from her eyes. I killed her and I'm going to have to live with that.

I retch at the overpowering stench of blood and shit and worm my way out from under the truck. My hearing is all fuzzed from the explosion and the gunfire, which has died down. I've got a job to do, dammit. The fire is suppressive, to convince the people holed up inside to stay down. That's the plan, anyway. What were Steve and I meant to do, in the office . . . ?

Oh, *that*.

I kneel, then stagger to my feet and lurch forward, slip-sliding on a loop of intestines until I catch my balance and crunch down on the dead woman's rib cage. There's another dead body behind the desk, wearing a security guard's uniform: he's been dead for some time, going by the way he's dark to my vision. I briefly consider raising him and using him as a proxy, but it'd take too long to summon a feeder.

There's a fuse box on the wall beside the inner door, the one that leads to the archive. I open it and look for the circuit breaker I helped the electrician connect this morning. It's still open.

Flick.

Inside the archive, the string of ultraviolet lights we laid along the top of the storage racks this morning blink on.

And then the screaming starts.

THE REST OF THE MOP-UP OPERATION GOES SMOOTHLY ENOUGH, modulo the mopping up. Which is . . . disturbing.

The screaming from inside the warehouse is continuous, high-pitched, and terrible. It's the kind of sound you associate with cats being skinned alive, or slasher movies, or mediaeval torture-fests.

I open the door.

Alex is moaning with fear, not screaming. He lies curled in a ball on the floor beside the doorway, hoodie pulled up, hands and face tucked in. *Clever boy.* His ward's toast, so I have to assume he's been turned, but right now he's focussed on keeping his hands and face out of the light that burns. He's smoking, but the duck'n'cover drill combined with his hoodie seems to have saved him from going the full barbie.

There's the characteristic black dome of a powered-up ward at one side of the warehouse. *Later.*

There is one other body in here, exposed to the eldritch purple glow of the booby-trap lights. It is making a hoarse screeching sound—almost a teakettle whistle. Its spine is curled over and its jaw gapes wide, and there is smoke pouring out of it, with pale fire flickering in its eye sockets and burning within its rib cage, where it is visible through the clothing that has scorched away. I can see the pallor of bone through the tattered charcoal of his trousers. A bell is ringing, and after a while I realize it's the fire alarm—our friend must have tripped the smoke detector. The worst thing about it all is that he's still alive and screaming.

Observe, Orient, Decide, Act.

I touch the press-to-talk mike attached to my helmet. Hope it still works. "Bob here, Howe is down, repeat Howe is down. Unidentified female oppo is down. I'm in the back, lights on, repeat, lights on. Alex is neutral, I can't see Pete, unidentified oppo is on fire but undead. I need hands here."

About a quarter of a ton of heavily armed specops soldiers tackle me onto the floor—forming a rugby scrum with me as the ball—then my earpiece crackles: "Awaiting orders, sir!" (Silly me, I guess I got in front of them again.)

"Get a tarp over Alex and get him into the front office, handcuffs and sedation—assume he's been turned. Find the vicar. That dome: point your guns at it; if it collapses and anything comes out of it, shoot them. Then get off me."

The weight eases momentarily. "Yes, sir." I've got tinnitus, dammit. (I feel a momentary pang. I can still smell the contents of Steve Howe's guts all over me. Taste that awful woman's weird craving for sex with paralyzed vampires. Someone made her that way. Surely?) I shove the thoughts aside for later. "What about—"

I stand up. So does the burning man.

"*Freeeeeze*," hisses the burning man. We all freeze. Our wards simultaneously buzz violently, then give up the ghost and start to smoke.

"Missssster Howard." Bits of carbonized cloth and flesh drip from his bones as he straightens up and turns to face us, like a walking skeleton with pale red worms writhing in the back of his skull. He's not hissing just because of the flames: there's something wrong with his dentition. "We meet again."

"Name, rank, and number?" I ask.

"Don't you recognize me, what-what?" Skeletal jaws grin, and now I realize I'm hearing his voice *inside* my head: he doesn't have lungs or larynx with which to laugh. "I really must thank you. I *do* appreciate a warm welcome: it affirms my sense of self-worth."

The blood-sucking Terminator impersonator steps around the table. "One of you fine upstanding chappies—yes, you—is going to go back there and *turn out the bloody lights*. Wait. Before you go, give me your gun." The soldier he's pointing at jerkily unslings his MP5 and extends it, butt-first, towards Basil. That's when I realize how terribly pear-shaped this op has gone. "You've had your little jape, ha-ha. In case you were wondering, we get harder to kill as we get older. This confirms something I've suspected for a decade or two, but lacked the inclination to idly test: mind over matter and all that. It'll be fun to go out in daylight again when all this is over. Now go and stand over there, in that corner. You've been very naughty boys."

I stumble along with the other three heavies. I am ashamed to say I'm shaking. Unlike them, I'm faking obedience: his will-to-obey is amazingly powerful, but so is my will-to-resist. On the other hand, he's pointing a submachine gun at us and I need a few seconds to think. What's worse than an elderly vampire? Answer: an elderly vampire with a submachine gun and sunburn-induced bad attitude. He's clearly a whole lot more powerful than the run-of-the-mill newbie PHANGs I've been dealing with up to now, and unless my middle names aren't Oliver Francis I'm only going to get one chance to lay Basil the Self-Propelled Barbecue to rest. While my back is half-turned to him, I cross myself, banker-style: spectacles, testicles, wallet . . . and camera?

Ah. Camera.

I pull the battered little Fuji 3D camera out and flick the power button. Mhari's lot didn't break it, even though it's a bit scratched and beaten up. I am going to assume it's still loaded with the basilisk firmware rather than the normal happy snappy variety, because if I'm wrong I am going to die in the next few seconds. I'll just have to trust my lack of any memory of having swapped out the memory card for the one with the regular boot image.

"You're going to wait in that corner until I receive a phone call from the New Annex," explains our chatty death-about-town: "There's a bit of mopping up going on there right now, but once it's over we can all get in your truck and go home." *Mopping up? That doesn't sound right,* I think fuzzily, stealing a surreptitious glance at the camera back. *Have we just been mousetrapped?* Yes, it's showing the gunsight display, not the camera focus graticule. "And then, ah, yes. Most of you can just *forget* you ever saw me—"

The ultraviolet lights go out, and there is an immediate blood-curdling scream from the front office.

"What-what?" says Basil, turning and raising his gun.

THERE IS THIS THING ABOUT MATHEMATICIANS AND PROGRAM-mers: they come in several flavors, often overlapping, but with distinct strengths and weaknesses specific to each type.

Alex's talents are multivariate and recondite, but he has a particular aptitude for language lawyering. That is, he takes great delight in exploring the nooks and crannies of formal languages and understanding how and in what circumstances they exhibit side effects or anomalous behavior that a naive or inexperienced programmer would not expect.

Alex is also very intelligent. He is under Basil's control, but he is not happy about his long-term survival prospects if this situation persists. Especially as his entire face is on fire and it feels as if his nose will fall off if he sneezes. Basil is not, in Alex's estimate, an entirely thoughtful employer: certainly he is unlikely to prove as accommodating or merciful as the Laundry's HR department.

Alex cannot disobey Basil's direct order. But he can creatively interpret the instructions he has already been given. And he cannot help but overhear what Basil is saying next door.

And it occurs to him that when Basil said, ". . . stand by the door and kill anybody who comes through it," Basil didn't specify which direction they had to be going in.

In the normal state of affairs, a fight between a highly trained soldier from the Territorial SAS and a pencil-necked geek will tend to end with a de-leaded geek. But in the interests of rebalancing the equation, the highly trained soldier has just handed his principal weapon to the vampire overlord who has turned him into a shambling robot whose motivation is the overriding order to *turn out the bloody lights* rather than defending himself. And the pencil-necked geek is a fully juiced-up young vampire who has rules-lawyered himself around to some very interesting conclusions about his own freedom of action within the constraints Basil specified, and who is extremely pissed off right now because he has third-degree burns across most of his face.

Alex isn't stupid. He lets the soldier pull the circuit breaker, and *then* he tries to kill him.

I DON'T REMEMBER THE NEXT BIT TOO CLEARLY.

The light flickered and something of its quality changed: it reddened, or lost something from the blue end of the spectrum.

There was a scream, and the nightmare figure turned towards the doorway and raised its gun. That's when I began to turn, and raised my camera, and pushed the shutter release immediately: not even aiming at him, just relying on the firmware to lock onto the person-shaped object closest to the center of the focal area and do the rest.

I suspect I was in shock at this point, because my memory of the camera is that it felt as if it was made of solid tungsten, and my knees were shaking, and my vision was blurred and I could barely focus on the screen and I felt sick and hot and cold simultaneously. But that's nothing compared to how Basil felt when I took his picture.

What happens when you point a basilisk gun at a semi-skeletonized vampire elder?

Basil *sparkles* electric blue for just a moment. There's a loud *bang!* A fragment of skull whizzes past my ear. And then the pile of red-hot bones collapses across the floor, as does the submachine gun they were holding a fraction of a second ago. (Thankfully, there is no accidental discharge.) One of the hot pieces of bone lands on the edge of the warded bubble, and begins to burn a hole in the paper, scorching the letters and linkages away. The bubble flickers and vanishes, revealing an apprehensive-looking vicar contorted over a chair holding a child. (Thankfully, Basil's instructions to Scary's men have overridden my orders to shoot anything that comes out of the bubble.)

A voice calls, from the office: "Is Basil dead? Can I stop killing this guy yet?"

What? "Yes, stop!" I shout. *On second thoughts*: "Alex, I want you to lie down, with your hands behind your back. Wrists together." I realize I'm still pointing my deadly little camera at the opposite wall and force myself to lower it. I turn and see the soldiers turning away from the wall, shaking themselves and focussing. "Go and restrain him in case Sparkle Boy here implanted any post-mortem commands," I tell them. "He'll need burn support. I'm going to sort out the vicar."

I'm shaking and shivery but I know what needs to be done. Pete is straightening up and saying something about untying the kid, about V syndrome and needing to get him to a hospital. I blink, feel the shuddering sense of exultation *that woman* would have taken at the moment Basil's skull exploded, almost enough to give her a spontaneous orgasm—she hated him and lusted for him at the same time—and I bend over and spit on the floor, because I can taste blood on my lips. I'm soaking in the stuff, actually. I nearly throw up. It's Steve Howe's. *Poor bloody Steve.* It's scant consolation knowing that if I'd gotten in front of him I'd have taken the vampire hunter's booby-trap right in the face.

I stumble and go over on one ankle as I walk towards Pete. He's saying something else now, something urgent, something about Basil storing his prey in the MAGIC CIRCLE OF SAFETY archive. I shake my head. Something is coming into focus, something huge and nasty and vile: Who added reviving MAGIC CIRCLE OF SAFETY to the training-wheels project list, I wonder? As if I can't guess. More importantly, *why* did Basil do it? "We've got to get back to the New Annex," I say. Then I remember I've got a phone. "Wait." I pull it out but iPhones don't work too well when they've been sprayed with blood and rolled around on. "Shit." I turn and stumble towards the front office, past the guys who are apologizing to Alex as they apply the handcuffs and leg restraints, ignore *that woman*, shuffle past the dead security guard who is staring unblinking at the ceiling with gunshot-wound eyes, and see his phone on the desk.

I lean over the corpse and dial a number from memory, finger shaking so badly that I have to stop and start over twice before I get it right. It's picked up on the second ring.

"Operations."

"Howard here."

"Transferring you now—" They've been pre-briefed.

Two seconds later, I hear a familiar voice. "Speak, boy." It's Angleton. He sounds distracted.

I dry swallow, trying to ignore the taste in my mouth. "Code Red," I manage.

We don't use Code Red very often. In fact, I've never heard of it being used before. Code Blue means there's an off-site emergency, probable hostile action on our soil. Code Red means there's *on*-site hostile action. Like the attack I expect Basil to have arranged, to take out everyone who might suspect his existence.

"You're a bit late," Angleton says laconically. I hear banging in the background. "We'll talk later," he adds. Then the line goes dead.

18.

A NAKED LUNCH, WITH VIOLIN

THE CATASTROPHE UNFOLDED IN MY—AND MO'S—ABSENCE. IT was rapid and devastating, and it's quite possible that the only reason I'm around to record this account of the event is because I wasn't there.

I feel compelled to raise my hand and admit that I'm partly to blame. I'm no more to blame than everyone else on the Senior Auditor's ad-hoc working group, but no less. If we'd realized that Basil had infiltrated the DRESDEN RICE committee—hell, if it had occurred to us that our mole might come in the guise of an elderly, low-level administrative employee—we might have paid more attention to reducing the threat surface of the working group. But he'd been working his mind-fogging magic within our halls since before I was born. He predates the Senior Auditor; he was certainly here during the organization's salad days as part of SOE during the Second World War. He predates *Angleton*. He was a careful planner, and although he operated at a relatively low level he had access to all our non-current HR files and declassified internal records. Consequently he got inside our event loop, with fatal consequences.

While we thought we were very cleverly mousetrapping our adver-

sary at an off-site location of our choice, our adversary was simultaneously mousetrapping our away team . . . and tricking his oldest,
deadliest enemy into a suicidal assault on the New Annex, promoted
by a trickle of cunning lies and assisted by the loan of a warrant card,
keys, and a floor plan.

Actually, this had been on the cards for a very long time. Months,
certainly; possibly for years, maybe even for decades. After all, the
first rule of vampires is, vampires don't exist, and the elders take its
enforcement as a matter of deadly importance. So a corollary of this
rule is that any viable strategy for eliminating an old and powerful
rival is going to be non-obvious.

There are a couple of long-term survival strategies open to the occult practitioner who has let the wrong symbiote in. One of these is to
hunker down and squat, invisible, in the center of a miasmic mist of
misleading magic that befuddles and bamboozles anybody who spec-
ulates about your existence. The leading proponent of this strategy, the
strategy of the hedgehog, was the late Basil Northcote-Robinson, and
it served him well—up to a point.

The other leading strategy is to turn the PHANGs' ability to compel belief to the accretion of wealth and power, and to use those ac-
cumulated assets to build a pearl, layering protective nacre around
your sand-grain heart. This strategy, the strategy of the fox, is the one
that Old George Stephenson employed. What kind of vampire elder
owns a founder's stake in one of the nation's largest investment
banks? Answer: one who is not afraid to take risks in the pursuit of
profit.

First Basil nudged us into taking Old George's Scrum-shaped experiment away from him. Then he bamboozled Old George into loaning him not-Marianne the assassin, by presenting a common front.
Finally, he removed himself from the firing line, warned Old George
that the Laundry working group on PHANGs was coming for him,
and thereby triggered a game of "let's you and him fight."

Foxes are fast movers—and they *bite*.

*   *   *

AT PRECISELY THREE MINUTES PAST SEVEN O'CLOCK, AT EX-
actly the moment that I'm rolling around in Steven Howe's intestines
with ringing ears as a demented vampire hunter with a pistol and a
selection of explosives tries to kill me, Old George launches an assault
on the New Annex.

If he was able to call on the support of all his minions, you would
not be reading this account of his attack; but Basil has cunningly
stripped him of his deadliest proxies and waved the flag of an immediate threat before him. There is insufficient notice to prepare adequately for the offensive. Old George is therefore winging it.

Old George is very well-informed, for an outsider. He knows
about the night watch. He knows about our alarm systems. Finally,
Old George is armed for bear. He may be desperate, but he's also a
two-hundred-year-old ritual magician and occult practitioner who is
immune to K syndrome, *and* a vampire on top.

At this time of evening the building is largely deserted. The cleaners have been and gone; a couple of night watch bodies roam the
ground floor and basement level. Lights burn on the second floor, in a
couple of briefing rooms and the duty officer's den. So it is that when
a black Mercedes pauses briefly outside the main entrance and a man
gets out, nobody is paying enough attention to the external CCTV
feed.

Old George wears a charcoal gray trench coat with its collar
turned up, and a homburg pulled low over his ears. The trench coat
conceals a multitude of sins, not least of which is a silk lining that Old
George has embroidered by hand himself over a period of many
months, with enough defensive wards and charms to armor an aircraft carrier. The hat has properties of its own, its brim casting a
shadow that renders the wearer's face unrecognizable. Anonymous
and all but invisible, he marches up to the front door of the New
Annex and touches the keypad. The pad smokes as he lets himself in.

In the darkness of the lobby, a shuffling caretaker hisses as it approaches the intruder. Old George has heard of these revenants, the
Residual Human Resources that gave their all for the organization
and now give even more, and he is amused to see the faint swirl of

green luminosity within the sunken eyes of the shambler. "Lie down," he suggests, not unkindly, and, reaching out with a gloved finger, he taps the night watchman on the forehead, right inside the span of its outstretched arms.

The corpse wheezes faintly as it collapses, the breath fleeing its flaccid lungs for the last time. Old George turns towards the staircase. Then he begins to climb.

GEORGE IS HERE BECAUSE BASIL HAS MANEUVERED HIM INTO A coffin corner, and the shortest way out is through the Laundry with guns blazing.

This latest move in the game they've been playing for seven decades began almost by accident, with the Laundry's move out of Dansey House. For the first time in more than half a century, Basil found himself unprotected by the subtle, powerful, and extensive geas that he had spent so much energy constructing—the compulsion to disbelieve in vampires. Many people would react to this as a threat. Basil, however, chose to view it as an opportunity.

Over the years, Old George has settled into a routine of sending his proxies to crush his enemies. Over the years, his proxies have become increasingly dangerous and unstable; the woman who is not called Marianne is the latest of these, a fearsome instrument of destruction—to vampires. Normally Basil would avoid both of them like the plague. There is nothing to be gained from messing around with Old George. But once outside the walls of Dansey House, a plan suggests itself to him:

1. Tempt Old George to create a nest of baby vamps.
2. Bring them into the Laundry, who will ultimately realize that Old George is their creator . . .
3. . . . Thereby threatening to overturn the law of secrecy.
4. Borrow not-Marianne on the pretext of suffocating the babies; seduce her with the gift of fresh meat, buying her temporary collusion.

5. Stripped of his most powerful catspaw, Old George is now in a position where he can only silence the security threat by attacking an organization he has been aware of (but has avoided any connection to) for a very long time.

6. Make sure that Old George believes Basil to be on the premises when, in fact, Basil is elsewhere at the time of the attack.

If Old George is killed, Basil will shed no tears. And if Old George succeeds, those of us who might expose Basil will be eliminated. From Basil's point of view it's a win-win situation.

It's cold-blooded, of course. But it's hard to make an omelette without breaking eggs.

I FIND IT VERY HARD TO WRITE THIS ACCOUNT OBJECTIVELY.

So I am going to quote extensively from the report of the board of enquiry, with added comments of my own.

AT THE TOP OF THE STAIRS OLD GEORGE PAUSED TO ORIENT

himself. Then he turned and headed down the corridor between the Operational Research Unit offices on one side and the Admin and Facilities cubicle farm on the other. Turning right he came to the general office fronting the Department of External Affairs, and here he encountered Doris Greene from Health and Safety.

We do not know exactly what Doris was doing outside Briefing Room 203, which was occupied at the time by the task alpha group established by the Senior Auditor to which she had been assigned. For obvious reasons, CCTV coverage of the New Annex premises stops at the front door. Jez Wilson indicated at the enquiry that she believes Doris was simply taking a break to powder her nose, but cannot provide definite confirmation for this theory. Certainly to get to the nearest ladies' toilet from Briefing Room 203, Doris would have had to turn right, walk past Briefing Rooms 204 to 210, descend the north staircase, turn left through the fire doors, and go through the corridor leading past the DEA cluster, which is exactly where her body was found.

Doris Greene (aged 56), leaves a husband, Martin (age 59), and three children, Peter (aged 31), Emma (aged 29), and Carol (aged 26).

Old George did not pause to feed or attempt to coerce his victims into obedience. He merely touched them with a fingertip and killed them. His touch carried an abstruse contagion, an anti-pattern for life—an invocation of a kind that can only be generated by someone who has consumed far too much of it. No soul-eating is involved: victims are simply thrown away, minds shredded, brains stilled, hearts stopped. There is no indication that Doris Greene offered (or was capable of offering) any resistance.

The board of enquiry located the next body just beyond the second-floor fire doors fronting the north stairwell, in the corridor outside the door to Briefing Room 210.

Four bullet holes were found, in two groups, in the left fire door. The gun that fired them, a standard issue Glock 17, was found in the right hand of Mr. Andrew Newstrom. One round was chambered and twelve more rounds were found to be present in the 17-round extended-capacity magazine after the weapon was made safe by forensic investigators. The ammunition load consisted of alternating rounds of hollow-point 9x19mm Parabellum and our own standard banishment rounds (essentially FMJ 9mm with an embedded banishment circuit in the base of the bullet). Examination of the spent rounds confirmed that the banishment circuits of the two bullets retrieved from the wall beyond the fire door were discharged by contact with a ward of class 6 or higher strength.

The board's conclusion is that the likely course of events was that Mr. Newstrom left Briefing Room 202 for reasons unknown, encountered Old George, and engaged him with his personal defense weapon at close range. He had time to fire four rounds and hit the target repeatedly, but the combined effect of the translocative compulsion wired into Old George's coat effectively rendered his target physically immaterial to bullets. Old George advanced at walking pace, covering six meters of physical distance, and touched Mr. Newstrom before he could fire again.

Andy Newstrom, aged 47, leaves a wife, Sandra (age 49), and two children, Alec (15) and Olivia (11).

Fifteen meters farther down the corridor, the door to room 203 was locked. Briefing Room 203 was occupied at the time of the incident by Jez Wilson and Gerald Lockhart, who had returned empty-handed from his errand to retrieve Oscar Menendez. The board's findings note that Wilson and Lockhart survived the incident principally due to their quick thinking in locking the door in response to the shots fired by Mr. Newstrom. As a result, Old George bypassed room 203. The board finds that neither Lockhart nor Wilson were equipped to survive a confrontation with Old George, or to impede his progress. Had they attracted the attention of the intruder, or attempted to engage him, they would certainly be numbered among the dead.

(Jez and Gerry were frantically piling furniture behind the door at precisely the moment my call to the duty officer's room connected.)

The next body was found just outside Briefing Room 203. It belonged to Dr. Judith Carroll, the ranking Auditor with internal affairs, and second in command to Dr. Michael Armstrong.

Indications of intense thaumaturgic discharge were found around this body. Dr. Carroll's ward of office was discharged: in the process it combusted and the metal trimmings melted. The body was extensively burned. Scorch marks were found on the walls and ceiling to either side, as well as on the body. A residual high thaum count renders a three-meter section of the corridor hazardous for traversal, and extensive decontamination and exorcism will be required if the second-floor corridor is to be rendered safe for normal use.

From the position of the corpse and adjacent spatter patterns, it is inferred that Dr. Carroll left Briefing Room 202 when she heard Mr. Newstrom open fire on Old George. A confrontation then ensued. During this confrontation, Dr. Carroll activated her entire repertoire of personal defense macros and spells. In doing so she caused extensive damage to Old George's coat and disabled the geometry engine supporting its translocative compulsion field. From this point on, Old George was no longer immune to gunfire. Old George attempted to apply his thanotic anti-pattern to Dr. Carroll. Dr. Carroll's ward short-circuited it, in the process discharging completely and, per subsequent evidence, inflicting fifth-degree (bone-deep) burns on Old George's right hand and forearm.

Old George appears to have responded with physical force, using his remaining (left) arm to apply torsion to Dr. Carroll's right elbow, first dislocating her limb at the shoulder, then inducing traumatic amputation. He then used the appendage as a bludgeon to apply blunt trauma to Dr. Carroll's head. The cause of death is unclear but may include a combination of blood loss, shock, and cerebral swelling secondary to a fractured skull.

Dr. Carroll, aged 62, was a widow at the time of the incident. She is survived by a son, Derek (38).

The door to Briefing Room 202 was open, and this is where the intrusion event terminated.

The last two bodies are unaccounted for but are believed to be located within the containment ward in that room. One of them is that of Old George; the other is that of DSS Angleton, also known as the Eater of Souls.

The precise sequence of events leading to the loss of DSS Angleton and the 227-year-old vampire known as George Stephenson have not been established, as of the date at which the board of enquiry issued their interim report. Briefing Room 202 is, as of the time of writing, currently inaccessible due to a residual necromantic thaum field, which is sufficiently intense (at 1200 milli-Parsons per hour just inside the threshold) to pose a high risk of neurophagic possession to anyone unwise enough to enter. A four-meter diameter, perfectly spherical, event horizon can be observed in the center of the room, but the thaum field rises exponentially as the singularity is approached. Detailed examination is not currently feasible.

It is believed that the bodies of DSS Angleton and Old George lie within the event horizon.

A narrative account of the encounter between DSS Angleton and Old George is appended to the interim report, but is marked as a provisional finding and some questions remain over its accuracy.

It is believed that, at the time shots were being fired by Mr. Newstrom, DSS Angleton was in Briefing Room 202, where he was occupied with a phone call from his operational assistant, Mr. Howard. On hearing shots, Angleton ended the call and spoke to Dr. Carroll, who volunteered to investigate. It is noted that Dr. Carroll's ward of office should have given her similar immunity to physical threats to that available to Old George, and Dr. Carroll's position as Auditor was contingent upon her ability to compel and command—she was, in her own right, a formidable operative (if somewhat rusty, her last field experience being over two decades earlier).

It is not possible to be sure of DSS Angleton's state of mind at this time (DSS Angleton not being entirely human to begin with, and having occupied his body for at least eighty-two years at the time of the incident). However, it is inferred that DSS Angleton was aware of an imminent threat from multiple sources: from the sound of gunfire, from Howard's Code Red warning, and then from the Auditor's radiative emissions and subsequent screaming as Old George beat her to death with her own arm.

It is unclear why DSS Angleton did not immediately enter the corridor and engage Old George. It is speculated that DSS Angleton required time to prepare himself for combat—again, as with Dr. Carroll, Dr. Angleton's last active field operation (if the fiasco two years ago at Brookwood Cemetery is excluded) was over six years ago. It is also speculated that DSS Angleton assessed Dr. Carroll's triage status as irretrievable and decided to spend almost a minute preparing Briefing Room 202 to receive Old George.

Witnesses trapped in Briefing Room 203 claim to have heard Angleton call out, "In here, George!" in a tone of voice that one bystander described as "jolly" and another described as "chilling." It is not known at this time how DSS Angleton was aware of the attacker's identity.

Subsequent witness reports are unreliable and subjective, but paint a picture of a subjective sense of extreme existential dread, nausea, bone-deep aches and feverish chills, hearing arcane chanting in unfamiliar languages (identified by one witness as "like Old Enochian, but different and much scarier—Old Enochian with Tourette's syndrome, perhaps"), inhuman groaning, and an intense and eerie sense of jamais vu.

The precise nature of the exchange of thaumaturgic firepower that happened in Briefing Room 202 is unclear, but it should be noted that items subsequently found in Old George's possession, both on his person and at his home, indicate that he was a proficient ritual necromancer even before his contraction of PHANG syndrome. Furthermore, Old George had the benefit of nearly two centuries to perfect his technique without fear of Krantzberg syndrome. DSS Angleton, in contrast, was the dead soul of a "Hungry Ghost," bound into the living body of a man whose mind was sacrificed to provide a vessel for the *preta*. Both these individuals were combat sorcerers of great age and experience, fighting for their lives: and they paid the ultimate price.

DSS "James Jesus" Angleton (not his real name), aged 102 (or: uncountable aeons), was single at the time of his departure. He is survived by an assistant who, in the wake of a destiny entanglement accident two years ago, shares some of his abilities.

And I am now going to stop writing, in order to observe a three-minute silence for the dead, before I bring this sorry story to its close.

THE POLICE FINALLY MOVE IN AND SECURE THE SCENE. SCARY organizes; Pete sees to Alex, delivering soothing words while one of the squaddies works on him from a field first aid kit equipped with morphine and burn dressings. I go through the motions of an after-op report, but it's very hard.

I'm back on the phone almost as soon as Angleton hangs up on me, but it takes me a minute to get through to someone who knows what's going on, and by that time I already know what they're telling me: Angleton, they say, is dead. Or, I infer, if not dead then discarnate, beyond recall unless someone attempts the TEAPOT BARON TYBURN invocation (which will happen over my dead body).

At the moment of his death I feel a great disturbance in the force, as if millions of voices suddenly cried out in terror and were silenced— well, no, actually. It's not like Star Wars *at all*. (And there is no luminiferous ether either, dammit.) But it's as if I've been wearing a pair of too-tight gloves for so long I didn't even notice anymore, and they're suddenly gone. And if I flex my mental fingers it's like I've been performing resistance exercises and suddenly I've acquired the grip of doom.

So I'm not the apprentice trainee Junior MythBuster Eater of Souls anymore. I don't know if you could accurately describe me as the real thing yet, but I'm the nearest we've got now Angleton's gone, and I'll just have to do my best to live up (or die down) to his standards. It's a lot to come to terms with, especially as I'm shocky and disoriented, covered in blood and other bodily fluids, upset and disturbed by the fallout from Basil's little party, and trying to hold everybody else on the KGB.2.YA site together.

This shit is highly distracting, even in the absence of knowing that there's a Code Red in hand, and people keep buzzing around my head like summer bluebottles, nagging me with stupid questions. I will confess to snarling a couple of times, and one or two of the cops push back with a bit of attitude—they're used to their authority being respected, even without the assault rifles and the Darth Vader stormtrooper gear—but it turns out that all I have to do is stare at them and they urgently remember something else they need to be doing.

And, in truth, Scary can handle this circus from now on. Basil is roadkill, Alex is gibbering and confessing to the vicar, Little Miss Serial Killer Squared is giving me a very bad taste in the back of my mouth, and there's a Code Red in progress back at base. So I walk over to the nearest crimson BMW with Christmas tree lighting and locate the occupant, who is by coincidence conversing with Scary. "I need a ride," I say.

The cop turns on me. He's something senior, inspector maybe.

"You wait your—" he begins, then I make eye contact and his tongue freezes.

"*I need a ride,*" I say, reaching deep inside myself for the power and authority that goes with my new job. "Do not make me repeat myself."

"Uh. Um . . ." The inspector reels and looks at me like I'm the Grim Reaper: maybe I need to dial it down a notch or two.

"He needs a ride," Scary says, not unkindly, "and he's *my* boss. I reckon you should give him a ride. It's the easiest way to get rid of him."

"Uh, right. Where do you need to go, sir?"

I give him the New Annex's address. I hope to hell I'm not too late.

If a motorbike or scooter is the second fastest way to get around London, then a police armed response car with blues and twos comes a pretty close third. Unfortunately there's no room for a chopper to set down by the New Annex or I'd requisition one, and fuck the budget. I spend the next twenty minutes in a weird hypnogogic state, eyes registering the blue highlights reflecting off the shut shop windows to either side as we hurtle along high streets like the proverbial chiropteroid making its exit from Tartarus. My mind's a million miles away. All I can think is, *Someone killed Angleton,* which means they need me because I'm the next in line. Or maybe they need Mo with her instrument, but she's in the North Sea right now. Funny: whatever killed Angleton will probably make short work of me. So she won't even get to yell at me for getting myself killed—

My driver begins to slow down, and I realize I recognize the roads. We're nearly there. Then I see more flashing lights, red and blue and white (which is worse), and we round the corner to see a small herd of ambulances drawn up, more police cars, and another OCCULUS truck setting up a mobile command center, outside a building with strange lights in one of the second-floor windows that make the skin in the small of my back try to crawl off and hide . . .

. . . And *stop.*

I'm clearly too late, which means I'm going to get to live a little longer.

Somehow it feels wrong.

*   *   *

IT'S THREE O'CLOCK IN THE MORNING IN THE BACK OF THE
OCCULUS truck parked outside the alleyway at the back of the New
Annex. It's chilly and winter-damp in the back of the truck. I'm cross-
eyed with exhaustion as the Senior Auditor turns to me and clears his
throat. There are bluish-purple bags under his eyes, highlighted by the
flickering overhead neon tubes. I've never seen him look so frighten-
ingly mortal before. "Nothing more to do here," he says. "You should
go home."

"Thanks," I say, then pause. "You're sure?"

He stretches tiredly. "Colonel Lockhart will come in early, in about
another half hour."

"Lockhart's a stuffed shirt."

"Yes, but he can handle mop-up. And that's what we're down
to. My colleagues will take over in the morning. You've done your
bit, you're covered in"—he hesitates momentarily—"*stuff*, you're
bone-tired, and you should get some sleep. We will be conducting
debriefings all day tomorrow. Don't come in until you've had at least
six hours' sleep. Preferably twelve."

"Is that an order?" I jab.

He looks at me without the customary twinkle in his eyes. "You
know better than to ask, Mr. Howard."

Oh great. I stifle a yawn. "Okay, six hours' sleep before the fatal
incident enquiry. Check."

Angleton is dead. Andy . . . Andy's dead, too, and that's worse, in
a way. In a lot of ways. Angleton was an ancient monster, but Andy
was just another guy, with a wife and kids trying to kick his smoking
habit and learn something new for his ten-percenter project. And now
he's dead, and some poor bloody cop is sitting up late with Andy's
wife and children and wondering how the hell to make a decent withdrawal. Maybe if I hadn't volunteered to help him he'd still be alive.
Then again, if I hadn't volunteered to lend a hand he was all set to
zap himself on that stupid summoning rig he was working on . . . I
don't know. I'll never know. And the terrible part is that right now

I'm so tired that I'd rather get some sleep than stay up an extra hour to find out the truth, if that was somehow possible. The SA is right. I need to go home.

I stand up. "See you tomorrow afternoon," I say. I strip off my filthy overalls, then stumble down the steps from the back of the OCCULUS truck, shivering in a tee shirt and jeans. I've got an app for a local minicab firm on my phone, and even though the shattered glass screen crackles when I touch it, it's just about usable—I've got my home address and the New Annex bookmarked, and at this time of night there's not much competition for fares.

I LET MYSELF INTO THE DARKENED HALLWAY OF MY OWN HOME like a thief in the night, skulking and shivering in unshod feet.

I'm tired, with a bone-deep fatigue to which is added a layer of despair and depression. I've lost co-workers and, dare I say it, friends tonight. To start with: Howe. Well no, he wasn't a friend. But I've ridden along with him a number of times, from that crazy hole in reality that opened in Amsterdam to training sessions on Dartmoor. He's helped pull my nuts out of the fire more than once. Now he's gone, just a smelly stain on my damaged-beyond-cleaning Google tee shirt to remember him by. And my life is smaller as a result.

I shuffle through into the kitchen and switch on the lights on the cooker extractor hood—dim enough not to hurt my eyes or wake up the neighbors. I am a mess. I shrug out of my clothes in the middle of the kitchen floor. There's a basket of clean laundry next to the washer-dryer, and I begin to rummage through it for something clean to wear against my skin for the long trudge upstairs when—

"Bob?"

I spin round: "Oh! Hi. You startled me."

It's Mhari. Hair tousled, still fully dressed. She's staring at my hands, which are the only things between her eyes and my wedding tackle. She yawns, puffy-eyed. "What is this?"

"Would you wait outside for a mo?" I turn my back and bend over the laundry basket again, trying to pretend I'm not bare-ass naked. "I fell in someone. I'm filthy."

"Why didn't you say? Wait a second!" She turns and hoofs it up the stairs, and returns while I'm hopping around with one leg in a pair of boxer shorts, clutching a bath sheet. "Shower. Now. You'll feel ever so much better for it." She throws the big towel over me, then gets a good look at my dirties. "Eew. You'll have to tell me all about it!"

"Why so lively?" I complain, fighting back another yawn. "Can't it wait?"

"I was dozing on the sofa, with Spooky. Who has been demanding unconditional love and complaining about your absence all day. I was waiting up for you." She's flittering about, casting shadows, getting on my tits. I can't cope with people who are bouncy at four o'clock in the morning. "What happened?" she chirps.

"Ops clusterfuck." I turn and head upstairs, climbing slowly. "There's going to be a fatal incident enquiry tomorrow. I need to get some sleep first."

"Ops? Oh. Oh dear. Anyone I know?"

I bite back the urge to snarl *probably* and close the bathroom door. I lean my forehead against the inside of the door with my eyes shut for a minute, but push myself upright when I feel myself beginning to slide. She's right about the shower. I shed the boxers and towel and step inside, then turn it on from cold. The water warms up quickly enough but the initial icy shock is positively painful, and goes a long way towards temporarily descrambling my brain.

After a couple of minutes I'm done: squeaky-clean but exhausted. I step out of the shower, towel myself dry, then wrap the bath sheet around me and step out onto the landing. "I'm going to bed now," I tell the airspace above the staircase. "Help yourself to tea and coffee." I turn the landing light off, shuffle into the bedroom, then drop the towel and slide into my regular side of the bed, which is clammy in the predawn chill. My eyelids slam shut as my head hits the pillow—

Delicate fingers form a cup around my balls, as a lithe, warm body spoons up behind me, flattening her breasts against my spine and sliding a knee across my hip. "Gotcha!" She breathes in my ear.

I'm so drained I barely twitch. "*Not* funny. I want to sleep. Go 'way," I grunt. It's Mhari, of course. Who is no less unprincipled than ever, if somewhat more single-minded and a lot less obviously crazy—vampiredom suits her down to the ground. But she's always had a hotline to my libido, and she's rather good with her hands: *I* may be sleepy, but my wedding tackle isn't.

Mhari squeezes, and I groan quietly. "Not cool," I say. I can feel her presence, both with my skin and with an inner sense—the inner eye, dark-adapted and far more penetrating than before. And I can see what she is, the dim red spirals in the void behind her eyes. I begin to struggle, finally waking up and resisting: "No, seriously, I want you to *stop now*."

Her hand stops moving. "Bob, what's wrong?" she asks, sounding confused.

I want to say, *I'm married and unavailable.* And I want to say, *What we had has been over for years.* It'd be better to say, *I think you misunderstood the context of my invitation*, but that's too complicated a construction for me right now. What comes out is, "I'm exhausted and a bunch of my friends are dead and I don't want this."

"Poor Bob—"

"And my wife gets home tomorrow, and it's nearly tomorrow already." I yawn. "And yesterday I killed a vampire-hunting psychopath and then an ancient and powerful vampire, and I feel ill. Mental indigestion."

"You killed . . ." She pauses. "Oh my. God. Bob." She's shaking; I can feel it through my misery. "What have they *done* to you? What have they turned you into?"

"We can't go back. Can't rewind and become what we might have been if we'd done the last decade differently. Please get out of my bed, Mhari. The thing that wanted you dead is gone. You're safe. You should go home now. It's not safe for you to be here. Make sure you get under cover before dawn. If you don't go you'll be stuck here all day tomorrow."

A moment passes, then she lets go of me. I feel the covers peel back, and she climbs across me. I feel her brief, cool kiss on my forehead before she leaves. Then darkness descends, leaving me alone in the night with my despair and the memory of her lost humanity.

Even if I wasn't married, I don't think I could sleep with her now.

Something in the back of my head thinks she's the sort of thing I eat.

DOORS SLAM: "HI, HONEY, I'M HOME!"

I open my eyes on darkness. The bedside alarm says it's six o'clock; thanks to Mhari I've had only two hours of sleep. I try and shake my head to clear the cobwebs, then blink painfully. My eyes are sore. "Hi?" I call out, rolling over towards the edge of the bed. I tend to sprawl in the middle when I'm alone. Except I'm not alone: something warm and furry chirps indignantly and jumps out of the way. *Blasted cat.* At least Spooky doesn't seem to be a face-hugger. (Mum's old cat used to do that: sneak into the bedroom and sleep on my pillow. Sometimes she'd fart in my face.) "I'm up here," I add.

I get my feet on the floor and sit up, then nearly double over in pain. There's a clattering thump from downstairs, and a muffled scream, and the base of my right middle finger throbs painfully. It's the counterpart to the signaling ring I gave Mhari. An uncanny musical tone wobbles up from below, clawing at my eardrums.

"No!" I yell. I make a dive for the staircase and slap my hand on the light switch. The note dies away to a distant hum. But it leaves a metallic stink in the air, like high-voltage switchgear, or an electric chair just before it is switched on.

Mo stands in the hall, just in front of the porch, the ivory-hue violin braced between chin and shoulder, bow resting lightly across the strings. It's aimed like a gun at Mhari, who is crouched in the living room doorway. She's half-dressed, and in the green-tinged light from the CFL bulb she looks as pale as the violin. Lithe and bone-white, her canines extended, she cringes away from Mo, whose posture reminds me of a junkyard dog on the edge of exploding in a murderous frenzy of biting and clawing.

"*Stand down!*" I shout. Instinct makes me duck back round the bedroom door, grab the dressing gown hanging on the back of it, and throw it around myself before I set foot to stair. The foot of the staircase is between the living room door and the kitchen. I reach the bottom and turn. We make an odd triptych: me, in dressing gown and bare feet; Mhari, huddling in the living room doorway with something between a snarl and an ingratiating simper on her face; and my wife, the avenging angel, red hair and gunsight eyes staring over the bridge of her weapon.

But she's not moving the bow across the glowing, barely visible superstrings that thread her instrument. Not yet.

I try to keep my voice level, speaking clearly and slowly, to be as unthreatening and unsuspicious as possible. "We had an internal threat. I told her she could stay here. The threat situation was resolved about three hours ago at the New Annex. She's about to leave."

Mo says nothing. But her eyes narrow, almost imperceptibly, and I see her tighten her grip on the violin.

"It's true," Mhari says, words tumbling out: "there was an elder inside the Laundry he was sending a vampire hunter to murder all the PHANGs Bob said he must have access to the personnel records this would be the last place a vampire hunter would look for me I've been using the living room I'll just get my stuff and be going—"

Mo breaks eye contact with Mhari and looks at me. There is death in her fingertips. "Is. This. True?"

Behind my back, I cross my fingers. "Yes," I say firmly. Because it *is* true. (Even though a suspicious little corner of my mind is reminding me that I didn't offer Mhari the living room sofa, I offered her the spare bedroom, and what is she doing still here? *You invited a vampire into your home,* it nudges, *you deserve the consequences.*) It's not the whole truth, but it's the truth, and the full truth will have to wait until the weapons are safed and the tempers are tamed.

Mhari shuffles backwards into the living room and from Mo's disinterest and the rustling sounds I gather she's pulling her clothes together in a hurry.

Mo continues to watch me. "You didn't email," she says, deceptively calmly.

"I thought you were on a—" My eyes involuntarily track towards the living room door. (Mhari has no need to know.) "Out of contact."

"That's not the point," Mo says, her voice even and controlled. She's at her most dangerous when she's like this: chilly and judgmental and poised and calm. Like an angel of vengeance. "You invited that—*thing*—into our house." The violin turns away from me, facing into the living room. The ring around my finger throbs: I think even the brief note Mo drew before I shouted at her to stop may have injured Mhari. She whimpers quietly, afraid.

"She's a member of non-operational staff who has contracted an unfortunate but controllable medical condition, Mo. We have a duty to look after our own."

"Yes well, I can see exactly how important that is to you." Mo abruptly glances away from me. "You," she hisses. The bow rests lightly across the violin. She tweaks gently, between two fingers. The instrument moans like a soul in torment, shivering very quietly. "Keep away from him, you bitch." Another note, another moan—this one from Mhari. The ring throbs, fiery pain that feels as if my finger's about to fall off. My skin crawls and my hair begins to lift. Static electricity everywhere.

"Stop hurting her," I hear myself saying.

Mo's fingers continue to move. She looks puzzled.

"*Stop,*" I say, and step towards her.

"I can't—" The bow drags slowly across the strings, and Mo's left fingertips begin to bleed. The strings are glowing now, and Mhari screams in pain. Mo's eyes widen. "It won't let me!" The bow is dragging her hand: she fights back but she can't let go.

I reach deep inside myself and speak again, dredging up a memory of an ancient language that I didn't know I had: "**Stop.**" As I say it I reach out and grab Mo's right elbow, pinching it right around the nerve plexus. I'm terrified; terrified for Mhari, terrified for Mo, terrified for me: but most of all I'm terrified of the violin. To touch it is death. To hear it is death. *And it wants to feed.*

A gust of chilly winter air blows in from the living room: there's a thudding rattle as Mhari bails out of the front window. She's obviously had second thoughts about being trapped in the middle of a domestic argument between the Eater of Souls and a blood-cursed instrument. (Hopefully she's taken all her stuff.)

The scroll at the end of the violin turns towards me, dragging Mo's hands with it.

"**Stop,**" I repeat in Old Enochian, looking Mo in the eyes.

The pale red glow begins to fade from them, but the violin still quivers, hungry for blood. I close my eyes and look at it with my inner vision. Now I can see it for what it is: a ghastly, filthy, cursed thing, a vampire of the second order. Exactly the thing Basil warned us about. *Why couldn't it be a blancmange? I could eat a blancmange. But then I'd inherit the curse . . .* a part of me is babbling inanely.

"You're hurting me," she says, distantly.

"I'm sorry." I relax my grip on her elbow, but I don't let go. I don't want to give the violin a chance to take over again.

"Did you have sex with her?" she asks.

"No."

Her fingers, nerveless, release the bow. It clatters to the floor angrily, but separated into its two halves the instrument can't stop her from lowering its body. Blood trickles down its neck, across the pegbox, pooling above the scroll.

"You're bleeding," I say. "Let me get a towel." She nods, and I hurry to the kitchen and grab the kitchen roll. By the time I get back she's laid the violin on top of its open box, so similar in shape to a coffin. I tear off a couple of sheets and she wraps them around her hand. The violin is spotless already. I glare at it: it's difficult to be sure, but I have a feeling it's watching me the way a hungry lion watches its prey. "Kitchen," I add.

All our most significant conversations happen in the kitchen, or over food. It seems to be one of the rules of our relationship. Another rule: don't even think about lying. It's difficult to slip one past someone you've lived with for a decade at the best of times; unbelievably harder if they're a practitioner.

Being good at spotting lies also makes one prone to false positives: mistaking truth for falsehood. It's the besetting curse of counterespionage. Mo chose, for a few seconds, to believe I was telling the truth. *I did not have sex with that woman.* Right. But will she still believe me in the cold light of morning?

"She's a vampire," says Mo. She sounds almost surprised.

"So is that." I glance towards the hall door, and she follows my eyes.

"That's . . . different."

"The difference is, now it wants me dead." I suspect it tolerated me previously, as a necessary support for its symbiont. But now . . . with my inner eye I can see it quivering in the darkness, coiled, ready to pounce. "You know that, don't you?"

"When it turned on you, it was horrible." Her shoulders are shaking. "Oh God, that was awful." She peers at me. "Bob, how did you stop it? You shouldn't have been able to . . ."

"Angleton's dead."

"*What?*"

"The Code Red last night. The intruder was a, an ancient PHANG. He killed Angleton."

"Oh my God. Oh my God." She looks directly at me and actually takes in my face for, I think, the first time since she walked in the door. "Bob. Oh my God." She reaches out across the table, and I take her hand. It's shivering like a frightened bird. Bits of white tissue cling to the still-raw slashes that criss-cross the older scars on her fingertips. "You're him now."

"Not really." *Not even close.* "But I have access to a lot of, of—" I trail off. The files stored in Angleton's Memex are waiting for me. I'm probably the only person who knows how to use the bloody thing, much less is authorized to use it without spontaneously catching fire. That's all the knowledge I've inherited from him. But knowledge and power aren't the same thing. "Stuff."

"What are you going to do?"

I look past her shoulder, at the elephant in the room. Or rather, at the monster in the hallway. With my human eyes, it appears to be a musical instrument, albeit made from unusual (and grotesque) materials. But with my dark-adapted inner eye I can see what it is. It's the color of all the blood that it's drunk over the years, bloated and turgid, bulging against the walls and ceiling like a tick sized to feed on tyrannosaurs. It's not shaped like a violin at all. It's got too many legs, and a proboscis, and other organs. It's as alien as a parasitic wasp seen under an electron microscope. And it's watching me with patient hatred, because it wears a choke chain and leash, and I'm one of the buzzing irritants that keeps its handler from letting it off the lead. Or maybe it just recognizes its own kind.

It's a naked lunch moment. The instant when you freeze and see for the first time what's on the end of your fork. Or in my case, Mo's tuning fork.

"I should destroy that thing."

She looks at me with pity and cynicism. "They won't let you. The organization needs it. It's all I can do to keep squashing the proposals to make more of them."

"Yes, but if I don't it's going to try and kill me again." I know it's true the moment the words leave my mouth. It'll wait. It's patient. But she has to practice, daily, in an elaborately warded anechoic chamber. And she carries it everywhere, takes it to bed. I don't think she's a natural sleepwalker, but I wouldn't put it past the violin to make her: sometimes she mumbles and cries out in her sleep.

"I can't let go of it." She bites her lower lip. "If I let go of it— return it to Supplies, convince them I can't carry it anymore—they'll just give it to someone else. Someone inexperienced. It was inactive for years before they gave it to me. Starving and in hibernation. It's awake now. And the stars are right."

The picture she's painting doesn't bear thinking about. I feel like I'm being backed into a corner by the inexorable logic of the situation. My skin feels clammy and my heart is pounding. "What are we going to do? It wants me dead."

"If I let go of it a lot of other people will die, Bob. I'm the only thing holding it back. Do you want that? Do you really want to take responsibility for letting it off the leash with an inexperienced handler?"

Our eyes meet. Ten years of love, pity, and regrets are all wrapped up in a single moment: I take a deep breath and say the words that I've somehow known were coming for the past few weeks, ever since our sushi date with destiny.

"I'm going to have to move out."